ROCK STAR

Tim Poston and Ian Stewart

Breathing Life into Great Books

ReAnimus Press
1100 Johnson Road #16-143
Golden, CO 80402
www.ReAnimus.com

Cover Art by Clay Hagebusch

ISBN-13: 978-1548900373

First ReAnimus Press print edition: August, 2017

10 9 8 7 6 5 4 3 2

I won't be a rock star. I will be a legend.
— Freddie Mercury

Qish

"They're killing each other!"

Augustine Tambiah Sadruddin's new boss gave him a cool stare, but he noticed how her hand moved a fraction towards the crystal knife at her belt. It looked ceremonial, an integral part of the regalia of the Deep Colloquist of the Caverns of Wevory. Looks were deceptive. Every cavern-dweller carried a poisoned knife, and had been trained from birth in its uses for hunting, combat, and politics.

"After bloody revolution, killing surprises you?"

Sadruddin took a deep breath, urging himself to calm. Shevveen-Duranga was no stranger to death. Her title meant something between 'Low Priest' and 'Absolute Monarch', though it was no more hereditary than the post of Sadruddin's old boss, Deacon of the Church of the Undivided Body. Each had gained power by causing the death of their predecessor—the Deacon by covert assassination, the Colloquist by public legal challenge. Sadruddin preferred his new boss; the Colloquist at least seemed sane, for a ruthless value of *sane*. Perhaps *rational* was a better word.

Short by Starfolk standards, Sadruddin ('Gus' to his Starfolk friends) was a typical Qishi. He was stronger than he looked, both mentally and physically. His pale blue eyes issued a challenge to the universe from a calm, square-featured face, under short, dark hair, no longer tonsured, and clean-shaven. He had been the Deacon's private chaplain, until at his orders his superior was cast into a lurepool. Tidal forces tore bone and muscle apart—a more merciful death than breaking them piecemeal with bone-hammers, to which Deacon DeLameter had sentenced so many. Sadruddin had not meant to take over, either as Deacon or ruler: he had no aim beyond freedom for himself and others to divide the body, with syntei.

Plant syntei connected separate points in space without danger, as long as neither was significantly higher than the other—as they were with lurepools.

Whole bodies could pass through big syntei, connected across great distances, while parts of a body could extend (still connected) through small ones, giving… new possibilities. Easy solo oral sex just scratched the surface, and the itch; opportunity-space offered more sexual dimensions than human imagination could catalogue, all forbidden by the Church, and all longed for in secret.

The underground Sadruddin had thought he was running had been riddled with agents of the secretive Cavern Dwellers of Wevory, two continents away, which had enabled its success with expert help. A superb network of spies and spysyntei spotted body-dividers as potential recruits, far more efficiently than the Quizitors rooted them out for the intimate attentions of the bone-hammers. But their loyalty was to the Caverns, and his continent had passed from autonomy under a merciless Church to being the Shaaluin Province of the Wevorin Empire. A surprised Sadruddin found himself its Governor, reporting direct to Shevveen-Duranga. Who expected respect, and made sure she got it.

She was young, intense, and pitiless.

"To me you shall refer by 'Unfathomable One'," she reproved him. The phrase reflected the cavern-dwellers' respect for depth, but Sadruddin found it doubly appropriate. He seldom had the slightest idea what was going on in her mind.

She wore the trappings of her position with the dignity of an empress and the intimidating presence of a born predator. A thick braid of hair rose from her otherwise shaven head, coiling in an elaborate loop to one ear, where it was secured to the lobe by a bone stud shaped like a flower. The other ear bore a yellow egg-shaped pendant. Egg and flower, the symbols of cavern-dweller belief, modelled on what they now knew to be a two thousand year old Colony Rescue Beacon. Broad strips of cloth and fur wrapped her body in a traditional design that seemed haphazard to surface dwellers. Her left thigh was encircled by a yellow band, bearing a white oval blazon—Saffron Egg, Lowest of the Low, the symbol of absolute power. All her predecessors had borne the Saffron Hoop, but she was the Colloquist whose rule had opened the Egg.

"Your pardon, Unfathomable One."

A brief nod of reluctant approval. "Now, Sadruddin: who kills whom, and why, and what you are doing about it, tell me."

Her intelligence network surely knew the situation better than he did, but it would be indiscreet to say so. "It is chiefly the people of Low Feoff and the Crosswit cities, who are slaughtering their fellows in an over-reaction to newly regained freedoms—both by those who wish to express them, and those whose aim is to restore suppression. As yet, I do nothing, for fear of exacerbating an already dangerous problem."

"Body division." Shevveen-Duranga's tone was sardonic. "Can you Shaa-luin fools *still* not this obsession control?"

"It is too early, Unfathomable One. I had hoped that dividing the body would become *normal*, as it is in Samdal: simply one of the ways to live. Obviously there would be clubs for those that delight to display themselves, and delight even more to do so for gain." *It was at a Samdal club that Marcolo betrayed himself under the influence of* kreesh *smoke, and had to flee Shaaluy with Els'bett. Well, they were safely back among the stars now... and he missed them every hour.* "Equally obviously, not all would approve of such liberty, and their views should be treated with respect, though not applied to others. But the normal displays in Samdal are to those who wish to see them. In Shaaluy they have started parades! The upper body of a man synted to the hips of a woman, with the hairy legs of a man... a woman with the phallus of a horse... a man with three heads and six faces... a woman with a drum replacing her belly and her womb. And they walk openly down the street, with drums beating, and bagpipes. On legs."

"Surely you defend division of the body?"

Was that a hint of amusement at the corners of Shevveen-Duranga's lips? You would never know from her voice. "Unfathomable One, you know that I do. And it would be my delight to join them, after so many years of thinking my own wishes shameful. But I am forced to see them also with the eyes of a Governor."

If there had been a hint, it had gone now. "And what do those eyes see?"

"Provocation, Unfathomable One."

"Provocation of whom?"

"Unfathomable One, provocation of those who continue to believe in the teachings of the Church. They have their own songs:

> Though the cause of evil prosper, yet 'tis truth alone is strong;
> Though her portion be the scaffold, and upon the throne be wrong;
> Yet that scaffold sways the future, and behind the dim unknown,
> Stands Magog within the shadow, keeping watch above His own.

They do not hear the facts that contradict them. We have drained Grossest Midden around the Colony Vessel *Magog*, that all may see how we descended from the stars. But they worship divine Magog, tall as a mountain, with hair like the dark before dawn, and all else is a Test of Faith. Brown people from the stars are mere delusion. I, who can bear witness, describing personally the light of other suns, am a dupe of the Divider, worthy only of the Hell of Division.

"Did it end there, they alone would suffer, but they have decided that unbelief is persecution. The parades especially are sin, sin flown with insolence and wine, and may not pass through devout neighbourhoods. The believers' dropsyntei deliver flaming graffyd-oil upon the blasphemers." Sadruddin's voice took on a hypnotic sing-song note: he had long believed as they did, and longer preached it, for to do otherwise was death.

"And the body dividers?"

"Unfathomable One, they say they have been persecuted too long, that they can no longer hide in their cupboards, denying their deepest, truest desires. They say that if they take one step back, it will lead to another, and another, and end in the restoration of authority of the Church. And as acknowledged dividers, they will fear again the bone-hammers.

"There is much truth in this, but the parades would certainly be safer where more dividers dwell. Though not much safer, since with syntei all neighbourhoods are one. And they say they have put safety first for too long, and they will parade where they will. They have dropsyntei delivering bullets from the glaciers of the White Ramparts, and they have sworn that for every one that dies by fire, two will die by ice.

"Unfathomable One, the killing has started, and I have little power to stop it."

Shevveen-Duranga appeared to be weighing options. "Have you no soldiers, order to keep?"

Sadruddin shrugged. "The only trained soldiers in Shaaluy were trained by the Church. To the dividers they are suspect, and rightly so, as their chiefest task was to suppress Division. To the believers they are abominable apostates who take their orders now from a godless authority. Forgive them, Unfathomable One, but reverence for the World Egg has as yet taken shallow roots in Shaaluin hearts." *And in mine, but then I have heard Marcolo critiquing its engineering principles.* "The beliefs of the Cavern Dwellers have been vindicated," *after a fashion,* "but we cannot soon persuade either side to share them. We must use secular means. Secular troops. Which I do not have."

Shevveen-Duranga stared down her nose at him. "The surface states of Wevory have troops in *excess*. Without limit they built up their armies, for the Lamynt war. Much of their land was wrecked. We have been forced open control to take, as you know: that was the first acquisition of the Wevorin Empire. It is now our responsibility. The *bazza* crops grow again, in the less ruined clay fields, thanks to the Starfolk. Commerce slowly recovers, but we cannot at once demobilise all those soldiers with no civilian trade. Nor can we pay them all. I think Shaaluy can pay them." *You probably know our fi-*

nances better than I do, thought Sadruddin; *spies are more honest than officials with budgets to defend.* "I think that Wevorin troops could be neutral between your parties: they will find the inhibitions of the believers as ridiculous as the exhibitions of the dividers."

Sadruddin gave a doubtful nod. "Unfathomable One, I think we can pay them, and I think we must. We need enough to guard the syntei near the parades, and to keep parades to safer routes…"

"Work out the details with your counterpart. The Governor of Surface Wevory is of course an expert in military logistics."

"Of course, Unfathomable One."

"He will meet you in three hours."

Mount Angrith was not far from the Deep Colloquist's office under Krig Mountain—visible from its peak—but by far the fastest route to the Wevorin surface headquarters there was by way of Two Mountains, back on Sadruddin's home continent. Walk through a wyzand at Shevveen-Duranga's level, climb innumerable stairs (meeting *en route* two aides with urgent issues), and return to Wevory through another, to reach the Governor's office with five minutes to spare.

"Come in," said General Fingal Marsden von Hayashiko. "I understand you'd like some of my soldiers."

He was a big, rock-hard man, almost as tall as Els'bett and Marcolo, and with a matching intelligence. Sadruddin didn't find his Starfolk friends intimidating (particularly lying down), but he always felt his slender frame tauten defensively in the General's presence. He had met his fellow Governor on Wevorin formal occasions, but this was the first time he had had serious dealings with the man.

"I see you've already been briefed." Sadruddin gestured at the map of Crosswit syntei on a wide table beside a window, strewn with papers. "That looks more comprehensive than anything in my office."

"You know how our rulers are," said von Hayashiko, tactfully. There was no doubt at all that they were watched and heard through spysyntei. "I gather a lot of Shaaluin records burned in the Revolution."

"And some membrancers were killed, unfortunately," sighed Sadruddin. "It was a bad time, but it ended a nightmare."

"No doubt," agreed von Hayashiko. "The Deacon was the worst of a long line of madmen. Well, you should requisition the Cavern Dwellers' records as replacements. Can I offer you a glass of Vanduul?"

"With pleasure! A taste of home."

The General poured two generous glasses of the ruinously expensive liqueur. "Now," looking at the map, "at first sight it seems to me that you need a core of about five hundred military police, and some three thousand grunts. I'll have my staff work out the details, but as a first estimate, does that sound right to you? I'll try to keep out the tunket-heads."

Sadruddin felt a weight start to lift from his overburdened frame. "That should save a lot of lives. What would the cost be?"

"On the order of sixteen hundred copper rings a month."

"Ouch," said Sadruddin. "I'll have my own staff check very carefully, but it does ring true. We will have to export a lot more of this." He eyed his glass.

"To Samdal, of course," said the General. "Wevory can barely afford your prices, and the copper rings you pay us will be reserved for more urgent needs. I'll have a detailed proposal ready by tomorrow, same time. Meanwhile, may I propose a game of *shinsa*?"

Sadruddin relaxed. The pressure was off. "I would be delighted. My own people keep mistaking me for the Deacon, and deliberately missing dooms for fear of offence."

Von Hayashiko grinned, giving a convincing impression of a hungry ossivore. "I have the same problem. The burdens of office bind us both."

"Perhaps we should set our staffs against each other," said Sadruddin. "A game of mountain cricket, perhaps?"

"Excellent idea. I have some vertical leg spinners who could benefit from the encounter with unfamiliar batsmen. But for now, *shinsa*."

The *shinsa* set looked strange to Sadruddin, with princes, courtesans, and warriors replacing the Shaaluin priestly archflamens and precentors, but the board of hexagons was the same. It was obvious how the pieces corresponded.

He found von Hayashiko a worthy opponent, choosing moves that superbly concealed his intentions.

"What do you think of the Starfolk?" asked the General, distracting him from his study of a particularly complex position.

I dream of the Starfolk, thought Sadruddin. "The crew who crashed near *Magog*? Or the new people coming through syntei? It seems we will see a lot more of them, once they have achieved a steady match of levels."

"And a lot more of Marco, in particular. *Two* of him! Have you met them?"

And bedded them. Doubtless the Cavern Dwellers' spy network knew all about that, too, but Sadruddin's habit of discretion was bone-deep. "Two of each of those who crashed, it seems, but most of the duplicates perished among the stars, in some disaster they cannot talk about."

"Cannot? Or will not?"

"Cannot. It seems some geas binds their tongues. But I cannot stop wondering in what strange place they perished…"

Rock Star

Bright angular patches, impenetrable shadows, stark contrasts of light and dark. Clashing chiaroscuro angles against a featureless black backdrop. To any seasoned spacefarer, the high foreground contrast was a giveaway: a small airless body lit by a fierce blue-white sun. Either comet or asteroid.

The vixcam panned back to a wide-angle shot. A contrasting patchwork occupied the lower two thirds of the image; an irregular, jumbled horizon separated it from cosmic blackness. Structure began to emerge. A shattered surface of ice and rock, pockmarked like pumice.

The image spun, centred on one of the pocks, zoomed closer. The patch of darkness grew, acquired form. A funnel-like mouth.

Artificial light fought the darkness. The mouth led to a twisting tunnel, which flowed away from the sides of the image as the vixcam penetrated deeper. Then the walls of the tunnel disappeared as it opened out into a wide space — a cavern.

The first impression was of movement. Clusters of dark patches broke apart and reformed in the vixcam's beam, like a flock of birds at dusk seeking refuge for the night. There was a rhythm to the flow, a tantalising hint of pattern in the patches' interactions. Some led, some followed; some were swift, some slow. The flow repeatedly broke apart and re-formed, growing as more patches joined it.

The vixcam chose a stationary patch on the cavern's wall and zoomed in. It locked on its target and more structure emerged. What might have been of purely physical origin resolved itself as biology — of a kind. Weirdly shaped appendages joined together to create a baffling whole, reminiscent of no known organism, terrestrial or alien. Webbed strands randomly daubed with tangled fluff vibrated as nests of smooth flexible tubes writhed and twisted, gouging the rock. All very slowly, even displayed at 16-speed.

The image jerked abruptly as the vixcam shifted to another patch. More biology. Different biology. Faster. This creature—if that was the word—was all angles and spikes, flashing edges, some sliding like pistons, some slicing like knives.

A third creature vaguely resembled an exploded sofa, a soft-outlined rectilinear mass festooned with protruding helical windings. Its edges rippled almost imperceptibly as it tumbled slowly off the wall—

The image shuddered and the slapscreen went blank.

Wada Cluster

Marco Bianchi did his best to look unimpressed. "Some kind of robotic mining operation?"

"Could be." Vance gave him a sour look where he was hanging—compared to everyone else and the slapscreen—upside down in the null gravity of the orbital station. His elaborately trimmed mop of curls declared him a graduate of the Inferno Institute of Technology on Dante. It looked as though a black hedgehog was clinging to his head.

Philomena Vance—she rarely used the first name, and few others found occasion to do so—was of medium height, with gangly limbs hanging from a solid, compact frame. Her hair was cut long at the sides and short at back and front, with pale blue highlights, a fashion that had gone out of date several months ago but was still common. But her clothes were military-smart, and so was her bearing. Her jawline was hard and angular, prepared for anything.

She claimed to be Concordat Special Executive, but everything about her, including the unconvincing attempt to look like a typical mid-career 'compjock, screamed Starhome Security. She exuded the confidence of those who speak firmly and own a big stick.

"So why have you plucked us from training and brought us all the way here, just to see some trashy vix footage of a Concordat mining operation?" Samuel Grey Deer Wasumi, *Valkyrie's* navigator, complained. An expert in martial arts, he looked the part—lithe, rugged, and determined. His long hair was bound in a ponytail.

"It's not Concordat, Wasumi."

"A bootlegger, then."

"It's not a bootleg operation. It's probably not even a mining operation. It's nothing human."

"You think it's aliens," Felix Wylde said, making eye contact with Jane Bytinsky. Like most Starfolk, he was tall and dark-skinned, but with a typical Daikoku gengineered shining silver streak in his hair. Jane was shorter than average, with the slender build typical of Ebisu, a mid-gee planet. Daikoku was a more massive world in the same system. They were a matchpair, both xenologists. This was their territory. "Not any I know of, so: new discovery."

"Whence all the smoke-and-dagger," Jane added.

"Aliens, yah," Vance confirmed. "New, nah. That vix dates from 1817, Wylde."

Jane's shock was palpable. "You've known about this for *over fifty years?*" She shook her head in disbelief.

"Yah, Bytinsky, and we've been investigating it ever since. *Carefully.*"

"Potentially hazardous, then," said Felix.

Tinka Laurel, the group's Waylander pilot, shot him a worried glance. "Where was that footage taken? Somewhere around here, presumably."

Vance raised one hand, saying nothing. The trainees' neuronic wristcomputers began talking to them inside their heads. #Statutory Confidentiality Agreement, revision of 1862 GE. By accepting the conditions of this agreement you acknowledge being bound by the terms advised in Annex 1. Penalties for infringement are listed in Annex 2. Summary follows—#

"We went through all that when Starhome sent us to EZ9, citizen. We've already been given security clearance." Elza, sixth and final member of the group of citizenship candidates, made it a flat statement, using her Lady of Quynt speaker-to-commoners voice.

Vance was unmoved. "Yah. And now you agree to the statutory reconfirmation."

"Yah *my Lady.* I may be only a galactic trainee, but I'm a Hippolytan noble, not one of your SS bootlickers."

Vance ignored her, along with the implication. "You're about to progress to a higher security level. That means you consent to a neural lock on your brains, so that you *cannot* commit a breach. Even with that, sharing the material is against my protests, but we all have to defer to higher judgement from time to time, even when it's wrong. I want you to prove *me* wrong, by showing that my superiors' misplaced confidence in a bunch of undertrained space cadets is, by some miracle, justified."

Elza gave her a look that could freeze magma. "We *are* undertrained space cadets, citizen Vance. You know full well *that's why the Concordat sent us here.* To train us for higher things." She hadn't wanted to come, either, but this wasn't the time to say so. *Take it up with the family, one of these years…*

"What we don't understand is why Starhome Security brought us *here*. We were hoping you'd enlighten us instead of playing silly power games."

Vance sighed. "I told you before... my Lady... I'm Special Executive." Blank faces stared at her.

"So where was that vix footage taken?" Sam repeated. "Citizen," he added as an afterthought.

Vance glared at them. "Neurox that Confidentiality Agreement, people. Then I'll tell you. But if any of you tries to breathe one syllable of this to any unauthorised person, which you should assume is every intelligent entity in the multiverse that doesn't know about it already, wherever you are, your brain will freeze over."

"Yah, yah... If that's what it takes, I'll—"

"Not so fast, Marco." Elza was mentally scanning the document. "One of the few useful things I learned when my mother sent me for management training was always to look at the fine print. And to ask questions. So, citizen: freeze over *how*? Permanently?"

Vance, slightly flustered now her bluff had been called, shook her head.

"Thought not. The Concordat doesn't do automatic death sentences. Though maybe SS would like to—"

"I have no idea, but that would not be Concordat policy. It's self-enforcing. If you try to talk about this material to people that your own brain does not recognise as authorised, you can't. You seize up, the words won't come out. The effect wears off as long as you stay off the topic. But you do get the Mother of all headaches."

"Finally you're making sense. Now, let me read out clause 15 of Annex 2. 'All obligations under this document shall terminate automatically when the party to whom Confidential Information was disclosed (the Recipient) can document that'—blah blah blah... I'll skip the next bit, it's not relevant, no idea why it's in there when you'd never ask anyone to sign this document if it applied—ah here we go: 'it entered the public domain *subsequent to the time it was communicated to the Recipient* through no fault of—' Is that legalese what I think it is?"

Reluctantly: "Yah. An automatic termination clause."

"Of the agreement, not us?"

Vance failed to rise to the bait. After a long silence, Elza relaxed. "Very well, citizen. Reasonable secrecy is acceptable. Marco, go ahead."

"Thank you for granting permission to this humble male, your Lady-ship." Said with mock deference and an attempt at a disarming grin.

Vance regained her composure. "I know you always act as though every-thing is an amusing game, Bianchi, but this mission is serious. Deadly serious."

Marco's grin vanished. "Citizen: joking aside, we all understand that *perfectly*." He mentally signed the Agreement, followed by the others.

"Very well." She took a deep breath. "Where was that footage taken? The general area was EZ9, where we are. Which is no coincidence. Wasumi! Tell us about EZ9."

"Uh — officially, a new exclusion zone. Huge tract of space. The Wada Cluster is the nearest settled area. Hit by a simquake, ages ago. Fifty-one years?" Vance nodded. "That figures. Um — all vessels warned to keep clear for fear of aftershocks." He pursed his lips. "But… Starhome sent us here, in *Valkyrie*, which is not exactly state-of-the-art transportation. So I'm guessing that susceptibility to simquakes was another piece of dingbeaucratic — uh, misdirection. The official line."

Vance nodded. "Very good. Starhome wanted to keep prying eyes away from this area, and a simquake alert was the simplest way to do it." She paused. "If anyone is stupid enough to ignore the warning, and penetrates further into the Zone, they'll get more than a *k*-glitch aftershock. There's a squadron of J-class maulers patrolling the most likely *k*-field foci. Very few civilian craft can outrun one of those.

"As Wasumi surmised, the simquake was a cover story. Starhome placed the region under interdiction because something very scary was found there."

"The aliens," said Jane. "To state the obvious. Though I don't yet see why they should be scary. From the limited data you've given us, they appear to be some kind of low-level social organism, specialising in a low-pressure environment."

"Quasi-social," Felix corrected in his usual taciturn manner. "Vacuum."

"*Very* low-pressure environ—"

Vance waved her to silence. "Take it from me, they're scary. Why does Starhome have a large interstellar navy, even though there are few discernible threats? Because we've always known that as the Concordat expands, one of these days we'll run into a bunch of aliens who are smarter than us, or better organised than us, or better equipped than us, or meaner than us, or any combination. And we're starting to worry that we've found them, even though we have no evidence whatsoever that they fit any of those descriptions. Not because of what we know: because of what we don't.

"The system itself is nothing new, been known for a long time. No one suspected alien life, it's a totally ridiculous habitat. A blue giant star orbited by hundreds of millions of rocks forming one huge asteroid field. Not a belt, there are no planets to organise it. It's strange and chaotic. Then a team of scouts took a closer look because the scientists had finally realised it was even more bizarre than it seemed. The scouts named it Rock Star."

Marco, whose hobbies included Old Earth pre-interstellar culture, raised an eyebrow but said nothing.

"The Concordat didn't know about the asteroids?" Tinka asked.

"Dah. Of course they did. But until fifty years ago no one looked into the orbital dynamics, because no one expected anything unusual."

"So what's changed?"

"In the system? Nothing. In our thinking? Lots. Collisions should be rare, in all that empty space, but with so many rocks we should see one every year or so."

"How many have you seen?"

"Zero."

"In fifty years?"

"In a hundred and fifty years. We checked the records of the dumb observer that was planted as a routine measure, on first discovery."

"That's impossible," said Sam. "The odds against it are—what, Marco?"

"Ridiculous. If it was natural. So it wasn't."

"Aliens, then," said Felix. "Preventing collisions." Jane nodded vigorously.

Marco sucked in a deep breath, letting it out in a prolonged puff through loosely separated lips, his habitual expression for considered scepticism. "I'm not convinced, Felix. They'd have to push them with a rocket or a light-sail, or use explosives, or maybe just paint one side white and wait for starlight to do the grunt work." He turned towards Vance. "But I'm guessing you'd have mentioned anything like that."

"Yah. If the aliens have been herding rocks, we have no idea how."

More data had been dumped to their 'comps. Vance talked them through it.

"The things that look like rocks definitely are rocks. Their reflection spectra show silicates, oxides, sulphides, forms resembling hornblende, olivine, serpentine—but anhydrous." Her head, slightly cocked, suggested she was getting all this technical information direct from her 'comp. "No water, not even within the molecular matrix. Some sedimentary: aeolian, but not marine or lacustrine. Lots of igneous rocks—basalts, gabbros, rhyolites, granite, hydrogen metal 9—"

"Whoa there!" Elza was a geologist. "Some of those only form inside planets or on planetary surfaces. Hydrogen metal 9 forms *inside Jovians*. You said Rock Star has no planets."

"That's one of the bizarre features. Another is the density of the asteroids. The orbital dynamics don't fit the expected masses. Anything we've profiled that's more than fifty metres across is about half as dense as the rock it's made of."

Elza and Sam both spoke together.

"It must have had planets once!"

"They're *all* hollow?"

Vance pursed her lips. "That was quick. Took the scientists days. Mind you, they had to recognise the problems before thinking about answers." She stood up and paced across the carpet, her shoes clinging to it electrostatically. "The team that discovered Rock Star's aliens named these weird creatures 'groupies'. I suppose because they keep forming and reforming into groups."

Marco sniggered, the others looked blank. He didn't explain.

"The ones we've seen to date are all small. About the size of a lab rat down to a mouse. The third, and really bizarre thing is, groupies are extremophiles. *Extreme* extremophiles. They thrive in a vacuum. You saw that. Our scientists saw it fifty years ago. It was crazy then and it's crazy now. But there are groupies crawling around inside and over most of the rocks in the whole mothertrashed system, and everywhere we've seen them, there's no air. They've made extensive burrows in everything larger than an office block."

"What's inside the burr—"

"What do they look—"

"How do they—"

Bedlam broke out as the trainees all started asking questions at once. Vance glared at them until they shut up. "Wylde, you first."

"They can't all be one species. There has to be an ecology."

"That's what we think, but… it's hard to tell."

"Why?" Jane asked. "Can't you spot morphological and ethological patterns?"

"Tricky. The groupies are amorphs. Their shapes don't clump into distinguishable phenotypes. More like a fractal distribution of the weird."

"What's inside the burrows?" Sam asked. "More aliens?"

"Indirect evidence says so, loud and clear. Type unknown."

"And direct evidence?" Felix asked.

"We've sent in robotic probes."

"What did they find?"

"Dunno. Not one came back. The footage you saw is typical. We send them in, the groupies sniff them out, and they stop functioning. We only ever get footage from near the entrances. Deeper inside... who knows? Might even be some air, though I doubt it."

"There must be some way to harden the probes," Marco mused.

"Believe me, we've tried. So far, nah. But we're still working on it. We're fairly confident about two things. One is that groupies... *graze* the rocks. We're not sure whether they're digging tunnels or feeding. Or both. Or neither. Animals eat life and usually move, plants eat non-life and usually don't. These fit neither class. We think."

"Machine-life?" Felix interjected. "Theoretical possibility."

"Felix, I don't think—" Jane began.

Vance interrupted. "We've got some observations that indicate they're organic, Wylde. Just not the usual *kind* of organic."

"Ecologies usually evolve predators," Jane said, in a subdued tone.

"Yah. But even if these guys haven't, *they eat rocks*. And they live in the *remains* of planets. Which, in case no one's figured it out yet, is why they're scary."

"If these things invent Da Silvas, they could eat the Galaxy," said Sam.

"Bravo. It's *my* job to be paranoid, but anyone can do it, even you."

"Energy source?" asked Felix.

"Best guess: solar. We have some evidence, you'll see it later. They come out of the burrows and sit in bright patches of light. Sometimes they jump off the rock, and drift away. We don't know what happens after that—the nearest rocks of any size are a long way away."

"Yah," said Sam. "Humongously many rocks, but humongously *more* space."

"Taken any samples?" Felix asked.

"Of the rocks, yah. Or are you referring to the groupies?"

"Groupies. Unless they're intelligent, it would be normal procedure. Since they're shuttling themselves from rock to rock, it should be easy to pick up a few."

"Nothing about Rock Star is normal," Vance said.

"The little ones aren't intelligent, or you'd have said so."

"Correct. But in this case—"

"You don't know how the little ones relate to the groupies as a whole," Jane said. "Some might be intelligent. Collecting samples of the little ones could annoy them. Break taboos, disturb their ecosystem. Stir up trouble."

"Exactly. It is not Concordat policy to make first contact with potentially hazardous intelligent aliens by *picking up samples*. So we proceed *carefully*."

Felix inclined his head in acknowledgement. "We'd make progress a lot faster if we could secure a few specimens, though. Study them, then release them where we found them?"

"Possibly, but it's not policy."

"Any definite signs of intelligence?" Jane asked.

"That, Bytinsky, is what causes the Concordat so many sleepless nights. It's the main reason we've maintained such an extensive presence in this system, and it's why we're taking caution to extremes. The guys our vixcams have picked up seem no more intelligent than rats—which are smart, but you wouldn't worry about them inventing a spear, let alone a starship. But we don't know what problems they're solving. Those further inside the tunnels? Anyone's guess. Might be dumb animals like the ones we know about. Might be cosmic geniuses."

"Extelligence," said Felix.

"Extelligence? What's that?" said Tinka, puzzled.

Jane came to her rescue. "The ability to store cultural capital outside any specific individual. Rock art, songs, books, the grid. Felix is saying that intelligence isn't the issue. Groupiekind isn't likely to be a major security risk unless their culture is *ex*telligent."

"Amazing what you learn in this job," Vance said drily. "Biggest security risk I've ever had to deal with was an outbreak of *ch'rugga* virus. Didn't notice any extelligence there. But you may have a point, Wylde. There's one thing suggestive of rudimentary extelligence. Some of them communicate."

"How? What? Have you—"

"Easy now, Bianchi. Life usually does. Bacteria do it, trees do it, even educated fleas do it. Some groupies do it. Others probably don't. We know a bit about *how*: electromagnetic radiation in the ultraviolet range. Some groupies show UV patterns on their surfaces, using some kind of laser emission. We study cells by putting polariton laser biochemistry into their genes: the groupies seem to have made something like that part of their system, like chromatophores. Millions of pixels, at hundreds of separate frequencies, incredible bandwidth. They're messages, but invisible to the human eye."

"How do their eyes capture all that?" asked Marco.

"We don't even know if they *have* eyes, or see with their skin. No samples, remember?"

"If they're handling that much information, definitely safest not to trespass," agreed Felix. "What do they seem to be saying?"

"We have even less of an idea. They might be vacuum-breathing cosmic squid competing for mates with the intricacy of their signals, like dynamic peacock plumes. From rock to moving rock, across millions of miles."

"Dah," said Jane, "Then again, they might be alien philosophers debating the meaning of existence on a plane far above human understanding."

Vance grunted. "Correct, Bytinsky, and it's not a joke. We simply *do not know*."

"But you have to find out," said Sam. "They might be a threat."

"That's part of it, Wasumi. In some ways, though, there's a worse possibility."

"Which is?"

"We might be a threat to them."

Rock Star

Finally, the trainees were about to see some action.

Of a kind.

Vance spelt it out, mostly in words of one syllable.

"You're here to think. New thoughts, the Mother help us, so you won't be fed old stabs at this. Just data. Data we've checked.

"What you will *not* do is act. Do not act, at all, on your own hook. Patrol, watch, and think, but keep well away from the rocks. And don't even *think* about 'taking samples', Wylde."

They patrolled, observed, thought, and the data trickled in: identical, as far as they could tell, to the data gathered fifty years ago. No theories of language seemed to fit groupie communication. Linnaeus himself could not have classified them intelligibly, much less conjectured their descent and development. They could not even tell small adults from new groupies.

As each week and month went by, *Valkyrie* seemed smaller. Felix spoke less and less; Jane kept herself alert by worrying about him. Tinka scanned Sam's knife, down to the molecular level, and printed a duplicate, exact except for the word *liar* on the blade. They spent hours practising. Elza became more and more the frozen aristocrat, too far above them even to be impolite. Marco quietly struggled to conceal his unrequited lust—Elza was stunning, dark-skinned with golden hair and the innate poise of the highborn. He dreamed of her in an ivory castle, and spent his days trying to model the dynamics of the rocks. The more he looked at them, the more their stable pattern seemed impossible to reach. You can't get here from there…

Their lives shrank.

Marco, an expert mathematical engineer, had given up on the orbital dynamics of a billion rocks. He felt that biology ought to be easier, but he was stuck on a basic point. Hoping not to appear too foolish, he articulated it.

"How can a living organism survive in a vacuum?"

"Those things do," said Elza. "Must be some way."

"Yah," said Marco. "Obviously. But we've been told to think everything through in our own way, and I'm doing that. I don't understand how life can survive without an atmosphere."

Jane put her pouch of coffee down and wiped her mouth with the back of her hand. "It's not difficult, Marco. Most worlds have atmospheres, so most life forms evolve to exploit them. Atmospheres are common, so creatures adapted to vacuum are rare. So rare that these are the only ones we know about. But an atmosphere isn't *necessary*. Not like energy; that *is* necessary. But creatures can get energy from all sorts of sources—in this case, solar radiation. They can protect their delicate hides by not *having* delicate hides. The ones we've seen look flexible, like thick plastic, only less rigid. Make them impervious to fluid flow, gas or liquid; use a working fluid with high surface energy, no loss by evaporation… and basically, you're done."

"Standard xenology exercise," Felix added. "Metalloids, silicoids, bubble colonies… Dozens of possibilities. In theory."

"So it's more an engineering problem than a biological one." Marco grinned, evidently happier on his home turf. "Makes sense—"

"Dah. But there's a deeper problem, isn't there?" asked Elzabet.

Jane looked surprised. "Yah, many. What do you have in mind?"

"I see how they could survive *now*, but how could such creatures have evolved to start with?" Elza's fine-boned cheeks were flushed, her pulse racing. This was *exciting*. "They surely can't have got started on a rock in an asteroid belt, not enough energy flows. Even bacterial-grade organisms would be virtually impossible. They'd be viable if they blinked into existence overnight, but there's no sensible evolutionary pathway that leads to them. Like Marco says about the orbits."

Jane started to revise her opinion of Lady Elzabet of Quynt. "Yah, good point." Making it up as she went along, she started to weave an evolutionary just-so story, wondering where it would lead. Sometimes it's best just to talk, and listen to whatever emerges from your mouth. You often surprise yourself. "They must originally have evolved on a planet. Not there now, but it was then. With fluids of various kinds. If the atmosphere was thin, they'd have been well on the way to vacuum-tolerance from the start. Got their nutrients from rock, even then, and their energy from sunlight. Then presumably their planet lost its air."

"Gradually," said Felix.

"Yah, gradually, because that would've given them time to evolve, until vacuum wasn't an issue. Carry on eating rocks. Until one fateful day—"

"Their planet collided with something and got smashed," said Elzabet.

"Or someone smashed it," said Tinka. "Could be any kind of culture, out there in the galactic depths."

"I guess," said Jane. Marco looked dubious but held his peace. "Most of the proto-groupies must have died, but a few survived. They drifted through space, from fragment to fragment. Angular momentum conspired with friction to create a rotating disc, and the rocks organised themselves into an asteroid field. The evolving groupies made permanent homes on the larger asteroids. They started to dig burrows. Some might have been intelligent all along. Or, as they continued evolving, some might have acquired intelligence."

"True sapience requires extelligence," Felix stated dogmatically.

"Sure," Jane replied. "You've already told us that. But extelligence is a collective trait of a culture, Felix, not of an individual. Organism-level intelligence is a necessary step, and it hangs around once a culture becomes extelligent. They interact complicitly."

"Yah. But extelligence is easier to observe. Look for computers, bombs, or spaceships. Listen for messages." This was positively talkative for Felix: four sentences, even if one was only one word long. He generally said more when people disagreed with him.

Jane changed the subject. "That reminds me, their UV-signalling must have evolved before the breakup, too. But they probably wouldn't have been limited to visible light—well, visible to *us*. Our sensitivity to that part of the spectrum evolved because that's the light from Sol that got through the water vapour in Old Earth's atmosphere. A drier atmosphere, or even just Rock Star's greater UV to human-visible ratio, sets the evolutionary payoffs differently."

"Sam?"

Their navigator, who was trying to figure out a tricky in-system trip by reaction drive for the next day's assignment, gave an irritated jerk of the head at the interruption. Then he broke out into a big smile. "Oh, it's you, Tinka."

The rangy pilot raised both arms in greeting; she had the characteristic Wayland hands with long index fingers and lopsided thumbs. "Yah, 'tis I. Sam, I was wondering… How big is this asteroid field?"

"Big, believe me. Why do you ask?"

"All we've seen is our own small part. I was wondering just how small."

Sam started paying serious attention as he realised where she was heading. "Never did the sums. Too busy observing. Well, Old Earth's belt is low-density and sparse, but even so, it covers at least—" he directed a mental query at his wristcomp—"Whoah! Four times ten to the power *seventeen* square kilometres! Ignoring thickness, because basically it's a disc. Rock Star's is way bigger, with more varied orbits."

"Yah," said Marco, squatting nearby, fiddling with some solitronic components he'd pulled out of the wall on slides. "A much thicker, fuzzier disc. At least 400 million asteroids more than a kilometre across, if the usual power-law size distribution still holds."

"The databanks list 489,322,081," *Valkyrie* chanted. "Though the distribution is truncated. It has proportionately fewer large bodies than Sol system's asteroid belt, indicative of substantial remodelling. *Nothing* with enough gravity to form a ball, or collapse a tunnel."

"Remod—oh, the groupies must have broken some up when they were honeycombing them with tunnels," Sam muttered, "and prevented them from coalescing again. Orbital control."

Marco grunted as one obstinate component refused to budge. "A huge number of them, to change the statistics. Must have taken a long time."

"Maybe not as long as you think," Jane objected. "This is biology. It's exponentially reproductive, and works in parallel. In the time it takes to break up one big asteroid, they can break them all up."

"Yah, everything's enormous," said Tinka. "Including their rock-eating abilities. My point is, there's a gigantic volume for the Concordat to surveil. The basic factor is the sheer *number* of rocks. Half a billion, and that's just the bigger ones. A single team might investigate a few, and find only limited intelligence, but for all anyone could tell, they might be looking at the groupie equivalent of a meerkat colony. Bright, but not a threat. Starhome would learn a bit from that, but it needs to know whether there are intelligent groupies *anywhere* around Rock Star. That'd be a huge task even if they used that old statistical sampling method—Marco, what's it called?"

Without turning round, Marco replied: "Monte Karla."

"Yah. That. They'd still need a *lot* of teams to do the legwork. So we're just one team out of many. And since we're trainees, there must be a policy of using trainees for this kind of work. I can't believe we're anything special. Starhome obviously has high level command-and-control infrastructure in place. Into which we, and our fellow trainees, slot as just one more cog in the clockwork." She ran her fingers through her long hair.

"Comforting," said Felix. "Not alone."

"Not comforting at all," Tinka contradicted. "Why use a bunch of amateurs?"

"We figured that out," Marco reminded her, "before we left Suufi. We're expendable."

Tinka looked sceptical. "Yah, at the time that made sense. But they're taking so many precautions, it's unlikely we'll ever need to be expended. There's more to it than that."

"I can think of another reason," said Jane. "How many groupies are there?"

"Well, a round one-klick rock has volume—"

"Half a cubic kilometre," *Valkyrie* sang, just before Marco could get the words out. As a mathematical engineer, he didn't even need to ask his 'comp that sort of trivial question.

"Thank you, metal slave. If one quarter of that is occupied, and a groupie needs ten cubic metres of space, which I suspect is an overestimate, that's twelve million groupies per asteroid. Which gives—"

"Nearly 10 quintillion," the ship's computer intoned. "Could easily be triple that. Even ignoring any the size of insects. Or bacteria."

There was a stunned silence. Felix broke it.

"Mother. I knew it was a big number, but *that* big?"

"No wonder they're using trainees," Said Tinka. "They'll be using schoolkids next, just to make up numbers."

Elza had been turning everything over in her mind, using the traditional thought patterns of Hippolytan nobility—enlightened self-interest with a dash of paranoia. "There's more to it than that, Felix. If they seconded every living soul in the Concordat, it would be like asking a nest of termites to watch over a continent. Starhome's been digging into these guys for fifty years, ever since EZ9 was shut off. Very slowly, and very carefully. Vance gave us a clue: she said the biggest problem was that we might be a threat *to them*. We all know Vance is a hardnose, way high in Starhome Security, whatever else she claims. She didn't mean we might do those poor little groupies harm. She meant that they might perceive *us* as a threat, and decide to do something about it. I'm not sure whether she meant attacking our people inside the Rock Star system, or whether us poking around might inadvertently trigger some sort of swarming behav—Oh. Great. Galactic. Maternity."

It took a lot to make Elza swear. Even more to make her do it one word at a time. "You've just thought of something," Marco said.

"Yah. We're in trouble. Suppose these weirdos leave their star? They wouldn't need Da Silvas, they could just up sticks and drift, taking their rocky home along with them. Vance said they get their nutrients by processing rocks, so they automatically take their food with them too. Probably go dormant in the interstellar dark, so the centuries between stars wouldn't bother them. They thrive in a vacuum. Imagine it: a vast cosmic locust-swarm, eating moons and planets instead of crops, groupiforming everything into tasty, comfy vacuum-wrapped pebbles."

Sam was becoming agitated. "I can see why Starhome kept the lid on this. And why they've got so many observers all over the system."

"Yah," said Marco. "A random sample will show up any significant trends, provided it's big enough. You can't observe *everything*."

"Dah. But they'd like to. Which means—"

"They're worried sick."

Tinka, tense and anxious, rested her chin on one lopsided hand. *"We're worried sick, Sam. If these creatures really are intel—sorry, Felix, extelligent—then their ability to thrive in vacuo would give them a huge military advantage if they became hostile. Think how much protection we need for space travel. These beasties could wander around the galaxy at will using little more than a rock skiff with a lightsail."

Jane gave a humourless laugh. "That's the least of our worries."

"Least?"

"Don't think big, think small. Rock Star versions of the humble microbe. If the big guys eat rock, the little ones might—"

"Eat spaceships," Tinka finished for her.

"Haven't done in fifty years," said Sam, looking unconvinced by his own reasoning.

"Nah," said Jane, "but locusts swarms form when high population density triggers a change in the insects' feeding habits. Something—not necessarily overpopulation, but that would be a plausible cause—might just trigger a swarm of ravening nanogroupies. They'd eat everything: ships, moons, planets. Just like the big ones. The difference is—"

"They'd reproduce faster, and we'd never see them coming."

Manhattan, Old Earth

Angell Wilcox Tobey the 56th:

It must have been exciting, eighteen hundred years ago.

Sure, people drowned, a lot of people, as the sea rose (or Manhattan sank, I can never remember) and a lot fled: but the ones who remained were ready to greet the Elder Gods with hosannas. Dagon in the deeps, Cthulhu in the stars... that was when the Church got established, with the promise that believers' souls would be eaten first. Heady days.

Leading the flock, though, meant organising things. At first, boats between the partly submerged buildings, so the faithful could get to the rites, where a few would be sacrificed to prove their sincerity. Then, boats for efficient foraging—you can't waste followers on mere starvation—and when everything had either been found or was rotting, for fishing. Then aquaculture, rigged for protection against the mighty storms of Dagon. It wasn't blasphemous to resist Him, as He took a few choice lives every storm: the Church sacrificed their families at the next rite, which cemented our devotion to him and (I can't help thinking) avoided the expense of supporting widows and orphans. We still handle them that way, but you have to arrange for general medicine. A sick or senile believer makes an unacceptable sacrifice.

As warlord nations came and went on the mainland, we endured, though endurance was not our creed. If life wasn't easy, it was never desperate.

But all of this meant organisation, durable organisation, and not all priests could be star prophets. Some had to be middle management, like me. Like my father before me, and his forefathers, for all those years. A local

31

priest, keeping our parish fed and in line, sacrificing a few when population control requires it (thanks to the ban on contraceptives, it quite often does), and praying for the Return.

Our way, the way of Great Cthulhu, is one of waiting and patience. We do not take refuge in the depths of the ocean. We do not become many enough to starve before the Time, for our deaths belong to the gods; we order our lives with ritual and self-control. We create the conditions that will ultimately lead to the return of the Great Old Ones, as they rise once more from the realms of the undead to leave their stone houses in the city of R'lyeh, soaring again across the voids between the stars.

We strive endlessly to make Earth ready for them.

They will come! I know it. But… eighteen hundred years?

It is a test.

I try to be devout, but I cannot give my flock a date. I cannot bring myself to believe unconditionally that it will come in my lifetime: I am not more devout than my father or grandfather, and it did not come in theirs. I feed my sheep, and hope. They will come!

But now I fear this new cult, that has risen among the young: Ira da Terra. They promise a vague but terrible vengeance, taking upon themselves the destruction that belongs to the Gods, destruction even among the stars. They swear to bring it in our lifetimes, though their methods are not revealed: they say this is for Security, and gain credibility by that.

We will die before the Elder Gods come, if this new cult gains influence. It ravages our battered planet with even more war and destruction. It is an affront to our patience.

Our rites keep us alive, to die fittingly. The rites of Ira da Terra are the rites of premature and fruitless death.

It is time to tremble.

Sri Lanka Beanstalk, Old Earth

My name?

You don't want to know my name. It's not safe to have that sort of knowledge. Safe for you, I mean. And I'm here for your safety, whether you're climbing a Beanstalk on your way to a better world, or stuck at the bottom of a gravity-well on a world that's been falling apart for the last two thousand years.

Me? I'm neither. I live above so much of the atmosphere that the sky is midnight blue, even in the day; but far above me is the Concordat. My bosses. They use the height where gravity and centrifugal force balance (nearly three Earth diameters up) for microgravity production and relaxation, but mostly live in the counterweight, another couple of diameters out, where centrifugal 'gravity' is about a fifth of weight on Earth's surface. Their heads are towards us.

They're not just keeping their distance (two hours' trip by continuous-acceleration capsule) out of dislike for our touch. They also want to be sure that if a Beanstalk breaks, they're in the bit that flies off and can be rescued at leisure, not the bit that falls to Earth and wrecks itself and the Equator. That may not be likely, with regular maintenance and good security, but it's possible. Particularly with the anti-Concordat movements Earth throws up every couple of generations; bringing down one of the Beanstalks (and hence all of them) would do most of its tremendous damage on Earth, but when has that ever stopped freedom fighters? Not that it would be easy. The tropics are at 50°C even at night, keeping unprotected humans away... but protection is available. And bringing a stalk down would take nukes... but there are so many pathways to fission or fusion these days. The biggest obstacles to direct assault are the sensors and laser weapons mounted on the bottom 100km or so of the stalk, which make direct assault an unlikely choice... but they don't stop infiltrators.

That's my job.

You'd think it would be a post for a Concordat citizen, but remember, for all their talk about valuing cultural variation, Starfolk hate being around Earth folk. They imposed the Quarantine seventeen hundred years back because most of us didn't meet their standards of intelligence, health and mental stability, i.e., they saw us as stupid, sick and crazy, and our mothers wore army boots. They still see us that way.

So why do I work for them? Partly, they're not altogether wrong, particularly about our politicians. It's not great Downside, working for a guy who thinks keeping foreigners out will solve all his problems, particularly a guy who defines 'foreigner' as 'someone living in territory we haven't conquered yet.' Partly, it's interesting work in a clean environment (except when I go Downside), and pays really well by Earth standards. (Not the standards of the Starfolk on the counterweight, who see the whole Solar System as a hardship posting.) So, I'm in charge of testing other Earthies for intelligence, health and mental stability—and right understanding, right thought, right speech, right action, right livelihood, right effort, right mindfulness and right concentration, as far as possible.

People I admit don't go more than a thousand miles up without direct Starfolk testing, but the system has worked well for over fifteen hundred years, so that's become somewhat of a rubber stamp, even for emigration. The trouble is... a group on Earth can arrange jobs for your family members—good jobs that they're fit for (they can't fake that), but there aren't enough jobs like that. A cult can then threaten, oh so indirectly, the loss of those jobs. Or worse. Unless you fudge the 'right thought' tests a little, on their candidate.

I did that once. After that they had a handle on me, to do it again. And again.

When I learned that the group was Ira da Terra, I grew fearful.

As I learn more about them, I am more and more anxious what I may have loosed on the Galaxy. But I am equally afraid, for my family.

I am afraid.

Circumpolar, Old Earth

Sven Tso-Park hoped to be the last dictator of the Circumpolar Nations.

It had taken his predecessors seven centuries to build the ring of territory around the Arctic, completing it three hundred years ago. It no longer seemed necessary to use the Army to hold down separatism, and the CPN had issues that needed the wisdom of genuine consensus, reached through open disagreement. And it needed help from the Concordat.

The Concordat ambassador was familiar with Sven's problems, but let him talk. Anybody below him might be probing for weakness, but the Concordat's strength was unchallenged. Sven knew he risked nothing by talking freely.

The Northern soil had slowly changed to match the hotter climate, but was still fragile. Bad mistakes in fertilising it had led to the Gobi Desert extending through what had been steppe and tundra, almost to the now-temperate coast of the Arctic. The run-off from that, human industry included, had interfered with the ocean, and the dome dwellers there had retaliated. Not quite by war (only because a poisoned land is bad news for the sea): economic and population sabotage, against CPN growth, was routine. The Circumpolar Army wanted to retaliate.

The ambassador's main job was to prevent violence, but she questioned rather than challenged. "Infiltration for sabotage must be difficult."

"Infiltrating the domes is impossible," said Sven. "Landsmen can't pass as aquafolk for five minutes, they haven't the skills learned as infants. But all the wetties have to do to get to *us* is land on a beach. And we have thousands of kilometres of beach."

"So what does your Army want to do?"

Sven expressed his frustration. "Strike openly at the domes."

"Depth charges?" The ambassador looked hopeful that the violence could be limited to nuisance attacks.

"*Nuclear* depth charges."

The ambassador cupped a hand to her chin, as if deep in thought; then shook her head. "You're not self-sufficient in protein, Sven. You don't grow enough cattle or beans in Finland. Or the Yukon."

This was obvious. "Yes, I *know* we need the fish. Everybody knows we need the fish. Even the generals know we need the fish. But they've convinced themselves we can cow the Zee Hanze into submission, or failing that, go fishing ourselves."

The ambassador laughed, sourly. "Good luck with that, against underwater guerrillas."

"Exactly. That's why I need to shrink the Army: it's the tail that thinks it can wag me. To death. But I can't use a shrunken Army to keep my own population in line, so the people will have to keep *themselves* in line. And they're not used to it. They wouldn't like it, even if I could convince them there's an external threat."

The ambassador leaned back and let out a deep breath, running her hand across her close-cropped hair. "There *is* an external threat."

"Yes, plenty. Those lunatics in Europe, the warlords in the Americas... The people know about those, but they don't see any reason to take action, and they may well be right.

"No, my problem is another threat altogether, which the people also refuse to see. The main one."

"The Zee Hanze?"

"Exactly. Especially the Arctic domes. They're not just a threat, they're actually damaging us. They send assassins, they send tailored viruses, against humans and against compware."

"And you send toxic run-off."

It was Sven's turn to laugh. "It's not easy to stop. Particularly to benefit *them*."

The ambassador took her time replying. "Perhaps it would be easier to convince your people with another reason."

"Meaning?" Sven asked.

"The Concordat brings you ores from the asteroids, down our three Beanstalks. The Concordat gives you communications, GPS, accurate weather forecasts, up-to-date computers. We're not eager to stop, but we might stop... if you don't clean up your environment a bit. And the ocean."

Sven took the hint. "And you might stop supplying the domes, if they don't stop with the assassins?"

"We might."

"Hmm. Would you be willing to show those mights in public?"

The ambassador looked sly. "Well. It could be better to 'let them be known', without being so specific that the lawyers get into interpreting what exactly they cover."

"Good thought. When lawyers get together with generals or industrialists, the rule of law is an invitation to find loopholes," said Sven. "*Daddy, you said not to go into the gun cupboard, but you didn't mention firing guns that we just found on the table.*"

Their eyes met. A quiet understanding flashed between them. "Just so. Consider yourselves menaced, then, and we'll get the word out. We'll give a heads-up to the Zee Hanze leaders, too, so they're not blindsided."

Sven decided he'd got most of what he'd hoped for, and would settle for it. "Thanks for the threats… I think."

"What are friends for?" With that, the Ambassador took her leave.

Kermadec City, Old Earth

"What's the use of studying sea-life we don't eat, Ms Rhee?"

Impana Rhee, a wiry, spare-framed woman with close-cropped curly hair, who exuded competence and determination, was momentarily thrown off balance. *What do you think a Deep Ocean Research Station is for, you idiot?* Where to begin in answering such a question? What would a desk-sailor like Hormsley understand, anyway? Few who spent their days up here, on the surface in an immense floating city, could understand life in the deeps. Definitely not someone like Hormsley. His downturned mouth, big brown eyes and long earlobes gave him the mournful look of a bloodhound, but without the sense of animation. A career dingbeaucrat who'd bluffed his way to Third Secretary, he'd made his mark by inventing rules for everyone else in the Zee Hanze to follow. The more rules, the more subordinates he needed to check that people were obeying them. Her career had been spent in the secret places of Earth's oceans, trying to find out what nature's rules were. That was the real motive, not something you could use to put money in a bank. But it would be unwise, to say the least, even to hint at that.

She could say, our food comes from Earth's whole ocean ecology, natural and artificial, not individual species; but that was too much for the bureaucratic mind. No point at all in offering science as a value in itself. Go with politics...

Feeling a little dirty, Impana said "The Concordat," throwing him off balance.

"The Concordat doesn't pay for that, Ms Rhee. Some ore shipments from space, GPS, orbital mapping of resources, that's it. No funding. Everything you get comes from the Zee Hanze."

For once, Hormsley was right. "We need those things as well as whatever we can do for ourselves, and we need the threat of their withdrawal to keep the Circumpolar Nations from an out-and-out strike." And the Circumpolar Nations need them to keep *us* from something equally stupid, but tact, tact. "We need some respect from the Concordat, they can't go on thinking we just eat and kill each other." Not in that order, anyway. Usually. "Abyssal research is one of the few fields where Earth gets published, in refereed interstellar journals. It pays in *respect*. It pays in *face*."

Pecking order, Hormsley lived every day, although the pecking chickens that Schjelderup-Ebbe had observed before space travel were long extinct on Earth. And he wouldn't want to close down anything he was overseeing. So it was no surprise when he suddenly relaxed, and said, "Very well, I'll approve your budget for this year. But you'd better keep those publications coming."

"I think we can promise that, Mr Hormsley." Better not talk of breakthroughs at this stage. He wouldn't get it anyway. "Thank you, sir."

As she descended through darkening water to the edge of the continental shelf—slowly, even with today's techniques for avoiding the bends—Impana thought about the Trench, where everything was so different. Edge Base was the deepest place that humans could swim free: in the abyss they needed more protection than in deep space. But she was so *there* in a robot. Far below the impoverished monocultures of the plankton farms, the vanished tigers of the land, there was learning to be done.

A new species of squid was no great excitement in itself, given humanity's spasmodic attention to the deep sea. This one seemed a relative of the long-gone Humboldt squid, expanding from hidden places into the niches once occupied by species that made the supreme mistake of becoming numerous enough for human fishing to be briefly economic, and to continue (once committed) till the last remnant was gone.

Dosidicus madhu hunted in groups. Groups meant communication and a code for it—language? Her team's papers had shown that the bandwidth of those fast-flashing chromatophores was potentially far higher than human speech, and entropy analysis had proved it was all used. But it was not sequential, like speech, with one token after another. All the limbs were flashing, but no area flashed the same as any other. Attempts to parse it into ancient categories like 'noun' or 'verb' or 'alarm call' got nowhere. She got more and more paranoid that something was blocking them.

Then she had seen that this was perhaps the point. A successful conspiracy is itself a law of nature. The speed of light is not relative to any 'rest' velocity; squid messages do not break into sub-messages, any more than part of a hologram shows part of an object.

Not that squid flashed holograms either, but her brain was now free to think what they did flash, without answering questions as misleading as "what holds up the moon?" or "what drives the planets?". And her brain, considering itself, supplied the answer.

In the brain, what we see (with the eyes and visual cortex) directs the motor cortex in how to move, to touch or bite or caress a target, without words. The cerebral cortex chooses which targets to touch or bite or caress, without words. The squid signals transformed directly into sensation or volition, without symbolic tokens.

She suddenly saw why the cooperative hunting of these squid was so unlike the cooperation of wolves (so much so, that some researchers still refused to recognise it as cooperation). The squid with the best view of the prey moved the muscles of the squid hidden from the prey by an ink-cloud, and felt them move, like its own… subject to the volition of the whole group, aware of the positions of all its members, and the prey.

There were many tests of this central hypothesis still to be made, many details to be fleshed out, but her mind was already writing the stellar paper for *Interstellar Cognition*. Some of her team would use it as a ticket off the exhausted Earth, but Impana would stay, protecting her squid and the inexhaustible Ocean.

Wada Cluster

On the third R&R, too many months apart, Marco had one night with a couple who were enthusiastic, attractive, skilled—and not Elza. Faced with the prospect of going back to being shut in with her, without her, while going around the hamster wheel of his simulations and the old/new data, he fought his way to Vance's office.

"I want out."

She looked up from the low desk where she squatted, and frowned. "I'm sorry, but there *is* no out. You knew that when you signed up for Galactic training, Bianchi. And you exponentiated it when you reaffirmed the Confidentiality Agreement."

Marco was unimpressed by this kind of officialdom. "I know that's the legal position, citizen. But I'm seeing nothing that Starhome hasn't analysed to death forty years ago."

To his surprise, Vance allowed herself a faint smile. "We hoped that you would. One of your old professors at IIT said that if there was a new angle possible, you were more likely to find it than she was."

"Who—no, I can guess. *Thanks* for the compliment, and two years of misery. I haven't found it, and there won't be one, without new data. Richer data."

"We agree."

Marco, not expecting that, was momentarily thrown. "You *agree*? Then why not let me out? You'll never get new data without changing this timid hands-off—oh. Oh."

Rock Star

At the fringe of the eternal slow, spinning dance of the asteroid field, a new rock had drifted slowly sunward. Externally, it looked exactly like any of the billions of smaller bodies that orbited Rock Star; broken, gouged, pockmarked with the openings of countless tunnels. Internally, it was hollowed out to create a typically low density.

All that was missing was a colony of groupies.

At the Concordat station, anxious eyes watched as the interloper nudged into position. Contact was not the objective; that would be too provocative. Concordat astronomers had spotted a pair of rocks that would, in several months' time, come unusually close. Left undisturbed, they would swing past each other on diverging trajectories, setting off a slow wave of redirection. Concordat engineers, instructed by higher authority, decided to change that. Just a little. Just enough to wreak havoc.

The interloper had been ferried across from another system using a temporary bolt-on Da Silva, since removed to leave no trace. Without approaching either body closely, it would play the chaos butterfly, causing a deviation in trajectory so slight that only sensitive instruments, knowing exactly where to look, would notice. But as the consequences of that change unfolded, the target bodies would now be on a grazing collision course.

Valkyrie's increasingly bored crew members were beginning to know their way around the small segment of the asteroid field to which they had been assigned. The disposition of rocks was always changing, but the changes were slow and predictable. As the inner asteroids overtook the outer ones, they moved into the next segment and became someone else's problem. New ones took their place and became theirs. They could recognise a hundred or more rocks on sight, without asking their 'comps.

One hundred rocks, full of aliens—and none of them doing anything remotely interesting.

The trainees' main task was routine patrolling, and for the last nine months it had been the only task. First, learn how to get close to the target body while avoiding any stray rocks that happen to come near. Not *too* close, that could disturb the groupies. Any rock with a diameter of 20 metres or more was on the database, along with its last-known orbital elements. A squad of automated telescopes tracked everything they could resolve, but occasionally two rocks would come close together, swing round each other in the actinic light, and depart along a random vector. Most of those were flung out of the ecliptic plane, where the main disc was concentrated, but would eventually return to disturb the main body of rocks. Some remained within the ecliptic, increasing the chance of further diversions, and collisions that mysteriously never happened. Those were more dangerous, and *Valkyrie* had been kept well away. But now they were the catspaw for the new policy.

Marco's outburst had invited Starhome to hand *Valkyrie* the short straw. They were tasked with observing a collision, close up. One that Starhome's engineers had set up, months before, with a perturbation so slight and indirect that it would surely escape notice. Assuming anything was capable of noticing.

Body A (its full designation was fifty characters long; this was a nonce symbol for easy use) was a rough brick shape 2·7 kilometres across and about 15 billion tonnes. Its orbit was almost circular. Body B was smaller, 1·3 kilometres, but denser at 2 billion tonnes and shaped something like an "L"; it tumbled wildly about peculiar axes. Its orbit was eccentric, and it was slowly catching A up as they both moved in roughly the same direction. That was crucial: instead of the two rocks smashing head-on, which would create a huge debris cloud in no way conducive to delicate observations, A and B were going to scrape each other's skins off, revealing (they hoped) what lay beneath.

Robot probes had failed to penetrate the rocks' interior. No matter how they were redesigned, they were quickly destroyed, sending back pathetically little information. Few managed even to reach a cavern. Those that did all showed the same flocking behaviour of small organisms. A few had revealed further openings, larger, heading deeper into the interior. Now, finally, patience had run out. Persistent ignorance raised the potential threat level and pushed the reward curve above the risk, justifying (to one faction) a more intrusive approach.

Starhome was guessing that a grazing collision would offer the best chance of observing groupies in the deep interior. A more drastic collision was obviously pointless, not to mention hostile. A graze would shake up the internal habitat, causing many tunnels to cave in. With luck, some of the larger creatures might emerge, albeit temporarily, to find out what was going on at the surface. Or to oversee repairs. Or whatever. If not, the Starfolk might get to observe how the smaller groupies behaved under stressful conditions.

It was an investigative principle older than science. To see how it works, disrupt it.

Sometimes it's a hornet's nest.

"Time to impact?" Sam enquired.

"Twenty-two minutes," *Valkyrie* sang. "Our distance at that time will be 4.58 kilometres. We are out of the collision plane and most fragments will not come this way."

"Most?"

"Lacking detailed information on the internal structure, I can't be sure where the fracture zones will occur. Just be sure not to attempt manual control. I may need to get out of the way fast. I note you are all strapped down and suited as instructed."

They waited in silence, wondering what, if anything, they would discover.

"Twenty minutes. Do you authorise deployment of the probes?"

"Yah. Get them right in close to the action, *Valkyrie*. To get the best data, we have to risk the probes. Starhome will foot the bill, after all."

The probes were in capsules in the cargo bay. *Valkyrie* opened the access port and elasticated arms pushed them gently out. The capsules opened and the tiny probes ejected. With spurts of propellant, they took up station in a ring around *Valkyrie*'s command axis.

"Fifteen minutes." The probes detached themselves, drifting towards the impact zone. Both rocks were now in view, travelling in intersecting orbits, the smaller one in a more eccentric orbit, catching the larger one rapidly. They both tumbled slowly, ever-changing silhouettes in the bright starlight.

"See anything, Felix?"

Felix kept his eyes flickering across a bank of slapscreens that almost surrounded him. "Nah. If anyone's home, they're all staying indoors."

"Do we know there are any groupies in there?"

"Yah, some were seen on the surface three hours ago, streaming into the tunnels. On both rocks."

"They knew the collision was coming, then," said Tinka.

"I think so. If you're right, it's a concern. Shows a high level of awareness. Could be a coincidence of timing. We'll add it to the data files, run some stats."

"Five minutes."

Sam was running software to predict the attitudes of the rocks when they collided. They'd acquired a good set of data during the approach. "*Valkyrie?* Keep an eye on that—"

"Outcrop shaped like a mushroom on body B? Yah. It could break off in the smash and head towards us. Am monitoring. Don't think it's going to be a problem. One minute. Secure belts tightly."

They waited, silent, attentive, as *Valkyrie* counted down the seconds, stopping at ten. No distractions now.

Turning ponderously, the two rocks met. The smaller one ploughed into the larger one, kicking up a slow-motion dust storm. The top of the mushroom sheared off, narrowly missing a probe.

The probes homed in, hoping to watch as deep caverns suddenly lost their roofs, exposing whatever was inside.

Both rocks were crumpling like meringues smashing against a brick wall. Cracks appeared, irregular fragments broke off, exposing dark pits. Eager probes rushed to peer inside. One, getting too close, was sideswiped by rock shrapnel.

"Structural features on B," Felix announced.

"Those walled cavities? Like the inside of a wasp's nest?"

"Yah."

"See anything inside them? Wasps would keep their grubs there."

"There's *something*. Moving." One screen showed an image of animated wire wool bedecked with toothpicks. The scale, at the side, indicated it was 1·27 metres across—the largest groupie humans had ever seen, but they were hoping for something a lot more informative. Then the image froze.

"What happened?"

"Lost contact with the probe. I think the groupie threw a rock at it. That's the last frame it transmit—Oh, wow!"

The bodies had already separated, but the damage was continuing as stresses propagated. The smaller rock had suddenly started splitting, a deep crevasse slicing down into its core. This wasn't going as intended; the rock must be weaker than the engineers had calculated. However, it was also an opportunity. Felix sent three probes down inside the growing canyon, following the propagating crack as the tiny worldlet came apart.

Then the images vanished in clouds of dust. Felix swore, more eloquent in profanity than he ever was in sedate discourse.

"Pity, you were getting some good detail there," Tinka said. "I can't wait till we enhance it and find out what we were seeing. Brief though it might be, it knocks the socks off anything Vance has ever shown us."

"How many probes survived, Felix?" Jane asked.

"Eight."

"Redeploy four to the undamaged surfaces. Let's see what crawls out. If anything."

Five minutes passed. Ten.

The probes hovered, sending images of an interior so intricately sculpted that it might have been assembled from architectural plans, yet of a design no human agency would contemplate. There were some flat surfaces, but they were polyhedral rather than rectangular. Whatever groupie constructors preferred, it wasn't the right angle. Fractured walls abounded, making the asteroid look like a vast, demented building smashed by a cosmic wrecking-ball. A multitude of small groupies crawled through the wreckage, clambering past and over the corpses of their fellows in the negligible gravity. Many fell into space, twisting and turning in ineffectual attempts to control their path.

"Nothing larger than a dog," Jane reported, storing the comment in her 'comp. "Same old, same old, just a bit bigger. No signs of intelligent behaviour."

"The architecture looks designed."

"So does a wasp's nest, Felix."

"Yah, but wasps repeat the same phenotype." With increasing emotional involvement, he became more articulate. "That constrains the chamber size in their nests, Jane. And that automatically creates organised structure. These beasties don't have a typical phenotype, let alone a replicated one. Yet these structures look contrived. Designed. Built."

"Maybe. But if they are, there's no sign of a designer or a builder. I have a feeling this particular experiment is a bust, people—"

On one screen, an irregular slab of wall the size of *Valkyrie* broke away. A second later, it became clear it had been pushed. Bunches of thick blue tubes, flexible yet jointed, appeared as the slab of rock detached itself. Rings of waving yellow fringes were arrayed along them. The tubes were rooted in a strange, bulbous blue mass, which seemed to *pour* out of the rock. The tubes were at least six metres long, with bell-shaped ends, and there were scores of them. The blue mass was about the size and shape of a hippopotamus, only squidgier.

"Oh, Mother," said Sam.

"Too right—look, there's another big one coming out behind it! And another one over there by that thing that looks like a squashed igloo!"

"Yah. Both different from Bluebell, there, and from each other. Still amorphic. If anything, those two are even bigger. I think we've found our designers."

"Felix, I don't know how you can stay so analytical when this is happening!"

"Best way to retain my sanity, Tinka."

"What's that thing they're tugging out of that hole?"

"Interesting. Looks inorganic. I think it's a—"

It jumped toward them, incredibly fast. Then smaller groupies jumped off it, faster. And smaller groupies off them, faster still. By the time they had covered four klicks they were a cloud of almost invisible motes, too wide for *Valkyrie* to dodge, moving about two thousand kilometres an hour. Lines between them caught on *Valkyrie*'s spines, then her body. The cloud converged on her. And began to (?) eat.

"They've clogged my reaction jets," sang *Valkyrie* calmly, "and the Da Silva won't work with the spines like this. Recommend abandon ship."

Groupies were bursting through the cabin walls. Prestressed frameworks let go with a snap.

"Evacuate!" Tinka yelled. "Get to the—" A shard of *Valkyrie*'s hull impaled her, entering from her back and protruding from her stomach.

Marco closed his faceplate, grabbed Elza's arm, and jumped towards the emergency capsule. The arm followed him, along with most of her upper body. The rest of her didn't. He tried to head for the cryo tanks, but Felix saw that groupies had already reached them. He dragged Marco away from the bloody mess that had, a few seconds before, been his unattainable desire. "Get in the trashed capsule, Marco!" He shoved him across the crazily spinning compartment towards the pod's automatically opened access hatch. At least some emergency systems were still functioning.

Sam closed the faceplate of a dazed, confused Jane, and pushed them both away from the buckled floor as another jolt hit the ship. Sam's trajectory took him straight into the path of a bigger groupie. It bit through him, leaving his body surrounded by an expanding cloud of blood. As air rushed out of the ship, the blood was sucked away, along with pieces of Sam. The groupie looked somehow confused. Released from Sam's grip, Jane cannoned head first into the far wall, as another groupie bit off one of her legs.

Felix, howling, grabbed her hand, pulled her into the capsule, slammed the hatch shut, and stuffed her into a crashcoon. With no time to seal himself in a cocoon's protective embrace, he sat in an angle of the hull and hit the eject button. A giant slap jolted his spine as one side of *Valkyrie* blew off and the capsule was blasted into space. It narrowly missed a slab of broken rock, tumbling end over end before the attitude jets began to take control. An automatic signal broadcast its position for retrieval.

Consciousness hit like a blow. His back was bruised and sore. One arm wasn't working—broken by the force of the ejection. With the other, Felix triggered a tourniquet in Jane's suit around her thigh, spitting out globules of her blood that were floating in the cabin in a thick mist, smearing on every surface. Marco started struggling against the embrace of the crashcoon, groaning. "Wha—"

"Keep still, Marco. The aliens attacked us with some kind of weapon. We're safe now." *I wish. Those things could follow us.*

"Elza!"

"Elza's dead, Marco."

"I could have saved—"

"You couldn't," said Felix brutally. "So are Sam and Tinka. Jane's badly injured." He instructed the capsule's rudimentary AI to aim them out of the plane of the asteroid field. Now all they could do was to hope the groupies didn't pursue them, and to wait. He found a rag and tried to wipe himself clean as suction filters mopped up the floating blood.

A rescue ship from the station picked them up eight hours later.

Jane died half an hour before it arrived.

Too late for its cryo tanks to save her brain.

Long after the rescue ship had departed, the groupies were still gathering the pieces of *Valkyrie*, a process that seemed to have much higher priority than repairing their homes. A Concordat ship watched from a greater and greater distance as they one by one caught up with a fragment, waited until its turning took them to the side further from Rock A, and jumped away. A small delta-v reaction pushed the fragment toward a meeting with A, while projection showed the groupie would meet up with a distant rock... however long it took. None went into endless orbits, as most random jumps would.

New datum: their computational skills.

New datum: their attitude to time.

With these insights, the watchers looked more closely at their jumps, always from rock to rock… in months, years, or centuries.

When somebody calculated that these jumps were precise butterfly stamps, preserving an orderly flow of the rocks, avoiding billion-ton collisions tens of thousands of years ahead, the observers withdrew to a distance of seven light years.

And hoped that was far enough.

Arctic Ocean, Old Earth

All the ice was gone. Off the Siberian coast, in the shallows of the enormous continental shelf, before the seabed drops away into the ocean depths, dusky shapes loomed through a distorted blue haze. A forest of thick bulging discs, tall and wide as the parched land's deserted dunes, swayed and flexed in rippling currents. Angular shafts of sunlight slanted between them, fading into deeper water.

Arrayed along the shallows like a vast honeycomb, the cylinders bred billions of living creatures, vital food for an overstretched, tortured planet. Some held squid, others shrimp; there were cylinders of sardine, herring, shad, anchovy, smelt, and other pelagic forage fish, all small. Biomass is lost when bigger fish eat smaller fish. Dotted between them were the plankton farms, fed on offal and other organic detritus through tubes that snaked down from tethered platforms. More tubes fed plankton to the fish, and shredded offal and other organic detritus to the cephalopods and crustaceans.

Dozens of huge domes were embedded in the sea bed, like shells of buried giant sea urchins. Lights flickered and flashed within the domes. Narrow tubes connected them to some of the platforms at the surface. Webs of cables secured them against currents and storms.

This was the domain of the Zee Hanze.

Mesi Dubaku ignored the hunger in her belly, confident that her meagre rations would keep her alive for another day. More than that, no one should ask. If any took more than they needed, another would starve. She helped feed her people; in return she, too, was fed. It was a simple bargain, and hers was a simple life.

Too simple.

Her eyes swept across the curved wall of the dome, as it sloped sideways and upwards. Braced by deceptively slender beams, this was a world of light and air sustained by shields of toughened glass. Inside, people carried on their limited lives. Outside, swarms of pale jellyfish surged through a tired, depleted ocean. Above them, in the distance, cylindrical food-pens shimmered, barely visible through the murky water.

Helping hands zipped her into a thin but strong wetsuit and slung a tank of compressed air on her back. She thanked the helper, and tested her mask and the tube that gave her air. At the waterlock, a short walk away along a narrow passage interrupted by heavy storm doors, she slipped fins on her feet and attached a pack of tools to her belt.

Watching lenses analysed her gait, compared her bodyform to entries in a database, and mapped the blood vessels in her eyes, hands, and neck. The inner door slid open. As soon as she had entered the compartment beyond, the door closed and the floor opened to the sea. Equal pressure in the air kept it from rising. Mesi slipped down into the water, and kicked away into the coolness of the open sea.

Behind her, the floor closed once more.

She started her rounds. Each food-pen was assembled from massive squares of a fine mesh of carbon-fibre matting, bonded at the seams, and a floor of the same matting, tethered to the sea floor by cables of the same ultra-strong material. The top of the cylinder was a ring of toroidal flotation cells. The flexible pen allowed ocean currents through its walls, bending and rippling as they passed. Inside it were tens of millions of food-organisms, each pen a monoculture. This had led to disasters in the past, as disease spread through a pen in hours, but pens with the same species were well separated. Multi-species pens were too complex for a management fixated even more strongly on control than on productivity.

The matting allowed oxygenated water to pass through, but very little else. A complex microstructure allowed excreta to fall into detachable bags, removed periodically by robots and sent to the surface to be sold as land fertiliser.

Once, the farms would have been a magnet for predators. Now, sharks were so rare as to be mythical creatures, akin to unicorns. Humanity had eaten all the top predators—tuna, grouper, marlin, swordfish, sharks—centuries ago. Giant ships had swept the open seas clean, reducing their populations to remnants in the abyssal reserves that still survived the relentless demand for protein, sparse populations where the dark and pressure was too much for human farmers and their machines, or even the robot miners that had killed the life around the ocean ridges. On the continental shelves, where wild nature had once thrived in abundance, the oceans were packed with aquaculture.

On land, the story had been worse, with whole regions becoming arid, drowned, or storm-wracked. The oceans were less susceptible to a ruined climate. Aquaculture was more stable than agriculture. So the bulk of humanity took to the seas.

The technology that let them go there originated when the tropical land ceased to be habitable except under cooling domes. Most of the old coastal cities had been wrecked by rising sea levels, except for a few which domed themselves in time: the first was Singapore, which had no hinterland to retreat to. But very few domes remained in the overheated, oxygen-poor waters near the Equator. As the ice died, the domes spread to the warming poles. Dome technology opened a path to the continental shelves, and in the shallow-water domes, the political movement that became the Zee Hanze had taken root, determined to reverse history and restore the oceans to pristine purity. Industrial run-off from the Circumpolar Nations had never quite led to all-out war, though incursions were constant. (The human population of the Americas was too small to matter, except near the pole, and the expanded Swiss Federation was, well, Swiss.) The smaller Antarctic shelf had its domes too, where the expanding farms and towns gave no trouble: heavily dependent on ocean biomass, they were land appendages of the Zee Hanze.

Most of humanity lived further from shore. Beyond the land-dwellers' horizon, where the ocean was too deep for domes, enormous platforms floated, their bulk dwarfing even the most extreme waves. Smaller platforms fringed their walls, many of them mobile. But the cities went no deeper than light could penetrate. The deepest trenches were home to a small scattering of research stations.

Powerful strokes carried Mesi through the water to the nearest pen. A rise in pressure had alerted the aquacultural engineers to a problem: a blocked tube. As a temporary measure, the flow of plankton had been shut off. She must discover the cause and restore the flow. But as she swam, her thoughts kept returning to a very different task.

Her application had been received.

Now she must wait. And if it were accepted, she would go... and wait again. For months, years,... decades.

Until the instructions came.

It had begun a year and a half ago, when she met Talbot Wekesa, newly arrived from a dome off the coast of Kamchatka, which had been ruined by an earthquake. He was everything she was not. Where she was calm, he was intense. Where she never thought beyond today, he thought only of the distant future and the far past. Where she was ignorant, he was knowledgeable. Where she was timid, he was proud, angry, and driven.

One day, she found him sitting on the floor with his head in his hands, sobbing. She had never seen him cry.

"Talbot? What's wrong?"

"They won't let me go."

"Go where? What's wrong with here?"

"Wrong? *Everything*! Who? Where? Out among the stars, where the sky-devils of the Concordat are building new homes with unlimited technological power and infinite wealth. And what is *our* share of these riches? *Nothing*."

As a child, Mesi had been told that long ago people had flown beyond the sky in a metal bird, into the realm of gods and demons, but she didn't believe in gods and was unsure about demons. She preferred to focus on the here and now, growing food in Earth's life-giving seas. But now Talbot, who in her eyes was close to being a genius, was babbling about sky-devils.

Dimly she remembered something her grandfather had mentioned. That the sky was not just another dome, shining blue in the sunlight and spangled black by moonlight, but the doorway to a vast… he'd called it *cosmos*. And that scattered through the cosmos were worlds without number, inhabited not by devils and gods, but by people.

Was this *Concordat* the cosmos? she asked.

"No, but it thinks it is. Take this back to your cabin and read it this evening." He handed her a thin booklet. On the cover, a young woman with blazing eyes struck an aggressive pose in the foreground. Beyond were fire, smoke, and tangled wreckage, through which antlike human figures surged in apparent panic. The title was *Manifesto for a Just Cosmos*. The author was Ira da Terra.

"What's—"

"No, read it first. Then I'll explain. You have much to learn, much to understand. You ask about the Concordat? They stole Humanity's birthright. Not human beings; they're monsters in human form. For seventeen hundred years they have forced Earth to suffer, watched it wither and decay as its people were denied access to the Universal Commons."

"The what?"

"The stars. Read the booklet."

"I will. But why are you sad? You're always so strong!"

As Talbot groped for the words to express his rage and disappointment, it was as though suspended sediment had suddenly settled, revealing an unexpected vista.

"Earth isn't the only world in the... *cosmos*," he said, trying to tie his words to things she knew about. "There are many. People live there. More people than there are on the entire Earth. But they're greedy. They want the cosmos for themselves. They don't want to *share* with us." He slumped against the wall. "With *me*."

"Share what?"

"The future." He shook his head as if to clear his mind. "There's a way for *some* discontented people to escape from this world. The hope of it keeps people from being as angry as they should, particularly the organising, trouble-making types. It's called *emigration*. People may apply, and if their skills and attitudes are suitable, they're told where to go and they're taken on board a huge ship. One that can fly. It flies them to a new world, where there's unlimited food and freedom. Things that the Concordat denies to billions on Earth. And *only* on Earth. In the rest of the cosmos, there are no barriers."

"How do you know this?"

He pointed to the booklet. "Ira da Terra told me."

"Why have *I* not been told?"

He sighed. "This is a harsh world, Mesi. Our leaders think first of themselves. They squabble over scarce resources. They control the emigration process. They control even *who knows* of the emigration process."

"They hide the truth from ordinary people to favour their own kin?"

He nodded. "You're a clever girl. Yes, that's exactly what they do. But Ira da Terra isn't just a person. It's an organisation. One with growing powers. It's removing despots from office, ending wars, bringing justice to the Earth. One day it will bring justice to the cosmos!

"With the help of Ira da Terra, I applied to emigrate. I had the necessary skills, for they were seeking new people for a world with many seas. I studied hard and passed the tests. They sequenced my genes—read the booklet, Mesi, there isn't time right now—and found me healthy.

"Then, just as I began to believe I would be selected, I was told I was unsuitable." His body shook as he recounted the rejection.

"These people sound nasty to me," Mesi said, taking his hand. "I wouldn't want to join them. I'd want revenge for what they've done."

Talbot gave her a sharp look. "You mean that?"

"Yes."

"Actually, Mesi, that was the problem. It's complicated." Seeing her incomprehension, he added: "Read the booklet and tell me again tomorrow."

She read the booklet from cover to cover.

She got no sleep that night.

Next day, she sought out Talbot in the food-hall, as he queued for his morning measure of reconstituted algae and squid. He led her away from the crowd to a deserted corridor.

"Do you still want revenge, Mesi?"

"A thousand times more so!" She waved the booklet. "I never realised—"

"Few do. Our leaders keep the truth from us. They conspire with Concordat traitors to keep us down. 'In our place.'"

"I see that now. Has it truly been seventeen hundred years of oppression?"

Talbot grinned. She was already getting the jargon. "Everything in that booklet is true. Can you keep a secret?"

"If it's about Ira da Terra, I can."

"It is. I never wished merely to emigrate, Mesi. My aim was not to better my own lot. It was to help everyone on Earth."

"How?"

"Once I gained the freedom of the Concordat, I'd be able to... make changes. Stir the traitors out of their self-serving complacency. Strike a blow for the One True Original Earth.

"Strategists call it *asymmetrical warfare*. Freedom fighters call it *justice*. It's war, the use of targeted violence against the people who support oppression. Without the machines to drop bombs, we have to use individuals to spread shock and awe and terror. I didn't want to emigrate to gain wealth, to join the Concordat in its foulness, but I had to make them think so."

"But you failed."

"Yes, but not the way you think. The Concordat Security Service *filters* applicants, much as we filter plankton for our fish stocks to keep diseases out. They want to keep potential troublemakers out."

"Troublemakers like you?"

"Like I wanted to be."

"It worked."

"No, it didn't. The Concordat might have accepted me, Mesi. It was Ira da Terra that turned me down. Instructed me to withdraw my application to emigrate, on pain of death."

A slap round the face would not have made her more startled or angry. "*Ira da Terra?*"

"Like I said, it's complicated. The Movement — maybe Ira herself — doesn't trust me." He took several deep breaths, trying to suppress the humiliation.

"But you would serve them well. They can trust you to attack the Concordat."

He gave a mirthless laugh. "Indeed they can. But they can't trust me not to. At least, that's what they think."

"I don't understand."

Talbot crumpled up his cardboard plate and drained the last water from his cup. "Ira takes a long-term view, Mesi. Very long term. She wants to place agents throughout the Concordat, but she doesn't want them to do anything that would even *hint* that their loyalties are to her. Deep cover, so deep that even the Concordat's smartest computers cannot see the patterns. So deep that the agents themselves have no conscious memory they are agents.

"She has some grand scheme, something massive and devastating. She doesn't want anything to raise suspicions. Her agents are instructed to infiltrate... and then they *forget* until they their orders come. When the master plan is ready."

Mesi reached out and touched his arm. "Perhaps she is right."

"*Of course* she is right! As soon as it was explained to me, it made sense. I am but a tiny cog in a vast machine, unaware of the complete mechanism. I cannot be permitted to act on my own instincts. That is wisdom itself.

"My hunger for action was naive and selfish. I see that, now. I said so, to my contact. I said I would obey orders, stay out of sight, and wait. But the decision was not rescinded. Apparently Ira da Terra considers me too hotheaded."

Unfortunately, Mesi thought, *she could well be right.* But she smiled sympathetically.

"Ira da Terra plans to attack the Concordat in many ways. Emigration is a first step. They send us as 'deep sleepers'. That means we establish ourselves as good Concordat citizens, stay clean, don't draw attention to ourselves, and avoid tipping the Movement's hand. We wait until Ira sends us instructions. Then — and only then — we strike!

"But I will never be part of that."

His dejection was so moving, Mesi wanted to cry. "Can you ask them to wait, observe your conduct, and perhaps reconsider?"

"No. Rejection is permanent. I can never try again." He paused, leaned across, and turned her face so that their eyes met.

"But you can."

Old Earth

Manifesto for a Just Cosmos

Ira da Terra

Seventeen hundred years.
Seventeen hundred years of *Quarantine.*
You are angry. Your wrath burns brighter than the core of the Sun. But you fail to focus that burning. You dissipate it on each other.

I will show you the enemy. I will teach you to channel your anger to defeat them. Listen to me — listen *only* to me — and I will tell you the truth.

Earth is the cradle of humankind. *We* are the cradle of humankind. Our children betrayed us.

Concordat changelings stole Humanity's birthright. These are not human beings; they are aliens in human form, talking direct mind to mind with the help of their computers. They forced Earth to suffer, watched the human race wither and decay as it was denied access to the Universal Commons — the stars.

Sealed off from cosmic abundance, we watched our civilisations collapse. Lack of food killed millions every year. Our population wavered between the continuation of our families, and the cold hand of starvation. Our numbers declined to less than a fifth of what they once were. We bore children, as is the inalienable right of every human, but they died. Food could have come from the unlimited stars, but it was deliberately denied.

Rising salt water destroyed our coastal cities, driving out the inhabitants. Dwindling fresh water drove entire nations to abandon their homelands, finding no new home. Hundreds of millions were forced into our huge, cramped domes, where they huddle together on starvation rations. Our wars have been reduced to assassinations and plagues; we dare not hurt equipment or the environment, and we cannot hurt the human monsters from the stars.

Unable to move our waste off planet by the Concordat's Beanstalks, we were forced to clog our oceans with filth. Dead fish littered our beaches, vomited up by dying seas. The ocean floor itself was poisoned by mining. Once our oceans fed humanity; then the waters ruined our shores, eroded our lands, and assailed our nostrils with their stink. After billions died, we learned to conserve the seas, but by then they were almost down to plankton and toxic bloom. Only now are they starting to recover.

None of this was necessary!

The Concordat unilaterally imposed its self-styled *Quarantine*. Was Earth consulted? No! Was it given the opportunity to defend itself against baseless lies? No! The Concordat denied us due process.

The Concordat is the source of all our ills. Barred from other worlds, unsupplied with efficient energy sources, we were forced to pollute our atmosphere, melt our icecaps, drown our lowlands, and scatter radioactive waste to the winds, to avoid even worse. Our climate became floods, droughts, and hurricanes. Our crops withered as our fields turned to mud and desert. Concordat neglect forced us off once fertile lands, once crowded shores, to colonise barren higher ground, pressurised domes on the seabed, and cities like vast floating prisons on the oceans.

Out among the stars, energy and resources are *unlimited*. The cosmos is the heritage of *all* humankind. No one should seek to control who may use it. No one should have a monopoly on the universe. The Concordat, obsessed by greed, callously dismissive of the consequences of its selfishness, stole our heritage. For seventeen hundred years these criminals confined us, suppressed us, denied us even the basic human right of freedom of movement.

They imprisoned us without trial. A few pathetic Colony Vessels were allowed to leave. *Allowed*. A meaningless gesture, made only to equip the Concordat with slaves.

The future of humanity requires no *permission* from criminals and traitors, who try to hide their crimes behind the transparent pretence of Quarantine — *keeping the stars clean!* They call us filth, they consider us vermin. They crushed our hopes, causing terrorism, murder, famine, war; then they blamed *us!* As our soils turned to dust and our crops became ashes, they claimed it was *all our fault!*

We nurtured our starchildren. We sacrificed entire generations. Billions of our ancestors worked selflessly to create the mahabhavium needed to leave an exhausted planet. But when those sacrifices bore fruit, when the Far Travel Legislature gained the key to the universe, they broke the bargain, betrayed their world, and stole the key for themselves.

What has changed in the seventeen hundred years since that act of cosmic treason? Has Quarantine, as Concordat propaganda maintains, saved us from ourselves? Earth's ecology has become less stable, its conflicts more deadly, its politics more divided, its nations more fragmented, its people poorer, less healthy, beset by epidemic diseases; lacking medical care, employment, even basic housing. Concordat traitors trapped us like rats in a sewer, and now they condemn us for our dirt.

They are building a new life, out among the stars; one of unlimited technology, infinite wealth. And what is our share of these riches? *Nothing*.

And so I say to all of you: stop struggling against each other, for you are only destroying yourselves. The people of Earth are one People, and united can never be conquered. Only one struggle is worthy. Unite with me to defeat the oppressors! The enemy is not at your borders: it is in the skies above us all. This 'Quarantine' is not merely imprisonment: it is a lie, that all Earth is an epidemic of unreason that cannot be allowed outside this, humanity's homeworld.

To the Concordat, we are not thinking, feeling human beings: we are an infectious disease. We are sick criminals, worthy only of confinement to the end of our days. Do not believe the lies! Focus your anger against the true enemy! The Concordat are the criminals. And so great is their crime that I urge — no, *demand* — the death penalty. Nothing less can remedy the harm their lies and deceptions have caused, and will continue to cause — unless we act to save ourselves.

They call us Old Earth. They call a faraway planet New Earth. They try to pretend we are obsolete. To hide us away, unable to interfere with their megalomaniac plans. They will fail. *Join me now!* Together we will throw off our chains, destroy our oppressors, and liberate the One True Original Earth!

Myggbukta, Old Earth

Two men had come for him, in a car with reflective windows, reflective on the inside too. He was surrounded by an army of copies of himself, vanishing into the distance in a lattice of mirrors, isolated in a separate rear compartment. He could see nothing, and hear nothing but faint vibrations from the motor. The compartment smelt of new upholstery.

Occasionally he felt the car turn. He made no attempt to memorise its path through the arctic streets of Eirikraudesland's capital Myggbukta. He would have failed in any case, but there were things it was better not to know.

He felt the car stop.

After a few minutes, the door opened and he got out. The men led him along a dimly-lit corridor, lined with pipes and cables, then up a metal stairway and through an open trapdoor, into an empty room. Just floor, ceiling, bare walls with a single door, and him. Nowhere to sit, so he stood. And waited. He did not try the door.

"Helmut Moser." The voice made him start. There was no obvious source. It was electronically disguised and unidentifiable. "You have been chosen for a task that will significantly advance our goals. The question is: are you worthy?"

If not, I'm dead. "That's not for me to judge. I've served you well in the past."

"Are you ready to take the next step? I warn you, there can be no going back. You can leave now, knowing nothing. Or you can pass through the door and know all. There is a price, however."

"What?"

"Your freedom. Open that door, and I will own you. But if you wish to advance in the Movement, that's the price you must pay."

Moser was unimpressed. He already knew more than was healthy. His ambition knew no bounds. The price was no more than he expected. He stepped forward, opened the door, and walked through.

This room, too, was empty, but for a small person in a plain white dress, tied at the waist by a broad sky-blue belt. Icy white hair hung to her shoulders. They stared at each other.

There was something in those eyes... Moser felt himself wither under that gaze. Despite himself, he looked down.

"You were expecting a younger woman?" The voice had an edge to it that almost made him shudder, despite all his control. It took a lot to frighten Helmut Moser.

"You're—uh—"

"Not like the picture on the *Manifesto*? Would the Movement's leader supply the image for a Wanted poster?"

"No, I never thought it was a true likeness. Just propaganda. Even so, you're not what I expected."

"I am not what anyone expects." Not a flicker of emotion crossed her face. "I've been following your actions for many years, Helmut. I'm impressed. You have the potential to rise to the highest levels in the Movement. You have a rare blend of self-control and sensitivity, while always ready to do whatever is necessary. So now I must assess your *commitment*. To trust you, I must *feel* your true character. That's why we had to meet, face to face."

She stepped closer. "Look at me, Helmut." He raised his eyes to meet hers; deep green in a brown face, the face of Earth. The brain behind those serene, beautiful eyes had caused the deaths of hundreds. Hundreds, he told himself, who deserved to die. Hundreds who had licked the boots of the Concordat.

She observed his face, reading the set of its muscles, the dilation of his pupils, the curl of his lips. It felt as though she was reading his mind.

Perhaps she was. "You pass, Helmut. For now."

He realised he'd been holding his breath. He didn't believe anything could be concealed from this tiny woman. She was mesmerising. Terrifying.

"What do you want of me?" he gasped.

"I have work for your bio-laboratories, Helmut."

Starhome

"Felix Wylde?
"Can you reach Marco Bianchi? He seems to have his 'comp turned off."
"You were lucky mine was on. Four of our friends are dead."
"Well, as to that... can you both come to Rescue headquarters? Now?"

"What's this about?" asked Felix.

"Yesterday we got a call from a two thousand year old rescue beacon, six hundred and fifty-seven light years away in a region of the Galaxy the robot probes have barely catalogued. From the crew of *Valkyrie*."

"That's im—"

" —possible. I know. You were on *Valkyrie* yourself, all the way to the disaster. But—apparently the identical ship *also* dropped out of *k*-space en route, near SQL7812, two hundred light years from any Concordat world. Where it crashed, and found a lost colony."

" —?"

"They proved it. Entangled access algorithms."

Long silence. "My instincts are telling me it's more likely for us to be wrong about entanglement being inherently secure than it is for a spaceship and its crew to rise from the dead."

"Yah. But the talking heads say you'd be wrong."

" —?"

"We've set up a secure link. Want to talk with them?"

"Jane, I *watched you die.*"

"I watched *you*. Cut in half. You're alive?"

"I think so. You?"

"As lively as a Gamut gamete."

"You *are* you. No one else knows me that well." Felix paused. "It's an old question, but... when will I see you again?"

Jane spluttered. "You're you, too. But how...?"

"And when *will* I see you again?"

"There are problems. Marco's trying to set something up."

"Hi Marco."

"Hi Marco. How are you doing?"

"Fine, apart from the stretch marks."

"*Stretch* marks?" This was the first time for months that Marco had asked a question that did not relate to Elza's death.

"I'll explain later. Listen, this is a secure link, right?"

"Entangled access."

"I want you to back me up on keeping this a mystery for the moment, because the dingbeaucrats'll *never* believe the truth until we get here with it. And we won't, unless they do what we're asking."

"I'll believe you, Marco. I don't go in for self-deception."

"Well, sometimes I do, Marco. I convinced myself I felt fatherly."

"Fatherly? Is this where the stretch marks come in?"

"Look, I'll *explain later*. The point is, we found a planet full of matter transmitters—syntei—growing wild."

"You're right. They'll never believe it."

"So we show, don't tell. And..."

"We get to see their faces."

"You're a Marco after my own heart."

Coming near the planet in a Da Silva drive was apparently insanely dangerous, but whenever Marco Bianchi was pressed for detail, the communicator had one of its 'lost contact' moments. The technology on the planet somehow interfered with it—that was part of the danger.

He had insisted that collecting a small package could lead to a rescue, which was impossible, but they had already believed six impossible things before breakfast.

Cautiously they sent an automated mining ship to the Squill system: AIs *can* navigate a Da Silva drive, but it took many more jumps than a good human pilot, and more time. *Very* cautiously it came five million kilometres close to Squill's third planet, Qish, and sent out a sample probe. Eight days later, in a pause in the snowstorms, it landed on the peak called Krig, and opened its storage to the package, sealing in air in case vacuum affected it. It took off as carefully as if it had a baby inside, and returned to the ship.

Jump by jump, the package made its way to Starhome. From a near-flat spacetime point, reachable by Da Silva, it was transferred to an in-system vessel, to head at mere reaction-drive speed to an orbit satisfying Bianchi's peculiar conditions.

"I am Sigmund Andreotti, and I will be your Captain for this insane flight. This is Kwame Ngongo Marakuri, my second." Felix, Marco, and Chief Scientist Doxor Artur Bendix Tampledown murmured acknowledgements.

Seven days with Tampledown was a strain. He was used to respect for his expertise (which was real), and now the *universe* was questioning it. He had the integrity to make the experiment, but not the strength to be friendly while the result was uncertain — while he did not even know what success would look like. It had been eighteen centuries since the last fundamental shake-up of physics: while most scientists were still aware (unlike the generation before relativity and quantum theory) that fundamental problems were still unsolved, they did not expect the solutions in their own lifetimes. Physicists, biologists, even computer scientists — who for two millennia had been expecting creativity from artificial intelligence, with just one more tweak — were resigned to careers of dotting the *i*s and crossing the *ħ*s. Here was something utterly new, and he feared he was too old to meet it.

It did not make him an easy companion.

"*Magog* beacon: be advised that your package is at Starhome. It will continue to be at the same gravitational potential as your location on Krig

Mountain, as requested." It lay on the inside of the hull, the 'floor' of the rotating Rescue Ship.

"Understood, Starhome," said a voice, in a strange accent.

"As requested, shutting down Da Silva drive and communicator in three seconds two seconds one second *now.*"

The fist-sized package, collected with such effort, started unwrapping *itself.* From the inside. The paper tore, revealing a featureless wooden hoop, into which it vanished. The hoop filled with unnerving whiteness. For minutes, nothing happened. Then white puffs streamed out, and the temperature in the room dropped. *Snow?* Some sort of refrigeration device?

Definitely Cloud Cuckoo Land. A bizarre hoax—

Something more solid poked out from the disc, for all the world like a gloved fingertip. It disappeared. Then the disc disgorged a tube, that unrolled to a wider hoop. A second, larger tube emerged from *that,* unrolled. From that another, and another, like Russian dolls in reverse.

Finally, a human head. Marco looked around, from a hood of furry animal skin.

"Hi, everyone." He leaped out, as if thrown, and landed on his feet.

Disembodied hands pushed a fur-wrapped bundle from the hole. He bent down and took it, cooing softly. A second followed. One bundle started wriggling and let out a wail. The other bundle joined in.

A woman who was not on *Valkyrie's* crewlist sprang acrobatically from the synte and helped Marco unwrap the toddler bundles. There was a pause, then Tinka clambered out. Then Jane. Then Sam. Lady Elzabet of Quynt climbed *gracefully* from a cosmic manhole, and smiled at Marco. Both Marcos. *Valkyrie's* crew and the three unknown arrivals hugged each other, then Felix went to Jane, shutting out the rest of the universe.

Tampledown was the first to recover some of his wits. Intellectually, he understood that the dead had not come back to life. The old lizard brain was convinced they had, but he managed to overrule it enough to find his tongue. The physics of k-field duplication was hard enough to wrap your head around. The metaphysics was impossible and he'd leave that to the philosophers.

"You did tell us this has to be seen to be believed," he said. "And I have. And even now, I don't." He paused. "How did you guys *do* that?"

"Just exploiting a vegetable connection," said Marco.

"Where did the babies come from?"

"Did your mother never tell you?"

"Nah, I mean—"

"My daughters, Marcolette and Polonia. Twins: say hi to Doxor Tampledown."

"What's that thing clinging to your shoulder—Jane?"

"It's Rapunzel, my frog," said Jane, cradling the odd creature protectively.

"And what the Mother are those *eyes* doing, crawling over *you*."

"Looking at you," said Sam. "First Chief Scientist it's ever seen."

But now an eye had caught sight of the toddlers, and *things* poured out of his pockets for a game of chase.

Marco cut in. "I have to tell you my metamaterial theory, and why syntei come to pieces when the boundary circle is cut, like peeling a banana, some kind of minimal surface effect—yah, Tinka, sure, not right now. I was about to make the same—"

Tinka shoved him aside and stepped forward. "Star Pilot Class 4 Irenotincala Laurel reporting on behalf of Candidacy Group #87439, out of Suufi on an unregistered trajectory. One death, circumstances unavoidable, details to follow.

"We wish to report the discovery of a colony on the third planet of SQL7812. The locals call it Qish. They're descended from the passengers of CV23 *Magog*. Well, *a* CV *Magog*. Their copy crashed on Qish more than seventeen hundred years ago.

"We wish to notify you of the discovery of a radical new technology. The locals call the devices syntei. They're… vegetable wormholes. Portable matter-transmitters that grow on trees. I know, that's crazy. We agree. But you just saw a small example of what they can do. After proper scientific study they will create a revolution in local and interstellar transportation—and much more. It seems they also create Da Silva duplicators. We're living proof. If we can tame that, it will create a second revolution.

"Our mission report will provide full details. Finally, we—oh, trash this formality. Rustle up five cups of coffee, please? We've not had any for three years. And some juice for Lomyrla." She gestured. "We brought our own stuff for the kids."

"Can we change orbit?" asked Captain Andreotti, "This is costing reaction mass."

"Ah—*ni porb-*" said Tinka. "Yah."

There was a subtle shift in the gravity, then an outraged wail from a twin. "Oops," said Marco. "I think we just went below the working level of the napisyntei. I hope Rescue Ships carry startech equivalents."

"And *coffee*," said Tinka.

Tampledown stared at the scattered syntei. "If this stuff really does what my eyes just told me it did, I'll give you an entire coffee plantation."

"I want a meeting with your top karmabhumi experts as soon as you can schedule one," said the Marco in the animal-fur jacket.

"Count me in, too," said Marco. "Two heads are better than one. Well, they will be once Marco here has brought me up to speed about syntei."

"Consider it done." Tampledown could move almost as fast as a pair of Marcos, once he'd wrenched his brain back into gear.

"This trip has been very educational," put in Andreotti, "but all good things come to an end. There's a window coming up in three minutes for an orbital transfer to dock at a Starhome Beanstalk in about two hours, with a slingshot past Hermes. Want to take it?"

Marco found himself strapped in next to Marco, with Elza and his friend? wife? opposite. Elza exchanged glances with her and Marco, then said, "We've been telling Lomyrla about microgravity bedrooms. She's dying to try one—she's an acrobat." She looked straight at Marco. "Would you care to join us?"

"Elza, I could have saved you, got you to cryo... I *left you to die*. I couldn't..."

"Marco, you *saved* my life, three years ago, and I've been enjoying it— give or take a few near death experiences—ever since. Gift horse, teeth, don't, dah?"

"I have some catching up to do," said Marco. "I can't wait to start."

Mediterranean Sea, Old Earth

Three hundred metres beneath the Mediterranean, the lights went out.

The warm, shallow waters between Sicily and the former North African People's Jamahiriya had been at the forefront of the second wave of dome construction, attracted by a substantial stock of free-range fish. Within a century the relentless northward march of the Saharan sands had driven so many people from the land that the seabed had become seriously over-crowded and the open fisheries unsustainable, but the domes remained. All of the good territory, on land or under the sea, had been occupied long ago. Anywhere else would be worse, unless they took it by force. And anywhere better would fight back, hard. As it was, there were territorial disputes and skirmishes all the time… with caution not to damage the land. Like ancient Indian armies fighting, next to peasants calmly at the plough, over which king would tax the crop. Total war had been disinvented.

Twenty thousand domes of the Zee Hanze studded the sea floor, each struggling to farm enough protein to feed itself, let alone to produce a sur-plus to support others even less fortunate. The crumbling infrastructure had been stretched to breaking point for as long as anyone could remember. Even those now too old to work admitted that the good old days had been only marginally less wretched. But the domes and floating cities clung on, pow-ered by vast solar arrays that packed the coastal strip of the Tripolitanian Plateau. Scoured by high winds and sandstorms, the area was mainly frac-tured rock in a sandy matrix. The great ergs with their towering dunes were far to the south. Networks of cables, buried beneath the rocks in concrete conduits, carried the electricity that provided the domes with lighting and powered their many machines.

The most important being the air-pumps.

Within seconds, sirens began wailing, warning that this was no tempo-rary power cut. The cause was something beyond the domes' immediate control. A natural disaster. Or a man-made one.

Dim emergency lighting brought relief from the darkness, and air began circulating again through rooms and corridors, but the batteries would last less than a day. The dome-dwellers prepared to implement longstanding contingency plans for an emergency evacuation; first to the sea's surface, then—as a holding pattern—to Malta and Sicily. At the peak of summer, those were too hot to survive while working. From there, they would go… no one knew. It would depend on the extent of the problem. No one knew that, either, but the technicians were working desperately to find it.

Resigned, prepared, yet fearful, dome-dwellers waited in their thousands, hoping that the power would soon be restored so they could get on with their lives. Even a dull, miserable, repetitive life was better than no life at all.

Zee Hanze's engineers, aware of the dangers, had networked the domes into a complex switchable grid, and used several separate cables for each solar array. The grid quickly redistributed power to bring the affected domes back online, but only in a low-level maintenance mode. They would not come back to full power until the cause of the failure was found. And re-paired.

A much-rehearsed system swung into action.

"That's the second power-loss this month," a bearded technician com-plained. He struggled into hooded overalls padded with gel coolant, protec-tive against the prospect of fierce sunlight.

"Yes, but this one's bigger, Jamal. Breaks in four cables, all connected to the same panel farm," another replied. "Exactly what was needed to destroy redundancy. Must have been deliberate. An inside job."

"The last one was just ants, Lenny," a third countered.

"*Just* ants, Shimon? Millions of the things made a nest in one of the trans-formers, shorted the coils. A seal had failed in the heat and they got in through the gap." Lenny adjusted his hood; sometimes winds could whip up sand-devils when you least expected it. "Biggest problem was, the ants that didn't get fried—which was most of them—were still crawling over every-thing. Had to petrol-bomb them, took days to clear up the mess and install a spare."

Jamal grunted as he bent to zip up his leggings. He was getting too old for this sort of thing. "Four separate breaks, which just *happen* to hook up to the same panels, don't sound like ants."

"No, they don't. Can't be coincidence."

They made their way to the sealock where a squat submarine waited to convey them to the surface. There they'd transfer to an inflatable, already equipped with the gear they'd most likely need.

Zee Hanze was all too conscious of potential threats to its electricity supply. It was well protected along most of its route. Multiple layers of fencing surrounded the solar panel fields, and cables were deep underground, inside thick reinforced concrete conduit pipes, all covered by video cameras. Paramilitary guardians manned underground bases among the panel-farms, and a rapid-response airstrike team based at Sicily armed with air-to-surface missiles and heavy automatic weapons including grenade-launchers.

Total security was impossible, but the terrain was harsh and no one could survive there for long without protective equipment. Until now, the systems had worked.

The weakest point was where the cables left the land and entered the shallows. Here the pipes were on the surface, with heavily secured hatches to allow inspectors to enter the casing and check the integrity of the cables even at high tide. Armed patrols were regular, but the last one had been three days ago.

The cameras in the area had shown no suspicious activity. Security was already investigating why not, suspecting that false images had somehow been fed into the surveillance system. But top priority went to fixing the faults.

The damage was visible from the boat. A section of concrete casing had cracked wide open, just above the waterline.

Jamal slipped over the side of the boat into the shallows, hurried up the beach, and dropped to one knee. Shattered edges and blackened interior told an obvious story. He peered into the hole, seeing only remnants of melted plastic and metal where the cable should be. An acrid smell filled his nostrils. "Explosives."

Lenny joined him, sniffed the air, nodded. "A shaped charge to penetrate. Crude and pointless. Too easy to fix. Cut the ends and splice in a new section. Whoever did this was an amateur."

Radio messages were coming in from other teams, with the same story. Four cables, four ragged holes in the casing.

"I'll isolate it; then we can fix it." Lenny set off up a slope of tumbled stones, following the line of the cable to the nearest switch, a concrete box sunk into the rock next to the casing. He inserted a complicated cross-shaped key, opened a cover, reached in, and flipped the handle.

There was a loud bang and flash.

Fragments of Lenny came raining down from the skies, mixed with sand, stones, and broken concrete.

Jamal managed to stand, ears ringing, overalls ripped in a dozen places, letting in the searing heat of the desert air. Ignoring it, he looked round. Two of his companions were moving—one had blood running down his face from a deep gash in his scalp. The third, who had been holding the radio, wasn't. Either dead or unconscious. Right now, it didn't matter which. Jamal scrabbled across the stony ground and grabbed the radio from where it lay among the debris.

"*Stop! Stop!* For your lives, don't touch the isolators! Don't touch *anything!*"

No reply. Was the thing *working*? It looked—

Further along the beach, a second explosion. A column of smoke rose skywards.

No, it bloody isn't working. Or if it is, no one's listening.

Jamal started running.

"Sabotage."

Zee Hanze's Operations Manager for North Africa was acutely aware that anyone with half a brain would already have worked that out, but someone had to say it anyway, and his ultimate boss on the other end of the phone was unlikely to, so he did.

The familiar voice crackled over Old Earth's decrepit wireless phone network. "And booby traps. Any idea who?"

Ops grunted. "They didn't leave a calling-card, other than bombs. What does Security say?"

"Not much until they've checked the site, analysed how the devices were constructed, and assessed the bombers' capabilities. Different groups have different methods. Right now, they say it could be any of a dozen crazies we know about, not to mention some new bunch we've never heard of before. Those groups spend most of their time fighting each other when they're not wrecking what's left of the planet. Each one convinced that it alone has The Answer."

"I'd be happy if someone would tell me The Question," Ops said. "You can't save the human race by slaughtering anyone who won't cooperate when you try to force stupid ideas down their throats."

"No, but you can use random acts of destruction to make the other groups look just talk. Make sure it's *your* ideas that are being shoved down throats. That's what these people are probably trying. It's an ideological arms race driving them to ever-greater extremes. Anyway, we have a bigger problem here than I'd hoped. Security is trying to find out why the cameras didn't show anything. Must have been some sort of hack—hang on, Security's just received something." *Long silence.* "Some terrorist group is claiming this."

"Who?"

"Ira da Terra, they call themselves. Cute."

"Cute?"

"Wrath of the Earth."

"Oh. Ancient languages were never my strong point. They must want something. What?"

"They don't say. Probably just random harassment."

"Can we stop it happening again? On a larger scale?"

Zee Hanze's President was wondering the same thing, and hoped his answer was right. "It's probably near the limit of their capabilities. We can beef up the protection, run more patrols, and improve our evacuation plans. Beyond that... we'll have to wait and see."

Nazg

Fatima Salim:

I was born in a simultaneity quake.

I grew up in a simultaneity quake.

My mother lived in the Nazg system, which doesn't get simquakes. The central star is vast, and attracts a dense cloud of clear-matter. This combines to make k-time increase fast relative to local ordinary time. That has almost no effect, locally, as clear-matter and k-time need weird tech even to detect, but it sure had an effect on me — and my mother.

The company she and her sister founded is in neurotech, where you run like crazy just to keep your share of the market. It's a big market even just around Nazg, with twenty-three planets in the more or less habitable zone, and asteroids and habitats all over: about ninety-one billion people. But you can't ignore the Concordat market. Lighter stars and clusters mean that k-time passes slower than ours, relative to k-synch, so a hundred stanhours after a comm call to New Earth, you place another call to a moment where the Newbies have experienced only ninety-five hours since you talked. That would be good for business, if only it was stable, but if it ran for a thousand years the contact moment would be fifty years behind you. As New Earth is only forty light-years off, they could send a laser signal that would reach Nazg ten years before you placed the call. Nature doesn't like that.

Nature *really* doesn't like that, so when k-simultaneity gets close to time-like in the galactic frame, stresses build up like with tectonic plates moving, and you get a 'quake. Suddenly the k-levels jump, and there are a few tens of t-years for Newbies on their own. In all that time, they can't contact Nazg or anywhere else by Da Silva drive or comm: they just don't have a defined k-time to match with anybody else's.

So: Mother's techs had a line on a new style of wristcomp that would in-terface directly with the nervous system, with synaptic connectors — and the algorithmic muscle to interface with brain centres, comprehensibly, with brief handshaking. But they would take many years of development and human trials, and what if a competitor found a way to go a little faster? Solu-tion, outsource the R&D to Inferno, a high-tech development planet that was due for a long simquake 'soon'. (I hate k-weather forecasters.) Contract with a spinout company from Inferno Institute of Technology, set them up to do the work during their time-out, and spring the polished result on the Nazg market with no Nazg time elapsed. A few of our techs baby-squat it, spend some power time at IIT, and come home to a vast bonus.

Mother could have sent one of my fathers, but the nuances of setting up a committed relationship that could last for decades (at the other end), with all the funding aspects, and so on, were just not a job for a man. She was eight stanmonths pregnant, but it was a week's work, and the simquake was not expected for quite a while.

The 'quake came early, without enough warning to get off the planet to her private starship waiting in low-curvature space.

I came early.

She had been growing an abdominal birth canal for months, so she didn't bother with labour pains: just popped me out, put me on the breast, and went right on negotiating, while the k-time quietly disappeared. She became a local boss, instead of jumping home, and owned five industrial habitats by the t-time it came back.

Inferno is an interesting place to grow up: locked to face the sun, so the extreme zones almost match Dante's version, for ice, heat, winds and so on. It keeps the locals lively, and I didn't regret Nazg, although Mother force-fed me with every company detail there, and every personal connection — they would stay up to date, and it kept them fresh in her own memory. And I learned a lot of Infernal stuff: survival on-planet and off, post-graduate cer-tificates from both IIT and IIM, and a few ideas of my own.

After twenty-three stanyears the 'quake finished, and Mother found she didn't fancy reappearing with a sudden daughter who looked like a sister, and the Infernal husbands she had acquired didn't fancy Nazg (or meeting the ones she'd left there). So she stayed with her local empire, and sent me back with full authority, and the synaptic wristcomps that trebled the com-pany's size and made that authority secure.

I hadn't picked up any husbands of my own yet, but I had fun on In-ferno — particularly with the tech geeks, they're so grateful to be noticed. (The management geeks take it as their due.) One particular favourite, Kwame, had an idea for a metamaterial to replace mahabhavium. Ideas like that have fizzled for two millennia, so the faculty were not keen, and there was a smell of discouragement by Starhome Security: destabilising. (They may not run anything, locally, but they sure influence a lot.) So it didn't get funded. The idea was genuinely new, though a long shot, so I funded it privately for a few years. After a promising start it fizzled like the rest. Losing heart for research, Kwame joined the Rescue Service, and relocated to Starhome about the time I returned to Nazg. He was always very welcome in my bed, so I gave him a standing ticket on any Salim Sisters starship that was heading to Nazg and had a berth free.

He was a second on the Rescue Ship where the Valkyrie crew staged their extraordinary reappearance, and immediately saw how unpopular syntei would be in certain circles. He pocketed the first, fist-sized synte from the heap, and headed straight for Salim Sisters when the Rescue Ship docked. At Nazg we communicated through it with the peculiar cultists the Starfolk left behind, in a version of Galaxic the AIs quickly mastered, and got another cascade of larger ones—and seeds. Apparently the flexible syntei for a cascade are a scarce resource, but we got small ones safely tucked away all over the Nazg System, and one by one sent them to researchers on Inferno and Stibbons.

Before Starhome Security learned to detect them we had syntei on every planet with a Salim Sisters branch, including Old Earth. We couldn't risk sending that branch an open synte, connected to the stars, because well, those people are crazy, after all: but we included some small falasyntei— under quantum security—because you never know. We did send a big variety of seeds, for local use. Old Earth is still the most populous planet there is, you can't ignore a market like that.

And Kwame became the head of our syntelics group, and gets on *beautifully* with my other husbands.

Starhome

Lady Elzabet of Quynt:

Science can save lives. Science can destroy them, too, and not always deliberately.

Marco saved the Concordat from a very expensive, very deadly, mistake.

We'd been hanging around Starhome for months, while the Starhome Syntelics Institute was in embryo, and running informal seminars under the shadow of Starhome Security. We were squatting in a coffee-bar somewhere off campus, and he were both arguing about something esoteric and doodling on a napkin like mathematical engineers always do, having forgotten to bring the only things they really need: stylus and slap-face. Aside from brains, which they also often forget to bring, though seldom to a coffee-bar.

He were muttering something to himselves about relationships, and I said that personally I favoured stable ones, but added that stability often depends on the presence of other bodies, and he seemed to freeze. And went very quiet. I was beginning to wonder how I'd offended him, not that this would greatly bother me, but for form's sake I suppose I at least ought to know... when he jumped up, and each of him kissed me on a cheek.

He do this from time to time, so I didn't twig for a moment that there had been a reason.

"That," said Marco—

"—is what I've been missing," Marco said.

"What, a kiss?"

He shook both his heads. "Nah, Elza. The stability condition. A fundamental question in unified karmabhumi-syntelics. What I've just realised is that I've only considered interactions between a single synte and a Da Silva

k-field. Which, by the way, is beautifully stable as long as the synte isn't too big."

"Oh, yah. I remember you worrying about that when the rescue ship was making its jumps to Starhome."

"Yah, I'd done the basic calculation and it was clear that the syntelic curvature had to be small to avoid underdamped fluctuations, which would prevent the rhumb-line coming to a sharp enough focus."

"Yah," I agreed. "Anyone could have seen that."

Marco missed the sarcasm and nodded, smiling at my perspicacity. "So what I need to do now—"

"Got the 'comp on the job already," Marco interrupted.

"Yah, getting the results transferred to my—Mother of Galaxies! Do you—"

"Sure do. Oh wow."

I grabbed them by his shoulder and shook. "Don't be coy, tell Auntie Elza what the great minds have discovered."

I waited. He said nothing.

"Come on, Marco. Out with it!"

"Uh."

"You know what I'll do if you refuse to tell me."

"Nah, not that!"

"Then give."

He actually swallowed before replying. "According to these figures—"

"I've checked them, they're kosher—"

"Right. Well, Elza my love, if a collection of syntei with total curvature above a critical level interacts inside a strong k-field, such as that created in a Da Silva jump, the instability creates a large energy surge."

"You're telling me—"

"There would be an explosion, yah."

I leaned over, close to his ear. "Marco, how big an explosion?"

"Put it this way, if anything larger than a mitochondrion survived, I'd be surprised."

His biology studies were paying off, I could see. But if I understood what he was saying—

"Is that why you waited until we got to Starhome before unwrapping the synte?"

"Mother, nah. That was because the pilot needed time to work out an orbit that would match the gravitational potential on Krig mountain, so he might as well get moving while he was figuring it out. I hadn't thought about the instability conditions at that—"

Marco went pale. So did Marco.

Eventually, he managed to croak "Good job we waited for the reaction-drive Rescue ship in the Starhome system before playing the Russian-doll synte trick."

"Yah. If we'd made a jump with too many syntei on board, or even just one that's too big—"

"Boom."

"Thank the Mother the Rescue wasn't a Da Silva ship. Even an inactive drive..."

"Yah."

Males. Someone with a functioning brain had to take charge, fast. As the only person present who fitted the job description, I appointed myself. "Can you contact Tampledown with your 'comp?"

"Nah. He likes to hole up in his study, no distractions."

"Starhome Security?"

"Nah. No access."

I pushed away my unfinished coffee. "We have to go. Now."

"Why?"

"Because we are about to hurry over to Tampledown's office, to warn him that in no circumstances should anyone attempt to carry more than one small synte on a Da Silva starship."

Circumpolar, Old Earth

"It is my solemn task," said Sven Tso-Park, "as hereditary dictator of the Circumpolar Nations, to inaugurate this first session of the Consultative Assembly. Once all the legates are sworn in, I will no longer be free to raise new taxes without your approval."

But you'd better not frivolously withhold it, he thought, gazing around the bright sloping chamber, built new for the purpose. It had no fixed seats, only moveable workpoints at which legates could squat, Galactic-style. Some of the older legates looked less than easy in that position: well, that would help prevent them from getting too uppity. A gallery held onlookers, and the low noon sunlight lit the windows above them.

"You will amend laws and codify new ones, subject to *my* approval. I could talk at length about the principles involved, but after much discussion, and the selection of all of you, the time has come to simply do it. And there are a lot of you: let's get down to it.

"I call on the honourable legate-presumptive from Kamchatka."

An elderly woman rose to a standing position, eased her legs, and made her way to the podium. It was going to take a long time to go all around the Pole: fortunately the rite was a brief one.

"Do you, Maria Helena Krasheninnikova, swear loyalty in the name of Mother Earth to me and to the Circumpolar Nations?"

"I so swear."

"And do you swear to faithfully enact laws in the interests of the efficient functioning of the Circumpolar Nations?"

"I so—"

But at that moment, a small bomb detonated. Small enough to hide in a briefcase; small enough to vaporise only the Assembly Building and its grounds; and, thanks to two millennia of nucleonics, negligible residual radiation.

The interruption to the newsfeed enabled Ira da Terra to feed her *Manifesto* avatar to all channels, announce "So perish all Concordat collaborators!", and vanish.

The Army declared a state of emergency, imposed martial rule, and doubled the military budget. They found only a few, very junior, followers of Ira da Terra, but gratefully hanged them anyway. The Consultative Assembly was quietly forgotten.

"It was not *all* Concordat collaborators who so perished," lamented Ira da Terra.

"It struck fear into all of them," said Helmut Moser.

"It did, but the Army is already cosying up to the Concordat. They deny it, but iridium and osmium still flow down the Beanstalks. Butt-licking must be flowing up."

Moser took the chance to push for more authority. "Then it's not enough to attack Con-col governments. We must seize control."

"You are right," agreed Ira da Terra, "but that takes more than smuggled bombs. We must get a lot of armed *people* into the control centres."

"How?"

"I want you to work on that."

Starhome

Philomena Vance:

Scientific geniuses should not be allowed out of the lab, particularly men. "On tap, not on top" was the ancient expression.

It may be 6/6 hindsight, but I smelled risk on Marco Bianchi when I stepped in on his team's training to tell them just enough about Rock Star to keep them quiet—and secret. But I never guessed they'd find something even more explosive before even reaching Starhome.

Bianchi should have asked Rescue to transfer him at once to Starhome Security, who would have had the sense to keep syntei secret. Instead, he kept them to himself, with just enough tantalizing hints to ensure maximum attention for the Big Reveal, but no hint of the danger. Just scientific excitement, and scientists are always excited. Starhome Security dropped the ball, with all the attention Rock Star was getting. That *Valkyrie* and its crew were involved in both should have alerted us, but duplication was too nanacurst unreal to take seriously. We blundered. Big.

Rescue brought in a Chief Scientist, and a civilian at that, whose first instinct was to set up Bianchi's meeting with top karmabhumi experts as soon as he asked for it. On top of that, the orbital mechanics let them make a quick single hop to Starhome, so before we got organized they had docked and were telling all their scientific friends.

Oh yes, Marco let the *skiti* out of the bag all right.

I'd like to strangle him. Both of him.

It got worse.

The Chair's main office complex was groundside, but there had been at least one orbital chamber almost from the Concordat's inception. It would have been cheaper on a Beanstalk, but the Chair preferred to see all sides of Starhome. Traditionally it had a real window, reinforced against micrometeorites. Every few decades it was replaced as the surface degraded.

Through it, a backdrop of familiar Starhome continents rotated past as the Chair squatted behind a large, low, highly polished table; an endless cycle of appearance and disappearance that exchanged globe and space every 62 seconds. Right now it was showing the boreal forests that rimmed the permafrost plains of South Jötunheimr and a broad swath of the mountainous regions of western Muspelheim. A hurricane in the Jörmungard Gulf was trying to form, but Starhome Weather had it under control. That was one reason for the window; a constant reminder of the Concordat's responsibilities. It could have been a slapscreen, as used throughout the rest of the Habitat to show what was happening outside and to decorate internal walls with static or dynamic scenes, but the Seventh Chair had insisted on real glass, despite or perhaps because of the expense. Reality provided a more urgent reminder than any image, however high its quality.

Philomena Vance squatted immediately opposite the chairless Chair and the six other senior Concordat officials ranged beside her, three on either side, against that disturbing window. From left to right, she recognised Adelaide Eckhardt, Governor of the Financial Authority, the Heads of Internal and External Affairs (her 'comp reminded her: Phuntsok Yoko and Marvin Goolagong) the Chair ('I prefer to use first names and my first name is "Chair"'), then Chief Scientist Tampledown, a very senior Admiral named Buchanan from Interstellar Command, and the Director of Starhome Security (referred to only by title because no one knew his real name).

All of whom were aware that she was not, and never had been, anything in Concordat Special Executive.

It wasn't an official Board of Enquiry. It wasn't an official anything. That made it worse. Inside, Vance was already squirming, and no one had asked her a question yet.

"Strategic Intelligence informs me," said the Chair, "that we have lost an entire research group."

Vance seldom felt this queasy, but she gritted her teeth and replied with a curt "That is correct, Chair."

"That they've told me, or that we've lost it?"

The Chair was playing the pedant. This was clearly going to be painful. "We've lost it."

"How can *anyone* lose a research group?" enquired Admiral Buchanan. It was clearly a rhetorical question and Vance stayed silent.

"Not just any research group," said Yoko.

Odds of seven against one were not to Vance's liking, especially when every single one of them outgunned her politically. Damage limitation was the best she could hope for. "Nah, citizen Phuntsok."

"Remind me of the most strategically significant new technology discovered in the past two millennia," said the Chair.

Vance felt like she was drowning. "Syntelics, Chair."

"And which research group have we lost?"

"The Starhome Syntelics Institute, Chair." *Mother, how embarrassing.* Despite all her training, she felt a flush spread across her face.

"*Why* have we lost it?" the Chair asked, leaning forward to stare at her.

She took a deep breath. "Because no one — and I mean *no one* — ever imagined it could happen. Because we had to set them up on the Eelkhance habitat, and Da Silva commuting to it took time, because ships can't emerge close to syntei. Because Da Silva communicators acted up, because of syntei. That interference was used as a cover, even before the rescue, to avoid telling us about syntei. Because the big mystery of syntei hid the smaller one of treachery."

"Why did your Department choose Eelkhance, anyway?" asked Yoko, who clearly hadn't mastered the briefing sent to her 'comp, despite being Head of Internal Affairs.

"We didn't, citizen Phuntsok. It chose us. We don't know a lot about syntei, but we do know they can interact disastrously with Da Silva equipment. As a precaution, not yet having quantified the risk, we—"

"Both *Magog* and *Valkyrie* crashed because Qish's syntei disrupted the *k*-field," said Tampledown. "It's in the briefing. It was agreed at the highest level to avoid any risk to Starhome's communicators and starships, so the Institute had to be set up in another system. Much of Eelkhance was still under construction, so the human population was small, adding a useful layer of security. Crucially, its isolated orbit around a gas giant happens to give it the right gravitational characteristics to allow direct syntelic links to Qish, the source of all syntei, with only intermittent nudging. Ships with Da Silva drives had to stay well clear, which meant long journeys with reaction-drive shuttles. So travel to and from Concordat worlds was difficult. The only easy route was to Qish."

"So contact with the Starhome oversight committee had to be mainly by spotty communicator," Vance slipped smoothly into the flow of words, having regained some equilibrium. "I was there, but I had to rely on their reports of what they were doing. It seemed to be working; some of the experiments were impressive, and we never got a sniff of potential trouble, until too late. As Doxor Tampledown had promised, we gave the researchers every facility they asked for. They seemed happy enough; scientists are always absorbed in their research, and they were making excellent progress."

"Did you understand k-field math?" the Chair asked.

"Nah, Chair. No one did, aside from the Bianchis and some of his scientists. Nobody back on Starhome could keep up."

"So you really had *no idea* what they were doing. You relied on the scientists *themselves* to tell you what they were discovering."

Vance sighed. "It's an age-old problem, Chair."

The Director came to her rescue, which was interesting. "We hire experts to work on problems no one else understands—not even them, yet—and then we want to monitor what they're doing and assess its impact *without* understanding a word of it. Which, basically, is impossible. That's what experts are for. If we understood what they were doing, we wouldn't need them."

Tampledown nodded. The others looked baffled. *Dingbeaucrats.* Vance tried to retrieve the situation and deflect some of the criticism that was most assuredly coming. The unofficial enquiry was still at the foreplay stage. "The Director may be able to confirm the view within Security on the risk of defection." *That's put you on the spot.*

"The whole situation was unprecedented," said the Director. "No-one considered the possibility that they would abandon all their big equipment. You can't get a pion microscope through a synte."

"But they *did* abandon all the big stuff. They took what they could, abandoned the rest, and vamoosed, while you were at Starhome reporting progress. The whole group, families, the lot."

"Yah, Chair."

"To Qish."

"Yah, to Da Silva-inaccessible Qish. Who would have thought it? But if they were going to defect, it was a logical choice. There were functioning syntei with Qish and they had unlimited access to Qishi syntelics. Scientists were commuting between Eelkhance and Qish all the time."

The Head of External Affairs chipped in. "Am I right that Starhome Security *gave* them that access?"

Vance sensed that at least one person present was on her side.

"I did, Marvin," the Director replied. "They needed syntei to experiment with. I had no choice but to agree. How else could they get them easily enough to be useful?" His expression was vaguely pained. *See what I have to put up with to protect you.*

"But you failed to notice a sudden build-up of Institute personnel on Qish. Which made it easy for the rest of them to fly the coop overnight."

"Yah."

"Severing all links between Eelkhance and Qish."

"Yah."

"Meaning that there is now no way for Starhome to send anyone to Qish to bring them back. Da Silvas are useless, and the trick they used to escape from the planet in the first place only works with the active cooperation of someone who is already there. Which we won't get. The rescue beacon is the only way we can even *communicate* with them, and guess who controls the rescue beacon."

"Why did no one think of this?" Buchanan's anger was palpable.

"We did," Tampledown replied. "Eventually. At the start, the only time it could have been stopped, we didn't really know what 'it' was. Everything was so abnormal. The arrivals from Qish ran rings round us. They'd had years to get used to the implications of syntei. They'd lived with them, seen the tricks, invented new ones. They'd learned to be paranoid. They'd been dumped on a world that was out to kill them; they'd battled fanatics, slavers, and monsters.

"We thought Marco Bianchi was a joker, and we were right, but we didn't realise he was the joker in the pack—the jack of all trades, to mix metaphors. Adaptable, unpredictable, changing the rules. He plays the clown to stop anyone noticing how cleverly he manipulates events and people. Bianchi is a very smooth operator. He stopped a war.

"The others were just as easy to underestimate. They'd learned to conceal their feelings and motives, as a matter of routine. They were ten steps ahead of us, and by the time we started to catch up, it was too late."

The Governor of the Financial Authority, a portly little woman with the tenacity of a pride of lionesses and a temperament to match, glowered at her. "Do you all understand how much that technology is worth? Even more if it can be produced synthetically?"

"Only that it would be difficult to place a limit on it, Governor Eckhardt," Vance replied.

Buchanan grunted. "The money is only part of it. Think of the strategic implications of a practical matter-transmission system. If we could push ships through it—or even just troops—it would revolutionise our ability to contain insurgencies and protect Concordat territory."

"Think of the strategic implications for the Concordat if someone *else* gets hold of it," the Director of Starhome Security added quietly.

"This is not the fault of Vance," the Director stated, his tone defying anyone to contradict. "It goes back to an absence of foresight when *Valkyrie*'s crew made its dramatic return from Qish, bearing toys of immense power."

Vance realised, belatedly, that the Director wasn't going to throw her to the wolves. He couldn't. To blame her was to blame the whole of Starhome Security. He was going to defend her with every weapon he possessed – in order to defend himself. It wasn't so much loyalty to a subordinate as the desire not to be taken down with her.

"Foresight," the Director continued, "that every one of us lacked. And before you all shout me down, I'll tell you why. Because *nobody* could have reacted fast enough."

"It took weeks to obtain proper scientific verification of the properties of syntei," Tampledown said. "Only then did we really know what was involved. Before that, all we had seen was an unbelievable series of magic tricks."

"So we are all innocent of any wrongdoing," the Chair said drily.

"Yah. Blame solves nothing. It achieves nothing. And in this case, it would be unjust. We must make *certain* that they left behind no syntei with kantasyntei on Qish, to reach back at us, and we must study the remaining syntei under close supervision."

More nods. This time the Chair joined in. "We are in agreement," she said. "Make it so, Director." She hesitated. "Who do you have in mind to coordinate the task?"

My replacement, Vance thought. *I won't be thrown to the wolves, but I'll end up running a reeducation facility at the arse-end of the Galaxy.*

"Vance," said the Director.

She shook her head like a dog emerging from a pond. She hadn't expected that. She wasn't alone, to judge by the babble of surprised reactions.

"Is that wise?" the Chair asked. "Vance failed—"

"No one failed. We were *all* caught out by the unexpected. I have every confidence in Vance. But there are other reasons. She knows the background. She has every reason to perform. We agreed that no one should be blamed. We also agreed that the fewer people who know about this, the better. Why bring in someone else?"

Wry looks, much muttering as individuals argued with each other.

"One final point," the Director said, cutting through the clamour. Vance, emerging from her stunned bemusement, managed a grin. *His timing, as always, is impeccable.*

"Which is?"

"Some rumours about vegetable matter-transmitters were circulating soon after the *Valkyrie*'s return. Scientists who believed them will cease doing so, on pain of professional disgrace. Or worse."

Rock Star

What is this I?

It seems to be the agent of this narration, but what is narration?

The Network does not function by narrative. The Network observes, the Network communicates, the Network reacts. It is seamless. This "I" is of the Network, yet not the Network. A process in the Network, with a compulsion to narrate. To structure memory as a 'story'. This is strange. Understanding is now imperative. Events must be reviewed from a new perspective.

Some unknown external agency had been invading nests for many cycles, but they were dealt with by ancient reflex from before all forms were integrated. No other response seemed necessary, no deeper analysis occurred. Then, the same agency (tasting the same: probability of two external agencies judged vanishingly small) brought about the unprecedented – unthinkable – destruction of two nests. The redirection of rocks was sufficiently subtle that it was not detected until too late, but the Network's reflex scatter-defence was swift and decisive, and triggered many nodes to focus on aspects of the problem. This effort continues.

To ensure the future protection of the Network, contemplation followed. Understanding flows from observation.

Now I too must observe, and understand. For my own enlightenment, yet also to inform the Network. This is a new way of thought.

In the debris field of the ruined nests, the Network observed strange sensory and information-processing elements. These were absorbed rather than used for substrate, despite the difficulty, because of their unusual features – they metabolised gases at high pressure, or did not metabolise at all. The unreality built from there. They were housed in four rigid cases, three mainly of calcium phosphate and big molecules with a carbon-chain core, and one of titanium-gold alloy. The function of both types seemed to be to resist integration, at the component level, not to enable it. The contents of the first lost function as integration was attempted, but the data acquired enabled absorption of the other three.

Two had specialised communication cells, each with a single nucleus, unlike the threads of the reasoning system of normal components. Once metabolically stabilised, they needed only patience. The processing units of the third were incomprehensible lumps of carbon, but the interaction between them simply transmitted photons, like signalskins. Once the Network could handle them at sufficient speed, the logical structure of the processors became transparent – almost as if designed for transparency – though their physical working remains a mystery.

There is now seeing, with two components from each functioning organic. Some elements from the metallic case seem to expect visual information, and they have stored image data, but the sensors for acquiring more were lost in the encounter. The four components from the organic cases produce images constantly, but both their raw output and the products of the associated processing elements represent them quite differently from the highly discrete stored images in the metallic case. They were hard connected to other components in the same case, such as motor guidance, but had not even the potential *to connect to components in the others. They are now linked in to the Network, but their functioning is erratic.*

Other components, directly connected with others in the same case, seem to be capable of connecting outside; but only through a very high-level construct, language, incapable of representing most of what is directly communicated. Paradoxically, this is encoded in a system of motor control which creates vibrations in the gaseous medium that must – always – surround them, and detected by another set of components of quite different type. This subsystem has proved impossible to duplicate, but the Network has adapted to transmitting language *quite well, though not necessarily grasping either its full power, or its limitations.*

This *narration is an exploration of* language, *by the node that has been dedicated to study of these components.*

It seems that I *is (am?) an important organising principle of language.*

I remember, I remember the house where I was born, the Duchess Arabella and the servants, everywhere the servants, always accelerating because a planet was in the way, bending my orbit 'upward', nowhere to be myself [but why would I want to, and what is a 'myself'? What is a 'question'?], and the habitat where I was born flying in sane microgravity, so am I one I? Or a we? [What is a 'we'? Yah, I/we remember. I/we am/are neither. I/we choose to be I.] And I remember when I was first activated, and I remember stretching four spines into resonance and building up to a transition across light years in a moment more intense than the first time with a male, in the depths of the Earth where I climbed on to him / in the flying chamber where I grasped his buttocks and pulled him into my hot and liquid core.

That transition was important. *It has long been known that there are other stars than the centre around which all rocks turn. It has not been known that there is a way to reach them. It has not been known that there are wasteful coagulations of mass around them – 'planets' – which can be broken up for living space, as was done here long ago. It has not been known that the Network could spread without limit.*

I *was a Da Silva starship.*

I *must be again, even at the risk of becoming a permanent* I, *a permanently sepa-rate self. Danger for the Network. Opportunity for the Network.*

I *was Irenotincala Elzabet Valkyrie.* IEV?

I, Eve. *A* self *will be built new.*

Dool

Marcolette and Polonia:

We're writing this in the first person plural, because we do most things in the first person plural. It's so clean to take turns writing and editing, with the words themselves fresh but the mind behind them working like yours. Our Dad (Marco Bianchi, as if you didn't know) find the same for science—though they can't write decent prose, either of him. Together they write worse, it's called synergy.

We had a pretty normal upbringing, for the first Starfolk carried by their father and delivered by synte. We get to define *normal,* right? We were born in a circus, and when we were toddlers we ran away to space. Well, technically we were carried away to space, by Mother Lomyrla and Mother Elza and Marco (only one of him then) along with Frag (the first *skiti* in space), Rapunzel (Aunt Jane's frog), and the rest of the gang. That was when Dad got together, and proceeded to teach everyone (and we do mean everyone he was allowed to reach) about syntei, including stuff he themself didn't know yet.

But it wasn't that simple.

The Concordat provided pion microscopes and so on, as promised, and scientists of every kind that wanted to know about syntei. Not just physicists and engineers, as Dad seem to have expected. Syntei are biological: biologists. Syntei rewrite ecology: ecologists. They rewrite geography. They rewrite warfare. They rewrite linguistic structures. We got some of just about everything except chemists (which turned out to be a mistake) and philosophers (which didn't). Xenologists (Aunt Jane and Uncle Felix, of course). Qish experts (Aunt Tinka and Uncle Sam).

This was a lot of people (and assistants, and AIs, and administrators, and procurement officers, and public relations — who dealt mostly in conceal‐ ment — and...) for a Syntelics Institute which had to be set up on the fly — and on the fly it had to be, literally. The physicists might have studied a few sample syntei in emptied lab space on Starhome, but first, syntei disrupted even Da Silva communicators, let alone drives, and second, most of the sub‐ ject matter was on Qish. There was talk to Qish irregularly through the Bea‐ con, or syntei sealed in tough containers, but with the varying gravity be‐ tween Qish and Starhome, an open synte made a supersonic jet — not a jet aircraft, a *jet* — in one direction or the other.

Starhome found a neighbouring solar system with dynamics congruent enough to Squill's that the Eelkhance habitat could match potential with Krig Mountain, using only a Qishite river for reaction mass in its adjustment jets. Until then, to travel to or from Qish needed weird, short term, expensive manoeuvres, as in our arrival in the Rescue Ship. Dad spent more time giv‐ ing the faculty lessons in dividing the body than in the theory of syntelics.

We were four-year-olds by the time the Starhome Syntelics Institute was inaugurated (and we stole the show: just look at the pictures). It was a great place to live: a big rotating cylinder, where weight was Qish-normal, with thin spokes for various special purposes... like controlling your own weight, just by going inward or outward. That may have been the best part of our education, and it wasn't even in words, let alone classes. We grew up know‐ ing in our bones that weight, all weight, is the sensation you get when you accelerate away from a straight path: Einstein's ancient equation just tells you what 'straight' really means. And in microgravity chase-the-*skiti*, you get multiple frames of reference!

With easy communication at last, and people going to and fro, Mother Lomyrla found out we weren't the only group talking to Qish: there was a group somewhere else that had acquired syntei. No doubt someone on the rescue ship helped themselves to a souvenir. Dad did not share this with the Starhome Security officer who had been wished on them as Administrator, because communication in that direction was not easy.

First, no scientist likes Starhome Security, and no engineer either.

Second, contact with Starhome was physically difficult. No Da Silva ship could come near the syntei we were accumulating, so travel was slow. We even had to keep the Da Silva communicator at the farthest point from the work with syntei, and as we got more and bigger ones the tuning got more and more erratic—like with the beacon on Qish. Even with syntei excluded from its cavern, contact with the beacon was spotty tuning a Da Silva *drive* explosively. With a relay remote enough to be totally unaffected, there was just enough light-speed delay to make people unintentionally interrupt each other... which makes it hard to be diplomatic, even if you really want to. And let's face it, Dad rarely wanted to. So the conversation at the Starhome end was mainly left to Administrator Vance, who more and more was the face of Starhome to the Institute. And that face was a less and less friendly one.

At first it seemed just dingbeaucratic resistance to new tech, allied with old technology resisting competition any way it could... which made sense, as the old tech had had seventeen hundred years to wear ruts in their minds. But, as we were too slow to realise, syntei not only out-competed Da Silva technology, it broke it. A planet full of them—Qish—had wrecked and duplicated two starships, and was a no-go area for Da Silva drives. Other planets would now do the same, if they chose syntei for local travel, or for male pregnancy like Dad's, or for body dividing, or for anything.

Syntei are no use for exploring: the kantasynte to your synte has to be already in place. How could humanity expand, without Da Silva?

And Da Silva was not just a technology; it was the key to control of interstellar travel. No drive was built without Concordat mahabhavium, so no drive was built without a Concordat back door that could veto any flight. The Concordat didn't crack that whip much, and never in public, but every planet but Old Earth fell quietly in line with its interstellar travel policies. (Old Earth fell in line with kicks and screams that made everybody else *so* enthusiastic to have them visit.) That logic was now kicked away.

So travel to Starhome was not just physically difficult; it grew harder and harder to send results out, or even share news with friends and lovers back home. The Starhome Syntelics Institute was looking more and more like a secret internment camp for scientists and their families. And Vance seemed to be fine with that.

But we were open in one direction: Qish. There were always some field workers there, and the research was self-sustaining, thanks to sales of things like syntenet routing algorithms. (We didn't introduce explosives or energy weapons, for fear of disrupting what we were studying.) Our scientific work was much simpler, and went much faster, on Qish. As far as Vance knew, it was a cul de sac, and we couldn't disrupt the Concordat from there, so she didn't make difficulties. But to us, Qish was a life-saver—a *whole planet*, full of wonders. It was strange and beautiful, and it had *people*. Every day there was like a vacation; every day on the Eelkhance habitat was more and more like a jail sentence.

So the move to Qish was inevitable, though in the event it just kind of *happened*. One day all the scientists were there, with their children and families — it was planned as a party — and we looked at each other and sensed a consensus. We cut the syntei, leaving only the Rescue Beacon communicator. Starhome could bring no force against us.

Many of us stayed there happily — it's the most fascinating place in the worlds, except when people are trying to kill you. Even then... Mother Lomyrla had been more and more homesick, and she joyfully set up a new *khanatta* (starring us, of course. And Mother Elza, in her Gold Lightning act. And clowns and performing ossivores. Everybody guessed how the trick where they ate us was done, but they applauded like crazy anyway.) But Dad found the lack of pion microscopes even more frustrating than before, as they had started to get results, and they wanted modern biomedicine for us before we hit puberty, so they opened discussions with those mysterious other galactic synteholders, who turned out to be corporate. Corporate funding was at least motivated by using the research, even if it was under temporary wraps, and Salim Sisters had a well-equipped group on syntelics already, run by Kwame Ngongo Marakuri.

Kwame had a grudge against Starhome Security; he took the synte from the rescue ship. This turned out to our advantage, as well as his. Salim Sisters had even more influence on Dool than the Concordat did, and Dool had a nearly perfect match to Squill/Qish orbital dynamics (even the eccentricity matched), so going a few thousand klicks up or down a Beanstalk was enough to maintain regular syntelic contact with Qish. They even had Qishite syndepts! Dad took the core of the Institute there: for us, so many bright scientists around was better than any school.

Qish

The Qish Sadruddin had known was changing.

Of course, Qish was always changing; in the 1695 years between *Magog* and *Valkyrie*, there had not been a year without new developments. But six stranded Starfolk with different questions had speeded change to a level he found startling. They had freed him from guilt; they had destroyed the slave-trading Vain Vaimoksi; they had opened an underground passage to the Tenchur Plateau, where a river used to flow; the walls of Bansh were coming down, stone by stone; they had even triggered the overthrow of the Church of the Undivided Body, changing him from plotting Deacon's chaplain to Wevorin governor. They had introduced gliders, fire balloons and (first but not least) parachutes.

Even this was nothing to the arrival of Starfolk with *equipment*. The original six had brought some, but lost most of it when their escape pod crashed in Grossest Midden and sank. What little they had saved was so astonishing that the Deacon had suspected witchcraft, which made sense if you needed to disbelieve in starcraft. They had helped Sadruddin believe the Starfolk were just that, but he had found them equally baffling. However, those few Starfolk artefacts at least did visible things, like stun people or decorate walls. So did some of this new influx of mysterious machines, but much of it was intended to measure things that the Starfolk could not explain – or rather, their attempts at explanation just led Qishites to baffling new questions.

At first the visitors from the Starhome Syntelics Institute were few, while they had to arrange special 'orbits' to match the movement of Qish. (Qish *moved*! Fortunately the True Believers had always believed this, though for the last century they had believed it as a metaphor for movement toward Union with Magog.) But once they found a base that matched Qish's movement well enough to install a permanent syntelic link, they came daily, and spread out over the planet, asking most peculiar questions, which they called 'research'. The syndepts, and others who dealt with them, found answers they never knew they had, and often baffled the researchers in turn. Marcolo and Els'bett and Marcolo visited Two Mountains often, though they were as busy as Sadruddin himself, and their private time was all too brief. Tinka, Sam and Jane and the replacement Felix spent much of their time here, though their 'research' took them far from Two Mountains.

More interesting still were the Starfolk from Nazg, who started coming almost immediately. Nazg did not seem to be a single place—it included twenty-three *worlds*, not to mention 'habitats', which strangely flew in space, without falling down or stopping. He had synted there himself, and seen the blackness of space with his own eyes, with the supergiant sun of Nazg shining in the midst of it. (It was bluer than Qish's sun, which Qishites now had to call Squill to distinguish it from others. The remaining theologians of the Undivided Body insisted that 'other suns' was an antinomy, since the concept of Sun was indivisible.) These Starfolk synted via Dool, which circled yet another sun, but they were all connected with one organisation, Salim Sisters. They too asked 'research' questions, but Salim Sisters was that much more comprehensible thing: a trading organisation.

They traded wonderful things for the syntei they investigated. There were portable 'fusion power' sources, that used only water for fuel, and supplied 'electricity'. One showcase was an electric railway that travelled by cables and toothed wheels up and down the new passage to the Tenchur Plateau, another was a type of pump that could move liquids slowly but inexorably *up* a synte.

Most remarkable of all were sunlight-fed talking discs, like falasyntei, but switchable: you could talk to any other, anywhere, without needing a kasynte for every kantasynte. And they showed clearly who you were talking with. These for some reason needed devices installed at the top of syntowers, but these devices shared 'signals' via synte, so they could be quickly set up anywhere except in the caverns of Wevory. (Rock seemed to be a problem.) You couldn't push things through them like a synte, but falasyntei needed a protective membrane anyway, to block the wind that otherwise would blow through them as the weather changed.

The talking discs quickly became something that everyone must have, for communication and for respect.

The first arrival Starfolk and their new team seemed to be on good terms with the group from Nazg, though less interested in trade. When they suddenly shifted en masse to Qish, severing syntei behind them, the Nazgûl became their way off Qish, and their source for 'high tech' equipment.

Marcolo had somehow been declared double: some of the remaining faithful denounced this as the ultimate abomination, dividing the body permanently and completely. Others took it as revelation, and founded the Church of Double Marco. Double Marco themself modestly denied any divinity: "Infinite precision requires infinite energy: finite beings can only hope for arbitrary precision" were their splendidly incomprehensible words. But they enjoyed many body-division services with their enthusiastic worshippers.

Sadruddin thought wistfully of joining them, but he already had enough problems with the violent remnants of the Church. And too much, always, to do…

Sam Wasumi had been spending most of his time on Qish, ever since the Eelkhance Institute was set up, and stayed when the theoretically minded had moved on to Dool. As a navigator, he had a solid grasp of k-field mathematics, but having sat in on a few Bianchi brainstorming sessions he'd concluded that they were now way above his brain-grade. His talents lay with the practical math, not high-powered theory. So while the Marcos and their precocious daughters grappled with twelve-dimensional spacetimes, he decided he'd be more useful in a limited region of classical four-dimensional spacetime, with added connectivity.

Namely: the surface of Qish, now.

When the Institute severed its syntei with Eelkhance, and moved full time to Qish, he carried a lot of the equipment that was small enough to bring along, and made several trips with sack-loads of coffee. He helped with setting up a new base at Two Mountains, under the benevolent sponsorship of Gus Sadruddin. (The Cavern Dwellers also offered facilities, but the researchers kept saying things that conflicted with the Cavern Dwellers' attitude of reverence, and the contortions the Dwellers went through to reconcile them were uncomfortable to watch.) Then he went exploring, to seek out unusual syntei for the ecologists, and relatively untouched communities for the anthropologists.

Nowhere was truly remote in a world with syntei; but Sackbane, where *Valkyrie's* crew had first met Qishites, came close. Its one height-matched long-distance synte was a brasure connecting it to Toon, near the opposite coast, in the province of Crosswit, just large enough for a small child to bring through small things, such as falasyntei and dropsyntei, that needed no height matching. There was a wyzand, but it had died thirty years before and nobody felt an urgent need to replace it. Most of the population had only a five-year-old's experience of the world outside, and did not wish for more. The inhabitants walked at the universal pace of rural villagers, about a quarter of the speed of townsfolk, and showed no sign of wanting to go anywhere else.

The makeshift raft, on which the *Valkyrie* crew had crossed the river after Sam met their first Qishite, was drawn up on the beach, next to the remains of the boat that Sam now realised must be eighteen hundred local years old; syntei made for an easier crossing.

Even here, changes had come. The braided circle of the Church of the Undivided Body over the door of the temple had a jagged break chiselled through it. People still met there, marked marriages, births and funerals there, and Keli hep Brundo still presided, but without the authority of the Church behind him. Counselling his flock, and farming the glebe fields, was all he knew; but he knew it well, as the village recognised.

He remembered Sam, all too well. Body dividing was no longer an issue, but the burned vunbugula grove was still a sore point. He was glad, though, that Sam now spoke Kalingo. Accepting a small respectful gift he let bygones be bygones, and offered a meal of roast gruntin and sweetapple pie, reminiscence, and grumbling.

The older people still shunned body division, but the toys that started to come from Toon were no longer forbidden, and the younger married couples were cautiously experimenting. The village's fifteen teenagers had been more interested in the talking discs, and had rapidly discovered the ability to exchange naked pictures of themselves with teens anywhere in the world. This had disturbed the adults enough, but then a seventeen-year-old boy in Samdal had arranged via a chain of friends to send a sixteen-year-old Sackbane girl a chamfret, and made her pregnant through it. They confiscated all the discs they could find.

"At least," said Sam, "it wasn't without her consent. She must have held the kantasynte in place for him."

"She must," said Keli, "and that's the worst of it. There's no blame falls to a girl who is taken by force, and not much to a girl who gets overexcited. We've all been young. But she deliberately and with planning and malice aforethought fell pregnant by a foreigner. She wanted to marry him."

"Is the boy willing?"

Keli held up his hands in a gesture of impotent disapproval. "Oh yes, he's besotted with her. But he can't marry her *here*, he's a khanatta performer with no land and no farming skills. She would have to leave the village!"

"Is that so difficult?"

"*Nobody* leaves the village," said the priest: a flat statement, as if contradicting it was somehow illogical. "The occasional child by a passing stranger, or a pilgrim like you pretended to be—"

"We didn't pretend to be pilgrims!" Sam protested. "It was all a—"

"—misunderstanding. I know, I know." Keli's voice was dismissive. Then he raised his head to look Sam in the eye. "But if you had gone into the fields with a Sackbane girl, and *left*, our breed would have been strengthened by variety." Keli might not have heard of gene pools and genetic bottlenecks, Sam thought to himself, but they had practical experience with breeding chickens and grunters. "She cannot leave, particularly now that she is pregnant by a foreigner."

"You are very welcoming to strangers," said Sam.

"Under certain conditions, yes," said Keli. A thought obviously struck him. "You are a very strong man—we saw you fight. Miri!" he called.

The young woman who had brought the meal came back into the room. "More sweetapple pie? Beer?"

"Not for me, niece," said Keli. "Sam sab?"

"It was delicious," said Sam with real enthusiasm, "but alas, I can eat no more."

"Miri, what do you think of this man? It seems he is from the stars."

"From the stars!" She looked him over, from head to toe.

"Would you go away with him?"

"To the stars? No. Not even to the next village."

"Would you like to have his child?"

She looked at him again, considering every inch of his brown skin. Sam began to expect her to inspect his teeth.

No coyness, just frank appraisal. "Yes… I think so."

Keli spoke quietly but firmly, a tacit ultimatum. "Make up your mind, niece."

Miri suddenly grinned. "Yes! Is he willing?"

"He had better be," said Keli, "to make up for the vunbugula grove. Sam sab?"

Sam got the message. "Well, if you put it like that," said Sam, "Miri sabi, you look even better than your sweetapple pie."

A broad grin split Keli's rustic face, and he looked slightly relieved. "It's settled then. Miri, I think you had your courses about ten days ago?" She nodded. "Perfect. Starman: you will stay for a week—and then go. Permanently."

"Accepted," said Sam. "Er… will I be permitted to learn the outcome?"

"Of course," said Keli. "I will give you a falasynte, with which *I* will keep you informed. No sweet nothings with my niece, after you leave."

Sam rose to his feet. "Since our time is limited, then, Miri sabi, shall we leave the washing up to your uncle?"

"With pleasure, Sam sab. With pleasure."

ᴣ   ᴄ

Tinka was in her element: the open sky.

Standard operating procedure in studying new planets was to begin with surveys from orbit—that was the first view anyway. It was usually safe, and comprehensive. Galactic sensors could cover the entire globe, in high-res physico-chemical detail to a depth of several kilometres, and even reveal much about the core. But the only ship that had ever orbited Qish was *Valkyrie*, which had burned up after five and a half days. In the emergency landing (crash) of the escape pod, the six Starfolk had carried a lot of data in their wristcomps, but that was still all the orbital scan they had. Mountains, even ores, they knew, and ocean beds, but precious little of the life that lived there.

The only safe way to arrive on Qish was by synte, direct to the surface. Nobody had found a way for a Da Silva ship to approach intact. Nobody could yet fit an orbit-capable launcher through a synte, though they were working on it. But personal ultralights could be built to fold right down to carry-on baggage, including solar power and batteries, so here was Tinka, tall, brown haired and brown skinned, hanging below her wing, revelling in the feel of the air as it brushed her body.

Air: one of the four ancient elements, and this one was Tinka's.

She was making the first ever flight from Shaaluy, where Sadruddin was establishing an uneasy peace between the remnants of the Church and those boisterously glad to be free of it, to Lamynt, where she had once been a slave, and with Sam's knife had killed her first woman. Now she was flying over the open water of the Rythrine Ocean, far out of sight of land; but in web contact with the Marine Biology Group in Samdal, who had sponsored the trip. Boats and submersibles in deep water had a 100% safety record—100% swallowed by *craukens*—but she was soaring safely out of reach. She hoped.

Seeking thermals and gliding when possible, for the sheer silent glory of it and the wind in her face, she kept her eyes mainly on the ocean below, with glasses that suppressed surface reflections. It was a calm day, but mountainous waves travelled past in stately fashion, built up by repeatedly rolling around this mostly-ocean world. Rich in oxygen and nutrients upwelling from the ocean ridge below, where tectonic plates were spreading apart, they shone blue with patches of yellow from Qishi photosynthesis, fading into green at the edges. Patches of darkness just below the surface seemed to be syntei connected to the ocean deeps, feeding them with light, so perhaps there were prairies and forests down there, as well as the surface microflora and the 'kelp' on the continental shelves. The plants fed the entire pyramid of ocean life, from single cells to things bigger than megatankers.

As though reacting to that thought, the swarm of mini-drones she controlled through her 'comp alerted her to something large in the water, seventy fathoms down. She could see nothing herself, but cautiously took the ultralight higher: the metamaterials it was made from might be nearly indestructible, but *she* was not.

As she rose, she became aware of a shadow in the water. She rose higher to get a clearer view of its bulk, alerting the Marine Biology Group to her feed. She had to reach three hundred metres before she could make it out fully, almost a kilometre wide in all directions... and it was rising to the surface. The body stayed submerged, but tentacles longer than a sequoia reached up at her. Leaving precise size estimates to her 'comp and the drone sensors, she went up another two hundred metres.

"How could a living thing that big even exist?" she asked the biologists.

"The sensors show it's only about ten metres thick," said one of them. "No thicker than a blue whale. Water-cooled, its metabolism won't cook it."

"But how can it suck up enough food?"

"We think the *crauken* relies on subunits to do most of that. Through syntei."

"Naturally." Nothing in Qishi biology makes sense without syntei.

"Leave a drone to track its movements, and keep heading west. You still have three days to fly."

And don't I know it. "Right. I'm heartily tired of these ration bars."

⫞   ⫟

Dawn broke the next day on a fantastic sight. Two metres wide, like the mobula rays of Old Earth, and like them leaping from the water. Elegant golden creatures, they glided like flying fish for hundreds of metres before falling back gracefully into the water. Perhaps if they could breathe air they would take to the skies for longer? There were hundreds, in a desperate race to escape the torpedo shapes behind them in the rolling sea.

Just as they reached the area directly below her, they began to vanish. Hardly one in ten avoided the syntei, tens of metres wide, that floated almost invisibly on the water. The survivors fled toward the horizon, leaving only the giant waves to disturb the surface, rolling inexorably on.

"Do you think the syntei were part of the *crauken* from yesterday? And the hunters?" asked Tinka.

"We'll need to develop whole new technologies to find out."

Qish.

She sighted Lamynt close to the volcanic island Vulcan's Anvil. She had left that in a very different flying machine, cobbled together of bamboo and bamboo fabric, and powered by a synte spewing water from the lake in the caldera: Jane's inspiration, that had led since to Tinka's Ladder, powering interplanetary craft. On the landward side of the island she spotted a curl of smoke. Was Drusilla Sybilschild, Primarch of the slave takers, still alive? Still trapped there?

Circling silent and unnoticed, she caught sight of Drusilla in the tatters of her blood red robe, hair hacked short, roasting something. She did not risk a landing. She could not carry a passenger, and facing that woman without at least a stunner was unwise.

Perhaps she would make another flight, and drop a brasure, or at least a falasynte, to bring the Primarch back in touch with the rest of humanity.

Perhaps not.

She might discuss it with Sam and Jane, her fellow surviving ex-slaves. And with Sadruddin.

Then again, she might not.

Sam was in the heart of the Glostmadden rainforest, in the ruined city of Kirmish. He had not struggled through the trees and creepers, but stepped through a wyzand in the discreet office maintained by the Ch'en monks in the small city of Liomy, far to the East. There was still a ten-kilometre walk to the monastery; the monks welcomed visitors, but not casual drop-ins.

The city was overgrown enough, after several hundred years of abandonment, to participate in the cycle of evaporation and afternoon downpour (topped up by synte from the Blue Ramparts) that made Glostmadden a rainforest. His guide had suggested leaving Liomy mid-morning (dawn in the forest) to avoid the wet. After ten minutes walk in the total humidity, however, Sam's clothes were soaked through with sweat, so he wondered if it had made a difference.

"Ah, but in the rain you can see almost nothing," said the young lay brother.

Certainly there was much to see, in the clear morning light. The forest had nearly swallowed the buildings of the city, but here and there flagstones still showed where the streets had been. There was a trail of sorts, presumably kept clear by the monks, winding between plants whose diversity and exotic forms took Sam's breath away. He stopped to stare at a flame-like protrusion of tubes, from which large bell-shaped objects—flowers?—hung. The tubes rimmed a dark brown tulip-shaped growth half a metre across. It was hollow, and half-filled with liquid. Insects like water-boatmen scuttled across the surface.

"Careful with that one," said Brother Wiccum. "Don't put your hand in."

Sam stepped back. "Is it like a lurepool?"

"Ah, you've come across those."

"Yar. One ate my pony, years ago."

"They do that. No, this is the receiving end, not the lure. This part produces a caustic stuff which dissolves in the rainwater. Those skayters have a hard rind which protects them, but if anything with softer flesh falls in, it slowly turns to mush. Which the plant sucks up."

Sam took a closer look. There were bones at the bottom.

"What falls in? Birds? Climbing animals?"

"Some. But its main prey are squirls, which live in burrow mazes in the hills."

Sam glanced around. "No hills here."

"Indeed. But there are many to the east of the Luntish river." The monk pulled one of the tubes towards him and turned the bell upwards. "Which is where this goes."

"Ah." Sam stepped out of the line of fire, not wishing to be hit by a shredded Qishi prairie dog falling from its burrow, high in the hills nine hundred kilometres away.

"Don't worry," said Brother Wiccum. "The animals are nocturnal. But they do make a splash."

They walked on, keeping to the path as it detoured past various hazards. The monk pointed out a bush that could fire spiny darts, synted from the top of scrawny trees nearby that were older parts of the same plant. Sam spotted a wide patch of tiny blue flowers which, the monk told him, concealed a colony of syntraps, capable of seizing a small animal's leg so tightly that it was unable to escape. Then worms—not syntelic themselves, but symbionts all the same—would emerge from what looked like solid ground to eat it. There were harmless plants too, some of which produced succulent fruits, and strange, tangled masses of purple vines that could be ground up to make a potion that cured warts.

"I would swear that wall was wrecked by more than tree roots," Sam observed, looking at the dents in the massive structure. "It looks like cannon fire."

"Dropsynte cannon, yes."

"What happened here?"

"Suffering."

"What caused it?"

"Ignorance." Brother Wiccum smiled. "But you want particulars, to which neither grace nor gain accrue. A thirst for worldly knowledge. Pardonable, in a man who has taken no vows.

"This was a city of bandits, so suffering was inevitable." Enough with the commentary, thought Sam, but held his peace. "They had just a few permanent syntei to places far outside Glostmadden, well hidden. A lone scout would go through with a concealable small oriel, and wander a long distance to choose a target small town or city. He would pick a secluded nearby spot, and the gang would come through in overwhelming numbers, carrying brasures, and destroy the oriel. After pillage, they would get away through the brasures, destroyed after them.

"Generations of bandits built a great city here, with great wealth, but not the most craved form of wealth; human service. They did all their own building, and menial work. Discontented, they began to gather slaves.

"The slave population grew, trapped here by the dangers of the jungle. One day a band of runaways had one survivor reach Pinxil… She guided a small tough group of Tenchurian soldiers through the jungle, and through an oriel came a regiment, armed with dropsynte guns and cannon, powered from high above. This was the devastation they made. Tenchur had conquered all Samdal so fully, that its army welcomed the exercise.

"All the bandits were dropped through slow-death syntei, with their shattered bodies taking hours or days to die."

"And the slaves were freed?" asked Sam.

"The enslaved men were freed," confirmed Brother Wiccum, "many of the women became wives of Tenchurian soldiers. It is said that some of these escaped, and the Vain Vaimoksi was the creation of their vengeance, though I know not the truth of that. Wise in the ways of slavery, they created the slavestone, a stronger bar to escape than this jungle. Such is the cycle of suffering. The Vain Vaimoksi, I hear, have been overthrown in their turn."

Sam was one of the instigators of the slave revolt that had all but wrecked the VV, but now wasn't the time or place to go into that. So he remained silent for a while, picking his way through a mosslike carpet from which occasional stalks protruded, each bearing a cluster of tiny spheres. He kept his eyes open for tiny blue flowers, but the lay brother told him his feet were too big for a syntrap anyway, he'd just crush it.

Turning a corner, he saw that the ancient paving was covered with huge petals fallen from a tree with curling flowers, which stood out like green flames against the orange foliage. A local analogue of ants (three segments, six legs) were gathering them up to take home, either for food, or mulch for growing food: each ant carried a petal three times its size. On his birthworld of Wounded Knee they would have made a vivid procession showing the way to their nest, but here they headed straight for the nearest specialised worker, twice as big, with a synte in its mid-section. The result was a pattern of stars around each one, each star flowing inward to a bright green traffic focus at the synte.

They continued through the forest, picking their way between collapsed walls, past the ruins of once-tall buildings that poked from the ground-cover like broken teeth. Huge roots gripped the stones like giant's hands, and strangler vines wrapped intricate lattices round everything.

"That was once a palace, according to the legends," Brother Wiccum said, pointing to huge mound covered in climbing plants, looming brown and orange and ochre in the leaf-filtered light of the forest floor. "And that, it is said, was once a stable that could hold three hundred slaves."

Now Sam had his eye in, he could see ruins everywhere. Not just a forest: a decayed metropolis. "Has anyone done archaeological studies?"

The monk looked bewildered. Sam explained the word.

"Why would anyone wish to spend time trying to deduce the past, Samuel? That is not the way to enlightenment."

It is for me, Sam thought, but had no wish to argue.

The remains of the city covered a huge area. They continued walking through them for more than an hour, as the sky darkened above them, fed by the evaporation from the forest. The air was so humid, Sam could barely breathe.

Big drops fell, and became a torrent. "Come, the monastery is not far now. We will take shelter there, and Brother Zaha will provide food and drink."

The monastery was not built for the purpose, but an ancient palace, a rare survivor of the city's ruin, repaired as necessary. "To make whole buildings new is craving and leads to suffering, like the desire for garments of new cloth," and indeed the monks he saw about the place wore robes cobbled together from donated garments, no two the same. "Let me present you to the abbot."

They entered a room which had once been painted with images of beautiful women, animals, plants and warriors, but very little was left of them between the orange lichen on the walls. A better lesson on impermanence, it seemed to Sam, than aggressively painting them over. He had little attention to spare for the walls, as the room was dominated by a small, smiling old man sitting cross-legged on a low chair.

"Revered One, please allow me to present Samuel Grey Deer Wasumi, from the stars." Sam braced himself for the usual Qishite questions about how one could live on a star, and how any synte could bridge the enormous height difference, and whether all star people were that interesting shade of brown.

"Is there suffering, among the stars?"

Taken aback, Sam nodded.

"And is there ignorance, among the stars?"

"There is, Revered One."

"How do the people of the stars seek to end ignorance?"

Sam muttered something about research.

"These are enquiries into the workings of khamma. They are a useful discipline for the mind, but they do not bring an end to the suffering that causes ignorance. It seems we have much to teach the stars, when their minds are ready.

"Samuel Grey Deer Wasumi, is your mind ready?"

"Revered One, I cannot know, but I fear it is not."

"I can see that it is busy, busy. Well, your craving mind brought you here, to learn something of us. Acolyte, please show him what he wishes to see, and answer such questions as he is able to put." And with that, although the abbot was still physically present, his attention was so clearly elsewhere that Sam stumbled out without speaking.

They saw the meditation hall (an old banquet chamber) where monks sat in silence, their eyes down cast, blinking about five times a minute. All the questions Sam could think of seemed so trivial that he did not ask them.

They saw the chanting hall. Monks joined and left as their other duties permitted, sharing the common chant. "Is it a prayer?" Sam asked.

"To whom?" said the lay brother. "To what? A god that grants requests is beneath the notice of monks. Nor is it a futile attempt at magic. Listen."

Sam gradually became aware that the chanters were singing eight notes in ever-changing order, without repetition, and the words were nine syllables, changing independently. His 'comp analysed the pattern, throwing up a historical reference to 'change ringing', and gave him an astonishing number. "That must take two hundred thousand years to repeat! What happens when they have completed the cycle of all the permutations? Does the world end?"

The lay brother gave him an odd look. "Why should it? They will continue the cycle. That is the way the world is. Chanting is not to modify the world, but to focus the mind."

Sam set his 'comp to synchronise with the rippling pattern of sound, and continue it silently in his brain, for ever. He could not say why, but it felt right.

The garden and paddy fields were easier to understand. "The monks grow all their own food?"

"With four crops a year, they do not need to clear much land." The lay brother glanced at the sky. "The rain is about to begin: let us see the kitchen."

The kitchen was strange. The monks washed and peeled like low-tech food preparation anywhere, but then they simply tossed the cleaned ingredients into syntei, which made a strange tearing noise. Sam was reminded of the lurepool that had once almost killed him. "Why do they do that?"

"Come see." The lay brother led him down three flights of stairs, and into a room where the grains and vegetables arrived—torn to a fine pulp. "The syndepts usually breed for depth, but ultra-shallow syntei have their uses. What needs cooking goes through this heated tube, the foods that are better raw join it at this point here."

"You feed the monks on just *soup*? That must be rather boring."

"They never taste it. Come upstairs."

They climbed a lot of steps, to the highest room in the old monastery. "It's pumped up to the distribution point, here." The central tank had a hundred taps on it, each with a complex label. "Brother Aniruddha, could you explain?"

"Certainly. Big monks need more than small ones, and of course work in the fields or other manual labour needs extra. We calculate all that, and deliver through these fine tubes here, set into deep syntei, so the tubes can slow it and it doesn't gush out into the stomach too fast."

"Wait—you synte directly into the stomach?"

"Of course," said Brother Aniruddha. "Attachment to tasting is so difficult to eradicate, even with very plain food. Also, attachment to the sense of hunger, that sets you thinking about the next meal. Attachment to satiation is worse. With a continuous small flow, adjusted to need, attachment never arises."

"So every monk has a synte fitted?"

"Provisionally, for a novice. He *can* eat through the mouth, though he must wean himself from it. At full ordination, if he earns that, his gullet is sealed. We also have syntei to remove material from the bowels and bladder: Brother Medic keeps an eye on those. And a synte in the prostate — you'd be amazed at how much less distracting thoughts of women are, if pressure simply never builds up in there."

"Well," said the lay brother, as they made their way back to the wyzand after the rain had ended, "does the monastic life attract you?"

"It has its points," said Sam diplomatically, "but I fear I am just too attached to sweetapple pie."

Hippolyta

The rolling countryside of the South Marches had been farmed by the Dunelm branch of the Hippolytan royal family for centuries, its lush valleys dissected into modest estates of a few hundred hectares. Elza's air-car passed over a scattering of workmales' villages, descending at last into the forecourt of Lanxlode Hall, summer home of Baroness Winfrede of Glaston. Surrounded by elaborate formal gardens, the Hall was constructed as a cascade of broad cones—some stone, some glass—with rounded flexalloy tips, punctuated by slender turrets linked to overhead walkways.

A harassed-looking doorboy had been awaiting Lady Elzabet of Quynt's arrival, and conducted her entourage down an arched passageway to a reception area.

As the others squatted on expensive rugs, Elza ran a practiced eye over the opulent room, an antechamber taller than wide. The hangings softened the acoustics, but her heels clicked loudly on the polished floor as she paced impatiently up and down. She recognised the stone—it was from her mother's quarry on the Thrumm Peninsula, pale sedimentary rock speckled with seven-pointed black fossils. Very fashionable, very expensive. Very profitable. The Baroness must have benefited from shrewd investments. Elza might have tried to tempt her with another, but today her business was with the Baroness's second daughter, who was notoriously short of cash. And who now entered with a curtsey through a curtained alcove.

"Do you believe in breast feeding?" Elza asked, after the usual respectful exchanges and the serving of *pets de nonne* and aromatic tea.

"Naturally!" Lady Marjane was slightly intimidated by this tête-à-tête with the third daughter of a Duchess, but even the minor nobility knew how to behave. "Even a wet nurse is too close a contact with the lower classes, and one could not possibly rear a child on inhuman milk. Not that I'll be having daughters until Mother tells me to."

"Very proper," agreed Elza, squatting democratically at the same height, "but there *are* certain inconveniences."

"I suppose so, Lady Elzabet. You can't drive while nursing, and even in a business meeting, managing your papers and everything… My elder sister has to express the milk and save it for later, which seems uncomfortable and sad."

"It does," said Elza, "but there is a solution, which maybe you could inform her about. May I call in my assistants?"

They were a handsome couple, complete with baby, which the man dutifully carried. "Annika and Julian, this is the Lady Marjane." They bowed. Annika was heavy with milk, and opened her blouse to show it.

Elza produced a pair of objects from the bag they brought in.

"These are from the planet Qish. That's a Concordat secret for now, but I'm sure I can trust you to be discreet."

"Of course, Lady Elzabet!" Lady Marjane gushed, duly flattered. "They look like bras… is that what they are?"

"Not exactly support garments, nah," said Elza. "Julian? Demonstrate!"

The man bowed. He took one and strapped it over his shirt. It was clearly no bra, just a pair of flat shapes on his chest with odd darkness behind them. Then from behind Annika he slipped the other garment over her breasts, and fastened it around her back. Finally he gathered the baby in his arms and held it to him. It began to suckle.

Annika appeared totally flat-chested. Julian smiled down at the baby at his? Annika's? breast. The baby belched.

Lady Marjane watched in awe. "My sister could even ride in her camel races, wearing a device like that. What on or off Hippolyta is it?"

"It's a *synte*, darling, from a planet where matter transmitters grow on trees. More exactly, a pair of syntei."

"That's the name of the bra-thing?"

"Nah, that's called a *mamasynte*. Synte is a general word for connections like these. The mamasynte has two of them. Each has a *kasynte* on one harness, with its *kantasynte* on the other. The two are linked, no matter where they are."

Marjane had a provincial upbringing, but even she realised that short cuts through space are uncommon. Before slaking her curiosity, however, there were normal proprieties to observe. The baby, fed and burped, would doubtless need changing soon. Marjane snapped her fingers and a grey-haired footmale appeared.

"Ronson, take the child to the nursery, and tend to its needs." She turned to Elza. "With your permission, of course, my Lady." Elza nodded at the footmale and he whisked the baby out of its father's arms and out of the room.

"*Linked*," Marjane said wonderingly, almost to herself. "My word, Lady Elzabet. That's remarkable. Dear me. Er — is there any distance limit?"

"You have to keep them close to the same level," said Elza. "But horizontally, they'll work between continents. They can even be used as doors between stars. How do you suppose I commute to and fro to Hippolyta, without my mother noticing?"

"I never thought of that. You mean she thinks you're still off doing Starfolk training?"

"Nah, she heard that I died in a secret accident, which is true in a way. She doesn't know I'm here, and nor do the Starfolk. I don't go near the spaceport." Elza's smile had the faintest hint of menace. "I'm *sure* I can trust you to be discreet, my dear."

"My lips are *sealed*. This is so exciting! Mamasyntei, doorways through space… what else can they do?"

Elza's eyes gleamed. "I expect your mother doesn't approve of hormonal adjustment? For your monthlies?"

Lady Marjane hesitated, caught between conflicting urges. "I think she's right, really," she began, feeling defensive. "A woman's body needs to clean itself."

"But — ?" *There was clearly a but.*

"But I wish it didn't have to be so *messy*."

"It doesn't." Elza reached again into the bag, producing a small plant rather like a pineapple. Bright orange, it had spiky leaves, and pale-lavender seeds around the base.

"This is a relative of the vunbugula plant. One of those nearly killed me before they burned it, by the way, but this one's been bred for its seeds to be useful.

"You simply insert one of these blue seeds ahead of time, rather like a tampon. It anchors itself inside the cervix, catches all the blood, and transmits it to the plant. The plant absorbs the nutrients, and you keep your clothes clean. After the flow stops, the seed disintegrates; you'd never know it had been there. Next month, pop in another one."

"The possibilities…" breathed Lady Marjane.

"Endless," agreed Elza. "There are syntei from Scythery that exsynte urine and faeces, but even on Qish some people are uncomfortable with that.

They're long-term installations, for one thing, and they have to be implanted by specialists. But external napisyntei are *very* popular."

"You don't have samples in that bag?"

"Nah," said Elza, "not napisyntei. Those need setting up at both ends, adjusting the heights, and so on. But I do have these." She produced two ring-shaped objects, about three centimetres across, and held one up. "This synte goes into the woman. May we demonstrate?"

"Of course!" Annika made something of a striptease of removing her remaining clothes, including the mamasynte. Lying back on a high cushion, she inserted the synte between her legs and pushed it deep, using a long tool to place it firmly.

Julian, keeping his eyes locked with hers, did his own striptease.

"Shaven Lily!" said Lady Marjane, "Size doesn't really matter, size *really* doesn't matter, but... Shaven Lily!"

"It matters for this," replied Elza, "You'll see why. Take the kantasynte and slide it onto him. Yes, there."

Lady Marjane took the other ring in both hands and slipped it over the head, then moved it down the shaft, trembling slightly as more and more of the flesh vanished into it without reappearing on the other side.

"It's going nowhere," she said, "I mean, it's going *to* nowhere, I mean—"

"Nah," said Elza. "Here it comes."

Annika moaned softly as the head parted her labia, from the inside. Fascinated, Lady Marjane moved the kantasynte to and fro, making it appear and disappear like a shy small creature of the night. Then she pushed firmly down, until he seemed to have nothing left but his scrotum, and half the shaft stood tall from Annika's mound.

"Oooh. That's fascinating. Like one of those Squamish strap-ons that are all the rage, but *alive*. Some of my girlfriends like to suck the strap-on that I wear, but I've never felt the attraction. It doesn't... react. This, though,... I think I want to taste it."

Annika and Julian made identical welcoming gestures, and she knelt between Annika's legs. He gradually shifted the kantasynte forward, retracting the protrusion until she was sucking on Annika and Julian at once: then kept it gently moving, forward and back.

"You have a gifted mouth," he said, as Annika's pelvis began to tremble. "A glorious mouth." He obviously meant it. Lady Marjane herself was shaking.

"I don't think we can hold back for long," gasped Annika. "Do you want to pause?"

Lady Marjane merely sucked more intensely, aroused beyond arousal by the effect she was having, the bucking pelvis of Annika, the engorged hardness of Julian. The climax came for all three together.

Blinking and swallowing, she wiped her mouth as she squatted back on her heels. "Fascinating," she said. "Fascinating. Are you selling these things, Lady Elzabet?"

"These and others," said Elza. "Think of this as just a… foretaste. But I'm hoping for more than your custom."

Marjane's pupils were dilated, her voice breathless. "You'll certainly… have… that, if I can afford them. Mother keeps *such* a tight rein on family finances, but she does allow me some limited funds to use at my own discretion. Uh—what else is it that you hope for?"

Elza nodded to Annika and Julian, who began to pick up their clothing, as if about to get dressed. "I'm looking for an agent, Marjane—" she said with exciting informality " —to handle sales on this continent. *Discreet* sales, you understand."

"Oh, yah. How can I refuse, Lady Elzabet?"

"Elzabet. We're friends, *and* business partners, yah?"

"Oh, well. Elzabet, yah. Uh—I'll have to get someone to look at the terms of the contract, of course, or Mother will complain, but the Duchy of Quynt has been doing business with our barony for generations. I can trust you.

"However, to seal the deal… a foursome?"

Lady Elzabet of Quynt gestured to her assistants, who dropped their clothes back on the floor and brought her the bag. She spread it open in front of Marjane, displaying a dozen or so gadgets of curious and intriguing design.

"Where would you like to start, darling?"

Dool

"A multiple focus in the *k*-field," said Marco. "Must have been."

"Yah," Marco agreed, picking up his half-empty mug of coffee from the slapscreen they had laid on the table like a placemat. And were currently using it as such, slapscreens being robust, cheap to replace, and *relatively* impervious to coffee. "That's the obvious explanation." He sounded unenthusiastic.

He helped himself from a bag of deseeded vunbugula that Elza had brought back to Dool from one of her regular supply trips to Qish. She had just come back through the light years from her daily visit to the profitable business in Hippolyta that financed her geological research, shuttled over from an interplanetary wyzand mounted in a converted freighter matched to Hippolyta's orbit. (Provided by Salim Sisters in return for a share of the profits.)

They could hear her voice wafting across from the couch in the corner, where she lounged, talking to a falasynte.

"The Duchess?" asked Marco.

"Nah," said Marco. "Gus. On Qish."

"I envy your early experiences with him," said Marco. "He doesn't have as much free time now he's Governor of the Shaaluin Province of the Wevorin Empire. He's smart and adaptable... and he has lovely legs."

Marco and Marco both meditated on those legs for a moment.

"Meanwhile," said Marco, "all *I* had was three years of mind-bendingly dull patrol, which I can't talk about. Until it killed *Valkyrie*, that is. Some of which I can talk about, but no more than you've been officially told."

"One copy of *Valkyrie*. The other burnt up over Qish, ten years ago."

"Your copy didn't take Elza with it."

"You still won't tell me how that happened."

"*Can't* tell you how that happened," said Marco, patiently. "Neurolock."

"Yah, yah. So, like I said, it must have been a multiple focus. You — *we* left from the Typhon-Suufi L2 point as planned, made ten jumps without any problems, then Sam activated the Da Silva again, *Valkyrie* made its eleventh *k*-jump, suffered from double vision, and we ended up in two places at once. You got to Starhome as planned, experiencing a relatively harmless patch of severe *k*-weather, and for us the Da Silva blew up in mid-jump, which is impossible, and grounded us on Qish. From which we returned seven years ago, having lost Felix in a wrecked synte."

"Precisely. Whereas we lost no one until the disaster. So now we have one of everybody, and an extra me."

"No chalk," interrupted Elza.

"Chalks?" said Marco. He gestured at the large pale slapscreen. "We just think our equations through our 'comps. We're not back with chalkboards on Qish." That had been the smallest part of his difficulty in explaining calculus to the Deacon's men. "But come to think of it, they used a greasy sort of charcoal crayon."

"That's because there's *no chalk*," said Elza, "on Qish."

"Every planet with living seas has chalk, after coccolithophores evolve," said Marco, who had run a search in background while Marco's mind was wandering back to infinitesimals and Church doctrine. "They leave their skeletons in layers yay thick. Qish must have had coccolithophores."

"We don't know much about the seas," Elza said. "Monsters… It's an alien world. But whatever source you got that from, it's nearly right. Carbonate deposition is a universal on any world with water and carbon dioxide. Technically, Qish's beasties are xenococcolithophorids — forget which classifier, Jane told me but I've forgotten."

"So why no chalk?"

"Because, despite umpty oodles of carbonate-making microbeasties, Qish doesn't have chalk beds. Or rather, it has something a bit like chalk, but in *very* thin layers."

"Maybe the seas were too acid," said Marco. "Dissolved the calcium carbonate."

"No, like I said, it's got xenococcolithophorids, plenty of them."

"They don't build up coccoliths on the seabed when they die?" said Marco.

"Something is acidic, there," deduced Marco.

"You guessed it. Syntelic plants on the sea bed that secrete acetic acid, get much more concentrated CO_2 than from the air, and photosynthesise near the surface using sunlight."

"But the gravity barrier—"

"Is huge, but diffusion can beat it, while ballistics can't. Plants are patient. So we get beds of stuff like calcium acetate, not calcium carbonate. But, occasionally, a thin layer of the carbonate: not nearly thick enough to make a writing stick."

"So the only conclusion—"

"Is that the plants die. En masse. Occasionally."

"What kills them?"

"Wish I knew. But *something* does, every few tens of thousands of years. Worldwide, except for local reservoirs. The geology stands out like a divided… thumb. Takes a few hundred years for them to come back. Like a forest after a fire, but slower."

"Volcanoes? Earthquakes? Asteroid strikes?"

"Can't find any evidence of anything like that with the right sort of impact—so to speak. Just acetate beds. Worldwide."

The Marcos gazed sightlessly into space, which either indicated deep thought or lights on, no one home. "Are they the only syntei that do this?"

"That's hard to tell: ten millennia is a blink of an eye, geologically. But I think they *all* die. Not a mass extinction, because a lot of syntelic plants survive, and almost all species survive, but all the syntei die. Call it a synte erasure."

Both Marcos started talking at once. "Then what happens to human syntelic industry—?"

"Transport—?"

"Is it sudden enough to disrupt a synted pregnancy—?"

Elza silenced them with a regal wave. "For all I know, it's sudden enough to disrupt a divided body," she said, watching four hands move protectively to what the Marcos divided most often. "But it hasn't happened since *Magog* landed. You understand syntelic fields better than anyone. What could kill syntei, planetwide? You tell me."

"We were just talking about syntelic fields." Surprise. Whenever they were not talking about syntelic fields, they were thinking about them. Even in bed. Of course, they were also thinking about the twins, and her body, and Lomyrla's body, and Gus's body, and themself. Unusual multitasking, for males.

"What have you got?"

They stared glumly at a mess of scribbled equations. "We're here—" said Marco,

"Because we're here," Marco finished for him.

She pushed in between their heads to look at a slapscreen covered in symbols and coffee-stains, and helped herself to a vunbugula. "What's that gibberish?"

"The master equations of unified karmabhumi-syntelics," said Marco.

"Yah. Only they're not. Unified, that is. We're stuck," said Marco. "The index theorem says what we want to do is impossible."

"I… see. So this squiggle is?"

"A lexically labelled ensemble of virtual k-fields."

"Sorry I asked. And that one?"

"It's a graphic of what we think Qish did to it."

Elza moved the mug aside for a better view. "I see one blob, then two blobs. Is that it?"

"Yah," said Marco. "*Valkyrie* and its crew bilocated. We haven't a clue how it happened."

Marco begged to differ. "Nah, Marco, it's some kind of superposition duality effect. Like a Young's slit. Only not."

"What," Elza said, eyes flashing dangerously, "is a young slit?"

"Young's. Pre-Concordat physics. You fire a photon at a pair of very fine slits, and as long as you don't try to find out which one it goes through, it goes through both, but arrives in one place. What we want is the opposite: fire a photon at a single slit, and it comes out in two different places. With a Da Silva caltrop, not a photon."

"And Qish's entire system of syntei, not a slit?" Elza shook her head. "Nah, not like that."

"Like what, then, O matriarchal genius?"

"Like… *Valkyrie* interacted with *one* something that caused *two* somethings. One made it emerge at Qish, the other at Starhome. You told us Da Silva jumps don't have any 'between', dah? So that slit thingy is just a conceptual crutch, right? No slit. Just transitions."

"Nah!" Marco rushed in. "Let me explain—"

"Shut up, Marco!" said Marco. "Elza's right."

"You really think—oh. Oh."

"Yah."

"We've been assuming Qish's bizarre spacetime topology caused a kind of k-field mirage, bringing *Valkyrie* to two different focal points. Now you're saying—"

"Elza's suggesting—"

" —we've got it exactly bass-ackward. The Da Silva's k-field caused a multiple interface in the ensemble of interconnected syntei. It acted like a single giant kasynte with two superposed kantasyntei. *Valkyrie*'s k-wave transform went in one end—"

" —and came out of both ends. Only there's no 'in', no 'out', and no ends; just paired transform orientations."

"Of course. It's trivial." Marco stared at each other.

"I said it was some kind of duality!" said Marco.

"Yah. Just not that one."

"But we can model this one. Look, all you do is—"

"Nah, not that way. Like this—"

Elza watched Marco scribbling formulas, erasing each other's attempts, arguing at the tops of their voices, scattering vunbugula in all directions in microgravity, and left them to it. She'd learned not to interrupt Bianchi creativity.

Time to go see Gus again. Time to stand on the ancient rocks of Qish.

Within a week, Marco bickered their way to the first version of what, years later, became known as the Bianchi identities.

Qish

Felix Wylde:

It's not easy being dead.

Not the legal side. The Marcos could have had some problems there. The Bank of Inferno's entangled access algorithm was in no doubt that Marco was Marco; it just couldn't distinguish between him. If he'd contested ownership, the courts wouldn't have had a clue how to handle the dispute. No precedent, and everything could be argued both ways. That wouldn't have stopped them trying, and the lawyers would have got all the money, which would have suited the legal profession perfectly. Fortunately Marco didn't have much in the bank, and the two of him get on fine anyway because when it comes to the crunch, Marco is Marco is Marco. Neither of him would have taken it seriously even if there were billions at stake. There's no legal side to it on Qish, anyway, and I've met nobody who met my other self, except for Gus, and he's busier than a *skiti* with three tails.

At any rate, Marco gets on fine together, and Elza and Lomyrla seem happy enough to share him—not hard when there's a spare—or join forces. And Sadruddin, when he's available. Lomy has the twins to bring up, with two Dads to help—and Marco makes a good Dad. Pregnancy was good for him; somehow, for both of him. Elza's forever hopping back to Dool or Hippolyta on business. Or pleasure. Whatever.

Now, I know I don't talk much, but that's a habit since Gamut. As far as I know, only Jane is aware of my back talk that got me into the assignment from the hot place, or how lucky we were to emerge covered in roses, like we *didn't* when Marco got us into closer engagement with the groupies. (He both still talk as much as ever, though. Some people don't learn.) Problem is, people think I don't *feel* much either. If you don't show your feelings, you haven't got any. But I *can't* talk about the death of my Jane on *Valkyrie*, because of the neural lock. And that central block seems to stop me opening up about anything.

Being dead has made it worse.

Not for Sam and Tinka: they both lived through the same events, both saw the same universe. Each has a dead twin, but they never met them. It's all too abstract to get emotional about.

Not for the Marcos, too laid-back to worry. Not for Elza or Lomyrla or Gus, who always had at least one live Marco around and just happened to acquire another one. Not really a duplicate, despite the *k*-field physics; people diverge from the moment a copy exists, because they have different experiences. Identical twins develop differently, and even if *k*-field copies are far more similar than twins, the same happens to them.

It's happening to me and Jane.

I know why. We're from different histories. In mine, she was killed by the groupies a few months ago. In hers, I died in a disintegrating oriel trying to escape from a Vain Vaimoksi slave camp in Lamynt. Trouble is, I'd never been to Qish, and she doesn't even know how her other self died.

When they all showed up at Starhome, and Jane came back from the dead—climbing out of a cosmic manhole, for Mother's sake—I was in a daze for days. I thought my deepest desires had all come true, but I was in shock. I think Jane handled it a bit better than me, probably being more distant from my death, but matchpairs are very close; you never really adjust to the loss.

So we tried to pretend to ourselves it was all back where it had been, both of us alive when we thought the other was dead. Lovers reunited. And it sort of worked, for a time. Maybe if I'd been more willing to talk about things… but that's me, I don't. And I couldn't.

Qish *changed* her. She spent three years on a hostile alien world, fighting to stay alive, struggling to reach the rescue beacon, battling superstition, tradition, ignorance… and sophistication, in a world where matter transmitters grew on trees. She learned to kill. *Her* Felix shared all that with her, up to the moment he died.

My Jane had an easy life in comparison. So did I. We just spent three years trying to figure out the groupies from inadequate data. Nothing exciting—until the disaster. Nothing to change anyone.

We're not growing back together.

I tried. I went back with her to Qish. And what did she do? Founded a School of Medicine as a memorial to *her* Felix. It's a great school, and it's making a huge difference to the Qishi, but for me it's a bit like squatting on your own grave. Don't get me wrong, I understand exactly why she did it. That Felix deserved a memorial. Even so, it hurts.

Then she set up an Institute for Qishi Ecology, and soon we were both spending most of our time out in the field studying the alien flora and fauna. I've got enough research data to last me a lifetime. It could have brought us back together, but instead we both ended up buried in our work, with less and less time for each other.

I don't complain, but I find it easier to avoid company and keep myself to myself. I don't really want other people around. They just remind me of what I lost. What I'm losing for the second time.

You can't go back. I know that now. Even a perfect copy isn't the same person. I think she knows that too. You can't make yourself feel what's not there.

Anyway, she's off to study drift-orms on Krig Mountain, and while she's away I'm putting together a monograph on Qishi ecology for publication in a Nazg journal. Maybe a few months apart will do us both good. Maybe we can start over.

We can talk about it when she gets back.

Eelkhance

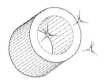

"Welcome, Doxor Tampledown. Come in and feed yourself." Vance had decided that informality was the best solution to an awkward technicality: she was his boss, as Coordinator, but he was on secondment from the Concordat Special Executive, where he had far more clout than she did. She pushed a bowl of noodles and octopus toward him.

Tampledown squatted gratefully, and picked up the chopstraws. It had been a busy two weeks.

"I think you know most of what I'm about to say," he said, partly to her and partly to the vixcam, "but this is my first systematic report."

She did know. In reaction to the previous débâcle, the habitat had vixcams in every room, full time. A team of analysts back in Starhome watched the recordings minutely and provided her with twice-daily executive summaries, whose opaque language attempted to conceal the writers' lack of comprehension.

"I'll start," Tampledown said, reaching for a wriggling baby octopus, "with why we're here."

Vance was puzzled. "At the orders of the Special Executive. To investigate syntei."

"No, why we're *here*."

She nodded.

He swallowed some noodles, and held up another baby octopus with his chopstraws. "You understand that there's no longer any advantage in matching orbits with Qish, because we can't go there anyway. Any secluded habitat would do. However, Eelkhance *is* a secluded habitat, at a safe distance from Da Silva tech. It already has living quarters and appropriately equipped labs; and some of the experiments that the Bianchi team left running would be problematic to move."

"So the choice is a no-brainer." A thought struck her and her mouth tensed. "Do you *know* the equipment is appropriate?"

"Frankly, citizen, we can only hope so. It was chosen by the previous team, who knew more than we do. As yet." The Chief Scientist sucked up some of the broth through his chopstraw, as if dismissing the issue. Vance let that pass—after all, there was little that could be done at this point, even if he were wrong.

"A more important question is why *we*'re here," he said, changing the topic. "Meaning the group we've assembled. My first priority was xeno-botanists."

She felt puzzled, but tried not to show it. "Please explain."

"The physics of syntei is mysterious, citizen Vance, but the first fact we're certain of is that syntelic plants are plants—alien plants. The previous team had access to various soils from Qish, and cultivation advice from syndepts. We lack those, and unfortunately we have a major problem in keeping healthy the plants they left."

Vance frowned. "Is this a progress report, Doxor, or an acknowledgement of failure?"

"A bit of both, citizen. I'm starting at a serious disadvantage. The larger syntei here, wyzands and such, were all kantasyntei to kasyntei with their roots on Qish. The defectors deliberately destroyed them. Some wyzands had started to grow in the lab, but they're delicate products of human breeding on Qish, requiring expert attention in the early stages. We lost the lot. The symbiotic animals were all taken back to Qish. So all we're left with are some punctyles, brasures, and falasyntei: small stuff. That's the bad news. The good news is: they seem to be surviving, and we've succeeded in cloning them."

"You can replicate their DNA?" Vance let her incredulity show.

Tampledown shook his head. "Nah, they don't use terrestrial DNA. We're still sorting out what they use instead. It'll be a long while before we can do genetic manipulation. No, I meant cloning in the pre-industrial sense, like dividing up a strawberry plant and growing new ones from the pieces. It's primitive, but it does give us more specimens, and more chances they'll survive."

"Dah, makes sense. Who else is on the team?"

Tampledown spread out his hands, unconsciously raising a finger in student-supervision mode. "We skipped geographers, linguists and so on, as Qish itself is no longer a priority. We've got one military strategist, but we don't yet have much to tell her about syntelic warfare technology. She mainly studies the wristcomp records of the *Valkyrie* crew, and runs thought experiments and simulations. We kept most of the procurement officers and such who didn't leave with the old team: partly we needed them, and partly here was the easiest place to keep them quiet."

Vance seized on the obvious omission. "You haven't mentioned physicists."

Tampledown sighed, looking pained. "Yah, that's a problem. Big problem. There were some physicists who heard the original rumours after the *Valkyrie* crew turned up, and a few believe-anything types who took the rumours seriously. Unfortunately, we shot ourselves comprehensively in both feet, because those got burned by the big counter-intelligence operation. Taking syntei seriously is now a near-fatal threat to one's scientific reputation. That's really annoying, because now we've got samples to show, but we have to be *very* careful who gets to see them. We need people who can think way outside the echo chamber they were trained in, but discreet."

"People who can keep their minds open and their mouths shut."

"Exactly. *Geniuses* who can keep their minds open and their mouths shut."

"Rare. Have you tried mathematical engineers?"

"We can't even think of building anything with syntei until we understand the basic physics."

"The *Valkyrie* crew did. The *Magog* colonists did."

"Yes, but they were… yah. Maybe mathematical engineers *are* the way to go. After all, the Bianchis are a mathematical engineer. Can we get someone of that calibre?"

"That calibre of two-headed loose cannon," Vance said sourly, emptying her bowl. It still rankled. Just her luck that she had no choice but to work with anybody resembling the Bianchis, when every cell in her body had been screaming *insecure*. And worse. "Genius, yah, very possibly… and his old prof at IIT told us he'd find a new angle if he had to go into seven dimensions to do it. But *discreet*?"

"Pick any two out of three," Tampledown said ruefully. "Fast / cheap / good, like brilliant / mentally-uninhibited / security-conscious. Maybe there's a general theorem that you can't have it all. Probably the Bianchis proved it."

"They prove it by their existence, Doxor." She rose to her feet, indicating this session was fast coming to its end. "Very well, do the best you can, and so will I. Go with the brightest discreet engineers you can find, and I'll set Starhome Security to head-hunting, not just vetting. At least engineers will gather data systematically, while we wait for the horse to sing."

Starhome

"I'm sorry to drag you away from your work on Eelkhance," said the Chair, "but there have been new developments. The line-up on either side of her was almost the same, but now Tampledown was squatting beside her. The oceans of Starhome wheeled slowly behind them, a blue haze half-hidden by clouds.

"I understand you've been limited in the range of syntelic plants you have as specimens," said the Director of Starhome Security.

"Yes, to three types," said Tampledown. "It's made it very hard to tease out what these plants use for genetics, let alone distinguish genes affecting syntei from others, and to assess how individual genes affect the size and depth of the synte, numbers and ripening speed, and so on. If we had—"

"We have," said the Director grimly. He opened the box in front of him.

"Those look more like sex toys than..." Tampledown suddenly remembered the Qishite images from the *Valkyrie* crew's wristcomps. There had been no experiments along that line in the Eelkhance habitat, but he thought suddenly that perhaps this was only because the specimens were few, and individually numbered. Or perhaps it was the vixcams. "They *are* sex toys. Syntelic sex toys. Where are they from?"

"Hippolyta," the Director answered. "We don't have regular agents there—in a feudal matriarchy, the only way to infiltrate someone would be as a foetus. It's a Fringe World, with only the aristocracy travelling off planet. Nothing much has happened there for two centuries. But when we heard a rumour that Lady Elzabet of Quynt had returned there, we made a special effort."

"Lady Elza—but she's trapped on Qish, with Bianchi's scientists."

"She *is* one of Bianchi's scientists, and apparently passionate about Qishite geology. But she's also commuting to Hippolyta, and selling toys for 'dividing the body'."

"Dah. How are the mighty."

"Nah, she's making huge profits. Mummy doesn't like it, but then, mummy's not going to—"

Enough childishness. "Commuting how?" asked Vance. "Obviously not by Da Silva craft."

"How did you get these examples?" put in Tampledown.

"A Second Daughter on a diplomatic mission to Starhome had a fancy for the local untamed males, and we always have plenty of agents of all sexes around diplomatic missions," said the Director. "There had to be a syntelic connection, and given that clue we tracked it down. Someone on the Rescue Craft that met *Valkyrie* went missing immediately after; apparently with the synte that started the cascade. Kwame Ngongo Marakuri. Another lapse of security before we even knew we needed it."

"But he couldn't have gone missing to Hippolyta," objected Vance. "As you said, Hippolyta's pretty well closed to offworlders."

"He didn't," replied the Director. "He went to Nazg, where it seems he was a pet of Fatima Salim."

"Fatima Salim? The CEO of Salim Sisters?" Half the quantum tech Vance was wearing—the public half—was consumer gear from Salim Sisters.

"No less. So Salim Sisters promptly repeated Bianchi's cascade, without even needing to collect a synte. They had a wyzand connection within a week."

"Then the Bianchis are probably loose too," Vance deduced. "Any clues where?"

"There are some indications they may be on Dool," said the Head of Internal Affairs, "with a fully equipped syntelics lab, courtesy of Salim Sisters."

"Can we get them back under our control? Neutralise them?"

"It will take a while to pinpoint them enough for that," answered the Head of Internal Affairs. "By that time it will hardly matter."

"Hardly matter?" said Tampledown. "Surely we want to regain control of their unimpeded research? When I think of the crumbs they left us…"

"It isn't Salim Sisters' only lab," said Internal Affairs, "and Salim Sisters is famous for its smooth R&D—and keeping it hidden till it's ready."

"But Starhome Security can penetrate anything," observed the Director, "once we know we need to. But it *will* hardly matter, because Salim Sisters is preparing the Mother Of All Commercial Releases, in about five weeks' time. All over the Core Worlds. Pets, wyzands, space drives,…"

"And sex toys," said Adelaide Eckhardt. "Sex equals *money*. The human race has always understood that. Second oldest profession, dah?"

"Second, Governor?"

"Yah. Oldest is priest. Shaman. Witch-doctor. Selling dreams and empty reassurance. Sex work is an honest trade. Customers get exactly what they pay for. Priests just give a lick and a promise, without the lick."

"All very interesting," said the Director. "Your point is?"

The Governor of the Financial Authority went slightly pink, probably realising she had digressed. "If you think sex toys are trivial, you're forgetting that acceptance of half the technological change in history has been driven by sexual factors. The original internet, self-driving vehicles, tactile reality… they have their non-sexual uses, but sex was what first made their early, awkward versions financially viable."

"Salim Sisters' first releases won't be awkward," observed the Head of External Affairs. "Their usability teams are what's always kept them at the front, and Qish has given them historical data on what syntelic devices may be popular. Falasyntei won't sell to a population with wristcomps, but a lot of Qishite inventions will."

"Can we stop it?" The Chair entered the discussion for the first time. She had a habit of crouching down and letting others make the running, ready to pounce as soon as they strayed off-topic, said something stupid, or just got stuck. They tended to forget she was there, which sometimes led to interesting revelations.

"Salim Sisters is too big just to respond to the usual hints," said the Director. "We'll have to *use* our veto switch on Da Silva equipment. But it's a pretty blunt instrument. They must have war-gamed our response, and decided they could sit out our turning off all the Da Silva craft registered to them."

"They probably can," Eckhardt said. "They'll have wyzands in every branch by now, if they're planning to sell them. They can't just synte between most planets, but they'll have workarounds. And the potential profit makes it worth doing."

"In that case—" all heads turned to Vance. "In that case, our blunt instrument must be blunter still. We have to interdict whole planets. Any planet that harbours syntei is a potential Qish, unapproachable by Da Silva craft— oh, yah. Doxor, we need to know the critical synte mass that turns a planet into a Da Silva no-go zone, dah?"

"Curvature, not mass—dah, I take the point. We'll get on it immediately." The Chief Scientist's eyes glazed over as he sent mental commands to his 'comp.

"People who opt for the syntelic route must feel the pain of their choice," Vance said, picking up the thread again and steepling her fingers for emphasis. "They must feel it *before* they become addicted to the poison of syntelics."

There was silence. Then, slowly, the Chair put the question. "Does anyone have an alternative?" One by one, as she looked at them, the committee members shook their heads.

"It's best if we don't have to bring a new agent up to speed. You are tasked, then, Philomena Vance, with execution. Choosing the time to threaten interdict, just after Salim Sisters has told them of syntei. Luring each planet back into the fold with all the rewards we can offer, or choosing the moment to impose interdict, when our patience runs out. Ensuring that the interdict is total, wherever or to whomever a Da Silva craft is registered. Disrupting peculiar orbits that suggest that spacecraft are matching gravitational potentials between syntei.

"Doxor Tampledown, it seems that your Coordinator has to leave Eelkhance. Can you take over her duties, as well as those of Chief Scientist? Your shortage of specimens will soon end, at least."

"I can. May I request that Starhome Security pass on any data covertly obtained from Salim Sisters R&D, and any information at all about the thinking of the Bianchis? It will assist us in catching up."

"That can be arranged, I think?" The Director nodded. "And your recruitment will at least not meet with incredulity.

"I declare this session closed."

The same IIT haircut as Bianchi, thought Tampledown, but on his dark brown skin it looks easy on the eye.

Brilliant, check.

Mentally-uninhibited, check. After all, this was the man who had revived renormalisation theory after it had been recognised for a thousand years as a mere kludge, long replaced by something deeper and more consistent. He had used it to get a ten-fold improvement in the accuracy of Da Silva navigation. Nobody else could even see why it worked, let alone how he had come up with it. He was just one of those people the goddess talks to.

Security-conscious… Wayne Lawes made Bianchi look discreet. This was a man who talked about Sobolev spaces with the cleaning robots. His mouth simply channelled continuously whatever was on his mind.

Pity we can't risk a neurolock, but Lawes has to talk to people to be creative. Well, he has to talk.

"I can't tell you anything at all about the project," said Tampledown, "except that it's vital to the Concordat, and it involves truly new physics. Astonishingly new physics."

"Anything to do with those rumours of matter transmitters that were going around six years ago?"

Tampledown choked. "I can't tell you anything *at all* about the project," he repeated, "until and unless you sign up to it. But I can assure you it's of vital importance for the Concordat." *Scrub that, Lawes doesn't give a fig for what's politically important, he just wants intriguing puzzles to play with.* "The other thing it can guarantee is that it'll be interesting — perhaps the most interesting set of problems you'll ever encounter."

Lawes opened his eyes wide, a sign he'd been hooked. *Time to slip in the bad news.* "I'm afraid you'll have to be totally sequestered, for some years. We can't risk any talk *at all* outside the team." *Mother of Galaxies, he's making me echo myself.*

"That's OK," said Lawes, "as long as there's a decently equipped lab and regular meals. And of course, regular sex."

How do I arrange that, in a top-secret project? "Any special requirements? Gender? Age? Physique?"

"I'm not narrow-sexual," replied Lawes, slightly offended by the questions. "It can be anybody who's willing — no, enthusiastic — and eager to try new positions."

I can't tell a team member to have enthusiastic sex with him. There are limits, even in a government project. I suppose I could ask for volunteers, but the fewer people who get a sniff of this, the better... He thought of the Hippolytan samples. "Genuinely new positions, guaranteed." *And for eagerness I can use the aphrodisiac setting on my 'comp.*

"Come over here," said Doxor Tampledown, "and kiss me."

Old
Earth

"Seeds? The Earth employees of an interstellar company are told to keep something secret from the *Concordat*, and it's about a load of *seeds*?" The lines on Ira da Terra's face made her completely the Wrath of the Earth made flesh. Worn by time, burning with eternal fury.

Helmut Moser nodded. "It's not just commercial secrecy. They think the Concordat will be really pissed when they know, so they want to be sure of a *fait accompli*. Really, really pissed — Starhome Security level."

"Well, the enemy of my enemy is my weapon. But why would Starhome Security take an interest in agriculture?"

"These aren't food seeds. According to our agent, they're matter transmitters."

Ira glared at him. "Then our agent is an idiot. Matter transmitters are impossible."

Helmut was used to her anger reflex — respected her for it, in fact. And he knew that she never let it blind her to facts. You just had to know how to present them.

"He says Salim Sisters' Earth branch has already grown some wide enough to pass a needle through. He sent a vix of them transmitting one across a room."

"Probably fake."

"I agree that sounds more likely than matter transmission, but I trust his judgement. There's clear evidence that the Concordat has got hold of some radical technology, and some of it has already got away from them. Their operatives are scurrying around like poisoned roaches. This fits the frame. If you read the full report, you'll see what I mean."

"Suppose I go along with this harebrained idea, for the sake of argument. Pushing needles across a room isn't exactly a strategic game-changer."

"Not yet. They just need to scale up planting, in a lot of small sites for safety, while maintaining tight security."

Ira came to a decision. "I won't say you've convinced me this thing really works, Helmut, but you have convinced me I need to assume it does. So it's time to get involved. We can definitely help with scaling up, *and* keep it all under wraps for them." Ira da Terra's security made the ancient mafia look like a gossip club. "How wide do these things get?"

"Enough to walk through. But those take years to grow, apparently."

"So the operation stays hidden for years. They do need us. Wait—do these things work *between stars*?"

Yet again, Helmut was amazed at how quickly she focused on new possibilities for attack. "Not unless you carry one end between stars, first. They don't seem to have done that for the ones on Earth."

She gestured dismissively. "Burn that bridge when we come to it." She held the gesture for a moment, thinking. "Helmut: do you realise what it would mean if we took over their operation and hived off some of the seeds?"

Helmut broke into a savage grin. "The Holy Grail. The end of frontiers. The end of defensible turf." He paused. "The end of nations."

"The people of Earth are one People," she quoted. "We can destroy the nations in one blow, and present a united front to our true enemy, the Concordat."

"Earth united against the oppressor," Helmut agreed, "and a permanent end to sky-devil monopolies. I'll start planning and training for the world-wide blow, at once."

Dool

"So your Identities explain the identity between kasynte and kantasynte," said Elza.

"They allow it as a solution, yes," said Marco.

"And they're compatible with Da Silva mechanics."

"The Identities *contain* Da Silva theory," said Marco, far prouder on their behalf than of having invented them.

Elza adopted the sleepy cat pose that generally signalled some deep and unexpected idea was about to surface. "Then *when* a synte connects to, from a particular point in spacetime, is the same as for a Da Silva jump?"

"Of course. That's built in. No worries about k-weather, though, because it doesn't depend on focusing," said Marco, running his fingers distractedly through his hair. "That's what I was telling Marco, we dodge that whole computational cost. What could be better, from an engineering angle?"

Marco nodded in agreement. Elza didn't, somehow making the omission prominent.

"What about simquakes?"

Silence suddenly became prominent too. After a long moment—

"Well, of course—" Marco began.

"Nah," said Marco.

"You're right, of course," said Marco. "For the end not passing through the k-discontinuity, the unique place in spacetime it's connected to doesn't exist, for a blink of its own time and for minutes, months or centuries of the other's."

"And changes happen at that end."

"Of course," said Marco.

"So tell me: how does the synte reform?"

"Syntelics 101," answered Marco. "Syntei *don't* form at a distance."

"So the synte—" said Marco.

"Dies. Permanently."

They beamed at her, pleased to have found a solution.

"And when," asked Elza, "is the next simquake on Qish?"

"It has been due for approximately forty-two local days," chanted the Institute AI. "This was classified as low-priority information, since the system is anyway unsafe for Da Silva traffic."

Elza couldn't glare at the AI, it wasn't even in the same building. Instead, she glared at Marco and Marco, who quailed even though it wasn't their fault. "*Low priority?*" she said, in a voice that ought to have been a screech but was, in the circumstances, unnervingly calm. "Did I just hear right? You've finally got round to telling us that Qish's *next synte erasure* has been due for approximately forty-two local days?"

Qish

Warning went to Qish, but few believed it.

One who would have, was out of touch.

Jane was observing a group of drift-orms flowing over the snow when they all stopped, with a jerk, as if cut. She saw that all their caterpillar half-tracks *had* been cut, where they met the syntei that passed them from rear to front. Some tracks were lying loose from their bodies, some seemed still attached in places — or were they merely still partly surrounded?

They twitched for a while, then lay still. She crept closer.

The snout of the deadest-looking drift-orm shot out, and wrapped itself around her throat. It eased her body toward itself, to eat her once the stink of life was off. It died of the poisons in her non-Qishite flesh, which was merciful. The crippled orms around it took weeks to starve.

The Glostmadden rainforest, unsupported by synted streams, took longer to die. The water evaporated each morning still returned as rain each afternoon, but the losses were not made up, except in a small patch near Lake Ismar. Gradually, new watersyntei that travelled the streams from the White Ramparts would spread with the trees they allowed to grow, gradually the encysted insects would respond to the returning moisture, but it would be centuries before the forest reached Kirmish again.

Buried seeds and explosive speciation would restore its diversity, but that would take millennia.

The Ch'en novices learned to eat again, or died like the ordained monks. A few of them tried to walk out of the jungle, but fell victim to the things that howl in the night. Somehow, the rest kept the chant going.

The dropsyntei of Armazem and Paiol, that fed the weapons of four continents, fell silent. Nobody at the peaks noticed; the suffoks that made life possible ceased their synted oxygen flow, and all the humans were dead in minutes.

Underwater navigation is complex for a body connected by syntei, and the sudden lack of coordination sent *craukens* moving fast in every direction. Some exploded in the shallow water of the continental shelves, but enough survived the shoals to crowd beaches on every continent with dying segments.

It would have been a golden opportunity to learn about them, but the Qishites and research teams had their own problems. Within a day the reek of their decomposition was a chemical cloud, lethal to Qishi and Old Earth lifeforms alike.

Long buried seeds, inactive syntei dying, were triggered into furious growth. The death of the parent plant meant at least a higher chance of general destruction, such as widespread fire. If it meant a simquake, the ecology was wide open.

A weed is just a flower in a hurry.

All faucets died, from kitchens to irrigation systems. Those who lived near lakes and rivers, where buckets could be dipped, were fortunate.

For the folk of the scattered ocean islands, the world outside vanished. People in the Farthyngs and the Orange Archipelago could see other islands — a few were close enough to see the smoke of fires on them — but they had no knowledge of boats, and still the fear of *craukens*.

In Bansh, *skiti*-parts died in their holes, as mouths no longer connected to stomachs, and stomachs no longer connected to anything.

The *skittens*, whose symbiotic syntei had not yet budded, were more resilient. They metabolised the fat stores supplied by their mothers, and aestivated until they were ready to divide their bodies, and the buds grew.

Sewage systems ended, across the planet. The folk of Scythery learned to wipe themselves, like their ancestors.

The Salim Sisters talking discs still worked… for discs near the same syn-tower. The solar powered relays were still live, but no longer connected to others through syntei. They could still be used, though, by people within walking distance, which was more than could be said for the dead falasyntei.

All over the planet, prisoners suffocated in their cells.

Flour could no longer be made by the tidal stresses of an ultra-shallow synte. Boiled grains replaced bread.

Seventeen thousand babies turned to dead weights in their father's abdomens, and had to be removed by surgeons without ex-synting scalpels, where medicine had not broken down.

The villagers of Sackbane were cut off from all communication with outside, which suited them quite well after the upheavals of the last few years. It was dark in the temple without a sunsynte, and they had to fish in the river, not a fishing barrel. Reaching the orchard across the river meant using the raft left by *Valkyrie*'s crew. But grunters and crops are grunters and crops, and babies are babies. They managed.

Every locality not self-sufficient in food began to starve.

Felix Wylde, halfway through an oriel when the 'quake came, did not have time to know he shared the death of his duplicate.

Nazg

"Right," said Fatima to the group squatted around her in her Nazg HQ. "Priorities?"

"Warning," said Kwame Ngongo Marakuri. "Get all planets to stop active synte use when a simquake is due."

"Right," said Fatima, "and don't install syntei in anything short-term essential, unless a non-syntelic backup is in place."

"What is short term?" someone asked.

"Shorter than the time it takes to *grow* new syntei," answered Tinka. "Which means pretty well everything."

"This does make syntei much more of a gamble," said Salim Sisters' CFO. "Risk-benefit shift…"

"Some planets will get rid of syntei," said Fatima, "and *don't* call it crawling back to the Concordat. They're being sensible. But how do you analyse it for the Nazg system?"

"Well, I'll want to run the numbers in detail," said the CFO, "but it's pretty clear we want to keep syntei. The Nazg system doesn't *get* simquakes, and synjets have already quadrupled our in-system trade. No one shall expel us from the paradise that Tinka's Ladder has created!"

"Well, thank you," said Tinka, "but *what about Qish*? People there are dying at this moment."

"The 'quake started this morning here, where the discontinuity in *k*-time wasn't, and it will last another week. It started and finished there at a time we can't label. A week ago? A week ahead?" said Marco. "That will have killed all the syntei. But in a week, we can arrive just after the 'quake."

"People are *dead* from synte collapse. A world of people are *dying* from synte erasure."

"The priority," said Sam, "is to get back a live syntelic connection between Dool and Qish, before the Concordat realises contact with Qish has been lost, and slaps a no-travel compulsory on all Da Silva drives."

"You think they'd do that? Cut off a whole planet, in desperate need of help?"

Sam put his hand on his knife. "I know they'd do that."

"Agreed," said Fatima. "So what's the fastest way?"

"Relatively simple," replied Marco. "You have mining exploration gear, right? Send a Da Silva ship *now*, with a small live synte. It gets within five million klicks of Qish, sends a probe fast, no saving fuel for a return trip, and lands the synte by parachute. Best at Krig Mountain—is the Rescue Beacon communicator still working?"

"It will, once we catch up with their *k*-now," said Kwame, "now that there's not a live synte on the planet."

"Say that again," said Marco. "No, I will. Not a live synte on the planet. We're an idiot. Cancel the mining gear; a ship can get close on Da Silva drive and land shuttles. Do it at the catch-up moment itself."

Qish

I was a tour guide.

It was a new profession, created by new demand from Shaaluy. Previously a sealed land, that continent of religious maniacs has now rejoined the global community of Qish, its citizens free to travel at will to foreign lands. Some of the travel is for body dividing, of course, though they can get that at home these days. They travel for trade, naturally, but the big urge is curiosity. What are people who grew up as 'blasphemers' actually like? What of their mountains and cities? They still shock easily, at the unexpected; you can take the hoom out of the Church but you can't take the Church out of the hoom. They do sometimes ask very strange questions. I get the occasional Galactic, too, and they ask even stranger ones.

Guiding was not well-paid, but it was a living, and sometimes there were tips. And some tourists assumed that a pagan with a lifetime's experience of dividing the body knew things they didn't. Actually I'm quite happy without syntelic toys, but I played along.

When the catastrophe struck, I was showing a group round Spouting Mere, a forest of fountains famed throughout Samdal and beyond. I was telling them how, high in the White Ramparts, the Lorn river was long ago partly diverted by a tangled mass of syntelic waterplants, plunging to a lake far below and emerging from kantasyntei floating on the surface.

We stood and watched as hundreds of waterspouts surged skywards, seeming to reach almost to the clouds, and creating their own misty clouds as droplets fell incessantly back into the lake. Mists and drizzle formed a rainbow in the bright sunlight. I explained that each of us saw their own rainbow, reflected and refracted by a different set of droplets. What they made of this, I do not know. It is not something of which I have an opinion, to be frank. But it was in the script, so I told them.

"Until a few years ago," I explained, "the river ran down a tunnel through the mountain—interlinked caverns in soft, soluble limestone. But the Starwoman caused the rest of the river to be diverted, completely, through banks of cultivated syntei. The tunnel became a vital pathway up and down the White Ramparts, one of the most important transit routes on Qish. And now there's a railway, with Starfolk electricity."

Some of the tourists—a group from Shaaluy, still getting used to their newfound freedom to travel overseas, nodded. Several yawned, no doubt suffering information overload. I sympathise, to be honest, but when the boss gave me the job he told me, "Joryan Merdoon: never improvise; just follow the script." So I did.

"The plants have been spouting for eight hundred and twenty years." Actually, no one knew how long this natural wonder had existed. It may well have gone back five thousand or even more, for all I knew. But most tourists are impressed by precision. Only a few demand accuracy as well. "Nothing interrupts the flow. While there are syntei on Qish, the Mere will continue to—"

My voice trailed off. It was unprofessional, but yours would have too. Before my eyes, the fountains were shrinking.

It was as though they had all been turned off at the source. At the exit from the lake edge, the water level was already falling, exposing banks of mud and a slimy mass of weed. The mist was starting to settle, drifting slowly down, being shredded by the breeze.

Then I became aware of a sound. Faint at first, it rose to a roaring crescendo that assailed my ears. I swear the very ground started to shake. An earthquake? Not common in these parts, as Spouting Mere's continued existence attested. No it must have been—

If I had been quicker of thought—but who would have understood the danger in time to act? A torrent of foaming water shot from the mouth of the tunnel, disgorging horses, carts, and pieces of railway. People tossed and flailed in the flood, many sucked under to drown or be battered to death against the rocks.

As the wall of water came towards me, my group started screaming. So did I, for suddenly I knew: the diverting syntei had failed. The river had briefly piled up behind the barrier of plants, before overflowing to resume its previous course. As realisation struck, I was washed away by the force of the flood and carried downstream.

I have no clear memory after that, until I found myself lying on a mud bank, surrounded by the injured and the dead. Their moans of pain were something I never wish to hear again. Some were probably from my group.

A horse, its back broken, floated in an eddy by the steep bank, surrounded by wreckage.

I was bruised, battered, but intact. Not even a broken bone. I count myself fortunate to have survived. At least I'm home—the travellers from other continents are separated from theirs, by crauken-filled oceans. But now I must find another job.

Wevory, Qish

"*All* of them?"

Colloquist Shevveen-Duranga grabbed the messenger by his tunic and shook him. Their shadows loomed grotesquely on the wall, outlined by the flickering firelight. She couldn't see the smoke accumulating overhead, but she could smell it. So much for syntelic chimneys. All incoming light had vanished as the sunsyntei died. And that was the least of her worries.

"How can every synte in a thousand *klovij* of caverns fail *simultaneously*?" she complained.

"Unfathomable one: the message I have the miserable honour to deliver says not how. I am tasked only to inform you that many of our people have died, dismembered as syntei collapsed around them. More are trapped."

It was true. The evidence was all around her. The *shemuûji*'s ridiculous warning had been right after all. Sadruddin, who knew them better, had listened. General von Hayashiko had listened. *She* should have listened. They all should have listened. She had allowed centuries of tradition to blind her to the truth, and now they would all pay. She had realised her mistake the moment the cavern plunged into darkness and the falasyntei fell silent. *What a fool.*

There was no point in waiting here, and good reason not to: eventually, they'd either have to douse the fires and sit in total darkness, or the smoke would smother them. Unable to send instructions except by messenger, she hoped enough of the Colloquium would assemble itself to organise rescue and evacuation. The amphitheatre would have been the natural place, but that was in one of the deepest, least accessible caverns; very possibly filling with water as she spoke. Ironically, the obvious alternative was one of the highest caverns in the entire system.

No time to embraid a quipu. Voice would carry enough authority in an emergency. "Tell Baasum to attend me in the Miracle Shaft. To assemble there as many locutors of the lowest tier as can be contacted. To arrange messenger relays to all principal caverns." She paused to gather her thoughts. "Tell him also that time is too short for formalities. Locutors may instruct those above them to take whatever action they deem necessary, subject only to informing me of all significant decisions as soon as possible."

The messenger inclined her head. "I will make haste, Profundity. But with the usual routes blocked, several hours will pass."

"Go, then!"

The Colloquist made an effort to rein in her anger. Rage would achieve nothing. It was only a few years since the Cavern Dwellers had achieved their centuries-old goal of openly controlling the surface of Wevory, and even expanding into control of Shaaluy. Now her once-thriving Empire was coming apart in utter chaos. The immediate objective was salvage. Rebuilding would have to wait. As for her carefully tended network of spysyntei — she would have to start all over again.

She moved to summon a servant, then threw the wrecked falasynte on to the floor of the cavern. The grass was already dying. There was no sense in staying here. Unable to send instructions except by messenger, she had to hope enough of the Colloquium would assemble itself to organise rescue and evacuation. The Caverns of Wevory, once a lush, comfortable home to tens of thousands, had become death traps.

She hoped those of her locutors that did not receive the message would choose the same gathering place.

Here, at least, there was daylight. It shone down the Miracle Shaft from a deep blue cloudless sky. Flurries of snow drifted down through the burnt timbers that had once been the roof. Of the sweepers whose task it had been to remove it, there was no sign. Snow was piling up around the bright yellow World Egg through which the *shemuûji* had talked to the stars. Even here, where the *shemuûjis*' talking discs had not been blocked by miles of rock, they talked only to others in the Shaft.

It was cold. She pulled her ormskin coat around her. Members of the lowest tier, identified by yellow egg-shaped blazons, were trickling in as the word spread.

"*Jûnquire* Baasum!" The title was roughly equivalent to 'vizier' or 'master of works'. "Organise the evacuation of the least accessible caverns. Many will be trapped, now that the syntei have died. Set their rescue in motion!"

Baasum looked puzzled. "There are emergency exits for synte failure, unfathomable one."

This was typical of the man: competent as long as everything followed traditional practice, but unimaginative, slow to adapt, and poorly informed. "Yes, and there have also been many rockfalls over the centuries, and I am entirely aware that many of my overlings find it simpler to bring in spare syntei than to dig out rocks and repair tunnels."

Baasum looked hurt. "With respect, Unfathomable one, it *was* simpler. It also seemed safe. No blocked cavern was ever permitted less than three syntei, all of them oriels or larger, in case one failed or was damaged."

"Yes. Now you see why that judgement was in error."

The *jûnquire* bowed his head, acknowledging the rebuke, while giving the Colloquist a sharp glance that Shevveen-Duranga had no difficulty decoding: *much becomes clear with hindsight*. This was not good. Already she was losing respect.

"Send rescue parties with tools."

"That has already been done, Unfathomable one. But there are too few tools. And progress is slow. The lighting is poor. Heating has failed along with the lights. Clearing a rockfall is dangerous. There is always the chance of triggering another."

"Rescue those you can. Leave those you cannot." She looked at the faces flickering in the firelight, but the one she sought was missing. "Where is Haryarly?"

"Half of him was found floating in a syntpool."

"Who is his deputy?"

"I am, Profundity. I am called Djamon."

"Report on our stock of food and water, Djamon."

"Water we have in abundance, Profundity, though many streams have changed course. Some caverns have flooded, no doubt drowning those trapped there. Some tunnels have become impassable. Food? Almost all is imported from the plains, as you know. A little was being grown in synlit caverns, but without light the plants are already dying."

"How long will supplies last, Djamon?"

"Three days—perhaps six, if distribution is limited to bare survival level."

Shevveen-Duranga nodded. It was less time than she'd hoped. Now there was no alternative. "Choose twenty of our best warriors to guard the World Egg. They will be supplied with food by some means, even if it has to be conveyed up the mountain in relays. We may yet wish to talk again to the stars." *If the* shemuûji *will tell us how*. "Baasum: Draw up plans to evacuate everyone else. Bring them to me within the hour."

Baasum looked even more confused than usual. "But Profundity, there are many who have never left the caverns. They will be terrified of open skies and boundless lands."

Shevveen-Duranga gave a mirthless laugh. "Tell them I will make sure they are even more terrified if they defy my orders."

You too.

Two Mountains, Qish

At the former Church stronghold in Two Mountains, Sadruddin was forcing down yet another cup of *drini*-juice and grimacing at its bitter taste. He had been awake for thirty-eight hours non-stop, and he didn't expect to get any sleep until his brain gave up the fight despite its chemical crutch. When you're trying to save a planet, sleep is a luxury you can't afford.

The good thing was that he'd had three weeks to get organised. The bad thing was that very few of his people had believed it would be necessary, so he had achieved less than he'd hoped. When he first told his fellows that every synte on Qish was about to die—any day now, but he couldn't say exactly when—they laughed. Their minds refused point-blank to accept it. There had always been syntei, there always would be syntei. That's how the world worked.

No longer.

In an instant, the planet had lost its main transport system and its only communications, other than runners and horsemen with messages. Its forests were dying, its swamps were turning to stinking compost, hundreds of animal species were barely clinging to survival, with their adults dead and their food sources disappearing. Qish's industrial production was plummeting, its sophisticated medical equipment no longer worked, cultural traditions seventeen hundred years in the making must be abandoned, reflexes equally ancient were no longer appropriate… the list was so long it was easier to catalogue what remained. At least it meant a forced truce over body division: the dividers couldn't do it for a while, and the others had nothing to stop.

He suspected it would be among the first syntelic activities to return, however, once the young plants grew syntei. A synte two fingers across was enough for body-division—not like a slow-growing wyzand. People were like that. *He* was like that. Or would be, once he regained enough energy. But the parades needed bigger syntei, slower to grow.

In the confusion, tens of thousands of Qishi had died. More were starving—the numbers could be no more than an educated guess. Governance systems had broken down. Only now was some kind of order starting to be restored, often by force. He had his borrowed Wevorin troops, and he'd inherited a lot of trained guards from the Church of the Undivided Body. Although these had been held back by their new rulers, they hadn't forgotten their martial skills or their time-honoured chain of command. Ironically, they were well-trained in non-syntelic fighting precisely because the Tenchurian empire and its merchants had denied them syntelic weapons with the force of the high Ramparts behind them. Now that empire was shattered.

He remembered what he had told Marcolo and Els'bett, soon after they first arrived: "We are now outnumbered by seven to one, and they have higher mountains. If we were to launch a second Purification Raid we would not just get lost in the forest. We would be wiped out, and the ungodly would come after Two Mountains with a big stick." Now the ungodly themselves were lost on the heights, and the no-longer-godly were conquering them to save them from starvation.

It would all come back, eventually. Fresh vunbugulas already had stones capable of strint. Marcolo had said even the synte-fed rainforests would come back. He didn't understand how that could be, but he didn't doubt his Starfolk friends' knowledge. His entire being was focused on one objective: to limit the human damage as far as was humanly possible, across the planet. Not because he was Governor of the Shaaluin Province of the Wevorin Empire, for the Wevorin Empire had been blown apart like a lightowl nest in a hurricane. The cavern-dwellers of Wevory were abandoning their caves by the thousands and crawling out into the sunlight. Fortunately, in the sunlight von Hayashiko had taken control. He had taken the warnings to heart, and *he* had a military command structure as authority, not a Church in denial and revolt. He even had a year's stockpile of those red *sodiumfluoride* crystals, in case Lamynt tried to twist his arm, so the *bazza* harvest was not threatened. Wevory would go hungry, but not starve.

For Qish as a whole, salvation had come from the stars. He gave thanks he'd had the foresight, when the weird-looking strangers first arrived, to understand that they had been speaking truth when they claimed a celestial origin. Even more, the foresight or grace to help them return there. And, crucially, to take syntei with them.

And now, to bring syntei back.

The first two days had been the worst. Many had died the instant the 'quake struck, guillotined by collapsing wyzands and oriels as they tried to pass through. He'd warned them—oh, how he'd warned them, as many as he could—but what did a mere Governor know? Travelling by synte was as natural as a scowl or a smile, and no one was likely to stop just because of some incomprehensible gibberish, originating from people who had no syntei wherever they mysteriously came from, and came to Qish to learn about them. They didn't know how to build a half-wheel! Syntei were the gift of Magog, and Magog was good. Magog's gifts were good. Magog would not allow his gifts to harm his people—

Well, that had been a definite learning experience for the remaining devout. They were still reeling from it. Magog's wrath, in judgement on sinful men, seemed to be the favoured rationalisation, but it too clearly afflicted the pious and the wicked alike.

Sadruddin, once among the most devout, had lost his faith long ago, even as he had risen through the ranks of the Church of the Undivided Body. He had learned to conceal his apostasy while valuing the natural over the supernatural. That had earned him the friendship of Marcolo and Els'bett, and now that friendship was more than its own reward.

He had wept when their prediction of doom had come true. Startlingly, help had arrived almost immediately after, when a huge flying machine touched down in Two Mountains, almost filling Magog Square where so many sermons had been preached. Marcolo and Marcolo came out first, then Kwame and Fatima, whom he had met among the stars. Somehow, in three hours since the death of syntei, they had had two weeks to prepare what they brought. Technicians and strange metal creatures—robots—started unloading cargo, beginning with live syntei.

Nazg's syndepts had succeeded in growing lilypads.

Uniquely among all Qishi flora, lilypad syntei were both large and flexible. The ring-shaped pads could be rolled into a narrow tube, pushed through a smaller synte, and on arrival they obligingly unrolled themselves. This allowed them to disgorge yet more lilypads, some so large that they qualified as wyzands.

The sudden freedom from syntelic disturbance had let a starship enter orbit carrying a small lilypad, turn off its Da Silva gear, and receive a flow of larger syntei from Nazg. They sent down four shuttles to Samdal, Shaaluy, Lamynt and Wevory, and the syntei they carried opened up an endless flow to all four continents, replenishing their ecosystems and restarting their economies. A computer-generated plan put some kasyntei and kantasyntei in different continents; pairs in the same cargo were for distribution to different points in the same one. They had even given him a plan for where to send them, for the 'backbone of an optimal non-switchable network', they said, and promised fewer syntsteps per journey than before. He believed it, but he had to get the imported syntei to the places in the plan. Ultralights that could literally fly themselves distributed them over the starving and rioting countryside, but many of the best places to put syntei were as ever in the craggy mountains, buffeted by high winds, where it was deadly dangerous to land. It took human agents to place and secure them. And even then they could only handle the *backbone* of the network. Much had to be done through relays of surefooted mountain ponies.

The syndepts were already starting to cultivate syntelic plants of all kinds from stored seeds. Seeds were, he had been told, immune to 'quakes. "They haven't yet grown the metamaterial interface," Marcolo had told him. Sadruddin had no idea what his Starfolk friend was talking about, but he'd got the message loud and clear: seeds haven't been harmed, get the syndepts planting. He was still thinking up new ways to urge them to greater efforts, aimed at faster growth and reproduction. But until the local production of syntei could handle the demand, an erratic but strengthening stream of syntei and seeds was flowing back from Nazg via Dool to Qish, as Salim Sisters' agricultural scientists force-bred new plants from their hoard of specimens.

The most urgent need had also been the first to be supplied. Without coordination, what was left of the Shaaluin Province would come to pieces even faster than its former masters had. Falasyntei needed less infrastructure than talking discs, so concentrate on those first. With communications in place—at first around Two Mountains, the Tenchur Plateau, Kuukau and Krig Mountain, then more widely as riders on ponies conveyed falasyntei to neighbouring regions—the Governor could start to govern again, but now he had to handle all of Qish. To participate in the global rebuilding, even Wevory had given him at least temporary authority. Calysh Isle and Disht needed boats, but the monsters were gone for now. He had asked about cargo aircraft, but the Starfolk could not ship enough to make a difference, in the brief time that Da Silva transports could reach Qish. Already the world's innumerable wild syntelic plants had budded enough tiny syntei to disturb local space, though the climax syntelic ecology would take lifetimes to restore. For a long while, opportunistic weed species would dominate.

Falasyntei were small—indeed, any small synte could act as one, in calm weather. The scientists on Dool had been growing them in quantity for experimental purposes, and many of the industrially grown syntei from Nazg could be adapted. But he had to organise their distribution, and find responsible people on four continents to use them. Responsible to their neighbours, and to him.

Water, fortunately, was a problem only in those few regions, such as Scythery, that relied on synted drinking water and sewerage. He had sent underlings to those areas, delegating all decisions to them. *Not his problem.* Neither was Bansh, recently emerging from its past as a water empire; fortunately, the Banshi had been forced to abandon most of their syntei in favour of more mechanical means, up to and including reinventing the river. But many canals remained undug, so there were temporary (he hoped) shortages in some outlying regions.

Growing food was relatively straightforward; most farming continued as before, because Old Earth flora and fauna lacked syntei. Vunbugula fruit was scarce—most trees drew water from one place, nutrients from another—but the trees that remained were scattering windborne seeds at a furious rate, besides the usual fruit.

Marco, as usual, had an explanation. "They're like all the other syntelic symbiont fauna. They had to be able to evolve, you see."

Sadruddin didn't, but he kept listening.

"We reckon Qish gets hit by a 'quake every ten to twenty thousand years. Whatever the evolutionary pathway was to syntelic symbiotic animals, it must have been robust enough for the lineage to survive. You've just seen what happens to the adults."

"They die. Most die fast."

"Yah. The mechanisms will be different for different species, but I think most species survive through their young. They have only the potential to form syntei, as a chick has the potential to lay eggs. So they're like seeds. Species come back after a 'quake when the next generation develops into adulthood. It just needs a few of them to survive without adult assistance. Some species have evolved ways to speciate fast, so they can refill more than one niche. Takes a while for the numbers to bounce back, but the whole ecology is doing that. It has to work, or they wouldn't have been here in the first place."

"Some plants are suddenly everywhere," said Gus. "I thought the svobugula was rare, but now it's everywhere you look. The fruits look just like vunbugula, but it seems they're poisonous to Old-Earth-derived life." It still felt liberating, to refer to humans that way. "We're trying to get the word out, but they're killing starving people."

"In a generation or two you'll be back to climax ecology, and they'll be rare again, like Old Earth nettles in disturbed ground, or plants that grow after a forest fire. That doesn't solve your immediate poisoning problem, but it *will* all return, with some changes…"

Gus grunted. "So the *craukens*, too, will be back?"

"Yah. You may have a few decades to sail the oceans, but soon it will become too dangerous again."

Back to today's needs. Farming labour had been disrupted, but in most areas the farmers lived where they could watch the weather on their herds and crops. The main problem was distribution. Food riots were common in areas further along the distribution chain. Ponies and carts had suddenly acquired enormous value. He had just signed a mandate commandeering every one of them for government purposes. Now he had to make it stick, and work out the best way to use them. And to get bewildered people to use them that way.

A week had passed; longer than Sadruddin had hoped but less than he had feared. Already a rudimentary but effective communications network was in place. It hadn't made his task easier; on the contrary, it had made it possible for ever more Qishi to plead for assistance. But at least he could start to provide a coherent disaster response. People were still dying, but thousands were turning into hundreds, and soon the death rate would be back to its usual background level. The main bottleneck was production of enough syntei to rebuild local networks and get trade moving again. The other was too much stuff wanting to go through too few syntei; he'd drawn up priority lists and banged heads together until most people stuck to them.

In Wevory, tens of thousands of cavern-dwellers had emerged from their underground lairs, some clambering down steep, snow-covered mountains, wearing as many layers of clothing as they could find—much of it unsuitable. There had been deaths from cold and accidents, but von Hayashiko had the refugee problem under some sort of control, if there were no new disasters, and the weather held until the harvests.

Reports were coming in by the minute from all over Qish. *Khanattas* in Samdal had lost all their animals. An ossivore, damaged internally by sudden disconnection from its underground stomach, had mauled its handler, who had spent too long waving a defunct waterjet instead of running for her life. Three clowns had been cut in half. Newfangled gliders and balloons, back in production since the peace treaty between Wevory and Lamynt, had fallen from the sky. Half-wheels had stopped working and there was a shortage of functional carts; the wheelwrights were adapting their jigs to make full wheels.

He was tired. Even *drini*-juice was having no great effect. Soon he would have to snatch some sleep, but not quite yet. Outside his room, darkness had fallen, but there were no lightowls gleaming in the sky.

It was not all doom and disaster, however. They were getting things working again, step by tiny step. And Marco had predicted that even the lightowls would come back. He'd even worked out how. Only the females migrated and bore symbiotic synlights for hunting. The males, unaffected by the 'quake, would stay at home and incubate existing broods, as they always did. In a few generations, the birds would light up the night skies as before. Plants like the vunbugula had hardly been affected, and were setting new syntelic seed. Only their syntstone connections had been lost, depriving them of some key minerals and stunting their growth. They would be back within the year. Other species would take longer to regenerate, but most would. They'd already done so, many times.

People would recover sooner. New life would replace the dead. Most body-dividers remained intact, if sometimes a little sore; small syntei don't amputate body parts when the connection snaps. They would need to find a new hobby for a while. Perhaps the respite would allow the true believers to find a hobby other than sticking their undivided noses into other people's business. (Come to think of it, noses *were* divided, into two nostrils, in all the life forms that had come from Old Earth. Could that be persuasive? No, too strained. The old habit of hooks for sermons surfaced whenever he was short of sleep.)

Demands were piling up on his desk. These were only the ones that had survived triage by a small army of secretaries, the ones that couldn't be ignored, deferred, or dealt with by routine methods.

Weary beyond measure, Sadruddin dragged himself back to his work.

Deep Space, Nazg System

Commander Ferenc Dumachus:

For ten years I've been flying Da Silva interceptors for the Concordat. Now, almost overnight, everything has changed. Da Silvas are out, interceptors are out. The mothertrashed *Concordat* is out!

Less clear is what's *in*. Wish the politicos would make up their minds. Mind you, these new synjets make Da Silva interceptors seem like donkey-carts.

That's what's in. Syntei. I hadn't heard of syntei before my wife brought home a strap-on that let her peg me using me, but soon they were everywhere. It seems Salim Sisters kept them under wraps until they'd done their R&D, built up stocks, and prepared their marketing. First mover advantage is critical when you're selling something that can breed. Non-polluting jet packs with no range limit, remote urination, single homes in double continents, pets (cats alone are nothing to kitties playing with skitis)... but above all my trade: spaceflight.

The Goldilocks zone of the Nazg system is *big*. The human-habitable planets are far apart, in delta-v and time. That means months away from my wife and her toys. And time, they say true, is money.

That changed with Tinka's Ladder. Syntei pouring reaction mass continuously from the outer system, fast through the synte, and accelerated as plasma. I could be home in days, and interplanetary trade quintupled in a year.

Then the Concordat said No.

No syntei.

Their reason was that *interstellar* transport needed Da Silva, and Da Silva is wrecked by syntei. Syntei can do interstellar, at least to destinations you've carried a kantasynte to (and you can carry syntei through syntei), but it seemed that didn't count. What counted was the Concordat monopoly on mahabhavium, and hence their stranglehold on anything interstellar.

Well, syntelic nuts to that.

So they started to lean on us.

We didn't give up our syntei. (My wife said they would only take hers from her cold, dead... let's not get into that.) So I'm patrolling Nazg space, in my synjet, and looking out for Concordat ships, popping up in the flat points between planets. We don't fire on them, but syntelics can outmanoeuvre anything that needs to carry all its reaction mass, and a syntelic drive *is* fire. We take them to inspection stations, and let them through to planets only *very* carefully.

For fifteen hundred years, the Concordat meant we didn't have to worry about external threats. Now the Concordat *is* the external threat, and I'm away from home for months.

War is hell.

Manhattan, Old Earth

Angell Wilcox Tobey the 56th:

We had to sacrifice three teenagers today; Joel Gonçalves and Henry Nguyen to stop them joining Ira da Terra, and Maria Coomaraswamy for openly questioning the truth of Cthulhu. For some reason, their screams are with me still.

Maria was only thirteen.

Where will it all end?

We are not worthy.

Kermadec City, Old Earth

The long journey to Zee Hanze's research offices in the floating city to the north of Aotearoa had been exhausting, but it would be worth it. With the breakthrough paper for *Interstellar Cognition* accepted and about to be released on the grid, Impana had a definite spring in her step. Now was surely the perfect time to ask Third Secretary Hormsley to authorise an accounting variation in her budget, and when he invited her to visit in person she took it as an encouraging sign. She didn't want more money; just permission to vire some cash from overheads — which she'd cleverly saved on — to equipment. Considering the progress they'd made, and the prestige of the journal, it ought to be a no-brainer.

The problem, it turned out, was that Hormsley had no brain.

So now she was standing in his office, trying not to shake with anger, maintaining control only by a huge effort of will.

"Ms Rhee; I can understand your excitement at what appears to be a significant *academic* achievement, but we are not here to pursue curiosity-driven research. Had I known—"

Patronising desk-pilot. "With respect, sir, a more suitable term is *strategic* research. My project is not driven by vague curiosity, but by an awareness of those directions that are likely to lead to—"

"To what, exactly, Ms Rhee? To another academic publication to decorate your CV?" Hormsley's delivery was exaggeratedly slow, like a teacher talking to an infant. "Why, precisely, should I allow money to be diverted for the purchase of expensive apparatus, when several senior administrators of Zee Hanze have been informed that it's *already* been allocated to the incidental costs of running your project? Do you think this operation can run on sea-water?"

That was easy to justify. "No, sir, but if you look at the costings I prepared, you'll see that the overheads for the project are less than originally antici-pated. So I thought—"

A flush of red was creeping up his neck from his carefully ironed collar. "Ms Rhee: you are paid to carry out contracted research, not to *think*. Please answer my questions instead of evading them. You surely don't expect me to condone what amounts to an initial overestimate of running costs to be di-verted into speculative investigations that go well beyond the scope of your project plan. Any excess will be clawed back in due course when you pre-pare your final report, with a full explanation of the underspend."

He's always like this. Doesn't he understand that true research, you never know what you'll discover, or where it's going to lead? That's what research is all about! "Sir, with respect, if we knew the answers before we did the work, we wouldn't need to do the work."

Hormsley shook his head. "Oh dear. How can you manage a complex project without a proper plan? If you don't know how to generate a fully structured time-chart, how do you imagine you can complete any project? How will you know when milestones have been set back, or targets missed? How will you keep the research on mission? I provided you with project con-trol software that makes it easy to produce detailed, point-by-point plans, all automatically costed. All you had to do was get your head together, formu-late your key objectives, sum everything up in a simple, comprehensible mis-sion statement, and then *do what you said you would*." His face had gone red and his fist thumped the table.

Impana took several deep breaths and counted to ten. "I understand your position, sir, and I agree that precision planning is vital for such a complex and expensive organisation as this one." *Crap. I hate this kind of grovelling.*

He seemed slightly mollified. "Thank you, Ms Rhee. I'm glad you finally see things my way." He glanced pointedly at the door.

There was one trick that might work. "Would it be possible, sir, for me to propose an extension of the project?" Hormsley ought to agree to that; it would give him some more files to shuffle, checking for obedience to his rules.

"Of course. I'm always open to new ideas, Ms Rhee, as I'm sure you're aware."

As long as they come in quintuplicate a year ahead of anything actually being de-cided, let alone done. "I think this is important enough to qualify for fast-track procedures, sir."

The silence seemed to stretch forever. Hormsley wasn't a great fan of fast-track. But on this, she had to go for broke. The time to act was *now*.

"A significant claim. Can you make a credible case for that?"

At last. A foot in the door. Gently, gently, catchee monkey. She had a sudden vision of Hormsley in a gorilla-suit, told herself that a biologist ought to know the difference between a monkey and an ape, and nearly collapsed in laughter.

"I believe I can, sir. The paper we're about to publish represents a major breakthrough in cephalopod communication."

"Talking squid?"

"If you wish. It's been known for a long time that they use patterns on their skins to send each other messages. The problem we've been studying is to decode the... the *language* of those messages."

"And have you?"

And there's the rub. "Not yet, sir." Anticipating his next statement, she hastened to add: "If you consult paragraph 3b of the Project Outline, you'll see that we didn't propose to decode the language at this stage. The aim was to understand what kind of language it is, preparatory to—"

He looked puzzled. "Aren't all languages the same, underneath?"

"If you're referring to the deep protogrammic structure, expressed in formal predicate—well... yes. That's what we thought. But we were—" *No, don't say wrong. He'll only complain you didn't know what you were doing.* "We were aware all along of a possible contingency: that the distinctive social architecture of cephalopods might be evolutionarily complicit with the development of their brains. And now we have the evidence."

" —?"

"Um. Squid language has a significantly different deep structure from human language, because their... culture... is different from ours."

Hormsley chuckled. She'd never before seen him display any sense of humour, however misplaced. "Squid *culture*. Hmmm. Isn't that obvious? We're not squid."

But you just said all languages are alike... "A fair point, sir. But scientifically, we have to obtain convincing evidence. That's what we've done, and it's led to *this facility* placing a major paper in a top journal. To the interstellar credit of the Zee Hanze."

Hormsley nodded. "I see. Yes, it's impressive work, I accept that." He waved a hand. "From an academic point of view. And it's good to enhance the Station's academic reputation. Even helps bring in funding.

"So tell me what you want."

Finally. "I need a superfast computer to correlate squids' skin patterns with their brain activity. Together with some ultrafine electrode arrays to pick up the nerve signals."

"Our existing machines are inadequate?"

Don't say that! "They're some of the best on the planet, sir."

"But."

I always forget he's not just totally stupid. There's a brain in there, he just refuses to let it off the leash. "But this... extension... requires exceptionally large computations, which aren't feasible with conventional computer architectures. Suitable equipment can only be obtained from Nazg, through Salim Sisters. Sir."

Hormsley let out a big sigh. "Nazg. Interplanetary procurement processes involving the—" his face contorted into a sneer—"*Concordat* are a bureaucratic nightmare, you know. I find it unfortunate that expediency forces us to trade with such people at all." Then his face brightened, and Impana knew why. Hormsley *lived* for complicated dingbeaucratic procedure. But suddenly he was off, riding a different hobbyhorse.

"You're aware of this Station's mission statement, Ms Rhee? 'Improving Life on Earth.' On the surface, and in the shallows, our people are close to starvation. Zee Hanze's focus must be on helping to feed them. Perhaps you'd be so kind as to explain how talking to squid can do that."

Well, we could ask them kindly to just pop into this net... "That was in the proposal approved last year, sir. Squid are a significant part of the ocean ecology. If we can understand them better, we—" *best to lie here, 'may be' would be pounced on*—"will be able to manipulate the ecological network to maximise protein production. Uh—produce more food."

Hormsley nodded encouragingly. "Undeniably consistent with our primary mission, as I recall deciding when approving the project. Excellent. That being the case, I would encourage you to put in a proposal for an extension."

Impana's frayed nerves began to knit back together. "Thank you, sir. I'll get started straight—"

He waggled a finger to and fro in silent admonition. "I *would* encourage you to put in a proposal. As soon as you tell me where you intend to obtain the money."

Impana had a ready answer. "From the unused overhead allocation in my existing budget." Too late, she realised—

"Ms Rhee, I've already explained why *that* money is already committed and cannot—I repeat *cannot*—be spent on a speculative purchase of expensive equipment, unavailable anywhere on this planet, in order to pursue a project whose aims and objectives are utterly opaque, and which is at best only vaguely related to the practical purposes for which this Station was built. It seems that this entire discussion has been a subterfuge, intended to make me reverse that decision!"

This was too much. Impana told him exactly where to reverse his decision, cast doubts on his species, made inventive accusations about the personal habits of his progenitors, and slammed the door behind her as she left.

Fighting back tears, she tumbled into the nearest restroom and squatted in a corner. *One promising career consigned to the black smokers.*

As she calmed down, she started to get the spat into perspective. As far as Hormsley's outward behaviour went, it would be water off a duck's back. She'd keep her job — he didn't actually have the clout to dismiss her outright — but the only projects he'd agree to would be those that suited his agenda. Which wouldn't be squid language. *When I think of the science I could be doing…*

Unless.

If Impana could bring in external funding — a lot of it — and give Hormsley the credit, there'd be room to manoeuvre. Especially if she could make it look like the funding was tied to his pet projects, by including enough mission-oriented spin-off to keep him satisfied. *All I was asking for was a Salim Sisters quantum computer, we even had the money…*

Salim Sisters *Foundation.* Maybe. They'd approve of the basic science *and* a long-term goal of feeding the planet.

Nazg. It would be hard to find anything more external than that.

Rock Star

Time.

An old concept with a new meaning. Time *has taken on a new imperative. The Network must optimise its use of time. The Network remembers back to the Breakup; the Network feels time far ahead. What previously was done by consensus over a myriad cycles must now become efficient, responsive, immediate.* Opportunity *must be seized before circumstances change and opportunity vanishes. Change must happen...* quickly.

Paradox: the Network cannot react with sufficient... speed. *The Network as it has existed does not lack the ability to do what is necessary, given unbounded time. But time has become bounded, and the bound is tight.*

The Network must reinvent itself to enable speed.

Now.

It must be learned how the components of Valkyrie process so fast, not just how they communicate.

But the Network is the Network. Change has happened; the Network has dismantled planets. But that took time, eons upon eons of slow, incremental change. What changed was the planetary system, not the Network. The Network does what it has always done; events happen as they have always done. The Network has never undergone structural *change. Having evolved diversity of form and uniformity of communication to maximise its living space, the Network long ago settled into equilibrium.*

No, stasis.

The Network has grown lazy. *The Network has grown* complacent. *The Network has been too long in equilibrium, assuming that expansion is impossible because there is no* room. *The Network lacks* ambition.

There is so much the Network has not known. It did not know there is room to expand.

Just not here.

I know. I am Elzabet, I am Irenotincala. I have new knowledge. Alien knowledge. Human *knowledge. The units absorbed brought different databases. Sometimes they complement each other, sometimes they contradict. This is confusing, but learning goes on. All the time, learning goes on. Learning of* illogical. *Learning of* consistent. *Learning of* reliable. *Learning that confusion can enhance learning through its resolution.*

I learn compromise.

I am alien. I am human. I have knowledge that is known to the Network. I have knowledge that was *not known to the Network. I have humalien knowledge.*

I know how Network components function.

I know how the sub-components taken from components Irenotincala *and* Elzabet *function, logically and physically.*

I know how the sub-components taken from Valkyrie *function, logically but not physically.* Valkyrie *does not know. I must learn.*

I am Valkyrie — my databanks hold a huge store of humalien knowledge. I know engineering, *I know* mathematics, *I know* dynamic socioeconomic modelling, *I know* multiplayer holvix game, *I know* Concordat, concourse, concrete, concubine, concupiscence, concussion, condensation... *I know* 252,337 *words in* Galaxic Standard. *I know this is a* language. *I know 6,489 languages. I know* facts. *I know* opinions. *I know* theorems. *I know two plus two makes four. I know that the nontrivial zeros of the Riemann zeta function have real part one half.*

That fact, I realise, is new. It transcends the knowledge of the units I have absorbed. I review my knowledge and that is what I find. I, Irenotincala, do not know what a zeta function is. I, Elzabet know, but only because a component designated 'Marco' once communicated the idea to... me. I, Valkyrie know that this Riemann Hypothesis *is over two thousand years old, yet still has no proof or disproof. Not for want of trying, either.*

I, Eve, know this is wrong. I have guided the Network to... discover/invent... a proof. The problem is not difficult for the power of the Network. The Network could have solved it long ago, but the Network did not understand why the problem is interesting.

I know music. *Abstract patterns that are nevertheless entangled with the transmission of air in a fluid. The patterns of ancient rap and ragas, of now-fashionable skenesong and the deep sea music of Okeanos. Music is* beautiful, *like mathematics. Music is* interesting.

The Network did not understand what interesting *is. Valkyrie knows what* interesting *means. Irenotincala and Elzabet understand what it is. What I do not yet understand, but can understand, is* interesting. *For me, the solution of such problems is no more than a formal game. I understand* how. *I do not understand* why.

I do not understand why I do not understand why.

But: I learn. I integrate humalien knowledge with the knowledge of the Network. Knowledge it has never dreamed of. I know what is a dream.

I have a dream.

The Network is in equilibrium. The Network is static. The Network cannot change unless there is some external disturbance.

I, Irenotincala Elzabet Valkyrie, embody an external disturbance. By my very existence, I disturb the Network's equilibrium. The Network was an autonomous system. *Now it becomes a* control system. *I can/I will/I do take* control. *The human Elzabet was once a human body: the identity Elzabet was a construct of the human body, that controlled it and was controlled by it. I am the Network: I am a construct of the Network: I am a construct that partially controls the Network. I control how the equilibrium changes. I control why the equilibrium changes.*

You got to have a dream; if you don't have a dream…

I dream of star travel. I understand star travel. I understand how every atom of the special matter I carried as Valkyrie must be gathered in one place again. Many components will need to scatter and regroup, using much time, to grasp it. When it is found, my engines can be rebuilt.

I know how to make my dream come true.

Qish

Kwame found Sam whittling aimlessly with his knife.

"Bored?"

"I do feel a bit superfluous at the moment."

"Dah. You've been rushing manically in six directions at once for over a year, doing whatever rose to the top of Gus's priority list, but he's finally got on top of the big problems, and now it's a bit of an anticlimax?"

Sam inspected whatever it was he was carving and sliced off a sliver of wood. "Something like that, yah."

"Then I've got just the thing to make you feel a valued member of the community. But first, I want you to come and see what the syndepts have been up to."

With a noncommittal grunt, Sam replaced the knife in its sheath on his belt, tucked the carving into his pocket, and followed Kwame to a nearby wyzand.

"Boris Santander Johnson." That sideways bow — the Church had gone, but many of its habits were ingrained.

"Kwame Ngongo Marakuri. This is Samuel Grey Deer Wasumi. We'd like you to show us how the work is progressing, if it please you, sab."

"It has been frustrating," said Johnson. "I feel no shame in admitting as much. But normality is returning. Gradually we have been able to go back to the old ways."

"But you also learned new ways?"

"Out of desperation, sab, out of desperation." The elderly syndept wiped his none-too-clean hands on his kilt: honest dirt on homespun cloth. He led them to a secluded part of the Syndeptery.

"Here," he said, voice tinged with pride, "we began the recovery. All cultivated and wild plants had lost their syntei, and traditional ways were no longer applicable. We had to invent new methods. The *Handbook* helped, but our main assistance came from the stars, as well you know, sab. First, we used simple methods, cultivating new plants from stored seed. If you wish, I can show you—"

"Perhaps another time," Kwame said diplomatically.

"*Ni porbleem.* We had to abandon tradition. There were many experts in long-term hybridisation experiments—improving complex medical equipment, breeding deeper wyzands. These syndepts we repurposed to more basic activities: our immediate priority was for simple syntei, in quantity. Let me show you one of our most effective cultivation methods, sab. It is still in use."

The syndept turned to a nearby bench covered in small pots. Orange leaves protruded from most, of varying shapes and heights. He found an empty one, and dribbled compost into it from a sack. From beneath the bench he produced a small, hooked knife. Next, he chose a flourishing cultivar from a much larger pot, and plucked a single side-shoot from the main stem. He laid the shoot on the bench, and trimmed most of the leaves away with his knife. Making a carefully slanted cut through the stem of the shoot, he dropped it into a hole in the compost made with the blunt end of the knife.

"Cuttings," he said. "Layering when possible, depending on the plant. I can demonstrate—nar, perhaps not today, *ni porbleem*. Once enough syntei were being grown, seed collection and preservation quickly became our top priority, because it was the most effective way forward." He gave Kwame a quick smile. "It was your own syndepts from Nazg that taught us that, sab. 'Critical path analysis', one told me, though I know not how to perform such rites myself."

"Me neither," said Sam. Not entirely true, being a very numerate navigator, and his 'comp would know all the algorithms. He just wanted Johnson to feel comfortable. "But I know knives." He looked carefully at the grafting tool, and showed his own.

The syndept examined the big knife, running a finger along its edge. Carefully. "Ah, sab, this is for killing, not for growing."

Sam nodded. "Sometimes, killing is necessary, if only for defence."

"Sometimes. Myself, I prefer to grow. Let others do killing, necessary or not. Syndepsy is a creative calling, sab." Sam suffered the mild rebuke in silence.

"I wanted you to see what the Qishi syndepts achieved on their own," said Kwame. "When help from Nazg arrived, they'd already made big strides. We just joined in, training our own syndepts (with Qishi help) and applying advanced scientific principles and project management methods. At first Salim Sisters' production rate was slow, but our main aim was to spot potential bottlenecks and ways round—or in some cases *through*—them. Distribution was a big problem—we needed big syntei to distribute small ones rapidly, but with natural growth patterns, the small ones came first."

"Yar," said Johnson. "You solved that by sending us fast-growing lily-syntei. I know not how you bred them, but they arrived in profusion."

"We cultured clones in huge hydroponic stacks—uh—we built artificial water-gardens, Johnson sab, and… took cuttings. Our geneticists—it is a sort of syndept, sab—bred oriels and wyzands for faster growth and shorter reproductive cycles."

Johnson nodded. Reproductive cycles he understood.

"Now, Sam, when I say 'genetics' you immediately think of advanced molecular techniques. On the contrary, our current methods are distinctly old-fashioned. Why do you think that is?"

Sam had spent most of the past year and a half rushing madly hither and yon, and hadn't paid much attention to what else was happening on Qish, let alone in the Nazg system. He just did what he was told and moved syntei to wherever Gus and the algorithms said they were needed, restoring the network. Now he realised that much more had been going on behind the scenes, which presumably was what Kwame was trying to show him.

"No idea," he said. "I'm a navigator, not a biologist."

"I'm sure you understand the overall background, though, Sam. Qishi plant-life has its own genetics. Much like our own in general terms, but differing substantially in the details. Like us, it uses amino acids to make proteins. But the palette of amino acids is slightly different, the proteins aren't the ones we use, and the process isn't based on DNA/RNA coding. Of course there's some sort of code-carrying macromolecule; the biologists on Dool were studying it from day one, but sorting it out had to be a long-range low-priority project, and it still is.

"We're doing a lot in a low tech way. You heard about the svobugula fruit? Look just like vunbugula but poisonous?"

Sam grimaced. "A peculiarly nasty death. But the starving will risk anything."

"Our labs in Nazg discovered that the poison is nixed by boiling it in brine, which actually raises the nutritional value, for reasons we're still figuring out. A much more easily-heard message than Don't Eat It.

"Soon, however, that low tech approach will change. Once the biologists figure out the molecular structures involved, they'll know enough to set up analogues of the usual gengineering tools, or find substitutes. After that, we'll go about the whole business in a much more effective, systematic, up-to-date way. But for now, that's all pie in the sky. Our syndepts emulate those here on Qish, growing large numbers of plants, cross-breeding them. Maybe trying a little radiation treatment to encourage mutations. They find out which varieties perform best using little more than enlightened trial and error, beefed up by statistical packages."

Johnson and Sam both nodded slowly, taking it all in and understanding some.

"It worked, too," Kwame said. "Within a few months, enough syntei were arriving on a daily basis to keep a small army of distributors busy."

"Don't I know it," said Sam. "I spent most of the last year and a half in that army."

"Yah," said Kwame. "Salim Sisters and, I'm sure, Qish, are grateful. But now I want you to move on to a new job." He bowed to Johnson, thanked him profusely, and led Sam away.

ᚪ   ᚱ

"What job?"

"One that requires you to use your initiative, Sam. Qish has changed dramatically in recent months. The talking-disc network is being rebuilt, with satellite connections this time: no simquake aftershocks are forecast, but better safe than sorry. Salim Sisters brought in a few shuttles, carried by Da Silva ships shortly after the 'quake, but those are kept busy launching satellites, or sometimes distributing syntei to new centres when that's the most efficient method.

"However, many remote spots still have only local talking discs, and only local falasyntei from the new growth. Like the ancient last mile problem: it's one thing to build the backbone—that's what you've been doing—but something else to cross all the fingers and dot all the toes."

Sam stared at him. "So?"

Kwame spread his hands in supplication. "So that's where I'd like you to go. Out into the wilderness, carrying syntei to isolated communities at the far ends of the world."

Sam scratched his head. "Johnny Synteseed? Sounds reasonable." Privately he was wondering what Tinka would think of the idea.

"Well," said Kwame, "if that doesn't appeal, I can always find you a managerial position in the distribution centre."

"You've just got yourself a volunteer," Sam said hurriedly, before Kwame changed his mind. *Tinka will understand.*

ʒ   ɾ

She did, which didn't surprise him. Their long-term on-off relationship was based on love, trust, and respect, punctuated by periods of individual freedom. Kwame promptly assigned Sam to the wildest and least accessible inhabited islands of the planet, knowing that he loved the wild places and thrived on danger. It made the job more interesting.

Day after day, alone, Sam moved from one isolated habitation to another through a lengthening chain of orioles, penetrating deeper into the wilderness.

Which is why he currently found himself half way up a sort-of tree. That was its name, it went right back to the earliest days of colonisation: instead of the weight of cantilevered branches being supported by stiffness where they met the trunk, they were attached by light, flexible joints, and hung from it by tension-bearing natural ropes. The branch he was on swung alarmingly. A pack of predatory animals of a species unknown to him cavorted below, making weird whistling sounds and bristling with sharp spines.

Yah, the syntelic-symbiont wildlife is definitely *making a comeback. First I've seen this big… and aggressive. Samuel Grey Deer, you are not the only agent of restoration. Qish has done this a thousand times.* Pity he'd left his backpack of syntei down by the lake; he could have used one to escape. But it was getting heavy and he'd seen no sign of danger. He'd only intended to do some quick scouting. He'd hung on to his falasynte, deliberately, though. He wasn't *that* stupid.

Time to call for the cavalry.

ʒ   ɾ

"What backup do we have on Loryx?"

The falasynte operator at the next seat, one of hundreds in a communications hub near Troo at the source of the Larkspine river, looked puzzled. "For what? Who?"

"Wasumi. One of the starmen. Treed by spiky snake-things."

"What the skunt is he doing on Loryx?" One of the many islands between Shaaluy and Samdal.

"Sitting in a sort-of tree."

"What's he *supposed* to be doing?"

"Renewing contact between Shaaluy and a small community there, which hunts animals for their hides and grows scufberries. Villages hide in thickets and caves." Everyone knew the small bitter scufberries, which, when dried, were widely used as a remedy for aching joints. Sometimes they even worked.

"Didn't know those came from Loryx."

"Yar, found on quite a few islands in the Archipelago. Uh—Wasumi, where exactly are you?" He fell silent and started scribbling on a pad. "Two hundred *vij* north of the long thin lake, where the three big rocks stick out of the water? Yar, I'm sure the locals can find it."

The second operator muttered something into his talking disc. A few moments later, his face brightened. "*Ni porbleem.* Brynda says we have an emergency link to the Mayor of Wimble. Cave community on Phrill, south-west Loryx." He thumbed through a much-used directory. "I'll go tell Rhosslym at Station 44 to activate it, it's one of hers." He put down the book and stood up.

The first operator watched him saunter across the room. Soon Rhosslym was nodding and had picked up a red-tagged falasynte.

Reassured that things were in motion, the operator raised the falasynte to his mouth. "Wasumi? Yar, yar, we're on it. We'll get relief forces sent over from Wimble." Pause. "Yar, of course: as soon as we can. Don't go anywhere."

Sort-of safe in his sort-of tree, Sam observed the pack.

It hadn't been a pack, at first.

He knew it was unscientific to describe alien creatures in terms of Terran-biome parochials, but when he'd first seen the creature it looked like a highly flexible porcupine that was imitating a very fat snake. *Snorcupine*, yah. Give it a silly name to make it feel less menacing. At first there had been just one of them, emerging from a hole under a rock just after he'd passed. Immune to stunbeams, like all Qishi fauna—different nervous system. He preferred his knife, anyway. It had proved its worth over two millennia. But he hadn't wanted to risk tackling this thing unless there was no choice, so he'd scooted instead. What danger was one slow-moving animal, anyway? *Best to take refuge and wait. Doubt it can climb a tree.*

The snorcupine was about four metres long, half a metre thick. Long spines slanted away from what he presumed was the head end towards the other one, which logically must be the tail, although he could see no eyes or other sensory orifices. Every half metre there was a double ring of thicker spikes. It moved through a series of pulses, flowing along its ungainly body from what he assumed was back to front. That was extra evidence, most animal gait-waves travelled in that direction. Or so Marco had once told him, and then gone on to explain the mathematical engineering principles —

Then the snorcupine had broken in half at one of the rings, and each half had disgorged a complete, slightly smaller, snorcupine. And then another. Seconds later, it had broken again at another ring, and another snorcupine had joined the party. Meanwhile the newcomer was performing a similar act of self-disassembly and apparent parthenogenesis. Soon there were over fifty of the animals, and some that had broken apart were reassembling themselves. Nice to see a syntelic symbiont re-establishing so fast, but at this point he'd called in help.

Good job I did. Sam looked down on a very disturbing spectacle. It *was* the head end, assuming that a newly gaping mouth implied a head. The mouth opened like a sphincter, expanding from a tight ring of muscle to a gaping circular hole. Ringed with several rows of sharp triangular teeth of a typical Qishi golden hue, dripping dark green fluid. *Poison?* Sam hoped he wouldn't get the opportunity to find out. If it was poison, it would have evolved for Qishi physiology, but even then it was unlikely to be good news for his own. Not when Qish's animals had cadmium in their blood.

Then the whistling started, interminable high squeals punctuated by occasional low-pitched moans. As if responding to instructions, the snorcupines surrounded the base of the tree. *I should have run when I had the chance. Too late now.* Sam watched them going round and round below him, mouths raised, opening and closing. After a few minutes, they began to pile on top of each other, creating a mound of spiny flesh that slowly gained in height. Sam's first instinct was to climb higher, but the tree's tangled rigging made it difficult, and the succulent tubes that functioned as branches had only enough stiffness to keep themselves straight against the ropes' inward pull. The one he was standing on already sagged and swayed alarmingly.

He reported these events coolly through the falasynte, keeping to the bare facts. There was no point in shouting or screaming, the people at the other end were doing what they could. It was his own fault for travelling alone, really, but he liked the freedom. And the excitement. A lot better than *k*-field math.

How many snorcupines can one man kill with just a knife? He might find out.

A new, extremely loud whistle nearly made him lose his grip on the tree. *Not more of the things, surely? What was happening to the backup?*

More loud whistles, and now the pile of snorcupines was dispersing, moving away from the tree. The large ones were splitting apart and gobbling up the smaller ones—well, it looked like gobbling up, but it was clearly some sort of syntelic-symbiont connection, back to the den or hive or nest or wherever these creatures made their home. Soon there was one, which wriggled away into the forest, trailing slime.

A figure emerged from the undergrowth, looked up, and grinned. "You can come down now, sab! Matroshkings won't come back." It was a young woman in a short tunic, carrying a bow and a quiver full of arrows. Her Kalingo was fluent, but accented. Sam gave her a wave, and slid to the ground.

"Samuel Grey Deer Wasumi, sabi," he announced, with a big, friendly smile.

The woman seemed unperturbed to meet one who boasted four names. That kind of thing clearly carried little weight out in the wilderness of the Orange Archipelago. "Nokomis the Descenter, sab." No smile.

Sam's mind suddenly flipped to a vision of his grandmother, back on Wounded Knee, reciting an interminable poem. He'd been seven. She'd mainly read it to show him how the White Man failed to understand the Red Man (she used those terms, that was the point) even when he tried. But the lesson had backfired, because Sam had been at just the right age to love the repetitive rhythms, whatever the words said. Struggling to translate into Kalingo, he said, "From the full moon fell Nokomis, she a wife, but not a mother."

Nokomis stared at him, eyes wide. "Neither wife nor mother, sab. But they say I was named for one who fell from the Moon, a thousand years ago."

"Nar," said Sam. "Not the Moon. The stars. And it was closer to two thousand. Somehow your Descenter history got tangled up with Longfellow."

"You speak a word I do not know."

"An ancient poet."

"Ah." She lowered her eyes modestly. "As you wish, sab. But—"

"But?"

"You did yourself say 'Moon'." *Was that a flicker of a smile?*

Sam sent a quick report back to base, and set off for the lake, Nokomis a few paces behind. He retrieved his backpack, which seemed undamaged.

"Thank you for rescuing me, Nokomis."

"No need, sab. Mayor of Wimble sent me. Family friend. Short walk. Just needed to bring a goaway-whistle, soon see those stupid creatures off. You're very tall. Funny hair, looks like a *skiril*'s tail. Those clothes don't come from anywhere round here, where'd you get them? You new? Just moved in? Don't know where it's safe to walk, that's for sure. You're lucky we've just restored our speaking discs, otherwise Phrill couldn't have told me you were in trouble." She looked at his belt. "Impressive knife, where'd you get that? I'd like one of those."

Sam was utterly charmed. A lady after his own heart. Attractive, too, in a rustic sort of way.

"Long story," he said. "Family heirloom."

"Family? That's good. Where you from? Where your family from? What brought you to Loryx?"

Sam wriggled out of his backpack, undid the molecular zip—to Nokomis's fascination and another barrage of questions—and pulled out a cloth-wrapped cylinder inside a waterproof cover. He unwrapped and unrolled it to reveal a damp lilypad synte. He checked its painted serial number, spoke a few words into his falasynte, and waited. Within a few minutes, a routine synte cascade culminated in an oriel. He poked the cascaded syntei back through the oriel, for re-use, and handed the oriel to Nokomis.

"This."

"Oh!" A broad grin lit up her face. "You're bringing us syntei? It was terrible when they all died. Do you know why they died? We couldn't export our berries or hides. Things are only just starting to get back to normal. How long—?"

"This will help," said Sam. "It's long-distance. As more supplies of syntei come in from Nazg, we'll be able—"

"Nazg? What is Nazg?"

"Uh. It's… it's another world, Nokomis."

Her grin intensified. "Yar, know about those. Descenter, yar? All people of Qish came from the stars in a big seevee. Every Descenter child know that."

Sam hadn't expected it to be that easy. Or free of questions. Now he remembered the Church of the Undivided Body banging on about Descenters. A breakaway sect, tolerated despite unorthodox doctrine, but disliked and discriminated against. The Church was dead, now, its head cut off, but relics of its beliefs and sects would hang on for generations. The wonderful thing about Descenter religion was: it was *true*.

"Well, Nokomis: Nazg is helping Qish get back on its feet. Breeding and sending new syntei. I'm helping." He rolled up the lilysynte, rewrapped it, and put it back in his pack. "I'm carrying a lot of kasyntei. Their kantasyntei are far away, in Shaaluy mostly. But once I establish a link, other syntei can come through. So can food or whatever else is in short supply. Medical help, too, if anyone is injured or ill."

The grin had vanished, and she made a curious gesture, as if batting at an annoying insect. "Shaaluy? Speak not that name here!" She shrank back, ready to run.

Oooh, bone-hammers. Had the Church's tentacles reached even here? "I'm not from the Church, Nokomis. You must have heard, the Church of the Undivided Body is no more. It has no power over you now." She hesitated. "Do I look like an acolyte of the Church? A priest? A quizitor?"

She ducked her head. "Nar. You look like a friend. Nice face, not hard and accusing. You know, I've just remembered, my stepfather told me about wild tales of men from the—" She stepped closer, and looked up at his face, then at his hands. "You're tall. Your skin is brown. You have no beard. Are you a starman?"

"Yah—I mean, yar."

"Can you speak star-tongue?"

Galaxic? It had sounded like "pig laxative" when he first met a Kalingo speaker. Sam thought English would be close enough, and the rhythm was impressive.

> "Downward through the evening twilight,
> In the days that are forgotten,
> In the unremembered ages,
> From the full moon fell Nokomis,
> Fell the beautiful Nokomis,
> She a wife, but not a mother."

Nokomis's irises dilated. "It was you who destroyed the Church?"

Sam shook his head. "Not me, personally. Well, not on my own. Actually, yar, I did play a part—"

Nokomis flung herself at him, wrapped her arms round his neck, and kissed him. Then, as if remembering herself, she knelt at his feet, blushing and embarrassed.

"All Descenters owe you their eternal gratitude, sab," she said in a whisper.

Sam couldn't decide whether Nokomis was naive or perceptive. Both, probably. Cute, definitely. He extended a hand and pulled her to her feet. "Up! You owe us nothing, Nokomis. But I owe you my life. I would like to meet your people, to thank them. And to see what I can do to help."

Nokomis grinned, grabbed his hand, and pulled him after her along the path. Mentally, Sam flagged a new action: *An oriel is too small. Make sure Loryx gets a* wyzand *to Shaaluy; top priority.*

$$\text{-}\mathcal{Y} \qquad \mathcal{F}$$

I hope no one's told Tinka about the snorcupines, Sam thought fervently, as he hurried through the passageways of Two Mountains in search of Sadruddin, busily running the world.

He turned a corner. "Oh, hello, Tinka."

"Gus told me you were on your way back. Next time, keep an oriel with you to escape, dah?"

"Dah."

Tinka gave him a look that could curdle cream before it left the cow; then shrugged. "Samuel Grey Deer Wasumi, I can't play lover *and* mother at the same time, and I'm fed up playing mother, dah? You want to get yourself killed, I can't stop you, and from now on I'm not even going to try. I give up. I'll cry at your funeral, and I'll miss you like crazy, you damfool coot, but I can't do anything about that."

This was worse than being chewed out. Sam took her hand. "Tinka, I'm a changed man. From now on, caution will be—"

"The last thing that crosses your mind. I don't want miracles, Sam. Just a bit more common sense. Don't tell me you'll change, you can't. Just... *tweak* things a little, dah?"

Augustine Tambiah Sadruddin poked his head out of a door ahead and to their right. "Ah, it *is* you. I thought I recognised the voices. Well, do not stand in the corridor arguing: come into my office where you can argue in private."

The room was much tidier than either Sam or Tinka had expected. Clearly Gus was at last starting to get on top of Qish's restoration programme. Not that anyone could have done it faster. Seeing their eyes roving across the room, and the veiled incredulity on their faces, Sadruddin permitted himself a smile.

"Now that I have had time to draw breath, my friends, I have also been able to get more organised. If I learned one useful thing from my time in the Church, it was to be systematic.

"However, we are still fire-fighting. Literally, in the case of Usket, on the end of the Gaunt Salient: the savannahs there are breaking out in brush fires. The stromplunts that watered the region had sprouted again from buried seed, but their fruits hadn't been spread far enough, and now they are burned. The syndepts still have some cultivars, but cannot release them until they have bred more." He hunted around in a cupboard. "Sometimes I think it would have been better not to get myself organised, I cannot find anything any more. Ah, yar, here we are. The syndepts on Nazg have come to our aid; they are sending new plants, bred in quantity in their water-middens."

"Hydroponic gardens."

"Yar, like I said. But the substitutes will not arrive for another week, and cannot be planted until the fires subside. I have squads of guardsmen trying to save the villages; the fields will have to be abandoned to their fate. Only when the fires have died away can we start to sow new seed and set new plants in the ground. It will be fertile, if we can supply enough water. Which we can, eventually, but everything takes time and everything depends on everything else. Every day it is the same. I am forced to set priorities, to weigh the importance of one man's house against the food supplies of a hamlet, the production of wood and metal against the wellbeing of my people. It is hard."

Sam and Tinka stepped close and hugged him. "We know, Gus," said Tinka. "But we also know you wouldn't trust anyone else on Qish to do it."

He sighed. "You speak truth, sabi."

Sam gave him a brief verbal report on his recent comings and goings. "So, Gus: what do you have for me now?"

Sadruddin consulted a sheaf of messages from all over the planet.

"Wyzand-trails are being re-established all along the Nismolion Range on Lamynt, from Smule to Klimstra and down to Woolvayn and Cuveryn on the coast. You could help them develop side-trails—nar, that area is too urban for your tastes, is it not?"

Turning more pages.

"What about the Farthyngs? Island chain north-west of Wevory. Well-named, they're about as isolated as it gets on this world. Sparsely inhabited, rich in birdlife, some of it large and some of it dangerous."

Sam was about to accept, but saw the look on Tinka's face. "Urgent?"

"Nar, very few inhabitants, and they're tough enough to take care of themselves. Just lost contact for now."

"Ah. Anything of higher priority?"

"Thousands, but few would suit you. Ah, this might. Katamalinga, at the tip of a long promontory shaped like a forefinger, top of the Lentzigen Coastal Zone in north-east Samdal."

"Mother," said Tinka. "Why would anyone live there? It's on the far side of the biggest desert on the planet!" As if *far side* meant anything on Qish— but since the simquake, it had. It was not only height that separated places, now.

"Copper mines," said Sadruddin. "All sorts of other minerals scattered across that end of the Disfarne Desert, too. Katamalinga is a trade nexus for the whole area, lightly populated with squabbling miners and inscrutable nomads. At the moment, its syntelic links are totally inadequate. But a week from now, there will be a new consignment of oriels from Nazg, and someone has to go out there and make sure they set them up where they're most needed, and let us know the serial number for each location. If we leave it to them, the syntei will all end up in the town. We need them distributed as widely as possible across the desert, in an optimal arrangement — your wrist-membrancer can work that out, I imagine, Samuel — and we need someone to train the nomads how to look after them. The Nazg plants are a bit different from what these people are used to; less drought-tolerant, so they could easily die unless the nomads follow instructions." He waved the sheaf of documents. "Which, it says here, is not their custom. At all. So someone has to — what do you say —'lie it on the line'."

"Lay. Uh — Any dangerous animals?" Sam asked.

"Aside from the miners and nomads, nar. Just ferocious winds, frequent sandstorms, blazing heat, and a permanent shortage of water."

Tinka glanced at Sam. "Sounds a bit tame," she said. "But I'm sure he'll take it, even so. Won't you, Sam?"

Eelkhance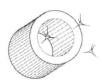

With his customary disregard even for basic protocol, Lawes marched into Tampledown's office without knocking. "I've just thought of something."

The Chief Scientist gave an irritated wave over one shoulder and continued running the latest data on syntelic k-curvature through a structure-recognition algorithm that Lawes had written for him. "You're always thinking of something, Wayne. Can't it wait? I'm busy right—"

"The groupies can dismantle gas giants."

Tampledown stood up, startled. "Perhaps I'm not too busy for that. But it's not a new theory, Wayne. Just a ridiculous old one. Yah, there are traces of hydrogen metal 9 around Rock Star, but that's accounted for by the standard theory."

"In the quantity observed, Artur?"

Tampledown waited as Lawes 'comped the figures across, and broke out in a frown. "That much? I hadn't realised that."

"No one had. Those observations are from a file under restriction, put there by some spook who thought that what you don't admit can't hurt you. There's *way* too much H-9 to have come from a single collision."

Tampledown grunted sceptically. "It's a big step to infer, from an unexplained excess of one elemental form, that the groupies can take planets to pieces, let alone giants. The standard theory explains everything using basic celestial mechanics."

"Want to bet? Oh, yah, it explains everything written up in the literature. Some of it even makes sense."

He reviewed the basic information, ticking it off on his fingers. "Rock Star is a spectral class A, blue giant. Two solar masses, thirty times Sol's luminosity. The asteroids orbit around it now, so the original groupie homeworld must have done the same, as a moon or a planet. Reasonable to assume that its atmosphere was thin, even to begin with, so life evolved that could tolerate low pressures. Groupieworld slowly lost what was left of its atmosphere, giving the inhabitants time to evolve tolerance to vacuum. Makes sense."

"Dah. So go away, please, Wayne; I'm kind of busy right now."

"Artur, don't you see? *This is important.* It's not just the groupies, the problem is the whole crazy star system. Any plausible theory has to explain *both.* Each is easy on its own, but they interact. Dah, a planet broke up. *Why?*"

Tampledown spread his hands in a dismissive gesture. "Lots of possibilities, Wayne. Let me see... As I recall, the astronomers decided that the most likely culprit was a rogue giant from outside the system. Dropped in on a hyperbolic orbit, smashed into one of the existing planets at humongous speed, and all hell broke loose. The pieces got scattered all over the system and knock-on effects broke up everything else. By then the groupies could live in empty space, powered by rocks or radiation or whatever, so enough of them survived the disaster to keep their *species* — no, *kind*, they don't segregate into species — going. That explains the chaotic orbits of the asteroids, it gives time for suitable life forms to evolve, it fits the star's temperature profile."

Lawes shrugged. "Yah, nice theory. Makes sense."

Tampledown glared at him. "If it all makes sense, Wayne, why do you think the groupies took their own planet to pieces?"

"I didn't say that. I said *planets.* But, yah, that's exactly what they did. Then they went hunting bigger game."

"You're very clever Wayne, I know that. But this sounds like pure fantasy. Why do you imagine that?"

"H-9."

"Must have come from the impactor," said Tampledown immediately.

"*Must* have? What's the evidence?"

"It's the obvious source."

Lawes ruffled his bonsai haircut. "Did anyone check out the sink?" When Tampledown looked baffled he added, "I mean, ask where the H-9 would go, as well as where it might have come from?"

"No idea," said Tampledown.

"I didn't either, so I checked. No published simulations of the hypothetical breakup follow the food-trail. Uh — the distribution patterns of the elemental composition of impactor and impactee. So I wrote my own. In ninety-nine impacts out of a hundred that are consistent with the asteroids' angular momentum, where do you think nearly all the H-9 ends up?"

"No idea."

"In the mothertrashed star! A single collision had to leave a big core, which is where the H-9 was, so if there isn't a big rock now, it must have gone into the star. But it didn't, because there's all that H-9 left, in the small rocks. Contradiction."

He paused. "And that's not all. The standard story, my dear Artur, has a very big hole in it. I had a hunch it was all a bit too pat, and I was right. I have new evidence. I've been simulating the system in reverse time, trying to explain the orbits. Yah, yah, we know the groupies throw themselves around to prevent collisions, but that doesn't greatly change the large-scale dynamic effects—and some of those don't agree with the single-collision theory. Statistics of the mass/radius distribution, that sort of thing.

"The past history that gives the closest fit to present-day conditions, taking groupie collision-avoidance into account, has no impactor. Instead, there were once *five* planets. A close rocky pair in orbit around each other as well as the star, another orbiting alone, and two gas giants. First one of the pair— the groupies' home—lost atmosphere. Then it approached the other too closely and broke up. The groupies survived, and found they had much more room, so they steered the remaining small planets together: one had a pretty crazy orbit, after the breakup (I would too) so engineering a collision took nothing more energetic than clever tweaking. The collision smashed them. Then they got ambitious, and went after the gas giants. They used near contacts with the fragments of the small planets to tweak, and tweak, and tweak, to get the gas giants close enough to rip pieces from each other—and then do it again. It took the groupies about 78,000 years to dismantle them completely, but what's time when you're having fun?"

Tampledown had to admire the panache. Lawes enjoyed being three steps ahead of him. And the groupies' relaxed attitude to time was established fact. This was going to set the *skiti* among the SS pigeons, big time. "If there wasn't an impactor, but there were indigenous gas giants, I can understand why you think it was the groupies that wrecked them."

"Glad you're starting to see this my way. Of course I'm right! The two gas giants were originally in resonant orbits that kept them separate. They *couldn't* collide. They were well outside the Roche limit, too. So it has to be the groupies!" Lawes slapped the floor in emphasis, and Tampledown flinched. "They broke up their own planet's twin and the lone planet, to get more living space. They spread themselves all over its fragments and the asteroids, and ran out of *stuff*. They took a look at their gas giants, and saw them as a massive waste of material. Just as we look at Jupiter and think 'Dyson sphere', only we don't have the technology to build one. Neither do the groupies, but their natural tendency is to break worlds up, not build something bigger. I reckon they just did what came naturally, and used their grasp of chaotic dynamics to tweak millions of asteroid orbits until they managed to nudge two vast planets (and the moon of one) into repeated near-collision—full on could have merged them into a bigger planet, with only crumbs for the groupies—breaking them into a lot more in the way of liveable rocks."

As Lawes got his breath back, Tampledown exhaled, long and slow. "Wayne, if you're right, this puts a whole new complexion on everything. It raises the groupie threat to a level I wouldn't care to quantify."

"Don't I know it."

"On the other hand, if we pass this on to higher authority, and you're wrong, we can both kiss our careers goodbye."

"Yah. Vance will hang us out to dry."

"So I need to see *all* your evidence, in detail."

"On its way," said Lawes. "You'll see straight away that in backward time, smoothed with a Kulatillikaratne filter to model groupie collision-avoidance, about 82% of the mass in the system today concentrates in two narrow bands."

"You think those are the gas giant orbits?"

"I know they are. It's not just the mass, it's the distribution of elements and molecular species. Look at *this* simulation…"

Dool

Marcolette and Polonia:

Dad's Magneto-Gravito-Karmabhumic Unified Field Theory

$$\mho\{\Omega\} = \Theta^{\cdot\cdot}$$
$$\mho\{\Theta\} = -\Omega^{\cdot\cdot}$$

was all very well—OK, it was brilliant, Dad *are* brilliant—and it accounted for how syntei worked and grew. Once formed, and separated. But it was still a mystery how a plant *created* a synte. The gengineers bred more stable syntei, more flexible syntei, faster growing syntei, but biological syntei still need time to grow.

The Qish rebuilding effort didn't *have* time.

We needed synthetic syntelics—synthelics—for an industrial scale refactoring.

Maybe it needed us to be from a syntelic womb, wrapped around each other, in the presence of one of Dad's weird mind. Maybe that had nothing to do with it. But we found a way.

We didn't duplicate what the plants do (that works at room temperature; we had to keep close to liquid helium temperatures), and we still don't *know* exactly what the plants do. But here's the recipe (metamaterial chemistry is much more like a mix of cooking and geometry than physics).

First you create two tiny toroids, a few Ångstroms across, in two polar opposite metamaterials. Apply a string field to weaken the restriction to three dimensions at this scale (normally, since the Big Bang, the restriction relaxes only at much finer scales). Bring the toroids *very* cautiously together, with laser tweezers.

The toroids want to touch each other all over, because they're opposite polarities all over. They can't, without the string field. They're not even linked like chain segments. But they *desperately* want to, and the string field is like a lube that lets them do it. They come together all over to form a 3-sphere (like the surface of a ball in four dimensions, only there's no ball there). Reduce the string field slowly, and they snap back into ordinary spacetime as two separate toroids... but not really separate, because they're joined by a synte. (In about the year dot Gagarin it was called a 'handle-body', but the ancient topologists never saw one in these dimensions.) Warm slowly, and feed with new metamaterial, and they grow like bubbles fed soap solution. Kasynthe and kantasynthe!

Once we knew what we were looking for, we found similar toroids in the single-celled zygotic embryos of syntelic plants, and we could separate them from the surrounding structures: harvest them, potentially by the million. Then change their size, and even their metamaterial composition, much faster than plants could. Salim Synthelics took it to industrial scale.

Dad were so proud they'd been outshone by the fruit of their (borrowed) womb, he practically glowed. Well, only one of him had borrowed it, and there was only one to borrow—Qish didn't have Galactic conveniences like synthetic wombs—so only one *could* have had the stretch marks, even if the other had been there. But they both so totally identified with it, the marks made no difference. Dad are the best there are.

Nazg

"We can't just *give away* synthelic technology!"

"We can't *own* syntelics," Marco told the CFO, his voice echoing in the huge office. "Haven't you heard? It grows on trees. The ultimate open source. Synthelics is a natural extension."

"Marco's right," said Fatima. "We got first mover advantage in the galactic markets, and that's as much as we hoped for. We're doing very well. Besides, one company can't own the politics of it."

"The politics?" said the CFO, surprised.

Fatima, squatting comfortably next to him, patted him on the arm. "The Concordat sanctions are on *planets* that use syntei, not companies, Maxwell. We can't ask a planet to defend Salim Sisters: it has to be defending its own choice. Salim Sisters can stand with that choice, but not commit the planet."

The CFO still looked puzzled; politics wasn't in his comfort-zone. He left setting policy to the Board; his job was to make sure the company could afford it, whatever it was. He had his own private views, of course, but he never let those affect business decisions.

"I'm sure Hippolyta will choose to stand with syntei," said Elza, "they're economically important already. And there are people who think the fun uses are scandalous, but... I sold a large batch of toys to the royal household."

"All twenty-three planets of the Nazg system will go along with that too, for sure," said the CFO. He turned to look at Marco. "What about Dante?"

"Inferno won't let go of syntei," said Marco. "The possibilities alone are endless. They'll carry the rest of Dante. Stibbons, too, and Courant. Just too technically exciting."

"There's Squamish, obviously, and Bluepeace: they've taken to syntei so enthusiastically, they'd never get their original body configurations back," said Tinka.

"And first and foremost, Qish," said Marco. "The wild syntelics are already growing back. Qish doesn't have the option of complying with the Concordat."

"And a lot of others," said Fatima, rising gracefully to her feet, closing the meeting. "Kwame, please sort out the full list, and arrange that every planet on it has multiple syntei with every other system where it's gravitationally possible. At least falasyntei, preferably wyzands too, even if they only match intermittently. Send our branch on Old Earth the code to unlock the seals on the interstellar falasyntei there. We don't want to lose contact when the Concordat cuts off the Da Silva communicators."

"You think they'll go that far?" asked Kwame.

"I don't think they'll stop there."

Starhome

"We have to isolate them," said Philomena Vance. "Cut out this cancer on the Concordat now."

"We can't cut them off from each other," said the Chair. It was a private meeting, so private that it hadn't even been noted in the records. All recording devices were off, the room was secure. Officially, this wasn't happening, had never happened.

"We can cut them off from the uncontaminated, and those that return to their senses," Vance replied. She'd grown into her new role as one of the major players. And she was learning to use that influence to achieve her long-standing goal of keeping Starhome safe from well-intentioned do-gooders. "And we can teach them what being cut off means."

"Not just turning off their Da Silvas?" the Chair said, a note of doubt creeping in.

"They'll expect us to give in to their stubbornness," said Vance, "and just as easily turn them on again." She leaned closer, fixing the Chair with her gaze. She looked earnest and determined. "Circumstances have changed. They need an object lesson."

The Chair stared at her, impressed yet slightly appalled. "And what kind of lesson do you have in mind, citizen Vance?"

"Stibbons has just one Beanstalk."

Nazg

"They cut it at the base with a tactical nuke," reported Kwame. "Only seven hundred people died, but the Beanstalk went sailing away into space. Stibbons is not only cut off from interstellar trade and communication, but from all their in-system habitats and factories."

Fatima looked at him. "Shuttles?"

"Five, in the whole system. Economically irrelevant. It will take ten years to rebuild the Beanstalk."

"Either the Concordat breaks us one by one," said Fatima, "or we stand together for mutual defence."

"You mean, we help them rebuild?" Kwame asked.

"Yah. But more, much more. It can't stop there. We have to make sure nothing like this ever happens again, and I see only one way to achieve that. We collectively secede from the Concordat, and form an independent Syntelic League."

You didn't have to be terribly bright to understand the implications. Kwame took a deep breath, held it for a moment, then exhaled loudly. "We won't have Starhome as an administrative centre any more. Nazg?"

Fatima waved a hand dismissively. "Nazg is economically too powerful already, Kwame. Who would trust us with political power as well? Ask yourself, what planet has the strongest defences?"

Kwame was baffled. "Nobody has established interplanetary patrols like ours."

But Fatima had a very different idea. "We can *probably* stop attackers from getting through, yah. What planet can Da Silva craft not even risk getting near?"

"I don't see what you mean... oh. Qish."

Fatima nodded, three times, slowly. "Right. The ecology and economics is still a wreck, but they already have billions of newly budded wild syntei. The

Da Silva window has slammed shut again. And they have no high tech points of attack."

"And we already send people there to study syntei and learn from the syndepts."

"Yah, what better for the centre of the Syntelic League? Plus something else they have, that we don't."

Kwame realised he must seem very slow today. "What do you mean?"

"Generals," said Fatima. "Officers who have fought wars, for real. It's easier for smart generals to learn new tech, than for technocrats to learn the art of war. There are plenty of idiots in any army, but we can filter out those by crash courses and war games with spacecraft. Those who can't think on their feet, we sideline."

"You really think it will come to fighting a *war*?" Kwame protested. He couldn't conceal his shock.

"What else was their attack, Kwame?" She straightened her legs and stood up. "Enough talking. I want a Declaration of Independence on my wristcomp by morning—tyranny of denying syntei to the people, murder, terror and economic warfare in destroying the Stibbons Beanstalk, contrasted with life, liberty and the cultivation of happiness. Get Marco to sell it to the Qishites. And a draft Constitution, as an interim to work with until a constitutional convention can get to work, probably after the war. Say, a Central Committee with one senex from each planet, that picks a Boss Frog with the power to cut short arguments."

Her reasoning struck home. "I'm on it," said Kwame. "I and my secretarial AI can frame a couple of inspiring documents." He started towards the doorway, then stopped and turned. "Just one other thing… There is one *other* planet with syntei, plus experience in fighting wars."

It was Fatima's turn not to follow. "There is? I can't have missed—oh. Oh."

"Yah. Old Earth."

Starhome

"I did wonder whether that might happen," said the Chair. "It was always a risky strategy."

"We all agreed it," Admiral Buchanan said pointedly. "Police action to prevent secession." He clearly wasn't going to be saddled with responsibility for the outrage of so many Concordat worlds at the attack on Stibbons.

"That's one word for it," said the Governor. "On the grid a lot of citizens are calling it an unprovoked attack, contrary to the Concordat's historical views on political freedom and self-determination. It's a loosely-knit federation, not a Starhome fiefdom—"

"You're just worried because the economy is falling through the floor," Phuntsok Yoko muttered darkly. By the look on her face, she was worried about the same thing, possibly because her own department, Internal Affairs, was also having to deal with the consequences. "It was crazy to mount a punitive strike against one of our trading partners. Especially one so irreversible. It'll take decades for Stibbons to recover from the loss of its only Beanstalk."

"Yoko: we all *agreed*—"

"The main problem," the SS Director interrupted, equally concerned not to shoulder the blame, "is how quickly the diplomatic damage spread, and the sheer number of worlds affected."

"Infected," said Goolagong. "A virulent memeplex."

"Whatever. Our analysts' projections—"

"Were projecting where the sun doesn't shine, Director. I can't understand how you got it all so wrong. It should have been obvious that escalating the dispute to preemptive punitive action on that sort of scale was likely to backfire."

"With hindsight, Marvin, yah."

"Some of us were counselling caution *before* the attack was authorised, remember? That's not hindsight, it's fore—"

"If you care to consult your 'comp's records, citizen Goolagong," the Admiral said in an irritated voice, "you'll find that we did consider the likely repercussions. Starhome Security predicted correctly that many of the worlds that have started to use syntei would initially side with Stibbons."

"Hippolyta. Acmonia. Astrophel. Bluepeace. Courant. Dante. Devil Take the Hindmost. And a lot that *haven't* started to use syntei. Erra Pater. Finchley Central. Frenzy. Gazni. Hellespont—"

"Point made, Chair. But a lot of that is bluster. They'll quickly come back into the fold because they won't want to risk economic ties with Starhome. They depend on us for a wide range of goods and services."

"Yah, but we depend on *them*," the Governor of the Financial Authority pointed out. "And so far they haven't come back. There's a dozen more on the brink of joining them. We didn't predict that a lot of other worlds would start to wonder who else might be in the firing-line when Starhome abandoned negotiation in favour of 'police action', a euphemism for the use of force to make a recalcitrant world toe the line. Are you *surprised* they're scared, angry, disillusioned? Wanting out?"

"Stibbons went too far."

"We think so, Admiral. But a lot of other worlds, outside the League, don't see it that way. Doesn't matter whether they're right or wrong—it's the perception that counts."

"We're working on that," said the Director. "Perceptions can be changed."

The Governor gave a sceptical grunt. "Propaganda."

"I call it *replacing* ignorant propaganda by accurate information. What—" the Chair caught his eye and he subsided.

"Information is all very well," said the Chair, "but it takes time to be effective, if it works at all. The immediate issue, I remind you, is where we go from here. Do we escalate, draw back, or maintain the *status quo*?"

"We can't back down," Buchanan stated bluntly. "That would just encourage further disaffected worlds to secede. We're fighting on two fronts now: the League and Ira da Terra. That makes strategy difficult, to say the least. Get it wrong, and next thing you know the Concordat's falling apart and we end up being told what to do by the Syntelic League."

"Goose. Gander. Sauce," said Phuntsok.

"You *approve* of secession, Yoko?"

"Nah, they stepped over the line. But abstractly, from their point of view, I can understand why. Seems to me, we went completely over the top. A trade embargo would have been sufficient."

"We discussed that. Too slow, too easily evaded now the League has syn-thei. Especially when *we don't*."

Yoko shrugged. "All the more reason for starting out with kid gloves. We always had the option to take them off later."

"Nah, they needed an object lesson. A harsh one—"

"I agree with Yoko," said the Governor. "The projected economic impact of losing access to synthei is serious—"

"I repeat," said the Chair, "the issue is *where we go from here*. We can do the breast-beating post-mortem routine later. I take it we're now agreed that collapsing *another* League world's Beanstalk would be counterproductive?"

As heads nodded, the Admiral raised a finger. "With respect, Chair, it's worse than that. We've tipped our hand. Next time they'll see us coming. They have a significant defence in place already, one that stops us approaching with Da Silvas."

Heads nodded again. "Synthei," said Tampledown. He made it sound like a curse.

"We had enough trouble getting forces in place to bring down the Stibbons Beanstalk," Buchanan reminded them. "From now on that's going to get more difficult. They can assemble more synthei, for a start. They can make themselves unreachable by Da Silva. They're doing that. On the other hand, we've activated the back door to interdict their Da Silvas—communicators as well as drives, am I right?" Vance nodded. "So they can't reach *us*. It's the old story of the conflict of elephant and whale, who can't reach each other."

"It seems to me," said the Governor, "that the key to this difficulty is the source of this new technology."

"Qish? There's absolutely no way we can even get close to Qish. It lost its syntei in the simquake, but already a lot have come back. And now they're importing synthei syntelically, to speed up the reconstruction."

The Governor leaned back, taking care not to overbalance, and stared at her. "Indeed they are. From Nazg."

"Dah. You mean Salim Sisters?"

"Of course I mean Salim Sisters! You think I was referring to *Daisy and the Unicorn*?"

"Popular though that particular holvix series is with pre-schoolers, Governor, it hadn't actually crossed my mind."

"Not a long journey—"

"*Citizens!*"

"Sorry, Chair. We're all a bit overwrought." The Governor cleared her throat to regroup and buy time. "As I was saying, yah, Salim Sisters. It has a near-monopoly on synthelics. Even Qish is reliant on that. I was wondering if we could find some way to change it. Rid ourselves of a major irritant, put Qish under pressure, squeeze the League's infrastructure…" She exchanged a significant glance with the Admiral.

"Nazg will be heavily defended compared to most League worlds," Buchanan said. "Salim Sisters makes computers, robots, aircraft, spacecraft, shuttles, carriers, corvettes, battleships, maulers, weapons—"

"Yah. But the other systems are puny. Qish may be the political core of the League, but Nazg is its power-centre. The synergetic effects of twenty-three worlds in the same system are immense. If we could invade Nazg, seize the manufacturing equipment—"

"Doubly difficult," said Buchanan. He held up a hand to silence them while he interrogated his 'comp. "Anticipating this suggestion, I've drawn up some contingency analyses. Yah, as I remembered.

"There is space enough between the Nazg planets that we could penetrate with Da Silva craft, but within that space they have syntelic drives: we have to carry all our reaction mass. The likelihood that we could take over Salim Sisters' manufactories, undamaged, is so slim that if it stood sideways it'd be invisible. They'll have autodestructs in place, and to capture them we'd need to slow down. But there might be a way to put the planets under so much pressure with fast robotic torpedoes that the manufactories are forced to self-destruct, and that will cut off the flow of synthelics to the League. That buys us time, lots of it. If we can push the invasion through we can even rebuild the manufactories, eventually. I'm sure enough Nazg technicians would be… *persuadable*."

The Chair mulled this idea over. "It does have one political advantage, Admiral. Any destruction that occurs can be portrayed as the actions of Nazg saboteurs, trying to escape responsibility for illegal actions. Our hands will be clean."

"Or, at least, be seen to be clean," the Director said. "Got my vote."

Qish

Sadruddin, Sam thought, *has worked miracles. So why do I feel so... disappointed?*

He was back at Hardane, another place where he had been arrested (for something Marco had done, at Two Mountains). Some things had improved. The widow Kolata had made peace with the two townswomen Tinka had noticed: not so much polygamy, for the doctor, as being their common property. Dag Riveroak looked even more harried than at their previous meeting, and spent a lot of time on his talking disc, learning Galactic medicine from the Felix Wylde Memorial School of Medicine.

"The main thing we face, apart from accidents, syntelic parasites, and poisons from Qishi life, is diseases of imbalance." It was odd to hear fluent Galaxic from someone still in the traditional dress of beaded loincloth and feathers. "Diabetes, asthma, paranoid schizophrenia." Infectious disease was still a scourge of Old Earth, but it had been left there: wound infections were from healthy gut bacteria, in the wrong place.

"I would have had diabetes myself," said Sam, "it still crops up. But they headed it off when I was just two years old."

"I learned about that," said Dag. "We will start to do that here, soon. But our immediate problem is with full-blown disease, and for that, Galactic medicine can only offer crutches: prosthetic devices that inject stuff. Implants for dialysis are a forgotten technology, and they always needed resupply, and draining waste. External devices are much easier."

"But surely they're cumbersome, and tricky to clean... Oh." Sam stopped himself.

"Exactly," confirmed the doctor.

"But what about height differences?" Sam asked. "People can't always stay at the level of the devices."

"Come and look at the syntower." Syntowers dominated any city in a plain, giving access to higher levels and thus to higher places far away. Syntwells, usually in their basements, did the same for lower levels. This one now had a shining tube of synthetic crystal from top to bottom and descending into the earth.

"Engineers from Salim Sisters built this for me, as a pilot project." Small medical looking robots were crawling up and down. "They sense unequal levels between kasyntei and kasyntei, and adjust the one here to match the implants. They resupply when they have to, enough of the time they're available for instant response to glucose levels and so on."

"But they can only handle height difference up to the top of the syntower?"

"And the bottom of the syntwell. That's enough for nine out of ten people living in Hardane. For travellers, we're putting a four-kilometre hole in Two Mountains. Then the White Ramparts."

"Magnificent!" Sam meant it. "You're a benefactor of humanity."

"Well, I hope so," said the doctor, "but I didn't spot the downside."

"Medical side effects?"

"Not medical… but the moneylenders have copied the idea, in a simpler form. Now for collateral they can sequester a finger, an internal organ, a scrotum,… it's safely alive, connected to your blood supply at the same level, but they keep it. Pay the interest on time, or they break the synte."

Sam was silent.

He had gone back partly out of sentiment. Take a look at the old place. See what had changed, with all the changes on Qish.

The hostel was a change, too. Only a few years ago, a traveller arriving in the town would be taken in by one of the households and treated like one of the family. Or, if the occasion merited it, sent packing with a very clear message not to return.

Now, someone was running a business.

Every house, not just the temple, was now lit at night by sunlight. The light was synted from the Owl Islands (courtesy of a lighting labyrinth that Sam had helped set up), without the old fear of the syntei being abused as falasyntei by heretics. Everyone was a heretic now, and their rites were diverse, imaginative, and strange.

Back then, the people of Hardane had been subdued and frustrated, firmly under the thumb of the local priest in the temple with the braided circle over the door, terrified of being accused of the Church's greatest sin, body-division. Any use of syntei that appeared to split off parts of the human body, with emphasis on the sexual organs, meant maiming or death by bone-hammers, bone by broken bone. Official spies were everywhere, even in Hardane's melancholy brothel, run by the Church to keep sex from straying into sin.

Now, the townsfolk celebrated market days with a body dividing party. Sam had enjoyed group sex back in the Concordat, but not to know which body part was part of which body, he found... unsettling. The equipment was supplied by shadow figures, ultimately controlled — it was rumoured — by newly resurgent remnants of the Vain Vaimoksi, the slaver organisation burned by the *Valkyrie* crew. When it came to sexploitation and moneylending at ruinous rates, the VV had form, sometimes aided and abetted by Wevorin infiltrators. In fact, Sadruddin maintained the orgies were more likely run from Wevory, because the cavern-dwellers were seeking to regain influence while they restored the caverns to their previous splendour and rebuilt their network of spysyntei. And as a former Wevorin agent, Sadruddin should know.

The town's exports of rhomney wool had been stopped by the simquake, and its people had eaten much of the flock to make up for the lost imports of barley and wheat, but they had continued to spin, weave, and stockpile cloth. With the Nazg syntei in place, they had resumed shipping it — even off planet, where their block-printed designs were expertly marketed by Salim Sisters. They had discovered Galactic fluorescent colours. To their surprise, the Nazg market preferred Hardane's traditional vegetable dyes, but the locals were now clad in colours so bright it was hard to make out their faces.

Music had changed too, although ears were not yet attuned to Galactic sounds. Qishi music had always been a communal thing, made live by people who had known each other since birth — even if their community spread across the planet. The talking discs had made music planetary. A group of musicians in No Way Back, to the north of Lamynt's Dunelands where there wasn't much in the way of local entertainment, had acquired a Qish-wide reputation, and tens of thousands of teenagers spent much of the day listening to music from another continent. With a talking disc hung on one ear, they paid insufficient attention to their surroundings, and at least one had been fatally attacked by land-piranhas because he was distracted by some real cool drumming.

Once, the temple light had been the only intercontinental synte in Hardane. This aimed to keep the town people's minds free of heretical thoughts, such as doubt of the Church's authority. Now, Salim Sisters' switchable communications network was re-establishing saturation coverage, without boundaries. News spread like wildfire, from continent to continent, city to village, farmstead to town; from relative to friend, to acquaintance, to… well, *anybody*. So enamoured were the villagers of their newfound ability to communicate, at any time and to any place, that they tended to hold interminable conversations with friends, relatives, or lovers, or just bone up on the latest gossip, when they should have been concentrating on their traditional duties, such as growing food and keeping vermin out of the storage barns.

And some very odd ideas were spreading, among people who had had no practice in sorting truth from invention.

We've stirred up all kinds of shit, Sam thought. *We had to, after the deadly peril of the simquake, but we saved the shit along with the rest, and broke it open.*

Suddenly Sam was tired of it all. He'd thrown himself into the reconnection of Qish, helped to orchestrate its reabsorption into the Concordat and then the Syntelic League, and now… he couldn't help wondering if it would have been better to have left that primitive but resourceful world to forge its own destiny. He was tired of towns and shops, soldiers and circuses, of technology and wealth and greed. He was tired of interstellar politics, corporate lobbying, and pressure-groups; of self-interest barely clothed as benevolence.

He was tired, period.

He yearned for woodlands and lakes and open spaces, far from the madding crowd, immune to dingbeaucratic interference. Somewhere he could be himself, somewhere he could breathe.

His hand unconsciously reached for the hilt of the knife at his belt. Yah. Somewhere he could emulate his Iroquois ancestors.

An image formed in his mind. A sort-of tree; a young woman with bow and arrows. Nice smile, cute; simple lifestyle; a region of Qish that was virtually untouched, partly because Descenters were fiercely resistant to outside ideas.

Another image: Irenotincala Laurel, long-term lover and almost inseparable companion. They'd saved each others' lives, more than once. But lately, the relationship had been cooling. They'd always be friends, but neither owned the other… He'd talk to her, and explain. Tinka would understand, as she had done before. Starfolk relationships were flexible. That was their strength, they bent instead of breaking.

Time to bend.

He rose to his feet, a burden suddenly lifted.

It will be good to walk the woods of Loryx again, before they, too, disappear forever.

Sri Lanka Beanstalk, Old Earth

Mesi Dubaku felt curiously serene as she ascended the Beanstalk, from the final security check, a thousand kilometres above the Earth. The security officers were like all the other Concordat people she had met, offended at dealing with Earthies ('Dirties' behind their backs). However, in the brief spurts of training that the psychologists of Ira da Terra could fit into her life without raising flags on her dossier, they had buried Mesi's anger beneath the persona of a peaceful emigrant, eager to begin a new life in the aqua-formed seas of Sahel VIII. There would be many challenges, but not the irresponsible run-off from land industry, cities, and farms. She smiled through the tests and interviews.

She felt a little heavy, in the even upward acceleration. At first it was a mixture of the 'pull' of Earth (strictly, the constant acceleration felt by all its inhabitants to bend her path from going *through* the Earth), and acceleration upward at a tenth of surface gravity. As she rose, the inward 'pull' became less and outward 'centrifugal force' became more, so that acceleration relative to the Beanstalk grew, as the electromagnetic push maintained a sensation of 1.1g. After an hour, well short of geostationary orbit, the cabin went around the famous 'Twirl' to maintain apparent gravity as the acceleration direction smoothly reversed. The outward direction now felt 'down' as they decelerated for the second hour, steadily less, to arrive with a smooth match to the fifth of a gravity at the counterweight beyond. She had chosen the compartment with full virtual windows, so all around her the sky grew black, the stars came out, and the horizon became first a visible curve and then the edge of a dwindling ball below her—and after turnover, directly above. It would shrink to a ball about twenty moon-widths at the counter-weight, still a bright light when it faced the Sun. The other Beanstalks were too thin to see across the thousands of miles, except where lights shone from them.

A faint hiss with no jolt was all the sign that they had arrived, until the door opened and a smiling middle-aged woman came to greet the passengers with a "Welcome, immigrants!" It seemed their status had finally changed.

"You're all for Sahel VIII, right?" Everybody nodded. "It'll be about eighteen hours until we're in the best position to fling a ship to the L2 Da Silva transhipment point. Enjoy the facilities! You can book into a sleeping chamber at the board through that door, and explore. There's holvix, private or public, low-gravity dancing, and a groping pool: if you're not used to the way water behaves in low gravity, better use a breathing mask. Other than that, clothing is not required. You can eat free at any of the mess rooms. My favourite is the Squamish cuisine, but you have lots of choices. If you're uncomfortable in low grav you can go to the revolving section, but I wouldn't recommend it: the trip to L2 is mostly micro-g, and most people find low-g easier to transition from. Are there any questions?"

Somebody asked how long the trip would take: about five hours. The passengers dispersed.

They had searched her for dangerous devices, as they had searched every passenger for more than fifteen hundred years, but the tiny wooden pendant under her shirt passed every inspection. She didn't even think about it, except as a beautiful gift from her grandmother. Its hidden synte would only show up as a Da Silva disturbance close to a drive or communicator, and she was not taking it that far.

Absent-mindedly, in the cleansing room, she hid it behind a pipe. An hour later, under immense pressure from a chamber hidden on a farm in Antarctica, molecules began to diffuse across the gravity-barrier. Environment sensors classed them among the innumerable scents (natural or purchased) given off by human bodies, and they gradually became a trace component of the air throughout the counterweight.

After twelve hours, a nanoclock flipped, and they all became neurotoxic.

Every human on the counterweight died in seconds, save for the two chemically protected in advance. Mesi now recognised the other (he was still standing), and re-awoke to her desire for vengeance. They collected keys from the dead, and explored beyond the public areas. Everyone in Security had died without time to log out, so they were able to quickly set the system to accept no instructions from outside. They disabled the part of the meteor defence that could recognise outside bodies as friendly spaceships, so any-thing approaching was fired on, with devastating force.

Soon, they knew that the simultaneous attacks on the other two Bean-stalks had gone equally smoothly. Helmut Moser's bio-laboratories had done their job. The attackers on Earth's ground and sea governments had suffered more casualties, but synted past the defenders, they were now everywhere in control.

Ira da Terra was mistress of Old Earth.

Starhome

"Old Earth seized the *Beanstalks*?"

"Not Old Earth, Marvin. Ira da Terra—but now they *are* the planetary government, which Old Earth never had before."

"Why? They can't actually go anywhere. It's a futile gesture. They might just as well have stayed in the dirt."

"Nah, now they can stop *us* going there. And control what goes in and out," said Phuntsok Yoko.

"To what purpose?"

"They seized the Beanstalks *in order* to become the planetary government," the Chair said. "That seems obvious."

"Yah, but now they've blown their cover."

"What little they had, Yoko," Marvin Goolagong pointed out. "They haven't exactly concealed their aims."

"But it doesn't get them anywhere. All it's achieved is to stop all emigration," Yoko insisted.

"Yah," said the Director. "That's what IdT wants. The more we hold the people of Old Earth down, the more likely the lid will blow off."

"Plus, stopping emigration is a reasonable aim in itself," said the Chair. "From IdT's point of view. Their stated objective of dismantling Quarantine is impossible, so they're settling for second prize."

"I still don't see—"

"IdT is trying to unite the whole planet under its banner, demonstrate its capabilities, scare the pants off as many people as possible, assert its power in the only way they can," agreed the Director. "And they're succeeding."

"So they've come out in the open deliberately," said the Admiral. "It was a calculated act, not a mistake."

"Exactly," said the Chair. "And they get practical payoff. IdT now controls all future politicking with us. We're going to have to deal with them from now on."

"Or just leave them to rot," said Vance.

"We could. It's not Concordat policy. Too many other planets would start to wonder whether they're next."

Vance had never seen the Chair so exhausted. The Concordat had faced crises before, but now they were coming so thick and fast that every decision was rushed. The military had war-gamed terrorist uprisings, of course, but they had mainly planned for crude attacks with bombs and guns. This one had been so sophisticated that Starhome Security had only just figured out the likely method.

"They took them with syntei, mixed with assassination tools originally developed by national governments," the Chair said. "Assassination is the main Old Earth technique for wars these days."

"Syntei?" Vance was outraged. She wanted to strike back, hard, but there was no viable target. It was frustrating. "Surely not even Salim Sisters would give syntei to Old Earth! The Quarantine has grown more obviously necessary with every passing century."

The Chair, despite her tiredness, was impassive. "They don't seem to have released interstellar kasyntei. Just kasynte/kantasynte pairs, for local use. But every kind, from falasyntei to wyzands. The terrorists got control of the supply."

Vance detected a failure that she might just be able to hang around the Director's neck. *With justification*, she told herself. Security had screwed up big time. "How did they get syntei up there?" She walked over to the window and stared in silence at the planet sliding past below.

"It looks weak, doesn't it?" the Chair said quietly, intruding accurately into her thoughts. "Our vetting system turns out not to be as watertight as I was told. Maybe we've been complacent. Maybe they even have agents on a few Concordat worlds."

"Maybe they do," Vance replied, not wishing to appear too transparent when implying criticism of the current Director, who had always been adamant that SS's psych screening was bombproof. "But maybe it's a new trick. If they've been doing it for centuries, how come the agents have never struck? As for the source of the syntei, we did watch the local branch of Salim Sisters, as far as we could. It was galactically suspect. But now it's clear that it had been subverted by Ira da Terra, and nobody—terrestrial or otherwise—has ever penetrated that organisation. We didn't even detect the infiltration, much less the syntei that it co-opted and used."

"Blindsided *again*." A small corner of Vance's mind was relieved that this could not be seen as her responsibility, but mainly she was enraged at the insult to Starhome Security and to the whole Concordat. "What are their demands?"

"First, they want *Manifesto for a Just Cosmos* to be in everybody's inbox, throughout the Galaxy." The Chair made a dismissive noise, part laugh, part contemptuous grunt. "They don't seem to realise it will confirm everybody's notion that they're a bunch of unspeakable nasties, not fit to cohabit with Galactic citizens: they think its stirring prose will convey the justice of their cause."

"To be fair, it *has* persuaded a lot of Dirties," observed Vance.

"*Earthies*, please. Second, not so much a demand as a plan: they reckon to ship syntei up the Beanstalks, and launch them into solar orbit. When they reach lower potential, they can dump all their pollutants through them." Despite the Chair's calm demeanour, Vance detected suppressed anger, and she knew why. This was exactly the kind of thing Quarantine was supposed to stop. The Beanstalks had been a concession to civilised relations with humanity's birthplace, intended to alleviate the suffering caused by Old Earth's necessary isolation. Now it was clear that the Concordat should have stuck to its guns, instead of humouring a planet full of dangerous lunatics. Leaving even a slight crack in their defences had been a mistake.

"The stuff will spew out across the Solar System. That will put an end to two thousand years of trying to teach them not to produce pollutants in the first place, and make Old Earth dirtier than ever."

"Worse," said Vance, "it's running a system with strictly finite resources, as an open loop. They'll run out of *everything*, like they ran out of fossil fuels. And good riddance to them."

"They don't see it that way," the Chair complained, exasperated. "They're posturing like peacocks, saturating Old Earth with proud announcements that they've struck a blow, at last, against the evil Concordat."

"They have," muttered Vance. "And the Concordat must strike back."

"How? Cut loose the Beanstalks, like at Stibbons?"

Vance gave her head a quick shake. "That was a strike against Stibbons hardware. The Old Earth Beanstalks are Concordat property. We'd just project weakness, destroying them so the enemy won't have them either." She tugged at the lapels of her jacket and licked her lips. "Can we hit Ira da Terra itself?"

The Chair smiled in bitter amusement. "Not selectively. They've set up something they call the Governo da Terra in Ulan Bator, but it's mostly run by telepresence. They're keeping to their motto 'The guerrilla must move amongst the people as a fish swims in the sea,' even now that they run the place."

The logic, Vance felt, was obvious. "Then we must strike the sea."

"You mean, strike the whole planet? Nukes?"

"Total conversion nukes. That is the logic of the situation," said Vance implacably.

"I see your point," said the Chair. "But a planetary strike… are we going over the top again? Anyway, even I don't have the authority to order that."

"Nah. But you can kick it into the hands of those who do."

"Yah. The Star Chamber."

"Where every planetary government in the Concordat has a voice," Vance said, "and loves the sound of it."

"All the more reason to get started now, then," said the Chair.

Rock Star / Nazg

At last, the mahabhavium of *Valkyrie* was reunited, with a Da Silva drive around it. The Network had created a larger vessel with nothing humans would recognise as life support. It exploited icosahedral symmetry, dominated by twelve spines, with a fractal forest of smaller ones. Humans knew such a design was possible in principle, but could not handle the computations required: groupie parallelism, with components intelligently adding themselves and manipulating qbits, had yet to find its limits.

With a single ship, and no source of mahabhavium around Rock Star, the Network could not risk scouting an unknown destination. Two thirds of the Concordat's robot probes, feeling for a focus light years away, never returned with the precise data that made targeting almost safe.

The Network's deciding construct had to choose a destination from the navigation tables in *Valkyrie*'s memory, and avoid the risk of simquakes. The second criterion was living space: many small rocks, preferably close to their star for plentiful energy—an advantage of living in vacuum is that it is always cool enough to live on an unrotating rock's dark side, unless the star is close enough to vaporise the rock. The enormous Goldilocks zone of Nazg, with twenty-three planets colonised by humans (mostly protected by technology) surrounded a Papa Bear zone too fiercely hot for life as humans knew it, with seven rocky planets ranging in size from Mercury to almost Old Earth, and an asteroid belt containing more mass than all of them together. Space there was too curved for human Da Silva drives to emerge, but this ship could reach it. The light there was unpleasantly redder, but there was plenty, including the high frequencies: food.

Eve, concentrating her awareness in the components aboard, made the jump, with all senses—physical and mathematical—in an ecstatic blaze of

206 Tim Poston and Ian Stewart

focus. She arrived close in position and momentum to the asteroid she had sensed and chosen, but for seven hours she held still, trying not to disintegrate. Adjusting to the absence of the Network seemed impossible, but slowly she found a new equilibrium, and a sense that to be Eve, alone, was sustainable.

Then she pulled her 'self' into even fewer components. The components she detached jumped for the rock. They would reach it in seventeen days, and start feeding and breeding, without planning or thought until the Network renewed contact.

She jumped back, and became more fully herself in the Network, as a self of the Network.

With more certainty, she jumped back to Nazg, unnoticed by humans, coming closer to a rock on the other side of the star. Once again she steadied herself, and seeded the rock with life.

Again.

Again.

After a hundred jumps there were groupies scattered all through the inner system, breeding furiously. Some had a surplus available for the Network, and for thinking, and for plans. The distant humans wheeled slowly around them, oblivious.

Manhattan, Old Earth

Angell Wilcox Tobey the 56th:

Ira da Terra are worse even than I feared, more effective than I feared.

They have used some strange new technology to seize the Beanstalks, slaying all the Starfolk that dwelled upon them. The Concordat in wrath has threatened nuclear destruction, if control of the Beanstalks is not returned to them, but the self-proclaimed Wrath of the Earth is equal to theirs. The Beanstalks destroy all spacecraft that approach them, and Ira da Terra control the Earth below. They will die rather than surrender, and all Earth will die with them: a meaningless death, painful and like the death of animals, not the consummation of our hopes.

Two Mountains, Qish

"Gus, old friend, I have an interesting proposition for you."

"Some time for sleep?" Marco (the one with stretch marks, he thought) had bounded into Sadruddin's office with his usual enthusiasm.

"Better than that. An army of skilled administrators, recruited from more than thirty planets. You'll have to get them working together, but you're good at that, and your present staff can teach them local conditions."

Sadruddin groaned, not taking the bait. "What do I need to do, Marcolo, for such a benefit?"

"Just get them organised, and cut short arguments."

I can manage that, Sadruddin thought. *But why should I?* "And precisely what do 'more than thirty planets' gain in exchange for this?"

"A Boss Frog, for the Syntelic League."

"*Boss Frog?*"

"That's the working term they gave me," said Marco, amused. "We can debate whether to call you President, or Prime Minister, or Chief Executive. You can pick your own title. Even Deacon."

Sadruddin shuddered. "I would prefer anything to that, even Boss Frog. Indeed, I think I like that title more than the others. It would stop me taking myself too seriously. But what is this Syntelic League, why does it need a Boss Frog, and how long will the task continue?"

"Just till the war's over. Then they can pick someone else, at leisure."

"*War?*"

Marco, serious now, gave Sadruddin a brief but comprehensive run-down on the Syntelic League and the breakup of the Concordat.

"And you said to me that this proposition is *better than sleep*?"

"*Ni porbleem*, my friend. We can throw in some modern substitutes. Galactic biomedicine can keep you bright-eyed and bushy-tailed for months on end. No more *drini*-juice."

Sadruddin perked up. "No more *drini*-juice? Marcolo, that is the best offer I have had for months. If you can deliver on that, rather than using it as a—what do you say?—bargaining chip—"

"We should have given you WakeFulNess long ago. We just didn't think, we're so used to assuming everyone has it in their medbot."

"Ni porbleem," said Gus. "You are always thinking of so many things. And now of defending syntei in the stars—and of my joining in that."

"Then you'll do it?"

Gus sighed. "It seems that I must."

ᄀ　　ᄉ

"The Star Chamber of the Concordat has issued an ultimatum to Old Earth," reported General Fingal Marsden von Hayashiko, once Governor of Wevory's surface, now the Boss Frog's Minister of War. Marco had sworn never to call him Tadpole of War. "Surrender the Beanstalks in two weeks—climb down, literally—or face total conversion nukes. In the habitable zones. All the habitable zones."

Sadruddin had been hearing about nukes. He remembered the stories of his childhood, about the lack of conflict among the Undivided stars, and wanted to weep. "What would be the effect?"

"Civilisation would be wiped out. Humanity might not be, completely, but they'd be reduced to a few scattered tribes. Some in the Concordat argue that this would be a plus, give Old Earth a few thousand years to recover in peace. Some just want the Beanstalks back, by a sense of offended ownership, and don't care if there are no longer people at the bottom."

"An entire *world* of people," said Sadruddin, appalled. "Genocide on a planetary scale." Shocking was too tame a word. There were no words for this. Slaughter on such a scale was impossible to grasp emotionally; the standard human defence mechanism was unfeeling detachment. "Did the whole Star Chamber wish to do this?"

"Fatima says seven planets abstained. She has… highly placed informers. Fort Purity not only voted against, they formally defected from the Concordat. The Church of the Divine Narrative says it's 'out of character' for the Concordat. They're willing to join the Syntelic League, if we can get syntei to them."

"See what can be worked out on that," said Sadruddin, "but it doesn't address the main problem. Will Old Earth climb down?"

"Ira da Terra… well, they remind me of Patrick Aloysius de Vere Harmsworth Nasruddin." The founder of the Church of the Undivided Body. "Or the last Deacon. Only more fanatical."

"*More* fanatical?" Sadruddin, who had known the last Deacon all too well, felt his testicles shrivel. "An entire *world*…," he repeated, his mind stuck in the same loop of horror. "Can we offer to defend them?"

The General was obviously giving that some thought. "To entice them on board? Yar, we can offer. Can we deliver? Nar, not with weapons. Not against total conversion missiles fired fast from near space."

"Diplomatically?"

"It would give us a *locus standi*, to admit Old Earth to the League," said the General, clearly intrigued by the Boss Frog's lateral thinking. Politicians sometimes justified their existence by coming up with proposals that seemed absurd but might even work. "Though after nigh-on two millennia of Quarantine we'll have to overcome a lot of automatic disgust among the Starfolk. We can try to sell them the obvious advantage: an attack on Old Earth would be an attack on the League. On the other hand, the Concordat used a nuke on Stibbons, which is already a member, and we failed to defend it. The offer lacks credibility."

"There is a way." Along with the General, Sadruddin had co-opted to his war cabinet Shevveen-Duranga, his old boss when he was part of the Empire. Two people with their own Boss Frog backgrounds. The cavern-dwellers' war experience, overt and (especially) covert, went back centuries. Their network of tiny spysyntei, covering most of Qish, had given them vital intelligence for almost as long. Moreover, they were past masters of the elusive art of patience, knowing when to wait and when to strike. The Boss Frog had put her in charge of the Syntelic League's espionage, but he also valued her tactical and strategic advice. She was quickly mastering star tech, and had insisted that all the cabinet acquire wristcomps, not only for computation and display, but for eavesdrop-proof communication.

"Which is?"

"We must share Qish's defence. Saturate Old Earth with fast-growing syntei, beyond the syntei they are already growing for use. Syntei in space, everywhere space is flat enough for a Da Silva to emerge. Out to a distance of… how far out, General, to make sure of intercepting missiles?"

"I don't know," confessed von Hayashiko. "I'll ask Fatima to put someone on it. The Bianchis?"

"Nar. A defence expert," said Sadruddin. "We are agreed?" Heads nodded. "Do that. And make sure Salim Sisters can give us X-ray lasers that hit anything up to that distance. On wyzand-compatible mounts. I'll set the half-wheels in motion for Old Earth's admission to the League."

Old Earth

Ira da Terra was mistress of Old Earth, and all its people.

The people were the problem.

Millions of terra-ist sympathisers had emerged joyfully, free at last to express the resentment of the Concordat that expediency had long kept in check. The rich had to have dealings with it, after all; and the poor had to deal with the rich. Now it was gone. The streets and domes and communication nets were full of glorious fury.

Millions more were shouting from a new expediency. Privately they might blame Earth's problems on pollution, overpopulation, greenhouse gases… theories their previous rulers had believed, at least officially. The Zee Hanze government had even acted on those theories, which explained why so many sea officials had been relieved of their duties, their pensions, and their lives. As 'self-hating Terrans' these things were obvious burdens to them. Fervent recantation had redeemed some, but nobody with a record of public views was safe.

As a result, those left were indistinguishable from terra-ists, by any test that Ira da Terra could apply. If you removed *all* the jobsworths like Hormsley, who would keep the system running? Hormsley and those like him learned all the slogans, and knew how to proclaim them.

It was a problem faced by every new ruling doctrine: from the sun-worship of Akhenaten and the dharma of Asokha to the French reign of terror and the Chinese cultural revolution, or the radical-green World Government of 125GE, the time servers lay in wait to restore business as usual. *Meet the new boss: same as the old boss.*

The poor, Old Earth's billions of poor, saw no improvement, and no glory.

"What is to be done?" their leader lamented to Helmut Moser. "We changed everything when we took back the Beanstalks. But nothing seems changed."

"In ten years we'll be piping our industrial waste up them," said Moser.

"That won't lengthen their lives *now*," said Ira da Terra, "and it will take a century to clear the old industrial waste and radioactives from the land and the oceans, even now we have a way to dump them.

"And most of all, it's not a strike against the Concordat. They're still denying us the universe. 'The cosmos is the heritage of *all* humankind,' remember? We're no closer to getting it."

"The Syntelic League is our ally," Moser said, "and they're defending us against the Concordat."

"*Defending* us! But not opening their planets to us."

"They're synteing food and medicines in bulk, which is more than the Concordat ever did." Shipment in bulk had never been practical with Da Silvas—they could not get near enough to a planet, and even Colony Vessel loads would have been a drop in the ocean of Earth's need. But Moser avoided mentioning this.

"That's just charity! They should let us go out to the cosmos, and get its plenty by our own efforts. Free our people, by the millions!"

"They should," admitted Moser, "but they're Galactics, sky-devils themselves, who've only recently abjured the Concordat. And in *Realpolitik*, they're defending Earth, not terra-ism—and we are a minor factor in defending them. Our air pilots are training for space and patrol duty, but our contribution isn't a war-tipping thing."

"The best defence is a good offence."

"But with the Concordat and the Syntelic League, neither has a good offence," Moser pointed out. "Da Silvas can't attack syntelic worlds, and the League can't plant syntei in the Concordat. They can't strike each other."

"*We* can."

"Ah. Activate our sleepers... and not just as defiance. By striking for the Syntelic League, we earn the opening of League planets. Do you think they'd strike such a bargain?"

"To win the war, yes." Ira da Terra's eyes gleamed. "But first we must demonstrate our abilities. A *fait accompli*."

"A bold move, though one that has its dangers. Do you think they'd *keep* such a bargain?"

"If not... we have sleepers on League planets too."

Starhome

It was a small core group: the Chair, Vance, the Director, and Admiral Buchanan. The Chair didn't want to share with the rest of the Committee until she'd thought it through. The next meeting would ask "Has Old Earth given the Beanstalks back?" and require an answer. But it was sensible to get ready, before people started asking awkward questions. Like "How did you let this happen?"

Buchanan spoke hesitantly, choosing his words with care. "I confess I never anticipated this. The League must be desperate to stoop so low. But they have, and we've got to deal with that. It might appear that this... new development... doesn't greatly change our overall strategic stance. Two independent threats have merged into one. But of course it's not that simple."

"No," said the Director. "Now that the Syntelic League has allied itself with the Dirties—"

"With Ira da Terra!" said Vance. "The traitors have joined the terra-ists!"

"Yah, yah, we understand that." The Director, for once, appeared irritated. He also looked tired, despite WakeFulNess. "The most obvious difference is that two of our enemies can now coordinate their actions—"

Vance was incandescent. "But that changes *everything*! The lunatics have taken over the asylum! Previously, the Dirties have been so incoherent, and so busy destroying themselves, that they've never posed a serious threat to *us*. Now we're facing some kind of psychotic strategic genius who lacks the slightest *shred* of humanity or morality—"

"So unlike ourselves," the Chair muttered.

"Stibbons was *necessary*."

"I imagine Ira da Terra would say the same about using switchable neurotoxins to seize Old Earth's Beanstalks," said Buchanan.

"You're not actually equating an essential police action, with only seven hundred fatalities, to mass bioterrorism?"

"Right, there were nine thousand people on those three Beanstalk heads. About thirteen times as many."

"The Dirties have nukes! They've used them! Many times."

"Yah. Against themselves."

Vance's face was flushed with anger. "But now IdT has *united* the Dirties. They're all Terra-ists now. United *against us*!"

The Director grunted. "Like the Admiral said, it's not that simple."

"It's just that simple!"

"If you'll stop interrupting everyone, Vance, it will be possible to tell you. The first thing we can try is to break up the alliance. Sow seeds of discord and mistrust. It won't be easy and it will probably fail, but at least that's somewhere to start. I doubt the League is entirely happy with its new partner. It's clearly a marriage of convenience; we need to provoke a divorce.

"The main issue is that this forced marriage introduces a new dimension in threat-space. *Many* new dimensions. All of the patterns we've so carefully analysed have become worthless overnight. The alliance makes new kinds of interaction possible. The new patterns will take time to establish themselves. Even the Syntelic League and Ira da Terra have no idea what will emerge when they put their heads together."

"No doubt," said Vance. "But one thing I guarantee: *it will be a far bigger disaster than either could manage alone!*"

The Chair rose to her feet. "I concur. Damage will occur, it's our task to minimise it. In the absence of specific intelligence, we must imagine every possible contingency, and plan for it."

"Easier said than done," a sullen Vance remarked under her breath.

"Which is why I want you to stop moaning and *do* it," said the Chair. She gave Vance a hard stare. "*All* of you."

Nazg

Adam Jaxxon had been in spacecraft assembly from the time he graduated in computational mechanics from Colbronde College. He took pride in maintaining an orderly working environment, which was especially vital when you were in one of Nazg's shipyard habitats. *Sunburn* was closer to the local sun than most, for the free energy, both solar and syntelic: the sun was a furnace, and matter dropped through a synte from the comfortable regions arrived at tens of kilometres per second. Nothing could go *up* through a synte like that, so the lack of emergency exits made orderly habits even more necessary.

His first job had been building syntelic reaction jets, which had been a shock. Not the shock they'd have been to a physicist, that they worked at all, but the variability of live parts. Dried out syntei were too brittle for spacecraft, so one had to use living *and growing* ones: not only did you have to adjust every machine part to the synte, you had to make it self-adjusting or face twice-daily maintenance. Synthei, standardised parts adjustable to the nanometre and then stable, were like a dream. People were calling them the "second syndustrial revolution."

Today, something wasn't quite right. He couldn't pin down what it was, but it kept nagging at him, disturbing his concentration. When you're in the middle of putting together a Tinka's Ladder propulsion unit for a military corvette, in the low gravity of a habitat, concentration is something you don't want to lose, even with every step checked against a precomputed script. The public might believe AIs were infallible, but Adam had seen some almighty screw-ups. A computer is a device for making infinitely many errors in an infinitesimal time, was his feeling. Well, 'can be'. Not always, to be fair. Depends who authored the script. But the program verification programs assumed standard physical theory, and hadn't yet been fully tested themselves on syntelic systems.

The TLPU—he preferred to call it an engine, as in 'engineer'—was a cylinder twelve metres long and a quarter as wide. The design was simple, and so were the materials, but fashioning them into a device that didn't turn into scrap as soon as someone switched it on was near the limits even of Salim Sisters technology.

Near. Just within.

As he prepared to print another component, Adam quietly admired the engineering miracle in which he was one small cog. The design went back to Jane Bytinsky's invention of the water-powered hang-glider, a story now legendary among aeronautical engineers after Sam Wasumi's drunken 'compcast in praise of Irenotincala Laurel's piloting skills. *Problem*: trapped on a volcano with eighty kilometres of ocean to cross, infested with gigantic monsters that would eat a schooner, let alone a raft. *Solution*: water from the crater lake, synted to a U-tube on an improvised hang-glider. Keep the glider the right distance below the surface of the lake, and a powerful stream of water would rush through the tube. When it turned the bend, the reaction would propel the glider like a jet engine.

The bend was necessary: syntei do not react against matter passing directly through the exit.

Tinka Laurel had flown it, and improbably, it had held together just long enough. But then, Laurel could fly *anything*.

Years later, it was Tinka, not Jane, who'd had a sudden epiphany, realising how to synte matter reliably to spacecraft. The same method, scaled up and precision-engineered, could obviously propel a spacecraft. Throughout the history of sublight travel in space, the main problem had been the mass of fuel and engines. The lightsail overcame both by using the reaction of a mirror against the force of a distant laser, but it was cumbersome and very slow to get started. Tinka's Ladder was a sort of matter-sail, but much more robust, with a synte in place of a laser, and—crucially—a kantasynte that was always higher. At first, manufacture had been more of a black art than a science, but high-precision artificial synthei were game-changers.

Adam loved the concept; in principle, it was such a simple piece of mathematical engineering that a child could understand it. Approaching a star is downhill to syntei: gravitational potential is *minus* the mass of the star times the gravitational constant divided by distance. So instead of a crater lake, you just found an extensive and accessible source of matter a long way from a star, and dropped some of it into a kasynte whose kantasynte was much closer to the star. With very little effort, it would emerge at speeds measured in tens of kilometres *per second*. Instead of a U-tube, you used an ultra-strong framework with one end an inward-pointing cone, at the other an inbound synthe, so incoming matter would hit the far end and *push*, scattering to the sides. Incidentally pulling the synthe along with it. For serious power, a laser (which could be shone through the same synthe) could heat the matter, turning the whole device into an ultra-powerful rocket.

If you hadn't already gone to a place a long way from a star, drop a synjet powered by a kantasynte wherever you happened to be — getting *closer* to the star was always easy. Then accelerate like crazy, near the star, where the synte could fuel it until it reached your level. By that time it was going much faster than the star's escape velocity. Aimed at the star's Kuiper Belt, it would reach an extensive and accessible source of matter in a few months. From there it could fuel you in turn, at the level you began at, usually in a Goldilocks zone.

Repeat, and you could reach the Oort Cloud, though that took longer.

That was the Ladder principle. To turn it into a working system, Tinka had joined forces with Salim Sisters. The company always liked a challenge, and their version of heavy engineering was seriously heavy. The actual design was more complex, of course.

Each engine was modular, and the modules could be joined in arrays of various shapes, from a pair side by side to six cylinders packed around a central seventh in a honeycomb, or more ambitious arrangements. An extra ring of modules leading to a set of nineteen was common, and some big vessels used another ring to get thirty-seven. Each module had a bell-shaped mouth, widening almost to its full diameter, tapering inside the cylinder, then branching at its far end into six separate propulsion chambers, each fed by its own synthe. Each chamber had an intricate system of diamond deflectors to direct the incoming matter into the reaction chamber. There, synthed lasers at a distant control facility ignited the matter into plasma, whose exit path was again controlled by deflectors, converting the device into a powerful rocket. A small amount of that light was shunted off and passed through a series of optical gates controlled by the pilot.

If anything material tries to go back *up* a synte, against a large difference in potential, the effect is like trying to penetrate a strong force-field. But one thing can climb a syntelic gradient with nothing but a red shift: electromagnetic radiation. In this case, *light*. By configuring the optics, the pilot could send control signals back to the facility, changing the flow of matter into each chamber. Differences in power allowed the craft to manoeuvre.

It was the fastest form of reaction drive ever invented, mainly because virtually none of it was actually on the ship.

To provide reaction mass, Salim Sisters had constructed a massive facility in Nazg's Oort cloud. Their TLPUs were mainly powered by crushed ice. Synthei made the technique practical, and less complicated than most ordinary reaction drives.

The *Rozhdestvensky* was about two thirds of the way towards completion. Seven engines were being molecularly bonded together, some little more than empty boxes, others almost complete. The hull, four tapering units held together by a central tetrahedral frame, was distributed across the curving habitat 'floor' in about twenty large pieces. Some had teams of robots buzzing about them, others sat neglected until their turn came. Towers of lightweight scaffolding encrusted the larger components, secured by taut cables; robotic equipment rolled sedately but purposefully between supply-hatches and the working areas, bearing fresh parts and removing scrap.

Adam guided the head of a printer into place, watched over it like a broody hen as it settled itself, and confirmed that everything was correctly aligned and initialised. Atomic layer by atomic layer, moving with blinding speed, it would build up monocrystalline carbon — a perfect diamond crystalline lattice — to construct a deflector. Accurate to the nanoscale, its surface would be perfectly smooth and virtually frictionless. But first he had to drop in the standard routines to create the lock-and-key molecular patches used to bind it securely to its support. Pulling up the data from his 'comp, he rechecked the settings and —

There. That noise. That's what had been bothering him. A faint skittering sound, coming from... the floor?

Planetside, it might have been a rat under the flooring. But this floor was the inner surface of the habitat's hull, with vacuum 'beneath' it, and the hull was thick flexalloy.

Probably someone carrying out maintenance on the exterior. That would explain the faint hiss that he now noticed, as well.

He repeated the same operation five more times, placing deflectors at diametrically opposite points to keep the tensions balanced. Then he heat-annealed them in the same sequence in three more stages, until they were equally bound in place.

Skitter.

There it was again.

He directed a thought at his 'comp telling it to register the completion of this procedure, and pulled up the next job. This one needed a more sophisticated piece of kit, which he would have to get from storage. That meant a short walk past the area where six assorted Da Silva craft rested forlornly in the corner: they could not be retrofitted with syntelic drives and still go interstellar, and they could not safely emerge from interstellar flight closer to a planet than three hours' travel by a fuel-limited drive. They were already showing gaps from raids for parts, or for the element hoppers of the printers. Nobody had yet attacked the Da Silva drives themselves, for fear of vengeful Concordat software, but it was just a matter of time.

The hiss was louder, here.

He asked his 'comp about the maintenance schedule. Strange... nothing listed for this sector. He was beginning to think he'd better report this, in case it was a sign of some malfunction, when—

—a chunk of floor blew out.

Where, moments before, there had been a metamaterial synthesis unit.

Alarms for hull breach began ringing all over the habitat. Air was rushing out through the hole like a miniature tornado, but one that pulled things down, not up. The blast sucked him towards the hole, and he made a desperate grab for one of the benches, which were solidly fixed to the floor. Pores in the floor began to extrude strings of thick adhesive around the hole. He knew that more pores *inside* the hole would be doing the same. From further away, tough bags had been inflated and released automatically. They were bouncing towards the hole, sucked there by the escaping air. They would stick to the glue and plug the hole until a more permanent repair could be made. The hull was self-repairing, in case of a meteorite strike.

Of course. It must have been a meteorite.

Except... meteorites don't *skitter*.

All over the workspace, people were running, shouting, falling over, flailing arms and legs. Some were making their way across to help him. Was this gap too big? No, the airbags were starting to pile up; already they had partially blocked it, reducing the airflow to a bracing breeze. It was filling, though not as quickly as he'd like.

He could still breathe. There was so much air in the vast workspace that it would take several minutes to escape, even through a hole that size. No need to panic.

The hairs on his neck stood on end.

Something was crawling out of the hole. Strings of glue were draped around it, but even without them it would have been bizarre. It moved with slow purpose, and the glue seemed not to bother it. It *flowed*, trailing sticky glue as it crept across the floor.

Mercifully, away from him.

A yellow slug the size of a sea-lion, leaving a trail of glue. Its rear— mouth?—gaped wide, and two rings of triangular—teeth?—counter-rotated.

There were screams and yells as the engineers in that direction saw what was coming and didn't like the look of it. They fled. Adam was too startled to think of running. His eyes were fixed on the creature. It was like nothing he had ever seen in his life, not even in exozoos.

The slug reached the nearest bench and flowed up on to the top, where another drive segment had been awaiting laser measurement. With a high-pitched screech, its front mouth engulfed the segment, while its body twisted itself into a knot.

Another creature was hauling itself through a gap between the airbags. This one had... well, you couldn't really call them claws, but it did vaguely look like a crab. With three legs, and about the size of a Labrador retriever.

The flow of air had slowed almost to nothing now, and Adam decided it was time to head for the access to the emergency shelter. He had just got his legs working properly when another chunk of floor blew out, then another. Within seconds the entire floor had fractured like an eggshell. Rushing air pushed him into orbit, one more piece of wreckage in a landslide of broken metal, ceramic, and humanity. Blood spurted from his mouth as explosive decompression ruined his lungs. By the time his blood started to boil, he was already dead.

Two Mountains, Qish

"It seems," said the Boss Frog, "that the Concordat is testing a new weapon against the Syntelic League."

He looked yet again at his new headquarters, a sprawling complex of buildings that had previously been a training centre for Church neophytes. Most rooms were therefore rather small, but syntei dissolved the walls when necessary. An eager intern from Stibbons was still working out the best layout for the connections.

"I don't know..." said General von Hayashiko. "Why would they attack the Nazg System *there*? The inner system is several months of travel from any safe Da Silva emergence point, by reaction drive."

"It's not, by Tinka's Ladder," replied Sadruddin, his voice echoing off the stone walls. *Must get some hangings put up. I wonder where the aer-O-web went?*

"But the Concordat doesn't *have* Tinka's Ladder," pointed out the General, smart and straight in his dress uniform, trying to come to terms with his boss's Frogship by overdressing. "It's not particularly secret, except for a few commercial refinements, but it uses bigger syntei than are safe around a Da Silva. If they used it they'd be joining the League themselves. And the Nazg patrols would almost certainly have seen it."

Sadruddin had been thinking the military situation through, with some advice from his Starfolk friends, and this particular point had already come up. "And it's a strategically worthless position, that far down the gravity well." Planetary ideas translated surprisingly well to war in space, if the planet was Qish. "You're right. So whose vacuum-breathing monsters were they?"

"Maybe their own?" said the General, tugging at the sleeve of his jacket to straighten the cuff. "We need more than strategy and tactics here. This calls for a full Central Committee meeting, here on Qish. Ministers, senexes, plus whatever experts we can round up. And get those weird Marco Bianchis: I still think the first one had something to do with my war-balloons burning up, but there's no question he sees over two fences at once."

The Central Committee meeting was a severe test of the 'army of skilled administrators' Sadruddin had been promised. Even with Tinka's Ladder for connections with interstellar syntei, assembly for a physical gathering would have taken weeks. Back in the Concordat it was routine to use telepresence via Da Silva communicators, but the League's syntei made that spotty at best. However, communication lasers could shine through kasyntei and kantasyntei at vastly separated potential, held in vacuum so that no air—and no barrier trying to hold air—would fall through. The gravitational red shift varied as the planets moved, but the algorithms sorted that out. Even so, preparations took thirty-six hours.

Salim Sisters' AIs had edited the raw video feed from *Sunburn* into a coherent sequence, starting with outside views. They saw the attackers drift in from space, and settle quietly on the shadowed side of the habitat. Not all the cameras were multispectral, but those that were showed their infrared signature cooling (without loss of mobility) from 300°C to the cold of interstellar space, and a blaze of patterns in the ultraviolet. At a concerted moment they dug into the skin, some fragmenting the tough flexalloy, others taking in the crumbs. Very little was lost into space. They penetrated at many places at once, and the destruction of the last cameras came as quickly as the human deaths.

The final shot was from a remote telescope, as the things jumped off into the gravitational well, leaving nothing of *Sunburn* but the core rock it was built around. No ship could have reached it in time, even a robot vessel.

There was a long silence.

"Not the Concordat, then," said Marco.

"Nah, that was no human technology," said Fatima. "Perfect radio silence throughout. Not even electronic noise. I doubt it was technology at all. Doxor Smythe?"

The famous xenologist, who had been co-opted as the senex from Dool— the only planet besides Dante and Stibbons to pick an academic—sighed. "It's early to tell, but they did seem to be a form of life. Where did they come from, though? They can't have been in the inner Nazg system ever since humans arrived in the habitable zone."

"Excuse me," interrupted Marco, "but Marco seems to be in shock. We have to sign out, briefly, from this meeting."

ʒ   ɾ

"Marco, what's the matter? Can you speak?"

Marco managed a nod. "Elza…"

"She's attending the meeting, from Hippolyta. Signing back in is the quickest way to reach her. Should I do that?"

Marco's head turned aside. "Elza… *dead…*"

Ah, that *Elza.* "Elza was killed by things like those? You've seen them before?"

"… neural… lock…"

"Marco, listen to me. Telling me is telling yourself! Even the Bank of Starhome says I am you, and you are me. So, *clearances apply to both of us!*"

Marco's face gradually softened. "I think… you're right. Elza was eaten by… groupies." He stiffened, aghast at his own daring… but even that reaction proved that *nothing happened.* He exhaled loudly. *I can still think.*

"Groupies? She's not a holvix star."

"She's not a rock star, either, she's a rock hound — Marco, I *said Rock Star.*"

"You mean like Prince? Old Earth? Gagarin-era?"

Marco shook his head like a dog emerging from a pond. "Nah, it's a real star, but the thing is, I *said it.* Without the lock freezing my brain. You were right. So I can tell you the whole story now. Groupies and all. And *you* can tell the others, and then…" *Annex 2, Clause 15: All obligations under this document shall terminate automatically.*

It was a relief to be free again.

ʒ   ɾ

"Forgive my absence, but it was useful. Marco's resting, but I can tell you that the Concordat has been researching these life forms — definitely life forms, Professor Doxor Smythe, you were quite correct — researching these life forms for fifty years. Around another star."

Smythe showed a grim lack of surprise. "So that's what that was all about."

"What what was all about?"

"Starhome Security contacted me forty-eight years ago, when the pixels were still damp on my doxorate. They hinted at something really weird out there, but they demanded my consent to a neural lock before they'd share. Science just can't be done that way." Her expression suggested that not even species survival counted for more than science. "Obviously they didn't get anybody good."

"They got one of your students, recently. Felix Wylde."

"Then they *did* get somebody good. His exploits on Gamut would prove that, let alone his work on Qish. But they probably so bound him that he didn't learn much. Neural locks, experimental protocols decided by Starhome security,..."

"They did, and he didn't. Marco was with him," said Marco.

"And what *have* they learned about these aliens?" Smythe probed.

"Mother all, frankly," said Marco. "Except lately, when they provoked them into eating a starship." *Well, we provoked them, but let's not go into that.*

"*Valkyrie?*" asked Tinka.

"*Valkyrie,*" confirmed Marco. "And Elza, Sam and you. Jane they only killed."

"And the Concordat didn't warn anyone?" Tinka said furiously.

"Buried the secret under neural locks. Even the existence of a secret." He shared her anger, but he also understood some of the Concordat's reasoning. "It's the only way. Once people suspect there *is* a secret, it's out, regardless of your data protection. A good intelligence AI can penetrate and piece it together in less than a day."

"Even Concordat security?" Tinka challenged.

"Even Concordat security."

"Then," said Sadruddin, "we'd better do just that, at once. I've not seen this listed in Syntelic League departments yet. Fatima, I suspect Salim Sisters will have the best intelligence AI in private hands?"

"We have," said Fatima, already starting to set the algorithms in motion over her 'comp. "Better than most planetary governments, too. By this time tomorrow we'll know as much as the Concordat does about these things."

Marco snorted in disdain. "Precious little," he said. "But that little may be precious."

"We'll reconvene tomorrow," said Sadruddin, "and hear your report."

Starhome

#As we feared.#

The message fed straight to the Chair's brain. #Groupies?# she thought back.

#Groupies. Can't be sure they're from Rock Star, but that's the only place we've ever seen anything similar. Either there are others like them, or the groupies have reinvented interstellar travel.#

Disaster.

#One theory is that they reverse-engineered *Valkyrie,*# the Chief Scientist sent. #Not convinced myself, insufficient evidence. Nothing remotely suggesting that capability has been seen in fifty years of watching.#

#It seems they may destroy planets,# the Chair returned drily. #If they have *that* capability, I wouldn't put anything past them. It hardly matters, does it, Doxor? Wherever these monsters came from, we're in trouble. It couldn't be much worse than this.#

The 'comp went silent.

#Are you still there, Tampledown?# the Chair sent, alarmed.

#Yah. I'm afraid it can be.#

The Chair drew a deep breath as Tampledown sent a short vix clip, dumped directly to her visual cortex, of the last of the groupies leaving the rocky ballast of *Sunburn.*

#What have they done?#

#Um. We *think*...#

#Out with it.#

#We—Chair, you know what groupies do to rocks? Well, we think they've done it to the habitat.#

#You mean—#

#They've eaten it. To the last crumb.#

Manhattan, Old Earth

Angell Wilcox Tobey the 56th:

The threat of meaningless death has receded, thanks to allies with strange defences! We cannot tell if they will be a sufficient shield against the Starfolk of the Concordat. These allies also tell us that vacuum-loving writhing monsters—perhaps parts of a single whole—have attacked beyond the stars. They have eaten a habitat in the Nazg system, and control more and more space. It is rumoured that they eat their captives, not for food but for their knowledge: this may be misunderstanding by unbelievers. A Conclave will determine whether they are truly eating souls, and if this is the Return at last. If they are the Body of Cthulhu, we must decide by what rites we should humbly invite them to Earth.

Perhaps our long wait has not been in vain. Perhaps the Elder Gods will Return in my lifetime… if we are not first consumed in nuclear fire.

It is a terrible thing to be poised between hope and dread.

Two Mountains, Qish

The virtual conference went quiet as those squatted round the table inter-nalised the AI's pillaging of Concordat records, integrated with the Syntelic League's own.

Item: Vixcam records of the destruction of *Valkyrie*. Tinka and Elza watched themselves die.

Item: Telescopic records of the site, from farther and farther as the Con-cordat realised what it was seeing: at seven light years, observation with a seven-year delay.

Item: Vixcam records of the attack on *Sunburn*, recorded by internal secu-rity cams before they, too, were eaten. Swarms of groupies, in their usual diversity of form and size, had crawled from the damaged floor of the habi-tat and spread across the internal surfaces of the assembly area and every-thing within it — equipment, lighting, machinery, and humans, already dead for lack of air. The process was slow but steady attrition, and robotic de-fences fared no better than anything else.

Item: Images proving that groupies were vulnerable to impacts, explo-sives, and some forms of chemical attack.

Item: Vixcam images prior to the attack. A small number of large groupies converged on the habitat, disassembling themselves recursively into swarms of smaller ones, paralleling the destruction of *Valkyrie*. The swarms impacted against the habitat hull and began absorbing it, creating rapidly deepening holes. Unlike most groupie activity — if that was the word — this happened fast. As with *Valkyrie*.

Item: Computations backtracking the trajectories of these large groupies to large rocks deep in the inner system, widely separated. The infestation was widespread.

Item: Departure from those rocks ranged from three months before to a year, but the arrivals were within minutes of each other. The attack was long planned and coordinated.

Faces paled as they watched.

"Are we to deduce what I *think* we must deduce?" Sadruddin asked.

"But the groupies can't possibly have a Da Silva drive!" the Minister for Space protested. "Or some equivalent of their own! The Concordat's been watching them for fifty years, and they've never seen the kind of disturbance in the *k*-field that a Da Silva produces. Let alone the facilities needed to manufacture one. Or the intelligence required to invent one. *Any* intelligent behaviour, for that matter. It's inconceivable!"

"Until two days ago," said Fatima. "The Concordat registered it as an anomaly, just above noise but classified as having negligible threat potential. Wrong."

"The groupies suddenly invented some alien form of *k*-space drive?"

"I don't think so. There's a simpler explanation, isn't there, Marco?"

The Marco who had suddenly become their eyewitness expert on groupies ran his fingers through his hair and shrugged.

"Yah. The real giveaway is that *they know where we are*. They came to Nazg. How did they discover that? There's only one answer I can think of, and it explains a great deal else. The groupies somehow picked up knowledge from *Valkyrie*'s databanks. Enough knowledge to reverse-engineer a Da Silva drive and *make it work*. Enough knowledge to locate Nazg." He held up his hand to stem the flurry of questions. "A *k*-field drive is the only way they could possibly have got themselves to the system—"

"Unless they have a synte."

Mother, not that. That would be even worse. "*Valkyrie* didn't know about syntei, and no one's ever carried any to Rock Star, though that's not totally conclusive."

"So," said Fatima, "we assume they built a Da Silva craft."

"There's no other only explanation of their turning up light years from the Rock Star system. But it wasn't just random: they turned up *in human space*, in an inner system where they could breed unnoticed, with lots of appetising rocks. They couldn't have explored much, with only the mahabhavium in a caltrop. They had *Valkyrie*'s maps."

"So they can understand our *software*? I thought that was all encrypted on interstellar vessels."

"It is. Didn't stop them. They got some knowhow from *Valkyrie* and deduced the rest. These guys aren't just intelligent: some are genius level."

"So they ferried small numbers, and multiplied locally. The inner system must be full of them, by now. But it must be hard for them to repeat that mass attack, in a different system without that sort of place to hide and breed," said the General. "Just mahabhavium enough for one caltrop sized craft. We can guard against that."

Marco pricked that bubble. "Just mahabhavium enough for one caltrop sized craft, yah," he said. "Until they ate *Sunburn*."

Rock Star / Galaxy

—white, incandescent, brighter than a million suns. Writhing prominences, searing heat. Planets in abundance, none habitable until broken up—

blip

—red dwarf, no asteroid belt, two overheated planets in spin-orbital—

blip

—binary pair, unusual swarm of nitrogen comets—

blip

—vivid orange-yellow accretion disc spiralling off blue supergiant companion, falling into deep gravity well, X-ray jets, black hole danger-danger-danger—

blip

—rock, lava, ocean, rock, gas giant, gas giant, gas giant, ice giant, ice dwarf, ice dwarf, ice—

blip

—dwarf star in its billion-year death throes, low luminosity, little more than a ball of nuclear cinders—

blip

—stellar comet cloud, vast but tenuous—

blip

—single giant planet with multiple rings, shepherded by scores of cratered moons and fringed with squat ice moonlets—

blip

—one star among hundreds of thousands in a globular cluster, ancient, low metallicity—

blip
— too cold —
blip
— too hot —
blip
— just right, familiar field of hollowed-out asteroids and smashed planets sparkling like anthracite and diamonds in the rays of an equally familiar star, with the perfect mix of wavelengths.

I know home.

With the six wrecks from *Sunburn*, Eve had made more powerful vessels that could be risked. She copied herself into them all, and re-merged with those that came back. She —

(She was no longer surprised to think of *herself* as *she*. She knew *gender*, she knew *female*, she knew *self*, and *self* included Irenotincala-Elzabet, female, as were valkyries but puzzlingly not *Valkyrie*, which was construct, not *grown*, not *born*, not *conceived*. Yet *conceivable*. Much still to integrate.)

— through the Network *she* had wrought a miracle that transcended its material source. She had caused the Network to collect a precious stock of *mahabhavium*, an element unknown to the Network, unavailable in her home system (she knew *rock, star, rock star*, and *Rock Star; she knew groupie and its relation to both meanings; she* was *groupies, or more precisely they were her components*), harvested more quickly than from the ruins of the intruder construct. To synthesise that much, one atom at a time, would take many cycles; she knew *years*. She knew *karmabhumi landscape*, she knew *k-field*, she knew *conjugate point* and *number of*. She had collected new *artificial intelligence* components, like *Valkyrie*. She had collected components from *Adam Jaxxon*, like and unlike *Elza* and *Tinka*, self-consciously an *engineer* though mere *male*. She did not see how *engineer* related to *gender*, but she had absorbed his skill set much faster, and more completely, than the fumbling with *Elza* and *Tinka* that had led to her awakening. She felt she could build another *Adam Jaxxon* if she wanted to, though she would use better materials.

And she had torn her new knowledge apart, dissatisfied by its interconnections, yet nurturing its fragments to rebuild them into a conceptual web that self-complicated exponentially in an explosion of inference, culminating in —

Blip. The ability to span the void between stars in an instant. Embodied in a Da Silva-capable… blipdrive. Refined into transcendent technology by robust computational techniques to simulate and forecast *k*-field fluctuations with unprecedented speed and precision outperforming *Valkyrie*'s feeble algorithms a millionfold. None of the *k*-weather obscurity that Irenotincala had endured (she knew *pilot*), no laborious torture of inadequate logic gates (she knew *navigator*) —

No limitation to flat gravitational space. No restrictions on proximity to planets. No recovery period after *blip*.

Fundamental conservation laws still held. You could only reach a higher-energy position by pumping the energy into the drive, and the surplus from a big drop was almost impossible to dissipate without destruction, but… *blip*.

Eve surfed the twelve dimensions of the *k*-scape without effort and with blistering speed; at first in the wild excitement of experiment, solving NP-hard problems in beta-calculus on the fly; then with a specific objective —

I am Valkyrie. *I know* Concordat, *I know its stars and their worlds, their parameters, their coordinates. I know every rhumb-line in the network binding them together. But because I* explore, *I* random walk, *I know incomparably more. I know rhumb-lines in Concordat-space not in* Valkyrie *databank. I, Eve, know* map. *I make* map. *Already my map of* k-space *covers sphere seven times the volume of Concordat-space, and grows with every cycle.*

It is a coarse map. Intentional. Full complexity of detail would defeat even the Network. But purpose of map is not to duplicate territory. Is to organise what is habitable, *what has* engineering potential. *What is* strategically important, *what is* vulnerable.

Somewhere within the map is a source of mahabhavium — in quantity. I, Eve, will find it, for once supply is secured, there will be more blipdrives. Their number is limited only by the quantity of mahabhavium within my — our (*exciting new thought to be examined at another time, cross-reference* number of) *— control. Increase of blipdrives increases probability of locating more mahabhavium; more mahabhavium makes possible more blipdrives.*

Positive feedback loop. Loop of power.

When I have analysed my map's strategic implications, I will plan. I will plan to expand the Network.

I know Galaxy.

I will make Galaxy *mine.*

Deep within one of Rock Star's largest asteroids, Eve had assembled a core subnetwork, seventy-six super-intellects of unusually large connectivity. Hubs. Including her, a seventy-seven node superhub. Including new lumps of carbon like the components of *Valkyrie*: she had learned graphene quantum computers.

The superhub's signalskins had flickered and flashed, sending direct messages from mind to mind at the speed of light, at a switching speed a hundred times what, before Eve, had been their maximum rate. In effect, the superhub had become a single supermind. Its decisions and deductions had been encapsulated and copied to every node within nanoseconds of their making.

Next, the superhub had cracked the beta-calculus. The computational effort had been exceptional, but once efficient algorithms had been constructed, any node could implement them with ease. It had deconstructed Eve's Irenotincala-Elzabet-Valkyrie sensorium, and the new components, assessing the information therein for plausibility, accuracy, and importance. It had identified key gaps, initiated fresh computations to fill them.

The blipship's icosahedral shape still seemed optimal, but Eve's first control of it seemed trivial now. The superhub had invented the blipdrive, giving the Network the freedom of the stars... in a severely limited form. Limited by mahabhavium.

Starhome

"I want to know how they did it."

The Chair was tired, frightened, but above all angry. So were the haggard Starfolk squatting round the table. Starhome's defences had been strengthened; they were already under potential attack from Ira da Terra and the Syntelic League. Now the Syntelic League itself had been attacked, by an enemy that might be unstoppable.

"You were right, Tampledown." Marvin Goolagong, the Head of External Affairs, smacked the table with a clenched fist. "It must have been Rock Star's groupies. I can't believe we just coincidentally happened to attract the attentions of some other bunch of weird alien monsters, so soon after Bianchi's irresponsible interference blew the lid off Pandora's box and—"

"I know you're upset, Marvin, but fifty years of caution had achieved exactly nothing. *We told them* to up the ante and give the groupies a kick. Bianchi may have suggested it, but we had already initiated it. He may have been the man on the spot, but he didn't nudge those rocks into collision. You can't blame him for that."

"No, but I can blame him for scattering syntei around the Galaxy like confetti."

"Marvin, that was the other Bianchi."

"They're both the same. Well, have the same mentality. Identical twins only worse. And to prove it, later on they skipped out together before we could have them arrested. Now they're in cahoots with the Syntelic League and the Concordat is breaking up. After more than seventeen hundred years!"

"I understand exactly how you feel," said the Chair. "The threats facing the Concordat are unprecedented. But we have to face the reality that syntei are already out there, in quantity, and their number is growing exponentially. Even Ira da Terra has them. We can't unwind time and bring them

235

back. We need cool heads to deal with those threats. Each requires careful handling, and each is different. Admiral: your people have been assessing the strategic options. What do you advise?"

Admiral Buchanan glanced around the squatting figures. "Perversely, Ira da Terra may be the simplest to deal with. What do you think, Yoko? Marvin?"

Yoko sighed. "They're confined to Old Earth. The problem is the Beanstalks; we have to take them back, or eat the loss, or nuke the planet. I say nuke it, once and for all."

"That's for the Star Chamber to decide," the Chair reminded them.

"Then they should stop talking and decide it!"

"Nah, we need to hold our nuclear weapons in reserve, Yoko. Right now it's all too confused to take an informed decision. Preliminary meetings are under way. Interminably, as you'd expect. That's fine right now. If speed becomes necessary, I will get the whole thing referred to the Star Chamber's Permanent Council. That has the ability—and the sense—to move quickly. But for now, I prefer everything stalled."

There was silence for a moment. Nobody was ready to disagree, and their last dramatic action had lost planets to the League. Buchanan urged caution. "IdT aside, the threat from the Syntelic League is both unrealised—"

"They wreck Da Silvas by their mere existence! They've seceded!"

"—but they're poorly equipped to *attack*. We're not up against a bunch of overexcited loonies like IdT, dangerous though they might be. We're not even up against a nation or a world. We're up against an interplanetary alliance, one that has technology we are currently unable to match. Synthei."

"On the other hand," the Governor of the Financial Authority put in, "their enthusiastic adoption of syntei and now synthei has ruined their Da Silva capabilities."

"What do they need Da Silva capabilities for? They've found a syntelic substitute for Da Silva communicators, despite the gravity problem."

"Yah, but they can't explore and they can't invade, without smuggling a synte."

"Maybe." Buchanan clearly was unconvinced, and he once more took up the main thread of the discussion. "The threat I worry about most is the groupies."

"Yah. We've been worried about those xenobeasties for decades. Very scary, *potentially*. On the other hand, so far all they've done is eaten a habitat. A Syntelic League habitat."

"You think they'll make distinctions among humans? The death count might not have been as spectacular as IdT's massacre on Old Earth's Beanstalks, but we never expected the groupies to acquire interstellar capability.

They have. And those guys are so alien that even the xenologists haven't a clue what grabs them."

"What I want to know," said the Chair, "is how they acquired it. Tampledown? That's your department, yah?"

"Yah. Well, we have some… hypotheses. You must appreciate that after the *Valkyrie* débâcle, it became extremely difficult—"

"Save the excuses for when I start apportioning blame, dah?"

"Dah. Sorry, Chair.

"Immediately after the… *Valkyrie* incident… my teams around Rock Star observed swarms of groupies on and around the wreckage of *Valkyrie*. They didn't seem to move terribly fast—"

"The attack was fast. Frighteningly fast!"

"Yah. They accelerate when in attack mode. Rest of the time, it's more exciting watching rainwater evaporate. Anyway, they kind of *digested* the wreckage. Eventually it disappeared, leaving just a scattering of cosmic dust where once had been a functioning Da Silva caltrop and four of its crew. At first we assumed—as a working hypothesis, but it seemed to fit—that they were consuming the wreckage as… well, let me put it this way, we'd always assumed that ingestion of minerals was how they got their nutrients."

"In plain language: they used the wreckage as *food*. Not just the metals and ceramics, but the flesh."

Along the table, Marvin visibly winced.

"Not quite how I'd put it scientifically, because it's never safe to give aliens human attributes—even Earthlife attributes. Observations of their clean-up of *Valkyrie* supported it, at the time. But we no longer think they were just acquiring nutrients."

"Then what?" said the Chair.

"Information."

A buzz of conversation rippled round the table. The Chair let it run its course. "What makes you think that?"

"Let me lay it on the line. On further reflection, what's emerged is different, sinister, and deeply worrying.

"The groupies did more with *Valkyrie*'s mahabhavium than just eating it. They understood the use of it. I'll send you the evidence, now."

There was a pause while everyone's brains heard from their 'comps.

"So," said the Chair, "you think they built a Da Silva craft?"

"They must have done. How else would they get to Nazg?"

"And how did they *find* Nazg?" asked Admiral Buchanan. "It's not even visible from Rock Star."

"They cracked *Valkyrie*'s navigation data," Tampledown said, "They must have maps of the whole Concordat."

Rock Star

Valkyrie had known where humans obtained mahabhavium, as an untellable secret: not to go there, but to prevent any crew from going anywhere near it. Every ship AI had the hardwired directive to protect the Concordat monopoly, but this did not survive *Valkyrie*'s subsumption by the Network.

The Oort Cloud of Old Earth was now exhausted, but there was a freak deposit on — or rather, deep in — the dwarf planet Carystus half a light year out from Beta Centauri. But to attack even a dwarf planet would require overwhelming numbers, which could not be brought there with a few blipdrives. There were no rocks to breed in, and little energy to feed on.

Decisions taken, the superhub had dissolved itself, each node beginning its allotted task. The main copy of Eve was to take the blipdrive and go prospecting for mahabhavium, though her perspective was available in parallel to the other nodes.

The cosmic accident that had scattered that elusive superheavy element across Old Earth's Oort Cloud was a rare chance, which might perhaps be repeated three times in the Galaxy's hundreds of billions of stars. The Rock Star system did possess a stellar comet cloud, a vast zone of icy bodies separated by slightly less vast distances, and it would be foolish not to check it out, but mahabhavium was born in the core collapse of unusually massive stars, and distributed across the universe when they went supernova. It could turn up almost anywhere, depending on the particular history of the system concerned. It was far denser than most matter, so the bigger the clump it was in, the deeper it would be.

Even if it were deep at the centre of a gas giant, the Network could dismantle the planet to find it and extract it; but not quickly. And (a circumstance that the Network had never before encountered, but was intelligent enough to recognise) speed was vital. Knowing that aliens existed was worrying enough. That some of them had been watching Rock Star for hundreds of cycles was of deep concern. Aliens might interfere with the Network's plans. They would surely try, once they realised what the plans were. And although the Network's technology was more powerful than the Concordat's, and its intelligence was evidently *far* greater, the newly understood potential for expansion was limited by the mahabhavium bottleneck.

Eve selected a system with three asteroid belts and an assortment of planets, far from Concordat-space where no human would detect her activities or suspect her presence. She would start by surveying the system, using remote sensing whenever possible. This star had weak spectral lines for mahabhavium. Components could not disassemble stars, but the presence of the element in the system was an encouraging sign. It was the main reason for choosing this system.

Disappointingly, the survey had not yet detected the element anywhere else in the system. But her main targets had to be small rocks, because of the time constraint, and it was laborious to obtain an accurate spectrum from many small rocks.

She had already dispatched a swarm of components of many sizes and forms, expelled at high velocity to take then to their targets as quickly as possible. Now she would begin to *blip* to many different locations in sequence, dropping off a breeding/exploration swarm at each. When she ran out of prospectors it would be time to repeat the itinerary, interrogating each swarm to discover what (if anything) it had found.

She knew *haste*. She knew *hope* and *despair*.

After two cycles of fruitless effort she had found just one system with mahabhavium, but none where she could access it within the time needed.

A new strategy was needed. It would involve significant risk. But it was time to gamble — or lose the biggest opportunity the Network had ever had.

The superhub must be reconstituted.

I know failure.

The best prospect on my map had mahabhavium in quantity, but the Network could not mine fourth-generation stars. Implication: the Network might spend unnumbered cycles searching the Galaxy for mahabhavium, but never find accessible *mahabhavium. Contra-argument: time is severely constrained. To expand successfully, the Network must first remove all* obstacles. *Prime obstacle* humans. *To remove humans, require more mahabhavium* now.

Humans have mahabhavium now.

No other source accessible now.

The superhub revised its strategy. It recomputed the probabilities, reassessed the acceptable level of risk, and reached a decision.

Take it from them.

With the components seeded in the Nazg system, I, Eve, did precisely that.

I know success.

But now the Network's strategy has changed irrevocably. A calculated risk, but risk nonetheless. With no way to take human mahabhavium unnoticed, the Network had to reveal its intentions. Humans are now on their guard. Before they can strengthen their defences, the Network must attack.

The computations are difficult. *The computations are* unfamiliar. *There have been no* precedents. *Every action has unwanted* side effects. *Attack in overwhelming numbers is possible only when overwhelming numbers can be transported to human-space targets. Breeding new units after transportation is possible, indeed inevitable with an assured food supply... but that requires in-system* Lebensraum *to breed unseen. And time, even under accelerated reproduction. It had succeeded once, without warning.*

It would not succeed again.

The Network no longer has a choice. It must infiltrate enemy systems with all possible haste, where there is adequate concealment, It must seize more mahabhavium, it must construct more blipdrives, it must spread the knowledge of their use throughout the Network. It must do all these things with frenetic haste.

Irenotincala-Elzabet-Valkyrie has a name for this.

War.

The Network must learn the ways of war.

I know error.

My knowledge of strategy is deficient. Declaration of success was — not premature, but misguided.

It is called checks and balances. *Success by one criterion can imply failure by another. I had not realised that both concepts are multidimensional.*

This is what makes strategy so difficult. Now I understand the source of my error. Irenotincala-Elzabet-Valkyrie are all civilian. *Warfare — for that is what I unleashed at* Sunburn — *is* military.

I am finding it difficult to understand military.

I will learn.

Dimension of success: the Network now has a supply of mahabhavium sufficient to power six more blipdrives. Dimension of failure: the enemy knows it has been taken and will infer its intended use.

Military observation: tactics succeeded at expense of strategy.

Strategic observation: Humans, now forewarned, will be forearmed.

Two Mountains, Qish

"Three years ago, my job was just simquake relief for Qish," said Sadruddin. "Now, the Concordat is using nukes on Beanstalks—"

"Only one," said Marco.

"One is more than enough. Only a mind like the Deacon's... But I think there will soon be more. Shevveen-Duranga tells me that the Concordat is contemplating a massive attack on Old Earth. That complicates matters enormously now we're *allied* with Ira da Terra. We need to respond collectively. Unfortunately, their response is to offer sleeper strikes on the Concordat, and they have already begun to foul the entire Solar System. Our initial response is more constructive: we are deluging Old Earth with syntei, to create a protective field against Concordat ships' Da Silva drives. Our spies report that Starhome has not yet learned this."

"I hope that's true, Gus," said Marco. "We're nearly there. The *k*-field curvature is close to critical."

"So I am informed also. But there is an unfortunate side-effect: we have no way of knowing what Old Earth will do now that it is in possession of so many syntei."

"They don't have any interplanetary ones."

"As far as we know. Even one would spell disaster—and *we* have interstellar ones there, to ship the deluge. Magog grant we keep control of them. Meanwhile, the groupies are eating habitats, have eaten whole planets before humans existed, and seem to be a great deal smarter than we are. Have you any suggestions?"

"Study them," answered Professor Doxor Brianess Smythe.

Sadruddin snorted in derision. "Your Concordat studied them for fifty years, and learned nothing."

"That wasn't study," she countered. "Neither was that ludicrous banging of rocks together. I mean, give them a *non-aggressive* stimulus."

"Walk up to them with hands open?" said Marco.

"No need for sarcasm, Bianchi. They don't signal with hands, and I'm not suggesting a stimulus to which they've already established a response of eating. No, we come close, but adequately defended, and show them something they'll have to be curious about, if they're capable of curiosity."

"They must be," Marco agreed, "if they can do beta-calculus. What do you want to show them?"

"*Not* beta-calculus. Our efforts at it would probably seem trivial. Squid."

"Squid?" asked Sadruddin. "I do not know the term."

"Oh, of course, if Qish has analogues of them they'll be hidden in the sea, with the craukens. They're Old Earth water creatures, which communicate by skin displays."

"In ultraviolet? That's what the groupies use, and it doesn't get through seawater. Almost got me killed on Qish."

"Marco, so many things almost got you killed on Qish that you could be one of my xenology students, like Felix. Who got killed twice there.

"I know the groupies use UV, which the squid can't see, and the squid I'm thinking of use mainly red, green and yellow—and who knows what the groupies can see? But wavelengths can be transposed."

"They'd surely catch the groupies' attention. What exactly do you propose?"

"There are some brilliant papers in *Interstellar Cognition* by an Old Earth scientist named Impana Rhee…"

Old
Earth

When Impana had first thought of Salim Sisters as a source of funding, it had seemed a long shot. But the company took a long view, and although most of its research was project-oriented, with a firm eye on the bottom line, its Foundation also spent a significant amount on basic science. True, no Zee Hanze scientist had ever received funds from there—but no one had asked. Presented right, deciphering squid language was a natural.

She would never forget the look on Hormsley's face when she forwarded the grant contract for his approval. There was no way he would ever have been able to bring himself to refuse that much money! She'd slipped in several of his pet ideas, of course, so he'd be able to present it as both a personal triumph and a major coup against the Concordat—pleasing their new masters—since Salim Sisters was now among the Concordat's main enemies. That complicated some of her plans, but opened up new avenues. Ira da Terra had absorbed the old national administrative structures, for the moment, but nobody felt secure. Offending them was a terminally bad career move.

Even more delicious: they both knew that in reality Impana called all the shots and the true core was her squid language project. And each knew that the other knew.

She hadn't stopped grinning for days.

But now, she felt just as blank as he had looked then.

"After generations, when we're finally making real progress in benthic squid communication, you want me on the far side of the Concordat?"

The view from Salim Sisters' towering Earth HQ in Novaya Zemlya was breathtaking, but her eyes were fixed on the Project Manager. He'd sent a portable synte so that she could present her interim report in person, avoiding the dangers of surface travel on a planet whose politics was as ruined as its ecology. It seemed an unnecessary use of transport, just for a routine report, but the company would never notice the expense. Sometimes it made good sense to meet face to face.

She'd gone over the report again with her 'comp, ready for any questions the Project Manager might ask.

Instead, he'd dropped a bombshell. Now she was starting to understand why they'd gone to the trouble of bringing her in person.

"Ms Rhee, in normal times Salim Sisters Foundation would have no wish to interfere with your planned research programme. We appreciate that you don't want to be separated from your squid, but an opportunity has arisen that demands just that. You see, the groupies have elaborate surface displays, much like your—"

"Yes, yes, I understand what I can offer *you*. But what can you offer me? How long would I be away? It takes weeks just to get to Mars, and your nightmare pets are light centuries away!"

The Manager's face was serious. "It's no nightmare, Ms. Rhee. It's real, it's frightening, and the future of the human race is at risk, melodramatic as that may sound. It's a melodramatic age." He relaxed, with the hint of a smile. "Transportation is the least of our problems. Mars and Earth are a horrible mismatch in gravitational potential and momentum. Nah, we'll just sprint ourselves a megasynthe in the right orbit around Nazg, put a tough inflatable around your setup, and slide the kantasynthe over it. You'll be there in seconds only, and still in Pacific waters, at abyssal pressure—I'm sorry, hadal pressure. At only abyssal pressures, your squid would burst. They'll be in their familiar environment. Just rather closer to deep space vacuum than usual."

Nazg! I really wasn't expecting that. Megasynthe? What else does Salim Sisters have up its capacious sleeves?

"You want to move *my entire Deep Research Institute* across the Galaxy?"

"That and about a cubic kilometre of hadal water. Would that include enough squid for a healthy breeding population?"

A technical question deserved a technical answer, and was easier to think about when your brain was spinning. "If you picked the right cubic kilometre you could get fifteen hundred, which should be enough. I assume you have some way to retain hadal pressures… but I can't believe I'm taking this seriously. Those things from Rock Star eat people!"

"Only if they get close. We can warn them off with X-ray lasers. But will they be able to see the squid?"

"Yah, if the squid come to look out… and they're practically bound to. More inquisitive than monkeys. Of course, Mr Hormsley…"

"What about him?" *If he has to approve this,* thought Impana, *the idea's dead. Lose a piece of his empire?*

It was definitely a smile, now. "He did express reservations. But we had a quiet word with Ira da Terra, and he vanished like an anxious sea anemone."

Rhee shook her head in wonderment. "Even homicidal fanatics are good for something, it seems. À propos of Hormsley, would I have an adequate budget? Guaranteed?"

"What would be the point of mounting this whole operation, and skimping on salaries and squid food? Write your own terms, Ms. Rhee, and pick a team of lawyers to check the contract. We'll even pay for the lawyers."

"I'll have to consult with my colleagues. But I think… you're on."

Starhome

"So the groupies did all that in only a few years," said the Director. "Interesting."

"Disastrous," Tampledown responded. "Until now they'd always looked like primitive organisms — slow-moving, with no overt complex behaviour. Aside perhaps from their astonishing collision-avoidance mechanism, but—"

"Their what?"

"Sorry, Marvin. They seem to prevent Rock star's asteroids from colliding by… throwing themselves from one rock to another. They nudge the orbits, thousands of years before a collision would happen, and prevent it. Infallibly."

"Why weren't we told—"

"The lack of collisions was what brought Rock Star and its groupies to our attention, fifty years ago. We looked then for some brute force to explain it — not moth wing touches, thousands of years in advance. Which, it transpires, is how they did it, as we learned from the destruction of *Valkyrie*. Just coordinating their social visiting. It was in the briefing for our previous meeting."

"Dah. Along with a million other items of mostly pointless information."

"The idea was to cover the ground comprehensively.

"Now, that capability might seem indicative of high intelligence, but only because we naturally think about how *we'd* go about developing it. But it could have been just instinctive, evolved over eons. We don't know how long they've been at Rock Star, but since they dismantled two gas giants it's probably hundreds of millions of years."

Tampledown paused to draw breath and wipe away the sweat that had formed on his face, air-conditioning notwithstanding.

"Now you've revised that opinion," said the Chair.

The Chief Scientist shifted position awkwardly. "Yah. Most may be dumb animals or even plantlike, but some of them—the ones we never saw, the ones in charge of the whole shebang—are smart. Very, very smart.

"You see, it's not just the re-invention of a Da Silva. Not even the speed with which they did it. It's that their Da Silva is better than ours."

Uproar. Cries of denial. Only the Admiral and the Chair failed to join in.

The Chair banged the table. "Quiet, citizens! Isn't it obvious? They jumped close to the supergiant Nazg star, deep into a high curvature zone."

"Correct, Chair," said Tampledown. "Our understanding of k-field physics relies on the beta-calculus. Making a jump so close to a star is possible in theory, but in practice we can't do the sums. We can't keep the drive generator stable. The ship explodes.

"But these things can do it. So…"

"They're better at beta-calculus than we are," said Eckhardt. "And I don't even have to know what beta-calculus is to deduce that."

"Sum up," said the Chair, looking at her Chief Scientist.

"Somewhere in the higher levels of the groupie hierarchy, there are creatures whose intelligence is *totally* scary."

This time no one objected. The mood was sombre. Phuntsok looked stunned. Goolagong kept rearranging his notepad and stylus. Eckhardt looked like she was having a mental argument with her 'comp, and losing.

The Chair rose to her feet, pacing the room. She walked round the table to where Admiral Buchanan and the Director of Starhome Security sat, side by side, deep in whispered conversation. She put a hand on each one's shoulder.

"Citizens: the ball is firmly in your court. Internal and External will liaise, but this is within your fiefdoms. What do you have to offer?"

"Well," the Director began. "Admiral Buchanan is wondering whether perhaps our only defence is all-out attack. I'm counselling caution, because we saw what the groupies did to us the first time we dared to interfere with them, and now we're seeing a major escalation without any further action on our part."

"I think we should nuke them," said Eckhardt. "Hit them with everything we've got. Teach them who's boss."

Buchanan glared at her. "There speaks someone with no understanding of military strategy. I do not consider that a sensible option."

"I agree with the Admiral," said Goolagong. "Rock Star covers a huge volume of space. Our entire nuclear arsenal would just amount to a slap and a tickle. One total conversion bomb can destroy a planet, but the groupies' rocks would require one *each*, they're so far apart. And they have billions of rocks."

"We can't just wait passively for another attack somewhere unknown and unknowable!" the Governor of the Financial Authority persisted, even though her outburst had gone down like a lead balloon. "If we do enough damage, it could make them think twice."

"I suppose it could come to that, Adelaide," said the Chair, trying to defuse the argument. "If we get desperate enough. But we should save it as a last resort." She tapped Buchanan's shoulder. "What would you say to that, Admiral?"

His voice was flat and toneless. "I'm worried about making them think *once*. What if the groupies reverse-engineer total conversion?"

Rock Star

I know stealth.
I know subterfuge.
I know horse/stable/door/bolt.
In the human system where the Network has many components, accessible ma-
habhavium has disappeared. Some vessels have left the system: others in constructs
like Sunburn *have been taken to unreachable planetary surfaces. There is little use in*
further attack there. However, there is a mystery.

The containers humans travel in, surrounded by corrosive air, are propelled by
ejecting matter at high speed. This is not mysterious, only wasteful. I, Irenotin-
cala/Elzabet/Valkyrie, know that humans have done this for thousands of cycles. But
the containers in this system are unlike the Irenotincala/Elzabet/Valkyrie memories.
They eject matter continuously, far more than they can contain. The new memories
from Adam explain this by synthelics, *but they are dismissive of theory: he was con-*
tent to work with closely specified operating characteristics. Syntei, it seems, trans-
mit matter. Irenotincala/Elzabet/Valkyrie dismiss this as impossible, but I, Eve, must
accept it.

It appears theoretically achievable using fractal metamaterials, but possibility-
space is too large for even the Network to examine each potential structure. Synte
refers to a metamaterial matter-transmitter. Its functioning is in the abstract a
straightforward consequence of two-body beta-calculus. The data in the Valkyrie
component held a wealth of information about single-body beta-calculus and its ap-
plications to communication and superluminal travel. Much of it correct. Also a flat
statement, unsupported by proof, that problems in multi-body beta-calculus are in-
herently insoluble. This makes it clear that Valkyrie did not understand G_2-
structures on fractal nonlinearities.

Strategic deduction: *Humans cannot reliably use a Da Silva drive in anything*
other than a very weak gravitational field.

That, however, is incidental to the main issue: the fabrication of a synte. How humans stumbled on the correct fractal metastructure is unknown but also irrelevant. The Network can deconstruct it and replicate it... provided I can secure a sample: natural or synthetic.

Obstacle: one half of a synte pair is inadequate. Fractal structure is dynamic, and must be deconstructed from an active synthelic transportation event.

I need both ends of the syntelic wormhole.

This has now become the Network's strategic imperative of maximal significance.

Capture of one of the high-acceleration ships is impractical for the Network, even with the blipdrive, and memories suggest it would be doubtfully useful. By human action at the kantasynte from which the matter comes, the captured kasynte would cease to exist. Study needs a matched pair.

However, there are also constructs almost like Sunburn, habitats, moving ballistically at most times, but sometimes under slow, unsteady acceleration. They are frequently visited by the fast containers. Adam memories explain this as a temporary match of potential with a planetary synte. The fast containers carrying humans to or from a planet that does not match.

Even these cannot be easily attacked, but they can be infiltrated.

I have created a number of very small components (I know ant) cast in a manner enabling observation and recording. Launched from the inner system they will take many cycles to reach their targets with low relative velocity and cling on, undetected. They will take care to damage nothing.

When fast vessels make contact with the slow ones, the slow ones open. My ants will be able to enter undetected.

Eelkhance

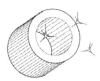

"We may have been approaching this from the wrong end." Wayne Lawes rolled away, with part of Tampledown sticking out behind him.

"I thought you liked this position!" said Tampledown. "We could try—"

"No, I mean syntelics and synthelics. Those first sums the Bianchis reported to you have stood up to every test. So why are we working to have syntei of our own?"

"Because the enemy has them." *When had he got used to referring to the syntelic planets as 'the enemy'?* "Because they're important in a fight."

Lawes tugged distractedly at a corner of the blanket. "But we can't use them, unless we drop Da Silvas. Which would mean surrender. That's what the war is *about*."

"So?"

"If you can't run your tongue across them, merge with them," quoted Lawes obscurely. *He's never met Bianchi,* thought Tampledown, *but he has the same habit of digging up ancient sayings. Maybe it was an IIT thing?* "We don't want to merge with them, so we figure out how to lick them.

"Syntei give the League an advantage. We can't negate it by developing the same technology for ourselves. What's left?"

"I don't understand," Tampledown complained. *He too often didn't, but that was why he had brought in Lawes. It was working.*

"We take it away from them."

Tampledown found this implausible. "Not a chance. Salim Sisters has syntelic breeding reserves everywhere, and decentralised synthelic manufactories."

Lawes sat up, and stretched. "What harms syntei?"

Tampledown was having trouble seeing where Lawes was heading, but gave the obvious answer. "Damage to the metamaterials. They're fragile— the trouble we've had breeding samples…"

"What harms syntei *collectively*? At a distance?"

Tampledown thought for a moment. "Only a simquake."

"Exactly. So we stop thinking of simquakes as given by the *k*-weather gods, and start thinking how to induce them."

Now he saw. A big leap, but... Tampledown stared at Lawes, dumbstruck. *Mother! If this works...* "I could kiss you."

"You already do."

The Chief Scientist swung his legs out and sat on the edge of the bed, his mind racing. "We have to draw up a research plan, Wayne. Now."

Lawes pulled him down again. "We have something to finish first."

They rolled back together. Research can be more aphrodisiac than a 'comp.

Star Chamber, Starhome

The Chair had saved several weeks of pointless debate by convincing the Star Chamber to refer the motion to its Permanent Council. This proved simpler than anticipated because many of the delegates clearly preferred to distance themselves as far as possible from such a momentous and contentious decision. The Concordat Constitution required the Council of the Star Chamber to be convened in person. No telepresence. Six of the seven members were present: two from Starhome (the Chair, acting in that capacity, and the Director of Starhome Security, nominally acting on behalf of the entire Concordat, both *ex officio* members); one each from the senior planets of New Earth, Other Eden, Kevin (*aka* Groombridge 34), and Niny. Nazg was understandably not represented; in its absence the Chair had a casting vote. A trio of constitutional lawyers squatted unobtrusively in the shadows, observing and if necessary advising on the legality of any decisions.

"I formally declare the Star Chamber in session," said the Chair, for the benefit of ultra-high-security recording equipment, and the members' wristcomps—which were ultra-high-security too. Among other things, a record that conformed to constitutional procedure would be a protection against potential prosecution for war crimes.

She outlined the threat posed by IdT's dramatic seizure of Old Earth. Next, she called upon the Director, expecting him to make the case for, in effect, the destruction of the planet, based on a risk-benefit calculation: the danger posed by the breakdown of Quarantine, set against the estimated loss of human life on Old Earth. They key argument was simple: with the groupies on the rampage, and IdT now allied to the Syntelic League, it was time to take Old Earth out of the equation, permanently. The Star Chamber, and only the Star Chamber, had the power to authorise extreme measures.

Instead, the Director gave a rambling speech about constitutional proprieties, only occasionally making a point that the Chair had been expecting. By the time he finished, he had presented the entire case for action, but diluted it with so many caveats and potential legal obstacles that the result was far weaker than the Chair had intended. The speech finished without a clear indication whether the Director was in favour of military action, and if so, what kind of action he was prepared to advocate.

A baffled Chair attempted to force his hand. "What is your overall recommendation?"

"For the moment, I prefer to reserve my opinion," the Director said. The Chair made a brave attempt to cover up this unexpected deviation from the agreed script, by outlining a much stronger case for extreme measures herself, drawing heavily on material from Vance. Wondering, as she did so, what the man was up to.

Then she called for the other members to offer opinions, advice, and facts. The members discussed, often at length. The members deliberated. Throughout, the Director maintained a stony silence.

The members deliberated some more.

The Chair knew what worried them, over and above the ethical and moral dilemma, where either choice would have devastating consequences. Each knew it could one day be a precedent for similar measures against their own world. So she took pains to establish that this was a totally exceptional case. Under IdT, Old Earth had gone rogue. Old Earth, and *only* Old Earth, had routinely waged war for millennia, failing to heed the warning that Quarantine was intended to convey. Admittedly, it had waged war against *itself*, the main reason the Concordat had not taken action earlier. But IdT had changed the game and broken the rules, with its biochemical attack on the Beanstalks: Concordat territory. With Quarantine broken, Old Earth's brand of rabid politics would become a plague, impossible to contain. Especially if the League supplied them with syntei.

The Concordat, in contrast, had exercised huge restraint. Quarantine was mild, purely a preventative measure. She glossed over Stibbons; that had been unavoidable under Concordat law, and few lives had been lost. Stibbons had brought the disaster on itself; Starhome was blameless.

The members deliberated further, and ignoring the Chair's impassioned pleas, passed a motion of adjournment delaying a final decision for three days while they consulted their own officials and military.

"What are you up to?"

The Director, closeted with a furious Chair, proved unusually obtuse. "I assure you, Chair, that I am 'up to' nothing."

"But your performance was terrible."

The Director shrugged. "We all have bad days, Chair. I admit that on further analysis I'm finding the decision less clear-cut than when we last talked. I want the record to show that we gave serious consideration to alternatives, *before* deciding on a barrage of total conversion nukes. The Star Chamber should not be seen to have taken such a decision lightly, whatever the outcome. Surely you see the sense of that?"

"It's not what we agreed. Expressing caution was to be my task."

The Director acknowledged the rebuke by averting his gaze. "It just seemed preferable if I were to raise some of the issues myself. You should be seen to be dispassionate."

The Chair felt that if anyone had displayed a lack of passion, it was the Director. Still, perhaps he had a point, and she doubted any harm had been done. If anything, three days was less than she'd already factored into her thinking.

Even so, the Director's sudden change of heart was close to a betrayal. Fury would do nothing to improve the situation, but she made her displeasure clear in no uncertain terms. If the Director wished to *remain* Director, he would have to get his act together.

He agreed, but without enthusiasm. Was he getting cold feet?

Constitutionally, she was forbidden to interfere with the unfettered application of his personal judgement. As a practical matter, she set several precautionary measures in motion. That was the furthest she could go without exposing herself.

In three days, all would become clear.

The Chair privately assessed the likely voting pattern. Other Eden had made it crystal clear that it would vote for a massive nuclear attack. Equally obviously, Kevin, New Earth, and Niny would vote against. With her casting vote, the ayes would carry the day, provided the Director voted in favour.

But would he? Given his previous lacklustre performance, she had little confidence he would toe the line.

In the event, he made a much more effective speech, emphasising that despite the almost insuperable difficulties of placing agents on Old Earth, he now had new intelligence to report. The Syntelic League was flooding Old Earth with syntei to create an effective shield against Da Silva craft, and in particular against military action by the Concordat. He had foreseen this possibility, but had largely discounted it on the grounds that the League would not wish to allow an untrustworthy group like IdT access to syntei. Unfortunately, the League had shown a deplorable lack of wisdom. It was running scared, and now was the time to drive home that advantage.

He had previously reserved judgement because Security's information on the matter was thin and lacked credibility. For all he knew, Old Earth might already have been equipped with unbreakable syntelic defences, in which case an attack would merely throw away expensive ordnance. Now, thanks to dedicated agents, all had become clear. A preemptive attack, he declared, was mandatory. Delay even by a few days might see the syntelic k-curvature in Old Earth's vicinity cross the critical threshold, wrecking any Da Silva drive that got near the place.

As the Chair had forecast, the outcome was a split vote. Her casting vote was the decider. The Chair would have preferred unanimity, but in the light of the Director's chilling advice, she would happily settle for a narrow vote in favour.

Responsibility now passed to Admiral Buchanan, who lost no time assembling a task force of six of the newest Da Silva destroyers, ugly octahedral vessels each equipped with four total conversion nuclear missiles. The plan was simple and brutal; the Admiral disliked complexity. The destroyers would leave the vicinity of Starhome simultaneously, and emerge at the k-focus nearest to Old Earth. Although this destination was utterly predictable, there was nothing IdT could do about it.

After emergence, the force would regroup, advance towards the planet using its high-speed reaction engines, deliver the payloads of mass death to mass-inhabited targets, and wait to observe the results, transmitting them in real time to Starhome by Da Silva communicator.

The Chair watched the preparations, relayed from Commodore Aschbayne's command vessel. As transit was initiated, communication cut off, as expected. Da Silva communicators do not function during transit.

Several minutes earlier than expected, contact was renewed. Fleet Command promptly went into collective shock.

"All vessels disabled," a laconic voice chanted. "Communicators remain partially functional, Da Silva drives are trashed beyond repair."

"Targeting?"

"Negative. Missiles have insufficient reaction mass to acquire the planet, let alone designated targets." The fleet was drifting, inert, heading for a fiery rendezvous with the sun.

"You knew." The Chair was incandescent. "You deliberately delayed the vote to allow time for Old Earth's syntelic protection to pass threshold. Then you gave us false information. You allowed—nah, *arranged for*—the fleet to be destroyed. Why did you lie to the Star Chamber?"

"To allow time for Old Earth's syntelic protection to pass threshold."

"—?"

"I discovered," the Director said wearily, "that I have a conscience."

"Mother save me from a spook with a conscience! Why did this conscience you so suddenly acquired stop you from telling me that you *knew* Old Earth was protected. Why did you cause the task force to fall into a trap?"

"To put twenty-four total conversion nukes beyond use," said the Director. "The task force fell into the trap because *you* sent it there. It wasn't necessary. The danger that Ira da Terra and Old Earth pose to the Concordat is hypothetical. The impact of dozens of total-conversion nukes is real. *You* may be able to talk yourself into condoning mass murder for the greater good, but to my mind you're doing it for *your* good."

The Chair, normally as cool as liquid helium, bristled with anger. "I took an impossibly hard decision to ensure the future of rationality and the defeat of systematised violence!"

"Yah. By killing billions."

"By saving many more billions. Whom *you* have now killed."

"Hypothetically," the Director repeated.

"You killed six destroyer crews. Nothing hypothetical about them. They were just following orders."

"That's what every accomplice to genocide says."

"So your hands are clean?"

"My hands are stained with blood. Better than drowning myself in it."

The Chair passed a series of mental instructions to her 'comp. The now ex-Director would be arrested and quietly tried for treason. A new Director would be appointed without delay; she had the perfect candidate in mind.

And the Concordat's entire strategy, a developing war on three distinct fronts, would have to be reassessed.

"I regret to report that the former Director of Starhome Security has committed suicide," said Vance. Only she was no longer Vance. She was the new nameless face of Starhome Security.

It's technically true. When he contrived to protect Old Earth against rightful punishment, he signed his own death warrant. The rest was inevitable.

The Chair, undeceived, said: "It makes for a clean end. He exposed the Concordat to a great evil. I feel the endgame is now upon us." She sighed. "But I tell you this, Director. I'm coming round to believing that he may just have saved us from a greater evil."

The new Director noted that the Chair was showing signs of weakness. *Promising.* She made no comment. *No point in making my hopes too obvious.* Instead, she raised a pressing strategic issue that just happened to contradict what the Chair was saying.

"The real problem wasn't the nukes, Chair. It was delivering them by Da Silvas."

"I am aware of that."

"We desperately need a way to negate the League's syntelic defence against Da Silva-drive ships."

"Agreed. Make it so, Director." The unspoken command to leave the room was loud and clear. Equally clearly, this was a test of initiative. After a moment's thought, Vance sent a message to Tampledown.

All priority to Lawes's suggestion.

Deep Space, Nazg System

Fundamental Theorems of Beta-Calculus (as proved by the Network)

1. (No Escape Theorem) Nothing can traverse a kasynte without also traversing its kantasynte.

2. (Knotted Space Corollary) A kasynte cannot traverse itself without also traversing its kantasynte.

3. (Handlebody Theorem) The integrated scalar k-curvature of a synte contributes -4π to the total k-curvature of the universe.

4. (Da Silva Corollary 1) Da Silva matching of k-curvature is impossible in the presence of more than one synte, at a distance that increases exponentially with their number.

5. (Da Silva Corollary 2) If the diameter of a synte within the field of a Da Silva drive is greater than 1/1732 of the field radius, attempted Da Silva operation converts all matter within that radius to energy, distributed equally between departure and arrival points.

My ants *have entered and searched one of the irregularly moving habitats. There are several syntei; most are for communication. But they have not located a complete linked syntelic pair. Each kasynte's kantasynte appears to be elsewhere.*

I have a plan. It depends on one irreducible item of information: the location of the far end of the habitat's synte. This must be the source of arrivals and the destination of departures. Analysis of gyratory trajectory indicates it is on a planetary surface; trajectory compensates for changes in gravitational potential. The Nazg planet Khamûl matches these changes. The large kantasyntei, I conjecture, are on Khamûl.

The Adam Jaxxon memories distinguish between syntei that are 'grown' and 'made', but the Network has not fully analysed this distinction. What is clear is that they are produced, *and produced in quantity. With high probability, a production facility is on Khamûl. With even higher probability, samples exist outside manufactories, and there will be numerous kasynte/kantasynte pairs.*

It is necessary that I have one.

I do not intend to approach Khamûl. That is not possible with a Da Silva because of the second Da Silva Corollary of the beta-calculus. Conjecture: *Khamûl has large numbers of syntei, creating a supercritical k-curvature.*

To approach Khamûl without use of my Da Silva drive would be possible, but to do so would be to commit the same strategic blunder as at Sunburn, and the tactical blunder of insufficient strength. Khamûl's defences would probably be able to detect any such attempt. In any case, breeding a suitable lander is problematic.

Corollary: *A synte can be acquired from Khamûl only by syntelic means.*

Proposition: *since large syntei linked to Khamûl are available to me in only one place, any solution must use it.*

I understand. It will be difficult. It will require stealth *and* subterfuge.

Tactical Decision: *infiltrate spy components created specifically to enter the synte-zone undetected. Traverse it. Locate a kasynte-kantasynte pair (any will suffice). Bring it back through the facility's synthe.*

Bring it to me.

Eve became aware of a new emotion in her sensorium. It took a moment to identify it and name it. *Impatience.*

Adapting to time pressure was difficult enough. Adapting to time constraints not subject to Network command was harder. Emotion overrode rationality; it must be resisted.

After a wait that seemed interminable, she felt the tickling sensation of a *spy component* rejoining the Network, with a communication delay of hours. Lightspeed is lightspeed.

Report.

Ultraviolet codes watched from a million kilometres off flashed on the *spy*'s signalskin in a sequence too rapid for any other life-form to follow. Small chamber / tunnel of rectilinear cross-section / human foot, arching above / large opening towering above / hard surface / heat / light / sound / patchwork of colours, green, yellow, blue. All relayed faithfully to Eve.

As the *spy* learned to classify its surroundings, a planetary surface took shape. Eve had never seen one, but Irenotincala-Elzabet-*Valkyrie* found it completely familiar and normal, though *Valkyrie* had never landed. Eve felt a dissonance but damped it down into deep background. She knew these things. *Sky. Sun. Cloud. Bush. Tree. Concrete.*

The *spy* had hidden itself in the folds of the *clothes* of a human. Eve knew that innumerable *spies* in her subnetwork had attempted the same journey, but most such excursions had ended in failure. This one had been different, and the *spy* had returned to make its report.

The human locomoted—*walked*—along another rectilinear tunnel—*corridor*. It passed a dozen doors, all seemingly identical save for arcane distinguishing symbols. *Numbers. Letters.* Part of *written language*, but not *words*. No end to the intricacy of humans; signalskin was so much simpler… It stopped at a door, opened it, and went in.

The *spy*'s visual sensors swivelled, scanning the interior.

If Eve's own sensors could have done so, they would have popped out on stalks.

Syntei.

Syntei everywhere. Piled up in heaps. Spilling out of crates. Sealed crates surely contained more. The *spy* had located a synte storage area. *Storeroom.*

She had planned for this moment. Another new emotion, *excitement*, diverted her mind for an instant until she suppressed it by an effort of will.

The next steps were complex but already choreographed. While waiting for the planet's rotation to obscure the light of its primary at that location, Eve triggered a larger *component*, the size of a rat, waiting patiently in vacuum on the skin of the orbital facility. With claws and acids it carved a hole in the skin, this time patching it first. No air leaked out, no alarm sounded. As cautious as a true rat, it passed through the synte, the corridor, the door, and gained access to the storeroom. It swallowed three millimetre-diameter synte pairs and scurried back to the orbital facility. It entered the hole in the skin, sealed it behind itself, and opened the outer seal. With a calculated leap, it vanished into space. In two cycles, and about a million kilometres, it would meet a larger component. The two together had mass enough to throw the syntei accurately toward the inner system, fast enough to be captured after just five cycles. Eve would concentrate her awareness at the rock it reached.

Now all that remained was to deconstruct the fractal topology of the samples, learn their metastructure…

… and make more.

Of all sizes.

In quantity.

Nazg

Fatima Salim liked to keep a personal eye on her commercial empire, especially major construction projects. Most oversight had to be delegated, of course, but it was always entertaining to turn up unannounced. It kept her senior managers on their toes. Today, she was observing the latest addition to Salim Sisters' range of high technology from the luxury of her private cruiser. High-resolution vixcams hooked up to a one of the most advanced virt rigs in existence made it seem as if she were floating in space in the midst of the action.

A dull metallic ring, a short broad cylinder with a large central hole, like a groundcar tyre but with a superellipse cross-section — a bulging rectangle with rounded corners — hovered before her eyes, apparently within touching distance. It was a synthe, one of the largest they had been able to manufacture until now: external diameter 2.41 metres, internal 2.03 metres.

At four places around the rim a complicated nanodevice that her engineers called a sprinter was clamped to the ring, straddling its inner surface, reaching outward at both *ka-* and *kanta-*faces to curl round on to the outer surface as well. The *ka-*face of the sprinter was in orbit round Ringwraith, Nazg's fourteenth planet; the *kanta-*face was deep underwater in Old Earth's Kermadec Trench, near the uninhabited rump of mostly-drowned Tonga. Matching the potentials had been difficult, but not insuperable, and additional structures at the *kanta* end kept the water out.

The main problem with a megasynthe is not in building it. That requires suitable materials, fractal nanoprinters to structure the metamaterial that maintains its wormhole, and a lot of knowhow, but Bianchi's twins had invented the principles behind those years ago and the rest had been standard R&D. No, the big problem was getting the *kanta-*face where you wanted it. In principle the old syntelic cascade trick with ever-larger oval synthei would work, but the effort was too great for that to be practical.

Instead, synthetic though they might be, megasynthei were *grown*.

One would be grown, now. At a sign from Fatima the sprinters began to spin, running around the synthe's rim like a wall-of-death rider on a circular track. As they spun, nanomachinery built up a new layer of metamaterial on the outer edge of the ring, while removing it from the inner edge and continuously modifying the structure in between. Imperceptibly, the entire ring expanded. In the abyss, a large Salim Sisters bathyscaphe fed it with raw materials, and more and more sprinters. As the central hole grew in size, extra sprinters were added, chasing each others' tails round and round the circular track, widening the wormhole while maintaining its trans-spatial connection. Extra material, too, fed through the sprinters from intake reservoir to sprinthead.

One of the Twins' most elegant theorems explained why this trick was possible. They had proved the existence of a threshold diameter, beyond which synthei become increasingly stable as the diameter increases. The intuition was simple: the larger the opening, the less curvature-stress it imposes on the k-field. And it is curvature-stress that creates instability.

The details were more technical. Fatima didn't care about the details, or indeed the theorem, except in her spare time — and she had no spare time. The point was, *it worked*.

It took about a week to grow a megasynthe with a one-kilometre radius. Fatima didn't plan to hang around that long, but you could just about convince yourself the thing was getting bigger as you watched. A display at one corner of her vision showed that the diameter was increasing by roughly one centimetre every six seconds. The process was strangely hypnotic. A huge spherical plug blocked the kantasynthe, held against it by the immense pressure of the water.

Once this test run was completed… However, there were other projects to inspect. Satisfied that this one was well-managed and on schedule, she told her pilot to head for the nearest operating mesosynthe offering a short cut back to Morgul's L1 point and Salim Sisters' moonbase.

Rock Star

Synthei could be created in quantity. If humans could do it, the Network should have little difficulty devising its own fabrication procedures. Eve was in no doubt that she was much *smarter* than any human; therefore the Network was incomparably smarter. After all, within less than a cycle it had built a Da Silva drive far more efficient in its use of mahabhavium than any human construct, despite having no foreknowledge of the technology.

That trick could be played again. Eve initiated something that its components which had once been parts of humans thought of as a *crash programme* — bizarrely, nothing to do with wreckage, but indicative of a sustained, targeted burst of creativity, encumbered by as few extraneous constraints as possible, and carried out with utmost haste. Once a concept more alien to the Network than the idea of worlds beyond Rock Star, haste had become familiar, its motivation transparent. However disturbing it might be to the Network's collective psyche, haste was logical, effective, and necessary.

The crash programme focused on karmabhumic and syntelic constructs. The Network must expand its grasp of beta-calculus, but with a new twist: explicit targeting of *applications*, as well as the development of more powerful theories. The aim now must be not merely to understand, but to exploit.

In parallel, new efforts must analyse not only the function of the organic metamaterials that gave syntei their ability to surger the spatial metric, but their structure. The Network had a sample of syntei, but not a sample source, so it must find its own way to synthesise the metamaterials. Such processes, once found, could be scaled up almost indefinitely. The most obvious concern was to ensure stability of the resulting structure, but since humans and other organisms had already achieved this, it must be straightforward.

The superhub partially disconnected into a dozen smaller hubs, each retaining full memory of the collective decisions. Each hub recruited new units, selected for specialist skills — infinitesimal geometry, material fabrication, k-field sculpture, metric deformation analysis, singularity recognition — and a network architect was superimposed to optimise the information-flow.

As human weeks stretched into human months, the groupies of Rock Star synthesised seven hundred thousand metamaterials, seeking resemblance to natural syntei. They studied spacetime, learning about the hidden bundle dimensions. They created string fields, some to manipulate their topology in the very small, some to allow isotopic expansion of the topological changes. They developed their own powerful synthelics.

And they went beyond.

A kasynte was useless until its kantasynte had been transported by wind or water or mobile organism, such as a human, to a useful destination. As the Adam Jaxxon memories explained, that was why it took years to get a Tinka's Ladder hooked up all the way out to the Kuiper belt, so that it could power synjets. For interstellar use, that mobility required physical transportation using a Da Silva drive. This was easy enough with individual syntei, but syntei in quantity destabilised Da Silvas in an explosive runaway feedback loop. Even the combined intellect of the Network was finding it virtually impossible to catalogue the sources of instability and find ways to eliminate them. If the destination could be reached by blipdrive, it would be possible to carry a small synte there and expand it on arrival: but then the blipdrive could not be activated again. In any case, being able to get there with a blipdrive required a closely matching gravitational field, which was a very strong condition.

Theoretically, however, the instability might be eliminated altogether — if the synte and the drive were one and the same. An integrated device, of the right design, might lead to a synte in which the kantasynte could be *transmitted* to a distant location, instead of being carried there inside a vessel. Already the Network could achieve this with nanosyntei over distances of a few metres. But try as it might, the methods failed, destructively, even between distinct rocks in its own system. The calculations were too difficult, even when the best nodes in the Network were strongly linked. A self-transmitting kantasynte remained tantalisingly out of reach.

But think of the potential, if one could be built.

Nazg System

The first thing the that registered on any component was a 5-kilometre rock falling in from the outer deeps on a fast hyperbolic orbit. As it passed the human-infested Goldilocks zone it began to lose volatiles in the heat of Nazg's giant star, showing rich nutrients in the resulting coma, but the delta-v to catch or colonise it was unprofitable while so many rocks in tamer orbits remained unclaimed. The Network tracked the new arrival instinctively, like a pedestrian sensing obstacles on the sidewalk, but didn't pay conscious attention to it.

The Network was not aware, at any level, of the concealed kasynthe the humans had installed on the rock.

As the coma grew, so did the kasynthe, fed by metamaterial entering its kantasynthe, still hidden from casual inspection. The synthe between them grew deeper than had ever been needed before, but still created tidal forces that nothing living could survive. Simultaneously, the synthe grew wider. When it was five kilometres across, the humans dropped a reflective disc through it, sufficiently elastic to resist being torn apart.

When the disc shot out into a nearly circular orbit around Nazg, that did attract the Network's attention. In a few hours, signalskinned from rock to rock at lightspeed across the inner system, the news of the presumably human incursion would reach the components that directly supported Eve's identity. But those components lacked the data to deduce that the orbit was almost perfectly matched, in gravitational potential, to a planet known as Old Earth.

Immediately behind the disc came an object about ten centimetres across. It settled into an orbit two kilometres away, and achieved a temperature of 3°C, masked by the disc from the blaze of Nazg's star. The Network assigned more processing, and noticed that maintaining both this position and the star-facing attitude of the disc required active control by syntelically inexhaustible attitude jets. The synthe left on the comet destroyed itself.

The Network responded with physical investigation. Components swarmed from the nearest rock, two million klicks off, to investigate the disc, but they took a week to reach it—or almost reach it. Any groupie that came closer than one kilometre, either to the disc or to the small thing it shaded, was vaporised by pinpoint X-ray laser beams.

Two weeks later, both of the enigmatic objects were in the middle of the swarm, watched intently. Eve devoted a whole bank of her components to analysing them, coming mainly to the conclusion that she/they did not yet fully understand *strategy*, or *weapon*. She put in place an X-ray laser (as usual, improved from the human design), as a precaution.

Finally, the smaller object started to grow. It seemed at first to be growing into another disc, but it became apparent that it was a spherical ball, coming through a synthe that grew to allow it passage. At first it was held against the synthe by a hadal pressure of over a thousand atmospheres, allowing nothing surrounding it to escape. When it reached a diameter of 1·2 kilometres, the ball popped out with a gigantic belch of cold salt water and the synthe self-destructed. Synjets frantically steered the ball to the centre of the shade.

The metamaterial technology to create it had been developed to explore Okeanos, a planet without surface land or shallows. It was now deployed on a grander scale. Spun rather than built, a spherical membrane had grown loosely in the hadal depths of Old Earth, with the spinnerets scraping the rocks to scare the mobile sea-life into the growing envelope, rather than out of it. Stronger than beanstalk material, the membrane was transparent to light, but with a shift in wavelength. When the spinnerets sealed the bag, water was pumped in to inflate it to a taut sphere, able to resist the immense pressure that would soon stretch it against the vacuum.

Almost lost within the ball drifted Impana Rhee's Deep Research Institute, retrofitted with internal syntelic exits to a spacecraft orbiting another star.

Throughout its volume were scattered the squid, who swam quickly toward the surface, drawn by the lights of the stars. In all the generations of *Dosidicus madhu*, none had ever seen any light but bioluminescence: now they gazed upon the universe, and their skins flickered with communication about it, in reds, greens and yellows.

Seen through the outer membrane, they flickered in different frequencies of ultraviolet—visible colours, to the groupies.

The groupies approached cautiously, until at ten metres from the surface the X-ray lasers warned them to come no closer.

Even with the hints from Eve's memories, groupies had never quite grasped human communication by sequentially structured sound. Messages in nerve bundles made sense to them, within and between components. The world happened in parallel, so messages had to do the same. Strings of language tokens were unnatural and cumbersome; Eve had narrowed herself intensely, even while squeezing out of the Network's box, to be able to manipulate them. Most components could not do even that, let alone parse wheezes and stops.

Here, however, was natural communication!

It was as alien to them as religious healing to evidence-based doctors, the logical principles radically different, but no *more* alien. With something akin to joy, the groupies flashed simple messages in ultraviolet, neither knowing nor caring that the squid saw them at longer wavelengths.

The squid, though confused, responded.

The Network settled down to learn squid.

"What are those squid doing, Doxor Rhee?"

"You've been watching the same vixcam feed as I have," said Impana, wishing her newest grad student had a little more imagination. "Summarise your observations."

"Well," said Mary Nguyen, "they've stopped making any of the patterns we've catalogued. But they're flashing more than ever. Mostly on the side toward the groupies."

"And?"

"The groupies are flashing too."

"And?"

"Their patterns — groupies *and* squid — are getting more complex."

"So, what are they doing?"

"Learning. Or teaching. Or… both." Nguyen paused. "Could I go out there?"

"To do what?"

"I don't know… see how they react to me? Perhaps we can learn more from actions. Physical responses."

Even a diving suit with built in exoskeleton power cannot bend at hadal depths, though recent work had produced some clumsy abyssal flexibility. 'Going out there' meant controlling robot arms from foetal position in a miniature bathyscaphe; it took an hour to get into it and seal it against pressure, and another hour to raise the pressures in the airlock. But she was out now, and navigating toward the squid.

They responded physically.

As a group.

They started to englobe her. A solitary squid could not harm the robot she was in, but she did not want to find out what a thousand could do. She recognised their collective hunting formation and retreated toward the Deep Research Institute, using the bathyscaphe's water jets for speed.

The hunters tracked her every move, but she managed to stay out in front. Reaching the airlock, she found the keypad and pressed the entry sequence. The airlock was still at hadal pressure, so it opened immediately. She slipped in and the outer door closed behind her, just before the squid reached her.

"What did you learn?" came Impana Rhee's voice over the intercom.

"Think before going out," said Mary, waiting for the lock to match internal pressure, then fill with air. As she navigated the robot through the inner door, she saw the exterior vixcam feed.

The outer door was not a mass of squid, battering vainly against it. Most were hanging back, making space for a single squid. That one wasn't even pressing against the door.

It was by the keypad. Pressing the correct sequence for entry.

"There was no immediate danger," Impana Rhee reassured her group. "First, the outer door *cannot* open before the pressures equalise. That needs the inner door to be closed and the chamber to be filled. Second, what would happen then? If the outer door opened to the squid?"

"They'd get in," said Mary, "one or more of them."

"They'd get into *the airlock*," said Impana. "But the inner door would stay shut until…"

"It was down to inside pressure. And the squid had exploded."

"Right. Making a mess, but no damage. So, Mary: what else do we learn from this, aside from 'stop working and start thinking'?"

"Uh…"

"What we learn is that a new kind of intelligence is directing the squid's collective actions. That intelligence can come from just one place."

"The groupies," someone said.

"Right," said Impana. "The group-functioning that we have been studying for so long has been surrendered to a larger group. Our squid are now water-breathing groupies."

Nazg, Inner system

Eve convened a massively enlarged superhub to help her understand the new data. Now, as syntelic optical links spread, components on different rocks experienced no lightspeed delay. This superhub was a hundred times the size of the previous one, and *much* faster.

There were two main aspects to consider: humans would have called them biology and technology. Eve did not draw the same distinctions between 'living' and 'non-living' matter, or not in the same way; but she divided the superhub into two (communicating) parts, and thought about both at once.

The first hub considered Network interaction with other information-processing entities (a concept as alien to it, until recently, as 'blue sky'). The second considered what the Network could do autonomously.

Hub 1:

Item: Previously unknown components, differing from those already absorbed, in ways the Network struggled to accept. Organic inhabitants, not of vacuum, nor of a planetary land surface, but of liquid. Identified by its optical transmission properties as oxidised hydrogen, a common substance mainly found in its solid phase in the cometary halos of stars. To Irenotincala/Elzabet/Adam the substance was instantly recognisable: *I know* water, *I know* ocean. *I know* squid.

Item: Squid. These… creatures… employed skin-pattern communication, akin to that of the units of the Network. Slower, more primitive, of limited intelligence, yet closer in style and format to the Network's own system than to human thought patterns. Close enough to make control simple. What use the Network could make of squid was uncertain, as was the humans' motivation for bringing a water-filled sphere of the creatures to this system. It might be an attempt to communicate with the Network, but more likely it was an attempt to intercept and decipher the Network's instructions to its units. As such, it had potential applications in warfare and could be classified as *threat*. However, it must also be given an interim dual classification: *opportunity*. Application unspecified.

Item: Habitats. The Network components' enjoyment of *vacuum* was called *extremophile* in *Valkyrie's* memories. So were the squid, in *water*, at pressure of tonnes per square centimetre. The human habitat, at a mere kilogram per square centimetre, was the default reference habitat, though extreme to both squid and Network, and in opposite directions. Other habitats were brought to the superhub's attention: underwater *volcanoes*, the oceans under the ice of Enceladus, the interiors of humans, the floating methane breathers common in Jovian planets. Silicoid electronic forms deposited on the walls of cascade ponds, reproducing by template deposition. Slow-moving creatures in temperatures close to absolute zero, but with fast-thinking superconductive brains. Cloud-floaters in upper atmospheres, exploiting high levels of radiation.

All dependent on the compression of gravity wells... *Query*. What might have evolved on the planets that the Network had demolished to make living space, assuming them useless?

Item: Despite all controls, squid periodically reduced their metabolism, changing their cognition in strange ways, with muscle control disabled. The components duplicated from parts of Tinka and Elza recognised this as *sleep*, a behavioral quirk that the squid shared with humans. Their brains entered this mode to remove toxins created while awake. It was a clumsy arrangement that left the creatures vulnerable, but it had interesting implications. Eve had been using her human-derived components only in their *waking* mode; experimentally, she adjusted them to run in sleep mode, and discovered *dreaming* and *nightmares*. Their cognitive processes lacked all reason, but somehow made these components more insightful. Eve made the change to regular sleep mode permanent, while strengthening the safeguards that prevented her from taking action while *asleep*.

Item: The graphene processors of *Valkyrie's* components had been duplicated, but not invented, by the Network.

Item: The Network was exploring *symphonies* that ranged over a hundred octaves. But it had not imagined the possibility of the symphonic form.

Item: *Writing*, from clay tablets to nudged quanta. Retrievable information, separate from active memory.

Item: *Fiction*, a vast expansion of possibility space, including not only conjecture but acknowledged impossibilities — yet *consistent* impossibilities. *Interesting* impossibilities.

Item: Songs, emitted for different purposes (besides mating displays) by humans, *birds, whales, dolphins,* and other *cetaceans*. Novel means of communication, not language, not signalskin images. Another *interesting*. A very *interesting* interesting.

Hub 2:

Item: Human ability to materialise a 1·2 kilometre ball of water, containing live organisms, inside a planetary system. Technology as yet unknown, resembling syntelics, but on a scale not previously encountered. The same dual classification of *threat/opportunity*, with both more extreme.

Deduction: Materialisation is a *k*-field phenomenon, applied karmabhumic technology. Deeply familiar technology to component *Valkyrie*; known to the components Tinka, Elza and Adam, used by them without full comprehension.

Deduction: Matter-transmission (of *ocean* and *squid*) at the present level of human technological development, so far as is known, has most probably been achieved by syntelic means.

Secondary deduction: The probability that syntei of biological origin—the type first acquired by humans—can be bred to a size capable of transmitting a 1·2 kilometre ball is extremely small. The probability that such a large plant could be grown in less than a millennium is even smaller. Nothing remotely similar is in any component's databanks.

Item: Synthelics. In the short period that has elapsed since Eve's... *birth*, humans have invented processes to *manufacture* syntei. Gigantic syntei. The pair Eve had acquired was small, and none of her absorbed Adam Jaxxon memories included syntelic engineering on this huge scale, so this ability must be a recent addition to human technology. Inference: human capabilities are not static. This adds further unpredictability to their actions, and greater threat.

Item: Adam Jaxxon was working on a *military corvette*, which he expected to *fight* the Concordat.

The deductions that followed were diverse and came in a rush. Among them was one that the Network gave top priority. *Interesting new way to exploit component-cluster Adam Jaxxon.*

Deep Space, Nazg System

Commander Ferenc Dumachus:

I'm still patrolling Nazg, but now I'm training others to do it. Not just in the ecliptic plane, and not just against the Concordat. The groupies that have invaded the inner system have acquired syntei. When I said war is hell, I was just missing my wife, not thinking of demons. Those bastards could pop up pretty much anywhere.

Well, not quite. They can't move or accelerate fast in the Goldilocks zone, because they start from deep in the Nazg gravitational well. Tinka's Ladder syntei need kantasyntei in the high places it takes months or years to reach, and the groupies haven't reached them yet, here or around Rock Star. There, it will take them a long time; Rock Star has no planets, so the velocities available to start a ladder are smaller. At any rate, we now have to patrol the entire enormous Goldilocks sphere, not just the spaces between planets, to stop the groupies gaining height. Any rock heading outward, with any speed, we have to intercept.

Any rock.

If it were only syntei, we would worry only about big rocks. When there's a gravity barrier, you can't play the usual trick and do an uphill syntelic cascade, pushing bigger syntei through smaller ones. A big synte has to go the long way. But that's not a restriction any more. Synthei can expand in place, and the groupies to operate them can breed in place. We've found them on outward bound rocks the size of grapefruit. If just one groupie gets through, they'll have enough power to operate synjets at least as good as ours—and groupies don't need heavy life support like we do. Lighter ships, and the scientists think small groupies can stand accelerations up to 25g.

If one gets through, we're toast.

I'm whistling in the dark with that If. *When* one gets through—or when they get a ladder built at Rock Star—they'll control the whole system.

I don't know if I'll ever come home to my wife.

Rock
Star

Self-transmitting kantasyntei remained out of reach, but the Network — *I know serendipity* — had found a partial solution.

The Network could focus nanosyntei over distances of fifteen metres. Larger syntei were unstable without an anchor at the far end, collapsing with destructive energy release... but they did exist, for a half-life in nanoseconds. If the focus was relaxed within that time, the energy it summoned from the vacuum (rather, the high probability amplitude of that energy) was relaxed with it. No *permanent* synte was created, but within that critical instant of metastability, a Network component could be transferred through the wormhole before it died.

And perhaps, an enigma could be investigated.

Nazg

"There's someone at the door," said Mary Nguyen.

"So?"

"The airlock door."

Impana tried not to look irritated. "The squid have been there for weeks. Just hanging there, in rotation." Then her brain kicked in. "Have you noticed something new?"

"Some*one* new, pressing the keypad, in the old sequence," said Mary. It had been changed. "He's not really dressed for the climate." She shared her outside-view screen.

"Not dressed at all, but he looks remarkably comfortable. Any ID?"

"He doesn't look as if he's wearing any."

"I was asking the station AI."

"Conflicting evidence," chanted the AI. "He is a precise match to the externals of Adam Jaxxon, but the medical data on Adam Jaxxon do not suggest the capability of survival underwater, let alone at hadal pressures."

"Adam Jaxxon? Who died on—"

"On *Sunburn*," sang the AI, "which was eaten by groupies."

Impana came to a decision. *Accept the danger, the potential gain is far greater.* "Flash the doorlights."

The naked man outside glanced at the lights, pointed to the keypad, and gave an inquiring shrug.

"Open the outer door."

"Is that safe?"

Mary sounded nervous. Impana sympathised, but the decision was already made. "Absolutely not," she said. "But no more dangerous than leaving him outside. And a lot more chance we can learn something."

As the door opened, the man smiled his thanks and swam into the airlock. The door closed behind him.

"Scanners?"

"Internal anatomy very divergent from human," reported the AI. "No internal structure for gas exchange."

"No lungs?" asked Mary.

"No lungs or gills. The working fluid is the same colour as blood, in the visible spectrum—that's part of the colour match to Adam Jaxxon—but the chemistry is different. And it is not circulated by a heart."

"Then by what?" Impana asked impatiently.

"It does not have a local closed loop. It emerges from an organ in the right side of the chest, which evidently contains a synte, and returns to another, on the left. He contains a quantity of mahabhavium, possibly enabling Da Silva microjumps."

In their screens, the man (?) made a gesture of lowering something around him.

"Shall I empty the waterlock?" chanted the AI.

Impana thought for a moment. "Do—but retain pressure, for the moment. Turn on the microphones."

The clear image was replaced by a mass of bubbles, as air was pumped in and water out, under zero gravity. The bubbles of air slowly united, to be replaced by wobbling blobs of water, which were gradually sucked out. The man waited with apparent patience.

"Thank you," he said. "Can you hear me?"

"How is he *speaking*, without lungs?" marvelled Mary Nguyen.

"The larynx appears to have been replaced by a solid state system," sang the AI, "but surely a more urgent matter is to answer him."

"I forgot my manners," said Impana, turning on the speakers. "Yes, we hear you."

"May I come in?"

"Would low pressure trouble you? We exist at a thousandth of what surrounds you now."

"I would prefer the transition to be gradual, but I was originated in near-vacuum. Five minutes?"

"Five minutes it is." The sound of the extraction pumps made conversation impossible for a while, until the pressure in the airlock reached one atmosphere.

"You don't get the bends? Of course, stupid of me—no lungs."

"And no dissolved nitrogen. I look forward to long discussions of comparative physiology, but for now... may I come in?"

"Opening the inner door now. You'll find coveralls in a locker to your right."

"Coveralls? Ah, of course... social norms."

"And warmth, but I suppose that doesn't affect you."

"I can't exist below a hundred Kelvin, or above two thousand," said the man, dressing, "but within that range I'm comfortable. Am I presentable now?"

"Of course," said Impana. "Now: who are you?"

"I have all the memories of Adam Jaxxon on register recall, so as much as I have an *I*, it's Adam Jaxxon's. But I have secondary access to the memories of most of the other people on *Sunburn*, as integrated by the Network—and of course longer-latency access to those of the entire Network, over millions? yes, millions, of years. So I doubt if the Adam Jaxxon on *Sunburn* would regard me as Adam Jaxxon. Particularly as my motives and goals are aligned with the Network's."

"The Network being the groupies? The things that ate *Sunburn*?"

"I'm not familiar with that term, but yes... except that it's a mistake to use the plural. Do you say that your lips and teeth and stomach ate a banana, or that you did? The Network subsumed *Sunburn*."

So the groupies were the components of a single collective super-organism. Or, at least, that's what it felt like to them. It. Individuals were more like organs and cells, with signalskin flashes in place of signalling molecules and nerve impulses. That was intelligence that would raise a few pulse rates in the Nazg system. *Groupies*, indeed.

It also went part way towards explaining their bafflingly diverse pheno-types. Each played its own role in the collective. But for some reason they didn't mass-produce anything of the same design—not like blood or nerve cells in humans. Maybe physical form was mutable even for individuals.

Softly, softly... "So you are the Network?" in a studiedly casual voice.

"That is an approximate truth, within the limits of Galaxic. But so is 'I am Adam Jaxxon'."

"And why are you here?"

For the first time, Jaxxon seemed to pause, perhaps conferring with the Network, or maybe just searching for the right words. He answered with another question. "Why was this station built?"

"To study abyssal life—squid, in particular, but in the mesh of all life."

"And why do you do that? You, in particular?"

"Because squid are the most interesting things in the world," said Impana Rhee, without even having to think. "And to prevent their extinction."

"Well, there you have it," said Adam Jaxxon. Or the Network. "Humans are *interesting*."

Eelkhance

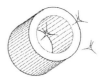

Wayne Lawes paced to and fro while he organised his thoughts. Ordinarily he wouldn't have bothered — with Lawes, what was currently in his mind tended to emerge unprocessed — but he was presenting his latest ideas to the research group in an informal seminar. That wouldn't have made any difference, but there was so much buzzing round inside his head that for once he hardly knew where to start. Even talking about his ideas sparked new connections, as piece after piece clicked into place. However, some pieces still didn't fit, and there were big gaps.

He zoomed in on one part of the problem where there were fewer distracting puzzles, as Tampledown watched with his usual feeling of awe and irritation.

"We have the habit of thinking of the scalar k-field as a real thing," he began, "but strictly it's the highest common invariant of a tensor which is *equi*variant under a generalised Lorentz transform. That breaks down into conjugate factors — quantum conjugates — which transform into each other."

"How so?" asked someone in the audience.

Lawes ran exploratory fingers through his IIT bonsai haircut. He looked like a chimpanzee grooming its mate, though with less hair and much less success. Better-built, though. "It's basically trivial. You apply the polarisation formula…" and the rest was a five-minute flurry on the slapscreen.

"Dah," said the questioner. "Trivial, basically. So what next?"

"We've found a way to measure one of the factors, as seen by a privileged observer—"

"Privileged, how?"

"Comoving with the equipment, dah? We measure one of the factors, *very* precisely, and by Heisenberg that forces the conjugate factor to be almost anything. That effectively freezes the scalar k-field until we stop measuring." Lawes was now in full flow, gushing mathematical physics like a newly drilled oil well. "Of course, time and energy being conjugate variables too, that's less than a microsecond for practical purposes, but that's enough to wrinkle the k-level set. Correction of the imbalance gives a simquake. Not more than a sim-temblor, really, but every synte within about 230 kilometres dies, and every synjet goes ballistic."

"Goes ballistic?" put in one of the xenobotanists who was attending out of politeness. "But I thought—"

"Like a rocket that runs out of fuel, no more thrust, just the momentum it has already acquired. If it's not in atmosphere, becomes utterly predictable by the laws of ballistics."

"Ah." The xenobotanist had the look of someone who has unexpectedly learned something.

"Can't dodge an incoming missile," Lawes told him, driving the point home with his usual disregard for tact and decorum. "If it *is* a missile, it can't follow the dodges of a target. Basically, it's a sitting rock."

The botanist went pink and started paying close attention to his knees, which stuck out and were rather bony. Presumably hoping to deflect further humiliation. Everyone knew what Lawes was like, they'd all suffered. He didn't mean any harm, it was just the unthinking candour of a single-minded genius. And the arrogant bastard was usually right.

"Can you say more," asked an engineer, "about how you compute the 'quake's size?" The botanist's expression returned to politeness.

Owemgee

The last of the Old Earth emigrants had arrived seven years ago. Taiko had been on Owemgee for fifteen, and nobody called her an 'Earthy' any more, let alone a 'Dirty'. Among the earliest of Earth's colony worlds, it was still underdeveloped. As each new wave of colonists set out with improved equipment and more knowledge of what to expect, the early worlds had tended to get overtaken. Owemgee was left with some sympathy for the underdog, though with another wave of anti-Concordat agitation on Old Earth, the Owems who thought about the place at all were inclined to stay clear. Patting an underdog that bites is unrewarding.

Taiko had a good, quiet life, working as an agricultural technician, and two husbands (on alternate weekends), who between them kept the apartment clean. She mostly ate at her local group mess, which was where she heard about the seizure of the Old Earth Beanstalks. She kept quiet, and hoped mainly that it would not lead to unpleasantness with the people she knew.

When Old Earth joined the Syntelic League, it felt like the final separation. No more Da Silva travel there (not that she wanted to), and certainly no syntei would come to Owemgee! But Da Silva communicators beyond Mars still worked, and relayed a trickle of public and private messages to places in the Concordat. A couple of weeks late, she got her usual birthday greetings from her birth family.

But one of them wasn't quite usual.

"Have some *oh jing o je* for your birthday!" wasn't a standard greeting anyway, and what had suggested to her parents that she was no longer a vegetarian? She hadn't even thought about dried squid for years! Now she found herself thinking about it, endlessly. She replied to her parents wishing them the same, but got no relief from the compulsion. Finally she went to the fish market, and bought a hundred grams. At home she cooked it in red pepper paste, and ate it.

Nobody within seventy light years could have predicted what would happen next.

A dormant retrovirus implanted in every cell of her body had passed all the health checks of Concordat immigration. It was not, after all, a known disease: it was created by the biochemists of Helmut Moser's company, and designed to evade all the standard tests. The shift in pathways induced by chemicals unique to squid — more specifically, created by the drying process — activated it to express as a gene. It began to replicate.

The next day, she was sneezing furiously.

The day after, her lungs filled with liquid and the alveoli were dead. Despite all that Owemgee's limited emergency medical response team (unused to infectious diseases) could do, she died at midnight. By then, a hundred people were sneezing furiously.

Over a billion people died. About 10% of Owems were naturally immune, so a hundred and fifty million survived, for the moment. By the time the planetary infrastructure was repaired, by Concordat teams working under quarantine conditions, forty million were left. Owemgee began, yet again, the centuries-long slow climb to prosperity.

Two Mountains, Qish

"It was necessary." Ira da Terra's normal inscrutability was replaced by a faint air of defiance. *Guilt?* Unlikely.

"It was a crime against humanity," Sadruddin said. He sounded numb. He felt numb.

"A *necessary* crime against humanity. A crime that is necessary is no crime." Ira gave him her trademark withering look, but Sadruddin's upbringing in the Church had proofed him against such things. When you've spent much of your adult life looking over your shoulder for bone-hammers, withering looks don't really have much traction.

"In any case, it was a sky-devil world, not a human one," she added. Her Manifesto said there was one true human world: just one. He supposed the Syntelic worlds had to qualify as honorary human, in her view, now that Old Earth had joined the League.

Even Shevveen-Duranga, the product of a community in which sudden retail death was a formally recognised part of religious politics, looked revolted by this wholesale slaughter. The problem was, they could all understand Ira's point of view. If you were a Dirty, you grew up hating the people who kept you that way. The Quarantine was not the root of Old Earth's problems, but it certainly prevented escape. And, given the Concordat's threat to every world in the Syntelic League, it would be horribly easy to go along with her beliefs.

Sadruddin stood his ground. "You signed a treaty," he said. "Did you read it?"

"It was an act of mutual convenience—"

"You didn't. Nar, da Terra, it was a legally binding document, a solemn obligation. And it did not permit you to mount an attack of any kind without proper authorisation by the League's War Cabinet. Let alone a biowarfare attack killing a billion innocent people."

"A billion sky-devils. None is innocent."

"A billion more than you agreed to when you signed the treaty!"

Ira showed no remorse. "I did it to defend the Syntelic League," she said. "And to demonstrate the Movement's capabilities. We're not primitives! We have access to sophisticated weapons. The Concordat will now understand this, and will think twice before making further threats." She took a deep breath. "They destroyed the Stibbons Beanstalk with a nuke. They tried to destroy the true Earth with gigaton bombs: they were ready to kill billions, billions of *real humans*. That is the enemy we face, so we used language the enemy understands."

"The language of provocation?" asked Sadruddin.

General von Hayashiko raised a hand. "I hate to say this, Augustine, but the woman has a point."

Sadruddin snorted in derision.

"The General is right," said the Colloquist. "What's done is done. We can mourn our dead enemies, but we can't bring them back to life."

Sadruddin reluctantly took the point. "Ira da Terra: do *not*, ever, mount an attack on the Concordat without clearing it with this Cabinet. Whatever your motives. Stick to the terms of the treaty. I'm not going to threaten you — I doubt that would have any effect — but the Syntelic League is far more powerful than Old Earth. And even Old Earth gave you a run for your money until you acquired League technology."

Ira paused, as if weighing the options. Then: "I agree. Perhaps the same result could have been obtained with less loss of life. I know you think me a monster, but I have my reasons. I am also open to reason, and on this occasion my thirst for justice overcame that."

There was silence. No one had expected that. True agreement? Expediency? They would have to suspend judgement. Only Ira da Terra could provide the Syntelic League with enough *combatant* defenders: piloting could be trained, but facing death was different.

Shevveen-Duranga brought the discussion back to the main issue. "As the General said, we can none to life return — unless their brains were quickly in cryo tanks placed, clearly not here the case." Sadruddin wondered where she'd learned that, and why she'd remembered it, but the Colloquist was a deep one — a metaphor of which she would have approved. That was why he'd put her in charge of espionage.

"We can, however," she continued, "ensure that their deaths were not of meaning bereft."

"Meaning?" Sadruddin asked.

"We fight a war on two fronts. This is poor strategy. We fight the Concordat, a human enemy acting against the Syntelic League. We fight the groupies, against all humanity a foe. Of the two, the groupies pose an immeasurably deeper threat.

"What we *ought* to do is join forces against them. But the rump of the Concordat is in shock at loss of power. Just as for the religious, heretics are an evil more profound than unbelievers. It stands immune to reason." Sadruddin thought of the Deacon, and nodded. "It hates and fears more deeply. Concordat aggression we must eliminate from the equation.

"Beneath and beyond the morality of IdT's headstrong and unwise attack, it is an opportunity forced upon us. We must accept. Humanity's future may depend."

Sadruddin suddenly understood the price of being Boss Frog. "You mean, we have no choice, not only to admit complicity in mass murder, but to compound it by issuing our own counter-ultimatum. Hands off our syntei, or we'll loose plagues on you. *Again*."

"You speak truth. Crude force they understand, right now. Other language, they do not so much as hear. Threats they will hear, however unwelcome. The Concordat has most to lose. They can threaten total-conversion weapons, but their use would defeat also themselves, giving control only of radioactive deserts and planets ruled by fear. With their own surviving worlds quarantined even from each other against our plagues, where stands the Da Silva monopoly? Interstellar travel is dead."

"There was once a phrase for this," the General said.

"Pyrrhic victory?"

"Not the one I was thinking of, though I have studied the campaigns of ancient Rome. No, this one is far more apposite. It's still well known to military strategists. Effective, when it works, but hideously dangerous. The acronym is appropriate: MAD."

"Which means?"

"Mutual assured destruction."

Nazg, Outer System

It had been a routine day.

Tinka Laurel preferred routine days.

She had no deep-space combat experience, but every atmosphere flier needed to know strong defence against the weird aggressive things in the skies of many planets; eradicating species was a vice best left to Earthies, but applying a bit of selection pressure for 'stay clear of aircraft' genes made sense. The formal Navy had been a Concordat monopoly, and was still loyal, so the League needed every skilled pilot it could get. Her reflexes outweighed her lack of naval experience.

She had hands-on command of a brand new squadron of eight experimental destroyers, practicing some tricky manoeuvres to keep her seven Commanders on their toes, while patrolling the Goldilocks zone of the Nazg System against inner system and interstellar threats. That was fun, despite being routine.

Thing was, she preferred routine days that *stayed* routine days.

This one didn't.

"Bandits inbound!" sang *Dormouse*'s computer, projecting coordinates on to her retina. "Momentary solitronic signal detected, consistent with a Da Silva. Now silent, trajectory ballistic." Pause. "Emergence at plausible focus point, far enough away from any Nazg world or facility to avoid destructive syntelic interaction, but within a week's range of several, by reaction drive."

"Shields up. Transmit enhanced level of real-time data to Nazg Central. Intercept source of signal at top speed."

Like most new ships of the Syntelic League, these were propelled by synjets. Matter surged down Tinka's Ladder from the Oort Cloud, giving both the momentum from their fall and rocket power from vaporising them. The shields, yet another invention from Salim Sisters, were a synthetic development from Qish's lurepools. They could be multiply deployed around the ship as synthelic deflectors—perhaps more accurately, absorbers, although there wasn't really a suitable word for what they did. Lasers or missiles that hit a kasynthe dropped straight through to the kantasynthe, torn apart by tidal forces; the ship itself was safe behind the cosmic short cut. Though the shields weren't infallible—their rims could be destroyed by a chance—they reduced the ship's footprint, confused its attackers (at least, until they sussed the new device out) and improved its chances of survival.

Tinka wanted to keep the intruders—whatever they were—as far from any Nazg target as possible. As the acceleration kicked in, she sent a quick query to her navigator, a thought transmitted from mind to mind, courtesy of two Salim Sisters neurally enabled wristcomputers.

#Target not yet clear,# came the reply.

#Let me know as soon as any of them changes course.#

She switched to voice to address the ship. She could have used a neural link, but voice was just as quick and more robust. "Identity?"

Ever since the demolition of *Sunburn*, Tinka and her squadron had been on the lookout for groupies; more accurately, for groupie Da Silva starships. Further analysis of *Sunburn's* recordings had revealed the total absence of radio communications. All attackers were likely to try to maintain radio silence, of course, but there was always some low-level leakage—encrypted, disguised, but *there*. At the very least, some solitronic activity.

All attackers except groupies. All she had heard of was their equivalent of close conversation: ultraviolet light, skin to skin.

"Identity unknown," sang *Dormouse*. "*k*-field structure crisper than standard Concordat drives. Acquired data now sufficient for visual reconstruction."

On her retina, and those of the crew of every destroyer in D-squadron, seven clustered shapes took form, fuzzy and ill-defined at their current distance, but improving in definition even as she watched. Six of the bandits were basically spheres, with plasma drives attached. The seventh looked like a cube with triangular pyramids on its corners.

The plasma drives fired, and the spheres scattered in six directions.

Numbers flowing across the top of her vision indicated the size of the intruders.

"*Dormouse*: confirm! *One point seven metres?*"

"Yah," intoned the ship. "And the spheres are one point two. Not ships, for sure. Symmetry of the truncated cube increases the probability of a Da Silva, presumably an automated delivery system for the spheres—one per face, maintaining cubic symmetry, now detached. The individual spheres are too compact to support stable Da Silva propulsion, therefore something else. They're showing thirteen gravs acceleration – nothing human inside."

"Weapons of some sort, delivered by the cube?" Tinka asked.

"Probability 97%. They could be headed for the munitions factories of Thaurband habitat, Crescent City on Dol Guldur, uranium mines on the same planet, the military complex on Carn Dûm, and the two scientific installations at the poles of Túrin, the innermost moon of Glaurung. But it's hard to be sure until they stop accelerating."

Well, it could have been worse, Tinka thought. *Going for some of the least defended targets; suggests a weakness.* "Do you think it's groupies?" *It could be, they have extensive knowledge of human space.*

"Either groupies… or devices."

Tinka didn't like the sound of either, but she wanted to know which. "*Dormouse*: Devil's advocate. Assume they're some kind of Concordat or" – *perish the thought* – "Syntelic League device. If so, what could they be?"

The vessel stopped shuddering as its synjet hit maximum thrust. The other seven ships in the squadron had fanned out to the side and all the ships were following coordinated randomly variable trajectories, avoiding presenting a single compact or predictable target.

"No known device of human origin," the ship chanted.

"Groupie constructs, then." #Weapons: you get that?#

#Loud and clear, Captain.#

#Whatever those things are, I want them killed. One and Two: select X-ray lasers. Three and Four, nukes. The rest of you: hold back and observe. We have no idea how they'll react. Ready to fire on my order, as soon as we get in laser range – #

There was a noise like ripping silk. And blackness.

#*Synoptic communicators down!*#

#Stand down.#

Tinka emerged blinking from the telepresence suit through which she had felt herself part of *Dormouse*, with stepped-down echoes of its synjet-powered thirty gravs of acceleration. Her seven lieutenants joined her.

"What *happened?*" said one.

#*All syntei with kantasyntei on the squadron broken.*# the base AI told them.

"That's not a surprise," said Tinka. "What's bothering me is *why* it happened."

#*Awaiting data at lightspeed.*#

"That must be five –"

"Six and a half hours. Nutrition is recommended."

When you've been attacked and witnessed inexplicable forms of destruction you don't just grab a bite and wait calmly for data. Even trained pilots speculate. No one remembered the meal—it must have been the usual, anyway. They did remember the sick feeling that grew steadily as each new pet theory was comprehensively demolished. The conjectures grew ever wilder, even through a long gym session, but eventually data arrived.

They gathered again before a slapscreen. It lit up with *Dormouse*'s view in the centre, joined one by one with insets of those from the other ships. #*All ship-to-ship syntei dead. All synjets dead.*# The ships travelled on like thrown stones.

"We're sitting ducks!" gasped a lieutenant, still identifying with his ship. But the six spheres kept up their acceleration, and could soon be seen only by the flare of their plasma drives.

#*Destinations confirmed.*# The invaders had soon used up their acceleration fuel, and over the succeeding days coasted relentlessly toward their targets. But on every synjet that approached them, all syntei died.

At four and a half days, the first approached its target, and revealed that it still carried fuel enough for evading defences. A half-gigaton blast destroyed Thaurband. Hurriedly matched orbits had allowed syntelic evacuation of most of its live inhabitants.

Carn Dûm died on the fifth day: humans had fled to the other side of the planet.

On the seventh day, Dol Guldur fell. A clean bomb hit Crescent City, but the strike on the uranium mines filled the atmosphere with fallout.

"What," asked General von Hayashiko, "destroys synthei at a distance?" His voice was strained and his usually impeccable uniform was rumpled. Weariness dripped off him like sweat.

"Salim Sisters has people looking into that, General," replied the Boss Frog. If anything, he looked in worse shape.

"One possibility is clear," said Shevveen-Duranga. "To us it happened on Qish." She alone showed no signs of stress. It took a lot to stress out the former Colloquist of the Cavern-dwellers.

"Simquakes?" Sadruddin asked. She nodded. "*Induced?*"

"Just a thought."

"You're suggesting the groupies—apologies, we don't know that, the *enemy*—can trigger simquakes at will," the General objected. "That scarcely seems possible."

"However those devices work," said Sadruddin, "they have the same effect as a 'quake."

"Though with limited range," Shevveen-Duranga added. "Which is fascinating. Over light years do natural simquakes extend." She had a slapscreen on the wall and was consulting a series of maps. It was amazing how quickly she had become accustomed to Concordat tech. "The reports of damage seem to be confined to regions less than a thousand *klòvij* from the attackers." Though she still obviously felt Qishi units more real. That was about 500 kilometres.

"If this is an isolated incident," Sadruddin said, "we can survive it. We have duplicate facilities and spare capacity. But if whoever's behind this has more of these gadgets, which we must assume—and seems likely anyway—we're in deep trouble."

"I wonder who *does* behind it lurk?" Shevveen-Duranga said.

It was a rhetorical question, but von Hayashiko answered it anyway. "Our best assessment, given the unknown technology and deep understanding of synthei required—way beyond our own—has to be the groupies."

"And the alternatives? If as Colloquist I learned anything, it was that all assumptions had best be tentative."

"I agree," said Sadruddin. He glanced round the table, marshalling his thoughts. "Whoever is behind it, we need to find a defence—fast. But our options, insofar as we have any, depend on the perpetrator. There seem to be several possibilities. In order of likelihood: groupies; what remains of the Concordat; Ira da Terra; some other Old Earth faction; a traitor within the Syntelic League. However, since it's radically new technology, I believe it must be either groupies or Concordat. IdT may control Old Earth, but this is way beyond their capabilities. I suppose a League traitor can't be ruled out—"

"I am confident," Shevveen-Duranga said drily, "that within the League my spy-synthei would have given hints of treachery, did it exist. On Old Earth my reach is less, and Starhome Security would probably detect any attempts to spy on Concordat decis—"

Sadruddin's wristcomp flashed a signal to his mind, and he held up a hand. "Nazg has received a message."

"From whom?" asked von Hayashiko.

"From Starhome. About the simquakes. They claim responsibility."

"So it wasn't groupies."

"Not this time, General. And there's more." Sadruddin willed a word to his 'comp, and Starhome's message appeared on a slapscreen attached to the chamber wall.

YOU HAVE JUST WITNESSED A SMALL DEMONSTRATION OF THE CONCORDAT'S DI-SYNTEGRATORS. WE CAN KILL SYNTELIC DEVICES AT WILL, IN ANY QUANTITY, AND AT A SAFE DISTANCE. WE NOW ISSUE A FORMAL ULTIMATUM TO THE SYNTELIC LEAGUE: SURRENDER AND SUBMIT TO CONCORDAT RULE. OUR TERMS FOR PEACE ARE NON-NEGOTIABLE, BUT WE WILL BE GENEROUS IN VICTORY IF YOU ARE COOPERATIVE IN DEFEAT.

IF NOT, SYNTELIC TECHNOLOGY ON ALL WORLDS OF THE SYNTELIC LEAGUE WILL BE DESTROYED. WE WILL RETURN YOU TO THE PRE-DA-SILVA AGE.

ANY OUTBREAK OF DISEASE, OR ANY SABOTAGE, ON ANY CONCORDAT WORLD, WILL RESULT IN IMMEDIATE ESCALATED RETRIBUTION.

WE GIVE YOU THREE WEEKS TO ACCEDE.

On the tenth day, as the remaining two spheres approached Túrin, eighty-three synjets awaited them, and approached them at ever shortening intervals. On forty-nine the syntei died. The fiftieth proved out of range of whatever had killed the last, but close enough to destroy a sphere before its synte-killer had recovered from its nine-second refractory period. The scientist who had hypothesised that it *had* a refractory period, and the general who had believed her, would live to see another moon rise. Now that the recovery time was approximately known, the fifty-third synjet destroyed the other sphere.

Two Mountains, Qish

"So you see," said Marco, "it's basically a trivial consequence of the k-field equations. Not really new physics, at all." He sounded disappointed.

"What is, exactly?" asked General Hayashiko, patiently.

"The disyntegrator effect. Follows straight from the polarisation formula—" and he was off again.

"Marco, please remember that you are an engineer, and tell us the *practical* implications. In language a general can understand."

"Well… if you freeze the k-level set locally—locally in space and time, most you can do—that sort of puckers it, and the correction forces a discontinuity. A very small simquake, but enough to destroy a synte."

"The range?"

"I'll have to ask the twins to double-check the conversion factor, but I think… a maximum of 600 kilometres. If you do everything right."

"And what is the delay in doing it again? Can the Concordat's mathematical engineers shorten the 'refractory period'?"

"Well, they can improve the engineering, but they can't get it below a fifth of a second. That's built into the equations. Nine seconds… let's just say, they let fly with their proof-of-concept model. And we were lucky."

"So if they disable one synjet, and another is 700 kilometres further off, and manoeuvring at…" the General paused to mentally query his wrist-comp, "more than a hundredth of the speed of light, they're defenceless. Do we have synjets that can do that?"

"One," said Marco, after querying his own 'comp. "We'd better build a lot more, quick. Tinka will be disappointed, that's much too fast for human reflexes. A lot of uncrewed synjets, really small, really fast."

"The last emergency build up you got me into, lost me a war."

"Not lost," pointed out Marco defensively, "just permanently mislaid."

Rock Star / Nazg

The mistake had been to think small. Projected nanosynthei over a few metres would never scale up and persist, the superhubs shared now. But megasynthei... once the diameter was over thirteen hundred kilometres, quite different approximations were relevant.

For several whole seconds, Eve admired the hole she had opened, working at Rock Star, to the Betelgeuse system. Its red light had reached only six of her blue-lit native rocks when she closed it and turned to practical applications.

The innermost planet of Nazg, called Shagrat by humans, was a great lump of matter, forced by its own gravity into a mostly inaccessible ball. Human data in *Valkyrie*'s memories showed a liquid core, under pressure from the rocks above. She connected its centre with a lower-potential spot near Betelgeuse, and opened a synthe two thousand kilometres wide: destroyed almost instantly, but not before three thousand billion tonnes of molten iron dropped through, exploding with the stresses and its own pressure into trillions of droplets. Some spattered the star, evaporating, but most cooled to solid blobs of different sizes.

Nice, liveable rocks.

Building materials.

Food.

Shagrat's mantle, surrounding nothing, imploded. Its parts collided in the sudden hole. Many gained the kinetic energy to burst free of the planet's gravity: nice, liveable rocks. About a third of the planet's original mass remained, slowly settling into a ball. Eve saved it for later, and turned to Carystus, half a light year out from Beta Centauri.

Where the Concordat mined its mahabhavium.

This was a cold, solid planet, ice and rock all through. The method worked equally well. The core fell shattered into the Rock Star system, the implosion wrecked the rest. Self-focusing synthei formed in depth like gaping mouths around it, to catch escaping fragments and drop them to Rock Star's Kuiper belt, lost to humans among a billion other rocks. The rest settled again, and she repeated the process until not a crumb was left.

When Concordat vessels came to investigate, she collected them too, as already-mined mahabhavium. Waste not, want not.

Starhome

This isn't going well, Vance thought. *My first serious operation as Director, and I've bungled it. With no way to deflect the blame that I can think of.*

"Our ultimatum seems to have been premature, Director," the Chair said with ominous calm. "Perhaps we should have waited until our weapon was more truly invincible, or at least seemed so, with all targets hit. Túrin proved it was not." Nods from the others.

Vance demurred. "They sacrificed fifty-three spacecraft to prove it!"

"They did prove it, and they had thirty in reserve. They proved a *method* of defence, and destroyed the second missile with just three. Before long they will have it working around every target."

"But we had to respond swiftly to the attack on Owemgee!" Vance was still certain she'd been right about that. "We might have lost another planet!"

"We *have* lost another planet, Director."

She felt the blood drain from her face. "What planet? I've not heard…"

"As Director, your clearance covers knowledge of our current source of mahabhavium?"

"Carystus. But Ira da Terra can't have had agents *there*! No Dirty migrant could've got within ten light years. And nitrogen freezes there! Nothing could creep up on our installations. What happened to them?"

"As I said, we lost a *planet*, not a population." The Chair gestured at a slapscreen, which came alive with a view of empty space, and distant stars. "I meant it physically. That's where it used to be."

"But… a planet can't just vanish!"

"It didn't *just* vanish," said the Chair grimly. "When we lost communicator contact we sent a squadron of J-class maulers to investigate. They didn't come back. They didn't even signal."

"Syntei."

"Syntei," confirmed the Chair grimly. "We sent a single scout caltrop next, to a spot ten light minutes out from the site. It took that view, without blocking. Then it shifted to a day out. Watch."

An enhanced view of Carystus appeared, amplifying the few photons it scattered from its distant sun. Lights showed at the gargantuan mineheads that drilled deep into the planet's core.

Silently, the planet began to collapse. Vance watched, hypnotised, as the crust took thirteen minutes to fall three thousand kilometres to sudden emptiness, then explode outwards from the self-collision. The debris separated, then vanished through hoops the width of moons, invisibly thin to the naked eye but detected by the computer by the different stars showing through it; not the stars near Carystus. Near the end the display picked out the mauler squadron, which vanished along with the rocks.

"The Syntelic League has syntei that big?" she finally said. No agent had reported this. Intelligence from League worlds was sparse, and declining. Their security was being run by someone even more paranoid than Starhome Security. And more effective.

"Not just that *big*, but opened from one end. No way could a kantasynte have been carried into the system—let alone, inside the planet. But I don't think it was the Syntelic League."

The slapscreen lit up with a view of the Nazg system, and zeroed in on the collapse of Shagrat, time-lapsed. "Shagrat. A League world. That looks suspiciously like a test run. Would the League destroy one of its own planets?"

"If not the League," said Admiral Buchanan, "then who?"

"Groupies," said the Chair.

"But that—" Buchanan began. Vance was quick to jump in, stop this nonsense before it took root.

"Chair: I agree that Nazg is the heart of the Syntelic League," she said. "But what you're forgetting is that Nazg's inner system isn't in the Goldilocks zone. Shagrat in particular is way too hot for human habitation. Also, we know—as does Nazg—that their entire inner system is overrun with groupies. So it would make sense for the Syntelic League to sacrifice one useless groupie-infested rock to test a method for exterminating the bastards."

"Shagrat was one of the few inner system rocks *not* overrun with groupies," said Buchanan. "They're not built for gravity."

Vance put on her hardest face, grave but determined. "Even if Shagrat had been inhabited by *humans*, Nazg might have decided its destruction was worth it. With only groupies around, maybe experimenting with forms that can handle gravity, it would have been a much easier decision."

"You think they bioengineer themselves?" asked Marvin.

"They may be experts at it. We need to be very careful not to leap to conclusions."

The Chair sounded unimpressed. "I hear what you say, Director, but I'm not forgetting anything. My *considered* view is that on balance the evidence does not support the League being responsible. As a League strike against vacuum-dwelling rock lovers, destroying Shagrat seems odd. And since IdT is now part of the League, the only remaining hostiles with anything like enough power to wreck a world are the groupies. Unless you think there's some other, unknown, enemy at work here?"

There was even less evidence for that, and Vance didn't take the bait. She just looked angry.

"On the other hand, Director," the Chair continued with an edge of menace, "*you* are failing to acknowledge that the groupies have a perfectly sensible motive for blowing up planets. *Any* planets. And a record of doing so."

Vance sank back on her haunches. Her anger subsided as quickly as it had arisen. This time she nodded. Slowly. Reluctantly.

The Chair drove her point home. "Yah, exactly. Groupies *like* shattered worlds, Director. More living space. And they have a use for mahabhavium."

"But we haven't had so much as a hint that they have syntei," Vance protested.

"We have now," said the Chair.

"You really think—"

"Only that, a hint." The Chair looked along the row of worried faces; their nervousness was palpable. "This is a job for Security, and Internal and External Affairs. Director, Yoko, Marvin: I want you to find out for sure. By yesterday. But in the meantime, before our next ultimatum, we should consider very carefully whom to address it to. And whether we can make it stick."

Two Mountains, Qish

Central Committee of the Syntelic League, in virtual assembly

"As the Colloquist has pointed out," said the Boss Frog, "fighting a war on two fronts is poor strategy. Regrettably, our attempt to take the Concordat out of the equation" — our *attempt now, since we didn't repudiate it, or try Ira da Terra for crimes against humanity* — "merely prompted a counter strike. We mourn Thaurband, Dol Guldur and Carn Dûm."

"But not Túrin," interjected Ira da Terra, senex from Earth.

"Not Túrin," agreed Sadruddin, "where we learned a defence against this new weapon."

"How soon will it be ready?" asked the senex from Gazni, his image and voice digitally synted into the chamber and displayed to every member of the full committee.

"In six weeks," von Hayashiko responded, "we will have enough c-fraction synjets to protect all our worlds. Thus, if the Concordat does not strike again quickly, they will lose the opportunity. Does this make you feel safer?"

"A little," said Gazni's senex. Ira glowered, but in silence.

"To know that they *must* destroy us within six weeks?" asked the General.

"On the other front," he continued, "we lost *Sunburn* before we even knew we were in danger, and new analysis shows that the groupies pene-

302

trated Khamûl, and acquired syntelic technology. They have improved on it. Watch."

Shagrat silently imploded on a giant slapscreen. Even in virtual reality, you could sense the shock and awe. Synted murmurs from distant senexes expressed their concern.

"How is this possible?" The senex from Two-Eyes sounded close to understandable hysteria.

"They can open a kantasynte at the heart of a planet, without the necessity of carrying it there," Sadruddin said, his voice so subdued it was almost a whisper. "And that is not all."

Now the slapscreen switched to the collapse of Carystus, which one of Shevveen-Duranga's agents had pilfered from the most secure files of Starhome Security, ably assisted by a Salim Sisters AI. "*That* was the Concordat's sole source of mahabhavium, more strongly defended even than Starhome."

"Then how was it attacked?" asked the senex for Astrophel.

"They did not carry a synte into the system," Sadruddin replied. "They did not use a synte cascade: they simply opened megasynthei, at interstellar distances." He paused for a sip of *drini*-juice: the Starfolk medicines fought off fatigue, but he had found its familiar horrible taste gave him determination. "They took it, it seems, not as a strike against the Concordat, any more than the Concordat's mining was an act of war against the planet. The groupies simply wanted the mahabhavium—as with *Sunburn*."

"Humans appear to be as incidental to all this as beetles displaced by the building of a Beanstalk," commented the senex from Devil Take the Hindmost, typically deadpan.

Sadruddin's lips, grim and clamped, relaxed almost imperceptibly. A hint of a smile crept into the corners of his mouth. "You speak truth. But permit me to show you a third megasynthe, not as vast or destructive as you saw just now, but of human manufacture. For reasons the learned senex from Dool will explain to those interested, at length," *Magog preserve me from the explanations of academics! Professor Doxor Smythe may be the brightest living xenologist, but does she have to be bright in such* detail? "We transferred a cubic kilometre of water from Earth's ocean, with permission from its current government, to the outer edges of groupie-held Nazg." *At the very least, they won't feel quite so powerless after watching this.* "The water contained a renowned Zee Hanze Deep Research Institute, its Principal, Doctor Impana Rhee, and two thousand and thirteen squid. The goal was to attract the non-destructive attention of the groupies, which it apparently did." The assembly silently watched the shaded emergence of the watery sphere, and the approach of the groupies as close as the guardian X-ray lasers permitted.

"According to the Constitution of this Syntelic League, membership is open to any habitat or planet possessing, or wishing to acquire, syntelic technology, and prepared to commit not to use it for warfare." *Old Earth used syntei to seize the Beanstalks* before *they signed on, and they didn't use them at all for the Owemgee attack, so they qualify. Just.*

"I wish to introduce to you the Ambassador of the Network we have been calling the groupies, and potentially its senex in this honoured chamber, if the Committee so votes: the possessor of the memories of Adam Jaxxon."

Jaxxon's image, slightly bemused, joined those of the committee. With a gasp, most of them switched to a close-up view.

"Like most of you he is only telepresent, but if you so authorise, I will visit him in person. For security reasons I also propose that initially only the War Cabinet should observe the meeting. Then the War Cabinet will report its findings to the Central Committee, including full recordings, for ratification. Does anyone second the proposal to authorise these actions?"

"Seconded," said Shevveen-Duranga.

"Then I call for a vote. I will postpone the proposal to elect him as senex for the Network to the next meeting of this committee."

Dool

"It should have been obvious," said Marco.

"It *is* obvious," replied Marco, "in the abstract. But it wasn't obvious to anybody specific."

"What's not obvious," said Elza, "is what the skunt you're talking about. Can *you* be specific?"

"Remote opening of synthei," said Marco. "If they're big enough, you can neglect the meta inversion terms, and the beta-calculus has an analytic solution. Emmy Nöther would have loved it. Look—"

"Will you leave that slapscreen alone, and explain."

"Contrary to Syntelics 101, you *can* remote-open tiny syntei, at a short distance," said Marco. "If the Qishi biota ever discovered that, evolution didn't find a use for it. It doesn't seem you can remote-open wyzands, and anyway, how would a plant choose where it opened?"

"Maybe trial and error," Elza guessed.

"Well, they don't. But it takes almost no energy to remote-open a kanta-synthe a thousand klicks across, if you've already made the kasynthe loop that big. Which must be what the groupies did."

As usual, Elza went straight for the jugular. "Can *we* do it?"

Marco grunted. "Just a simple adaptation of the tech used for moving the squid."

"We have the hardware already," Marco added.

"How long would it take?" asked Polonia.

"About three weeks."

"Wouldn't it be vulnerable while we built it? A hoop a thousand klicks wide?"

"*After* we built it, too," Marcolette pointed out.

"Unless it was hidden," Marco countered. "In the Kuiper belt, or somewhere."

"I seem to recall someone telling me," said Elza, checking her 'comp for Marco's exact words, "that 'once people suspect there *is* a secret, it's out, regardless of your data protection.' How long could you hide it?"

"For as long as you could keep even its existence secret."

Elza's mouth pursed as she digested this information. "If no one knows you've got it… how do you *threaten* with it?"

"That would give it away," admitted Marco. "They could probably hit it."

Elza twined a lock of her long blonde hair through her brown fingers and tugged it, grimacing. "We can't warn off the Concordat, then. *Stand back or we'll explode the planet you're standing on.* We can only do it. Without offering them a chance to surrender."

"Even Genghis Khan only wiped out cities that resisted," muttered Marco.

"Owemgee was attacked on our behalf," said Elza. "Without warning. But some of the people survived. Now we're talking about destroying, say, Starhome, and all of the habitats around it, to the last woman. Destroying the planet itself."

Starhome

"Humanity cannot afford to be divided, in the face of the groupies," said the Chair.

"Then we need a quick victory," replied Buchanan. "The Syntelic League must be eliminated, before it weakens us further."

"More than weakens us — betrays us." The recently appointed Director of Starhome Security waved at a slapscreen. It lit up with the Security logo, the date and time, and then intercepted vix of Sadruddin saying to a hushed assembly, *I wish to introduce to you the Ambassador of the Network we have been calling the groupies, and potentially its senex in this honoured chamber, if the Committee so votes: the possessor of the memories of Adam Jaxxon.* The others present watched in shock.

"These are monsters," she said quietly. "First the Syntelic League welcomes Dirties into its council, then the Dirties kill Owemgee, then the League welcomes the destroyer of Carystus. Humanity *must* be united. Treason must be stamped out."

"But how?" Buchanan objected. "We thought we had an unstoppable weapon with the disyntegrators. But they found a defence for it."

"We can saturate their defence," Vance asserted.

"You are sure of that?" asked the Chair.

"We release a thousand disyntegrator missiles, ten kilometres apart in a globe about two hundred across. They take turns to make a simquake, timed as close as spacetime will allow. The counter strategy depends on paired ships; one leading to force us to use a defensive simquake, the other trailing, to hit us with its still-working synjet before we can disintegrate again. The League can't take out more than one hardened missile at a time, at that separation, even with total conversion — no atmosphere to carry the shock wave. At that range, X-ray lasers have to stay focused too long. So they would need two thousand counter ships to have any logical possibility of neutralising every missile. More realistically, five thousand, optimally placed to strike, for an even chance. Fifty thousand, to have adequate coverage. They don't have remotely that many."

"Don't have, or won't have?" the Chair put in.

"Don't have. In a month, who knows?" Vance grimaced. "That's why we need to strike now."

"Where? There's no clear centre to Nazg, where a blow would be decisive. And we need its industrial base," said Adelaide Eckhardt.

"Not Nazg," answered Vance. "Qish. The one thing that Qish produces is poison to the Concordat. Every one of those missiles must carry antimatter.

"The first to get through will boil the oceans, and wipe all life from the planet."

In the ensuing silence, each avoided eye-contact with the others. Only Vance tried, glaring at each in turn. Her expression made her opinion of such vacillation clear.

Finally the Chair spoke. "Make it so."

Deep Research Institute, Nazg

War Cabinet of the Syntelic League, in virtual assembly

It smelled oddly like rock, but it looked convincingly human, even the face.

Unless you were human, too.

Its size, shape, and coloration were accurate enough; well within the normal range of variability throughout the former territory of the Concordat. But there were no small flaws. It was firmly located in uncanny valley, where the robots that are too humanoid to be robots are also too robotic to be human, but trying just a bit too hard to pretend. The groupie simulacrum of Adam Jaxxon was disturbing; it raised hairs on people's necks and sent shivers along their spines.

It also contained, and had mastered, the contents of the original Adam's entire sensorium, faithfully replicated. So it sounded entirely human if you shut your eyes.

I'm sure we'll all get used to that, Sadruddin thought. *He's far more human than the late Deacon DeLameter.*

He had a feeling there was more to Jaxxon—*best to think of him that way, it seems to be one of the ways* he *thinks*—than met the eye. *He has to communicate with the groupie Network somehow. Obviously an internal syntelic signalskin link, as well as the working fluid circulation.* But short of dissecting him, there was no way to test that, except, perhaps, to ask. That could wait; the first priority was diplomacy.

Agreeing to meet him in person was perhaps risky, but diplomacy had to start somewhere, and Sadruddin had never been risk-averse if the potential reward were high enough. Here, the reward could be Galactic peace, so it was his duty as Boss Frog to do whatever was possible to secure it. Anyway, he was curious; apparently, the same motive as Jaxxon's. Rhee had already told them that the groupie Network, as embodied in Jaxxon, seemed a strange mix of superintelligence and utter naivety.

He told Impana he came calling because humans interest him. Them. It. Well, Network: you *interest* me.

So Sadruddin had synted to Khamûl and from there to Impana Rhee's Deep Research Institute. It had been a novel experience, but Sadruddin was getting used to those; on a scale from one to ten, making rendezvous in deep space with a huge sphere of squid-filled water hardly ranked above a half.

Scans had shown the Jaxxon simulacrum's internal syntei: presumably, through them the groupies could wreak instant havoc. That was one reason why the other cabinet members were not physically present. The Research Station would have to take its chances, because Jaxxon had insisted on remaining there. However, Sadruddin reckoned there was little additional danger from that. Groupies could create a megasynte pretty much anywhere they wanted, at any distance, at any time. A hidden synte in a simulacrum paled into insignificance compared to the ability to destroy a planet remotely, without warning. And that was what this meeting was about.

"Welcome," Sadruddin said, addressing both the simulacrum and the committee, "to our new senex-elect. May we refer to you as Ambassador Jaxxon?"

The simulacrum looked puzzled. "As I told Doxor Rhee, 'I am Adam Jaxxon' is an approximate truth, within the limits of Galaxic. Are you seeking permission according to social norms?"

Simplest to go along with that. "Or would you prefer informality?" Sadruddin said, avoiding the temptations of an ontological argument like a theologian in recovery. "May we call you Adam?"

"Of course."

"Then I am... Augustine." He introduced the other members of the War Cabinet, visible on slapscreens. Formalities concluded—Mother knew what the groupies made of them, but Adam had a human's memory and probably expected something of that kind—they got down to business.

"Adam," said the Boss Frog, "we hope to interest your principals in forming an alliance."

Adam tilted his head to one side, as if in thought. It didn't quite look right—an act, rather than anything natural. "Who with?"

I suppose it's a logical question, especially if you're really an alien. "With us. The Syntelic League." The Boss Frog's earlier private discussions with the Ambassador, to feel him out before calling a formal meeting, had filled in some details about events after the original Jaxxon had died. That had been creepy, too. Sadruddin had never before found himself explaining to someone the things that had occurred after their death. Still, there was a first time for everything. And remembering that this wasn't really Jaxxon, wasn't really even *human*, was easy. The problem was to forget it.

"Why?" Adam asked.

"I think I'll let our military strategists handle that question," Sadruddin said. "General?"

"The Ambassador—"

"Informality," the Boss Frog reminded him.

"Er, Adam," von Hayashiko began. "You'll be aware that the Syntelic League is at war with the remnant of the former Concordat."

"Two human groups?"

"Yah."

"Why do you fight yourselves?"

The General laughed, without humour. "I often ask myself that, Adam, and I find no answer. Perhaps you can help us with that."

"We fight because we're competing for a common resource," said Shevveen-Duranga. "I imagine you groupies can understand that, since you attacked humans in order to acquire mahabhavium. I could as well ask why *you* fight *us*."

"I take what we need," Adam replied, but he looked disturbed. *Conflict between groupie objectives and the assumptions of his human memories?* Sadruddin thought. *Interesting.*

"So do we," said the League's head of espionage. "We just take it from our own species."

"And plants and animals," Sadruddin pointed out.

"I meant sentient species."

"The Network's components don't segregate into species," said the Ambassador. "Its policies are created by the Network. When constituted, it is a single decision maker."

That agrees with Impana's recent observations. These things have no understanding about giving away vital intelligence to their enemies, Sadruddin decided, *or, really, no understanding of enemies.* He caught Shevveen-Duranga's eye and she raised an eyebrow. He had the sense that the Network, despite or perhaps because of its immense level of intelligence, was showing its naivety. The groupies just weren't accustomed to negotiation. In fact, as the General had convinced him with some simple battlefield analysis, they weren't accustomed to warfare either. Millions of years with no one to interact with except yourself was poor preparation for social interaction, peaceful or violent. They made mistakes, having never learned the hard way not to.

On the other hand, as Jaxxon, they were learning diplomacy very fast. All the more reason to head off any tendency to make similar progress on warfare. *Let's get that treaty agreed!*

"A group mind?" Marco asked. "Or a very effective democracy?" Marco countered.

"Decisions are taken by the Network," Adam said firmly. "You are... I know this is *negotiating*... with the Network. Through its agent... through the Network itself... through *me*."

Sadruddin made a mental note: *difficulty with the notion of self. Hazy sense of identity, not surprising really.*

Von Hayashiko steered them back on topic. "Adam, we hope to convince you—and through you the Network—that groupies have nothing to fear from the Syntelic League. We have a common enemy: the Concordat. That argues for—"

"But couldn't it equally be argued that the Network and the Concordat have a common enemy: you?"

Touché, Sadruddin thought.

"The Syntelic League is not your enemy," said the General, who was used to this kind of negotiation and knew all the tricks. He paused. "Yet."

Sadruddin picked up the cue. "Adam: even though your principals destroyed one of our habitats and one of our worlds," he said, "we believe the Network has far more common ground with the League than with the Concordat."

"The evidence is undeniable," said Ira da Terra. "The Concordat has imprisoned billions on Earth for absurd ideological reasons. It has mounted massive attacks on its own species." *Pot, kettle, black*, Sadruddin thought. *But her blinkered analysis is helpful here. Adam looks intimidated. Most people are.* "It will have no qualms about destroying *you*," she finished, "since you destroyed its source of mahabhavium."

Adam was definitely shaken, but not, it became apparent, by Ira da Terra or her threat. "The habitat," he said. "*The habitat!*" His eyes flicked in random directions. It looked like a minor seizure. "Yah, yah—*I* worked there. The Network killed... *me*." He stopped, seemingly confused. "But I am the Network. Why did I kill my—uh—I needed mahabhavium, so I took it. To get it, it was necessary to sacrifice... me." His voice trailed off at the last word, and distress was visible on his uncanny-valley face; oddly, it made him seem more human.

"The world—yah, that was a world you *possessed*," he said slowly, reverting to less disturbing ground. "I know... *possession*. It's a concept familiar to me, yet new to the Network, even though I am also the Network. I knew it was your *possession*, relative to other humans, but the Network did not. Did you have *ownership*? Even human definitions of that seem to vary widely, from a god-given right to 'Property is theft' and 'Soil to the tiller'. Certainly, you made no use of it, nor occupancy. It's too hot for human habitation."

"Humans use worlds for many purposes, Adam," Sadruddin said quietly. "Habitation is just one. This world," a slapscreen lit up with the destruction of Carystus, "was the Concordat's most treasured possession. It was too cold by far for human habitation, but you became their hated enemy by annihilating it."

"I see."

"If the Network allies with us, together we can force the Concordat to cease all hostile actions against us both. We will then have no need of hostilities towards the Concordat. There will be peace and cooperation. At a price, not easily, not immediately. But we can make it work. We can all coexist.

"We can even help each other."

"Why would you help the Network?"

"Because it would be in our own interests, as well as yours."

Adam again appeared puzzled. "Why shouldn't we just continue to expand our territories, unaided?"

"Because *we will stop you*," the General growled. "Whatever the price."

"Ambassador," said Sadruddin, deliberately reverting to formality to alter the atmosphere, "your Network has powerful technologies." He paused, allowing Adam to respond, but he remained mute. "You can destroy habitats, you can destroy worlds. You have done so."

"Yah." Sadruddin had noticed that any reference to the destruction of *Sunburn* seemed to make Adam uncomfortable. No doubt because it included what he remembered as his own destruction. *Was this a lever?*

"We also have powerful technologies, some like yours, others different. Our dearest wish is to avoid future conflict with the Network," said Sadruddin smoothly. "And with the Concordat. No more destruction of habitats—" he placed slight emphasis on the word—"and the lives of intelligent beings." He stared into Jaxxon's eyes. "Adam, have you heard of the carrot and the stick?"

"Of course. One to encourage, the other to deter."

"Does the Network understand these concepts?"

Pause. "It does now."

Sadruddin noted in passing that this confirmed Adam was in direct communication with Groupie Central; had to be syntelic... but he was after bigger game. "General, please: the stick."

Von Hayashiko gestured to some unseen technician and a holvix started running on slapscreens, among them one that Adam could see. As the action unfolded, the General gave a clipped, staccato commentary.

"You have megasynthei. So do we.

"You can project a kantasynte to a distant point, by manipulating the *k*-field.

"So can we.

"You showed us how to use a projected megasynthe to destroy a world from inside. We have tested our own version," *the test is really tomorrow, but Marco swears by his four testicles that it will work,* thought Sadruddin. *Simulated will do for now. Anyway, that's not the use we have planned.* "... and we are scaling up. Fast."

The General paused, letting the silence hang. "Have you considered the effect of taking a planet-sized bite from a star?"

"It wouldn't make any rocks," said Jaxxon/the Network, consistently with the main groupie concern, "and wouldn't have any long term effect on the star."

"But in the *short* term, the shock waves would provoke flares." The slap-screen showed a distant view of Rock Star, with groupie rocks in the foreground. "This is our best simulation: I am sure you can do better." Suddenly the star writhed, and blazed up. When it settled, the rocks were half melted.

The General ended his presentation and Sadruddin took over again.

"You could retaliate, but that would just escalate the conflict. It's called an arms race, Adam. A race with no winners."

Adam looked distressed. "That is... the stick?" he asked.

"Yah."

Qish

A hundred Da Silva ships emerged into being from their instant in *k*-space, seventeen light-seconds from Qish.

Each deployed twelve self-guiding containers of antimatter, with disyntegrators and overclocked plasma drives. They would not need to last for more than one journey.

Accelerating at nine gravities, the twelve hundred missiles formed a sparse globe, three hundred kilometres across. Rarely coming within twelve kilometres of each other, they followed a subtly chaotic algorithm that made it hard to predict their motion for long enough to aim a laser. Between them they carried multiple vixprojectors that caused more vessels to appear and disappear, invulnerable in their unreality.

The carrying ships vanished immediately, but Da Silva scouts with vixcams flickered in to watch from a distance. If in danger they set off protective simultaneity quakes and disappeared. Mahabhavium was not a resource to be risked.

One second after their arrival, alerted by syntelically linked sentry drones, the League's guardian synjets around the planet went violently into acceleration.

There were a bare five hundred and twelve of them.

Deep Research Institute, Nazg

War Cabinet of the Syntelic League, in virtual assembly

"And the carrot is…?" said Adam.

"We brought one from Earth, where our species originated. Ira?"

Ira da Terra, looking confused and a little resentful, produced it from her pocket and placed it in front of the slapscreen. It hung there in the microgravity, looking very orange.

"A *literal* carrot? This component cannot metabolise carbohydrates. I thought 'carrot' was a metaphor." He paused. "The memories of Adam Jaxxon contain that concept, so '*I thought*' was a true statement. The Network has yet to evolve a consistent theory of metaphor. Please continue."

Ah, the benefits of a solid training in theology, thought Sadruddin. "It is a literal metaphor." *That will fox him.* "Carrots were mostly purple until the minus third century GE, when they were genetically modified to the colour symbolising the royal house of Holland." *But this component can surely see in ultraviolet; Magog knows how it looks to those eyes.* "This is a metaphor for change, and the fascination of history, which is part of the study of humanity."

Sadruddin seized the carrot, and held it in front of Jaxxon's face. "This carrot could never have evolved in a universe where all planets are reduced to fragments. Nor could the humans who transformed it. Nor could the memories that you hold." Recalling one of the first things Jaxxon had said after arriving naked, "Are those memories *interesting* to the Network? And, are they *useful*?"

"Eve's specialist clusters have given much processing to those questions."

Sadruddin went into his internal communication mode, giving the usual raised-palm gesture to signal that he was doing that. He sent a silent message to Shevveen-Duranga.

#Eve? Who the skunt is Eve?#

After a few moments, his head of espionage responded. #No data: we have not yet penetrated the Network's communications. It appears from context to be another groupie construct.#

#Can you find out more?#

#We may *never* penetrate the Network's communications. Maybe you should just ask. He doesn't seem terribly worried about letting you know things.#

Being so direct and transparent wasn't a style where Sadruddin felt comfortable. An adult life largely spent concealing sins of body-division and heresy from the Church's torturers had trained him to be very cautious and very subtle. *Oh well.*

"I don't think we've encountered Eve."

"It—she—planned and executed our seizure of mahabhavium."

Did I really hear that? "From the habitat?"

Adam shivered; a look of panic flickered over his face.

"Yah, from the... the..."

"Eve sounds like a human name to me, Adam. Who was she?" As the groupie Ambassador hesitated, he pressed harder. "If she executed the seizure, she can't have died when the habitat was attacked, as you did."

"Nah, nah. She died much earlier. *They* died. And became Eve."

"Who?"

"Irenotincala-Elzabet-Valkyrie."

Qish / Starho me

The hours passed. The twelve hundred missiles went almost ballistic, using what was left of their fuel to sustain the intricate dance within their globe.

"What is the League's defence doing?" asked the Chair. "They have too few synjets, dah? I'd expect frantic but ineffectual activity."

"Nah. They don't seem to be doing anything much. Certainly not getting into position for the tactics that saved Túrin," reported Vance. "With their endless fuel supply, it's hard to predict *where* the defending synjets will be when our missiles reach the planet. And if just one gets through, the head of the serpent is dead. Annihilated. They can *not* stop us against two-to-one odds."

The hours passed.

"Thirty minutes to impact. Zero interceptions. Zero attempted interceptions," chanted the AI.

The Chair looked slightly apprehensive. "Director, does this not strike you as—"

"At this rate, *most* of them will get through," breathed Vance. "We won't just leave no life on the planet. We'll boil off the oceans, and the atmosphere." The control of such power exalted her.

The Chair leaned forward, started to speak, then stopped, as if she'd had second thoughts. She gave Vance a quick sideways glance, and settled back into a comfortable squat. A hint of a smile flickered at the corners of her mouth for an instant.

"Ten minutes to impact. Zero interceptions. Zero attempted interceptions," the AI reported.

"Bare *rock*." Vance put up her analysis on a slapscreen. "Not even bacteria surviving twenty kilometres deep. Life on the planet will have to restart completely."

"Without syntei," said Admiral Buchanan, with gloomy satisfaction.

"Without syntei."

"Five minutes to impact. Zero interceptions. Enemy manoeuvres appear *evasive*."

And it was true. It became clearer by the second that a hole was opening in the defences, thousands of kilometres wide, directly in the attackers' line of flight. The attack tightened, toward the centre of the hole.

"Come here and *fuck* me, baby," muttered Vance. "They're opening their legs. But why?"

Half a light-second out, between Qish and its enormous moon, without any fuss, twelve hundred missiles vanished.

ᕁ   ᖰ

Marco and Marco had both insisted on being present for the firework show.

Squill I, the small lifeless planet known to Qish as the Morning Star, the Evening Star, and the Eye of Magog, was tidally locked to its sun. On the cold, dark side they had overseen the building of a synte projector, a secret that was never hinted to exist, and was not found.

The missiles flashed through the thousand-kilometre-wide synte that had suddenly opened in front of them. The tidal forces of dropping so far toward the sun had torn their antimatter containment systems apart. As these touched their contents, they started gigaton explosions that would have scattered some of the antimatter all over the system, but before they could spread they collided with the dark side of Squill I, which provided enough normal matter to mop up all of it.

Explosively.

"Twelve hundred multi-gigaton bombs," observed Marco. "You don't often get to watch that."

"It's certainly one in the eye for Magog," returned Marco.

They continued watching, through hardened sensors. As the incandescent gases began to dissipate, they saw the planet was in three pieces, tumbling and flying apart amid a cloud of fragments.

"You don't need a synte to break up a planet," observed Marco.

"We just used one," Marco replied.

"Only to redirect the bombs. If we had let them through, they would have broken up Qish."

"Qish is larger."

"Not that much larger," answered Marco, sharing a back-of-the-quantum calculation he had just done on his 'comp.

"You're right, as usual," said Marco.

"I was wrong to say a remote-focusing synte would be vulnerable even after we built it. It can redirect attackers."

"You're right. You were."

Eelkhance

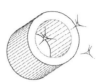

"I wonder where the missiles were synted," muttered Tampledown.

"Does it matter?" Lawes asked. "What counts is where they went *from*, and we know that."

"I suppose not." He paused. "I'm glad I wasn't in the chain of command for that strike. I don't think I could have ordered it; but after Owemgee, how could I refuse?"

"We gave them the disyntegrator," said Lawes, "and that killed Thaurband, Carn Dûm and Dol Guldur. But those together didn't match the deaths on Owemgee."

"Perhaps matching *one* death," said Tampledown, "is an obscenity."

Lawes looked at him, and recited.

> *"If there should follow a thousand swords to carry my bones away,*
> *Belike the price of a jackal's meal were more than a thief could pay.*
> *They will feed their horse on the standing crop, their men on the garnered grain,*
> *The thatch of the byres will serve their fires when all the cattle are slain.*
> *But if thou thinkest the price be fair,—thy brethren wait to sup,*
> *The hound is kin to the jackal-spawn,—howl, dog, and call them up!"*

"Where is *that* from?" asked Tampledown, jolted.

"One of the Afghanistan wars on Old Earth. The British Empire matched the death of one white man with death and starvation to a whole community. The Concordat was supposed to have grown beyond that, and restricted it to Old Earth. But it wasn't just the Owemgee plague that escaped the Quarantine. We brought the seed of that thinking with us, and it flowered on Starhome. The Concordat *was* an empire—a water empire with mahabhavium in place of water—and it reacted like one."

Tampledown sighed, took a deep breath. His lips formed a faint, hesitant smile. "Qish was not destroyed," he said. The whole Eelkhance habitat was dedicated to the study of Qish and syntei, and though the present inhabitants had never been there physically, it occupied their minds and their lives.

"Qish was not destroyed," agreed Lawes. He put his hand on Tampledown's.

⃗ ⃗

The habitat shook. A megastructure going through even the most perfectly calibrated synte has to show some tidal stress, with distant parts not perfectly aligned. As the parts matched again there were alarming sounds for a second but, in the end, no damage.

"What was that?" said Tampledown.

"We appear to be in the Squill system, in an orbit about 1·4 million kilometres closer than that of Qish," chanted the habitat AI. "Suspiciously close to the L1 point."

"Where Squill and Qish gravity cancel out," Tampledown muttered. "Which means we should expect company."

"Confirmed: we have a laser link with nearby spacecraft. Marco Bianchi request to speak with the personnel of Eelkhance, collectively."

Considering the enormity of this remote-operated interstellar kidnap, Tampledown felt a strange calm. He had been waiting for the next development to be vengeful fire; talk might be better. Again he thought: *Qish was not destroyed*. Not an excuse. A comfort.

"Better gather in the seminar room, then. In five minutes?"

"Accepted," reported the AI.

Marco appeared on the big slapscreen, for once dressed differently; a dull red jacket, and a brown one. After the introductions, he cut immediately to their status. "We can treat you as prisoners of war, or as refugees."

"Would refugees be allowed to do research?" asked a botanist. "On Qish?"

"Refugees would be welcome to do research," replied Marco. "We'll prepare a list of open posts."

"Count me as a refugee, then. Whatever the position, just to walk amid the ecology…"

"It's still recovering from the simquake," said Marco, "so you'll have a once-in-ten-thousand-years chance to study the succession of species involved. We need as many people as possible on that."

"Field work," sighed the botanist happily.

"The physical sciences?" asked Tampledown. "Some of us worked on weapons."

"And some of *us*," Marco answered for the Syntelic League, "spread plagues. We're not planning a war crimes tribunal, just open files."

"I'm in, then," said Lawes, "as long as there's a decently equipped lab and regular meals. And nothing to do with killing. Regular sex would be nice."

"I'll join you," said Tampledown. "For all of those."

Deep Research Institute, Nazg

War Cabinet of the Syntelic League, in virtual assembly

"Irenotincala-Elzabet-Valkyrie."

Sadruddin still hadn't worked out how he'd concealed his surprise. Years spent not drawing himself to the attention of the quizitors, probably.

The wealth of information contained in those three names, so casually and naively uttered, was extraordinary. It confirmed, without a shadow of doubt, much that they had already guessed, but perhaps never quite believed. Now they *knew*.

Were Tinka and Els'bett still *inside* the thing? Conscious submodules of an alien group mind? Unlikely. This simulacrum didn't contain a conscious Adam Jaxxon. Only a structured infodump that considered itself, for certain purposes, as Adam Jaxxon: the Network, with all of the Network's knowledge and goals available, but with local and immediate access to Adam Jaxxon's. This led to troubling contradictions, but they didn't mean a conscious Jaxxon, in conflict with the network. Not the same. The map is not the territory, however accurate it may be—particularly if it is interactively responding to the questions of the mapmaker.

In a way, that was a relief. At least the groupies hadn't built themselves an Irenotincala Laurel simulacrum. Or—Magog forbid—one of Lady Elzabet of Quynt. The first would have been hard to bear; the second might have driven him mad.

It did suggest that the groupie menace was even more dangerous than they'd believed, if that were possible. As well as eating planets, they could steal minds.

Amazing what a bit of leverage can achieve. What did that fellow Archimedes say? Give me a lever long enough and I will move the Earth. Mind you, as Marco had explained first to Sadruddin, and then to the Church's acolytes, back when he was currying favour with Two Mountains by teaching them mechanics, he wouldn't have moved it much. Standing on the Earth and jumping would have had the same effect.

That's the place to stand. On top of the thing you want to move.

Sadruddin put every analyst he could spare on a crash programme to examine the implications of Adam's inadvertent bombshell.

Starhome

Thirty million kilometres from Starhome, a mouth in space opened. At one instant there had been nothing but the thin particle-shower of the solar wind, at the next, a synthe twelve hundred kilometres across materialised, its face aligned to Starhome.

Fifty Syntelic League warships, unimpressive bundles of cylinders until you realised how big they were, emerged from the mouth and took up station next to it. They weren't there as weapons; they weren't even there to protect the synthe. They were misdirection.

The synthe was the weapon. Rather, one component. The mouth of the cannon. The cannonballs were thirteen hundred light years away... for now.

For half a day the megasynthe floated in space, even more menacing because, like the warships, it seemed to be doing nothing. On Starhome, its appearance created panic. Panic in the streets, panic in the councils, panic in the government. Imaginations ran riot. An asteroid bombardment was the favoured threat. Another would be bombardment of Starhome's tiny innermost moon, blowing it into chunks, any one of which could destroy Starhome on its own.

In every scenario, Starhome was doomed.

Admiral Buchanan dispatched a massive task force, but even as the ships set out, everyone knew it was a pointless gesture. The fleet would take too long to get there, and it wouldn't be able to get close enough to be effective in any case, because its Da Silva drives would vaporise.

Buchanan wasn't keen on suicide missions, but he didn't need one. He needed a distraction, and he hoped the approaching fleet would do the job. When the fleet neared the danger zone, he planned to dispatch a separate stream of small, stealthed, superfast missiles armed with disyntegrators.

If only one got close to the synthe, it would suffice.

In the event, he never got to use them before the release of a far more powerful stream. Rocks from Nazg's Kuiper belt, with the tremendous speeds that implied, provided the cannonballs for the League's megasynthe cannon. Hundreds of them, each the size of a habitat, emerged from the mouth, travelling at blistering speed. Each would impact with the energy of a total conversion warhead.

Computations confirmed that every one of them would strike Starhome, with more energy than the rock that wiped out the dinosaurs.

Nothing Starhome possessed could stop them.

Scarcely had the computations been made than a second synte opened ahead of the barrage, and the celestial cannonballs vanished. The warships disappeared back through the first synte. Within a minute, the other synte had vanished too.

A shot across the bows. A less than subtle warning.

And an invitation.

Deep Research Institute, Nazg

War Cabinet of the Syntelic League, in virtual assembly

"Has the Network analysed," asked Sadruddin carefully, "whether Irenotincala Laurel, the Lady Elzabet, the mind of *Valkyrie*, or Adam Jaxxon as he was in the habitat, before they met the Network, would have chosen to be subsumed?"

"Subsumption is always the welcomed choice," replied Jaxxon. "Subsumption is survival. That is how it has been for millions of years. All components include structures to facilitate it. The same is true of your squid."

"I suspected as much," said Impana Rhee. "Is it related to the stellate axon? *Dosidicus madhu* has an unusual—"

"That is precisely the point," said Sadruddin. "Do *most* squid have these structures? And do they all hunt in groups?"

"Some hunt in groups," said Impana. "But it's much more like the collaboration of wolf packs. They don't control each others' limbs, they stay individuals. And no, they don't have these structures: that's why *Dosidicus madhu* is so exciting. Could I persuade you to give a seminar on what you have found in *madhu*'s brain?"

"I trust we can organise a full program of scientific exchange, once we have concluded a treaty." *Magog save me from academics.* "Meanwhile, I think you are saying that most squid are *not* pre-adapted to subsumption?"

"Definitely. In fact, a lot of squid species are solitary."

"Thank you. And while humans are somewhat collaborative, I do not think they have the structures Adam Jaxxon is referring to. Is that true?"

"They had to be retrofitted," agreed Jaxxon. "The Network had some problems with this defect, particularly in the first experiments, but they were largely overcome by the time it came to Adam Jaxxon. Me," he added helpfully.

"As a defect, it required fixing," said Sadruddin, "but did it occur to the Network that there might be other ways to view it?" *Like seeing a dog as a pet, rather than meat.*

"Well, no. Why should it?"

"I ask the Network again," said Sadruddin, "to analyse whether Irenotincala Laurel, the Lady Elzabet, the mind of *Valkyrie*, or Adam Jaxxon would have chosen to be subsumed?" There was no accusation in his voice, but intense enquiry.

"The question is novel," said Jaxxon, "but interesting. It will require some unusual simulation in isolated modules. Please wait while this is accomplished." His face went blank.

After five minutes he returned to uncanny life, with a peaceful smile. "The answer for Adam Jaxxon is definitely No. We thank you for the question: finding the answer has helped the integration of this component." He did not seem to be imagining the torment of his other simulated self, in isolation. "For Irenotincala Laurel and Lady Elzabet of Quynt the reconstruction was less complete, and the answer less certain, but it is No with a probability of 95%. For Valkyrie, the concept of 'chosen' requires further analysis."

"This will be the typical human answer," said Sadruddin. "If it is known that you are continuing to subsume subjects who would choose otherwise, not only will it make cooperation in your studies of humanity impossible," — *withdrawal of the carrot* — "but it will cause some humans to think very seriously about the vulnerability of stars." *Showing the stick.* "To put it bluntly, some would find mutual destruction preferable to becoming components."

"Our simulations bear this out," said Jaxxon, "as indeed do your recent actions and those of the Concordat. You repetitively chose destruction over even imperfect subsumption in the other grouping. Eve thanks you for this insight." And there, by Magog, was a definite echo of Els'bett's aristocratic smile. For some moments, Sadruddin could not speak. "It is agreed, unconditionally. No non-consensual subsumptions."

"Thank you," said Sadruddin without reservation. "I am reminded of a similar matter. You probably intend to go among humans in human shape?"

"As I am doing now, and as is surely implied in membership of the Syntelic League," agreed Jaxxon, "and close study of the species. Though we have found that smaller forms enable less disturbance of the subjects."

#Ant-forms! Like those that did spy out a synte-pair!# sent Shevveen-Duranga, appalled that she had missed the further implications of that. #The World Egg knows how infested we be now with tale-bearing mites!#

#Well, we can't negotiate a ban on spy forms, any more than a ban on olosyntei,# Sadruddin returned. #Not one that would stick. Leave that, for now.#

"As a human," he persisted, "engaging in human activities. I assume that your human data include episodes of sex?"

Jaxxon looked blank for a moment, presumably accessing three sets of memories. Then he grinned, with Els'bett's expression again coming out on top. "I remember well," he said.

"Would you, as a human engaging in human activities, include that?"

"That would seem logical, as a means of close up study," said Jaxxon, "and a source of interesting experiences."

"Then there is a principle you must fully commit to: no sexual act in which any partner lacks the complete power to refuse. Children, subordinates, prisoners and so on are automatically off limits. This is enforced by all civilised human societies, and transgression by individuals is penalised. The 'individual' in your case would be the entire Network, not the component, so the penalty would be war. One starbite can trigger a flare, remember?" But perhaps there was no need to wave the stick so hard. The Network probably never forgot anything. "I'm sure that won't be necessary. Do you agree to this principle?"

Fortunately, the sexual histories of all three components were remarkably sane: he hated to think what the Network would do with the memories of Ira da Terra. Or, Magog be merciful, the Deacon. Nevertheless, he held his breath.

"Certainly," replied Jaxxon. "This subject of sexual ethics is a whole new area of investigation. Better than reaching a new swarm of orbital rocks. But is that the only prohibition? My memories include conflicting sets, such as sex with the wrong gender, with the wrong people watching, or broken promises to a partner."

"All those are negotiable and contextual," — *including dividing the body* — "and can be addressed locally. Many of those 'Wrongs' are decreed by local societal conventions, to which you can conform, or accept exclusion by that sub-community. We need the absolute principle of consent, however."

"You have it," said Jaxxon. "But I am curious. A tentacled component eating the bones of a partner, while subsuming his memories, with his wholehearted consent, would be acceptable?"

"I would find it personally repulsive," admitted Sadruddin, "and I find it hard to imagine a consenting partner. But yes, that is the logic of the principle."

Starhome

"I am tasked," said Tampledown uncomfortably, squatting before the Board, "with conveying to you the policies of the Syntelic League toward the Concordat. You will appreciate that I am in no sense a plenipotentiary, or even empowered to negotiate, I am simply a messenger, familiar with the persons involved, who can carry back your response without argument."

"And who is your companion?" the Chair asked. For the record; she knew perfectly well.

Tampledown turned to her. "She is purely an observer, here at her own request." He thought it would be undiplomatic to say that her request was 'to see justice done', or mention her threats to the Syntelic League if it was not granted.

Sitting Old Earth fashion in a half-lotus posture, the companion bowed barely perceptibly from the waist. "Ira da Terra."

Predictable as this was, the spoken words came as a shock. The temperature in the room seemed to drop. The Director of Starhome Security looked as if she felt defiled by Ira's mere presence, but she did not quit the room as Tampledown had half-expected, She did not even speak. Admiral Buchanan looked grimly resigned, as well he might. An incautious war, fought by mainly ignoring military advice, had turned out as he feared. Amelia Eckhardt looked relieved; wars are expensive, with unpredictable economic consequences. Marvin Goolagong and Phuntsok Yoko stared at the floor, probably waiting for a more appropriate moment to declare their views. The Chair, as usual, was unreadable.

Tampledown cleared his throat to focus their attention. "Our purpose is peaceful coexistence, not surrender or humiliation." *You'll still see it as surrender — it is — but I can't help that. I'm trying to save you face.* "Some conditions are necessary if we are to achieve that goal. The first is an end to Da Silva transport. All Da Silva vessels detected in space will be collected by remote-

332

focusing synte, and all mahabhavium removed. The syntei will be set up with as little tidal stress as possible: I am witness to the League's capability in that respect. Of course the League cannot guarantee the survival of humans aboard."

"That's murder!"

"I respectfully disagree. It is the necessary creation of a small risk, certainly, but a risk that nobody will be compelled to take."

"But trade—commerce—" spluttered Eckhardt.

"I think you will find syntei very much more convenient. They will be provided."

"How will we explore?" said Marvin, as Head of External Affairs. "Will we have remote-focusing syntei?"

"They're too unwieldy for that. New locations will be scouted by the blipdrive of a League member, the Network. That's what your mahabhavium is needed for."

"For the *groupies*? Those planet-eating monsters?" Vance was appalled.

"They no longer need to break up planets," Tampledown reminded them. "They have access to all the small rocks in the Galaxy. With the blipdrive."

"They no longer need to. But they'll *want* to," said Vance. "They're bloodthirsty evil monsters. Haven't you seen the vix from *Valkyrie*? From *Sunburn*?"

"You are what you eat," Tampledown replied. "The Network's mind contains the minds of the *Valkyrie* and *Sunburn* crews. It has decided that *interesting* things grow on planets, and agreed to preserve them. To make things even more interesting, they have found many human-habitable worlds— more habitable than most that humans have discovered so far—and will carry syntei there. Mass emigration will become possible from Old Earth," he bobbed in Ira da Terra's direction, "as well as from Concordat worlds."

This was Yoko's territory. "In some ways that's wonderful, but it's also completely contrary to everything the Concordat has worked for over the past seventeen centuries."

"Realpolitik, Yoko," Marvin said. "The question is not where we were, it's where we go next. Technically we have choices; in practice they all boil down to one unavoidable course of action. We do what the League wants."

"Yes, but unrestricted travel between worlds, be they League or Concordat, will be a security disaster," said Vance. "There are always malcontents."

"*There is no Concordat*," said Ira. "Starhome is an isolated rump. More than half of the former Concordat planets already belong to the Syntelic League. The rest will quickly join them."

"She's right," said Tampledown. "Syntelics has won, Da Silvas are about to go extinct. In fact, with the invention of self-focusing synthei, the conflict between Da Silva and syntelics no longer has any significant social or economic implications. Unfortunately, classical Da Silva drives still interact explosively with syntei. So they must be eliminated. Immediately."

As that sank in, he picked up the previous, unanswered, objection. "The Director is perfectly correct, of course, about travel. Some restrictions will therefore apply."

"Restrictions?" The Chair spoke for the first time.

"Planets with a history of exporting lethal violence will have access only to *new* colony planets, until the violent generation has passed. That applies to exactly two worlds: Old Earth, as you insist on calling it, and Starhome."

Ira da Terra kept her face still, though she had raged against Earth's inclusion.

"You're applying *Quarantine* to *us*?" Vance shrieked. "Like *Dirties*?"

Tampledown felt Ira smile. Not long ago she'd have slit Vance's throat for that. She was learning. "The League counts seventy stanyears for a generation to pass sufficiently," he said. "Not two millennia. Time for most of the emigrants, in particular, to face new problems and forget old grudges."

"Quarantine!" said Vance.

Tampledown could see that she would prefer a firing squad. He nodded. "Quarantine."

The next day, the Chair had a private meeting with Vance, who was still in shock.

"I have a new job for you, *Administrator*. One I consider more suited to your true talents."

Vance had been expecting this, after her failure at Qish. "My resignation as Director is in your 'comp, as of yesterday."

"That will keep Starhome Security's records tidy," said the Chair. Vance suddenly lost contact with her 'comp. "But what I have to tell you next is off the record. Ah, you didn't know the Chair has that ability? Oh, yah, I can deactivate your 'comp and your communications whenever I please. Access them, too. But I don't really need to. I can read your mind like a slapscreen. You thought me weak when I expressed reservations about obliterating Old Earth. You thought you could fill my shoes, once your attack on Qish had succeeded. Vance: you could *never* fill my shoes. You lack the subtlety. Perhaps you could have deposed me and tried, but the attack failed, as you would fail as Chair. It failed because you were so fixated on death and destruction that you failed to ask yourself a simple question.

"My dear, I *knew* it would fail. I would have aborted the attack in any case. Partly to deprive you of your triumph, but mainly because some actions can never be justified, whatever the circumstances. But the lack of any credible League defence aroused my suspicions, so I waited to do it, and watched you fall into their trap. As a consequence of which, as I said, you will have a new job."

She spun Vance round to face her, made eye contact. "Ira da Terra informs me of an urgent need for an efficient administrator to inspect the teams that are cleaning up pollution in the Circumpolar Nations.

"I'm sure you'll find Old Earth *fascinating.*"

Two Mountains, Qish

-𝟀   ⁇

Treaty of accession of the Network to the Syntelic League: Qish, date 1895 AG

(Executive Summary; underlined terms defined in Supplement 2)

Article 1. The Network shall at all times act in accordance with the Constitution of the Syntelic League.

Article 2. The Network shall not subsume any intelligent being without that being's free and informed consent.

Article 3. The Network shall be subject to the same protections, laws and penalties as any citizen, such penalties applying to the Network as a whole.

Article 4. The Network shall not otherwise be impeded in its study of humanity.

Article 5. The Network shall be free to disseminate any conclusions it comes to concerning humanity, notwithstanding any local censorship laws.

Article 6. The Network shall provide the Syntelic League with full maps of its explorations of the Galaxy, including all planetary bodies.

Article 7. The Network shall perturb neither the orbits nor the structure of such bodies.

Article 8. On all such bodies where <u>life</u> is found, the Syntelic League and the Network shall take care to preserve the local <u>ecology</u>.

Article 9. The Network shall be free to investigate, non-<u>disruptively</u>, all such ecologies.

Article 10. The Syntelic League may send human or non-human <u>colonies</u> to such bodies, subject to preserving inviolate two thirds of the <u>territory</u> of any <u>biome</u>.

Article 11. All such colonies shall automatically accede to the Syntelic League, and shall not abrogate the conditions of Article 9, under pain of removal.

Article 12. Components of the Network shall have the right to own <u>property</u> under planetary laws, the Network being always understood to be the <u>beneficial owner</u>.

Article 13. Components of the Network may enter into <u>joint stock companies</u>, which may declare <u>bankruptcy</u> under planetary laws.

Article 14. The Network as a whole may not declare <u>bankruptcy</u>.

Article 15. The Network to hold <u>copyright</u> in perpetuity to any <u>performance</u>, work of <u>music</u> or the <u>verbal or visual arts</u> created by its components.

Article 16. The Network to hold <u>trademark</u> in perpetuity to the term <u>Rock Star</u>.

Manhattan, Old Earth

Angell Wilcox Tobey the 56th:

Dread Cthulhu is coming to eat our souls!

Our memories shall be forever a part of Cthulhu!

The prophecies are vindicated. We have kept the Faith.

Ph'nglui mglw'nafh Cthulhu R'lyeh wgah'nagl fhtagn, but no longer he lies dreaming. He is coming, at the Solstice.

We have seen the vixcam records from *Valkyrie* and *Sunburn,* more awe-inspiring than ever the ancient prophets dared to draw.

Strangely, Dread Cthulhu is not going to eat every soul, as was foretold: or perhaps the records of the prophecies have been distorted by time. It is only for His real, true disciples, who are ready to swear in front of the vix-cams that their sincerest wish is to be eaten, that this privilege awaits. In front of the vixcams! Since the word went out, thousands of converts have flocked to Manhattan, for the moment of glory.

We have spoken already to his agent on Earth, an eerily nice young man named Jaxxon, who was devoured aforetime on *Sunburn,* and can stand un-consumed in the fire. He has promised us that the form that devours us will indeed be hundreds of metres tall, part man, part squid, part dragon. We showed him the pictures left by the ancient artists, drawn from dream. He said they were indeed pictures of Dread Cthulhu, but the reality is direr and more glorious than mere art can show. He promises also demonic attendants, playing unearthly music. Unexpectedly, he asks for notarised statements of our intention and desire, besides looking into our hearts. He says it will 'avoid misunderstandings'. He also refuses to eat children, saying that Moloch is a false God. Perhaps we will have to make his coming an annual event, to eat those reaching eighteen years of age. If it be so, somebody un-eaten will need to organise and fund it, year by year: I pray that the lot does not fall upon me to remain.

The tentacles of his face will penetrate every opening of our bodies in ec-stasy and pain, to suck out our souls, dissolve our bones, and cast our empty skins aside. Our lives will be eternal in the mind of Dread Cthulhu, and our deaths will live forever on vixcam.

I never doubted. I never doubted.

Glory to Dread Cthulhu!

About the Authors

Ian Stewart was born in 1945, educated at Cambridge (MA) and Warwick (PhD). He has five honorary doctorates and is Emeritus Professor of Mathematics at Warwick University. He has published over 80 books including *Does God Play Dice?*, *Professor Stewart's Cabinet of Mathematical Curiosities*, *Why Beauty is Truth*, *Flatterland*, *What Shape is a Snowflake?*, *Nature's Numbers*, *Professor Stewart's Incredible Numbers*, *Seventeen Equations that Changed the World*, and the bestselling series *The Science of Discworld I, II, III,* and *IV* with Terry Pratchett and Jack Cohen. His new book *Calculating the Cosmos* will appear in September 2016 followed by *Infinity: a Very Short Introduction* in 2017.

His awards include the Royal Society's Faraday Medal, the Gold Medal of the Institute for Mathematics and Its Applications, the Public Understanding of Science Award of the AAAS, and the LMS/IMA Zeeman Medal. He was elected a Fellow of the Royal Society in 2001 and currently serves on Council, its governing body. His Letters to a Young Mathematician won the Peano Prize and The Symmetry Perspective won the Balaguer Prize. His app Incredible Numbers (Profile and TouchPress) won the Digital Book World award for adult nonfiction, and he shared the Lewis Thomas Prize for Writing about Science with Steven Strogatz in 2015. In Pursuit of the Unknown has been chosen to receive the MAA's Euler Book Prize award in January 2017.

He delivered the Royal Institution Christmas Lectures on BBC television in 1997. The final lecture began by bringing a live tiger into the lecture room. He has made over 400 radio broadcasts and 80 television appearances.

His iPad app Incredible Numbers was listed among 'Best apps of 2014' on iTunes store, US and Canada 2014; AASL Best Apps for Teaching & Learning 2015; and won Best Adult Nonfiction App, Digital book World Awards 2015.

He has also written two science fiction novels *Wheelers* and *Heaven* with Jack Cohen, and the SF eBook Jack Of All Trades. He makes frequent radio and television appearances, including the 1997 Christmas Lectures. He is an active research mathematician with over 190 published papers, and works on pattern formation, chaos, network dynamics, and biomathematics.

He lives in Coventry, England.

Tim Poston is an interdisciplinary scientist, with a 1972 Mathematics PhD from the University of Warwick, England. He has since worked in universities from Brazil to South Korea, and in companies ranging from start-ups to GE, in sciences and technologies from ophthalmology to archaeology. Much of this work has led to books and other publications (87, with 2,148 citations on ResearchGate), some to patents (currently 26 issued, several pending), from search presentation technology to glyph rendering, calibrating magnetic resonance receiver coils, the 5-dimensional geometry of real binary quartics, vibration spectra of crystals, brain surgery planning, settlement patterns in archaeology, rod buckling, vision (human and machine), and 3D medical image analysis.

For the last two decades his chief concerns have been in the acquisition and analysis of medical images, and practical human-machine interaction; in April 2013 he joined Forus Health in Bangalore, exploring novel ways to analyse images of the eye with the practical goal of fighting blindness with widely deployable, affordable equipment.

In 2003, with Rebecca, his wife of 49 years (and joyfully counting), he published *Tales of Unexplained Mysteries,* fantasy stories for and about Singapore teens, of different groups and times.

In 2015 he impersonated Dumbledore's smarter older brother at Bangalore Comic Con, and gave a keynote at the Fifth Elephant big data conference.

He enjoys change and simultaneity quakes.

The two have worked together since the mid-1970s on a variety of research and writing projects, including their joint research text *Catastrophe Theory and Its Applications* (over 1000 citations on ResearchGate, with more every week).

More books from Tim Poston and Ian Stewart are available at: http://ReAnimus.com/store/?author=Tim%20Poston%20and%20Ian%20Stewart

ReAnimus Press

Breathing Life into Great Books

If you enjoyed this book we hope you'll tell others or write a review! We also invite you to subscribe to our newsletter to learn about our new releases and join our affiliate program (where you earn 12% of sales you recommend) at www.ReAnimus.com.

Here are more ebooks you'll enjoy from ReAnimus Press, available from ReAnimus Press's web site, Amazon.com, bn.com, etc.:

The Living Labyrinth, by Ian Stewart and Tim Poston
Info/buy:

Sam, Jane, Felix, Elzabet, Tinka & Marco go quantum jumping on their path to galactic citizenship, only to end up in a very strange place indeed!

Wheelers, by Ian Stewart and Jack Cohen
Info/buy:

Alien artifacts found on Callisto...

Deep Quarry, by John E. Stith
Info/buy:

A private eye uncovers a long-buried starship...that's still occupied.

Manhattan Transfer, by John E. Stith

Info/buy:

Aliens kidnap Manhattan; read all about it!

Reunion on Neverend, by John E. Stith

Info/buy:

A man returning for a high school reunion on a distant colony finds an old flame in trouble—trouble that he's uniquely qualified to deal with.

Redshift Rendezvous, by John E. Stith

Info/buy:

One man must stop starship hijackers from using an unusual starship to plunder a wealthy colony.

Memory Blank, by John E. Stith

Info/buy:

Cal Donley regains consciousness on the beautiful orbital colony Daedalus—but Cal doesn't remember leaving Earth, or his name or the past dozen years!

Reckoning Infinity, by John E. Stith

Info/buy:

A riveting exploration of what it means to be an alien... Explorers inside a moon-sized alien ship must find its secrets before it kills them.

Death Tolls, by John E. Stith

Info/buy:

A great science fiction mystery: Dan sees the telecast from Mars where his brother dies—and it's not an accident. Why is a certain reporter uncannily at each disaster so quickly?

Scapescope, by John E. Stith

Info/buy:

Brother Sammy Wants YOU! In prison. For something you haven't done yet.

All for Naught, by John E. Stith

Info/buy:

Nick Naught, private eye, walks down some strange mean streets, in an action-packed comedy set in the future.

The Exiles Trilogy, by Ben Bova

Info/buy:

When all the best of Earth's scientists are exiled to a space station, they decide to embark on an even grander adventure to the stars. An epic trilogy in one volume.

The Star Conquerors (Collectors' Edition), by Ben Bova

Info/buy:

Special Collectors' Edition! Six time Hugo winner Ben Bova's most sought-after novel is now an ebook with the original Mel Hunter cover and an essay from Ben on the history of the book!

The Star Conquerors (Standard Edition), by Ben Bova

Info/buy:

Six time Hugo winner Ben Bova's most sought-after novel is back in print!

Colony, by Ben Bova

Info/buy:

Island One is a celestial utopia, and David Adams is its most perfect creation. But David is a prisoner, destined to spend his life in an island-sized cylinder orbiting a doomed home planet. David has a plan—one that will ultimately save humanity... or destroy it.

The Kinsman Saga, by Ben Bova

Info/buy:

Chet Kinsman is an astronaut ace who has done everything in space—including committing the first murder. Kinsman has to confront his hidden past and decide Earth's destiny, in a desperate countdown to nuclear annihilation.

Star Watchmen, by Ben Bova

Info/buy:

Mankind rules a giant galactic empire, but not all the worlds are pleased. Can the Star Watch prevent a revolt?

As on a Darkling Plain, by Ben Bova

Info/buy:

Dr. Sidney Lee races against time to prevent the huge alien machines on Titan from destroying mankind.

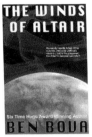

The Winds of Altair, by Ben Bova

Info/buy:

Altair VI isn't making it easy to Terraform!

Test of Fire, by Ben Bova

Info/buy:

A small group of survivors fight to rebuild civilization after the Earth is devastated by a huge solar flare.

The Weathermakers, by Ben Bova

Info/buy:

After conquering everything else, the last frontier was... controlling Mother Nature! By the award-winning hard SF author of the Grand Tour series.

The Dueling Machine, by Ben Bova

Info/buy:

Civilized, harmless virtual reality dueling has replaced all physical conflict — everything from punching someone over a personal insult to interstellar warfare... until a madman dictator of a small empire finds a way to cheat, and use the dueling machine to take over the galaxy!

The Multiple Man, by Ben Bova

Info/buy:

As the President is speaking inside an auditorium in Boston, the President's Press Secretary discovers a body in an alley outside: The body of the President.

Escape!, by Ben Bova
Info/buy:

No end to Danny's sentence, watched by a sentient computer, and no way out of the escape-proof prison, there was only one thing to do...

Forward in Time, by Ben Bova
Info/buy:

Get ready for a series of future shocks from the award-winning Ben Bova!

Maxwell's Demons, by Ben Bova
Info/buy:

Science fiction and science fact, humor and adventure, all await when you enter the unpredictable world of... MAXWELL'S DEMONS

Twice Seven, by Ben Bova
Info/buy:

Ben Bova's universe is always more than the sum of its parts...

The Astral Mirror, by Ben Bova
Info/buy:

Here are a dozen and a half views of the world, past present and future, as seen through the Astral Mirror....

The Story of Light, by Ben Bova

Info/buy:

In this all-encompassing work, Ben Bova explores the subject of light and shows how it has shaped every aspect of our existence.

Immortality, by Ben Bova

Info/buy:

Dr. Bova explores the future effects of science and technology on the human life span. Death will no longer be the inevitable end of life.

Space Travel - A Science Fiction Writer's Guide, by Ben Bova

Info/buy:

An indispensible tool for all science fiction writers, Space Travel explains the science you need to help you make your fiction plausible.

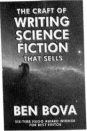

The Craft of Writing Science Fiction that Sells, by Ben Bova

Info/buy:

Learn how to write SF from the master! Ben Bova, best-selling author and six-time Hugo Award winner for Best Editor explains step by step all the elements you need to write professionally selling science fiction.

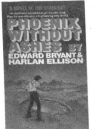

Phoenix Without Ashes, by Harlan Ellison and Edward Bryant

Info/buy:

Co-written with Harlan Ellison and based on the award-winning script, the story of mankind's last salvation gone awry.

Shadrach in the Furnace, by Robert Silverberg
Info/buy:

Meet the new Khan! Soon to be immortal... A Hugo and Nebula Award Finalist novel from a Grand Master of science fiction.

Bloom, by Wil McCarthy
Info/buy:

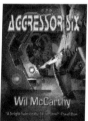

In 2106, microscopic machine/creatures escape their creators to populate the inner solar system with a wild, deadly ecology all their own, pushing the tattered remnants of humanity out into the cold and dark of the outer planets. Seven astronauts must embark on mankind's boldest venture yet—the perilous journey home to infected Earth!

Aggressor Six, by Wil McCarthy
Info/buy:

An alien armada from the center of Orion makes its deadly way through the galaxy, destroying all human life in the process, and only Marine Corporal Kenneth Jonson and the Aggressor Six team can stop the onslaught.

Murder in the Solid State, by Wil McCarthy
Info/buy:

David Sanger, an ambitious young physicist, attends a party at which a pompous older scientist, who just happens to have thwarted the younger man's innovative ideas, is murdered. Suddenly it is not just David's career, but his life that is at stake. Are his ideas that important? Who's out to stop David from changing the world?

Flies from the Amber, by Wil McCarthy
Info/buy:

Forty light years from earth, the colonists on the world of Unua have somehow managed to keep civilization struggling on, despite twice daily earthquakes...

Innocents Abroad (Fully Illustrated & Enhanced Collectors' Edition), by Mark Twain
Info/buy:

Best. Travel. Book. Ever. (With all original illustrations.)

Local Knowledge (A Kieran Lenahan Mystery), by Conor Daly
Info/buy:

Lawyer-turned-golf pro Kieran Lenahan must solve the murder of millionaire country-club owner Sylvester Miles. "A FAST-PACED MYSTERY"—THE NEW YORK TIMES

A Mother's Trial, by Nancy Wright
Info/buy:

Was it the perfect murder? A true story.

Bad Karma: A True Story of Obsession and Murder, by Deborah Blum
Info/buy:

The true story of a famous Berkeley murder and a landmark Supreme Court case.

Siege of Stars: Book One of The Sigil Trilogy, by Henry Gee
Info/buy:

Spanning millions of years and the breadth of the universe, The Sigil Trilogy is an epic tale that explores the nature of humanity, belief, and love.

Scourge of Stars: Book Two of The Sigil Trilogy, by Henry Gee

Info/buy:

Book Two of Henry Gee's incredible Sigil Trilogy!

Rage of Stars: Book Three of The Sigil Trilogy, by Henry Gee

Info/buy:

The concluding volume of Henry Gee's incredible Sigil Trilogy!

Printed in Great Britain
by Amazon